SATURDAY

Have you ever experienced that moment when you realize someone is so close to you, and the gaps between words have become so long, that a kiss is inevitable?

I hadn't – until now.

Sean: amazing, funny, smart, total fittie Sean, was millimetres from me.

After fifteen years and two months, it was really happening.

My first kiss was a nanosecond away. I crossed my fingers underneath the sofa cushion and tried not to freak out.

Every bit of advice I'd ever watched, read or picked up from bad films was running through my head.

Please let this go OK.

Please don't let me be terrible at this.

In fact, *please* just let me be averagely normal at this.

In fact, scrap that.

Please just don't let me pass out with nerves.

I opened half of my left eye. Phew. Sean still had his eyes shut, so couldn't see me squinting at him with total panic. He was so close that he was almost pixelated, yet somehow he was still intimidatingly gorgeous. How was he looking so calm?! Probably because he'd done this loads before. This was probably no biggie to him – but this was The Biggie to me.

I breathed him in. He smelt of the boys' changing rooms after PE (but in a good way) and cola bottle sweets and Lipsyl original and warm. Me? Well, Anita had just staged a best-mate first-kiss preparation intervention and made me emergency chew-and-spit twenty Bubblemints in a row, so I probably smelt like a dentist's.

And Sean was getting even closer. Any moment we'd have full lip-to-lip contact. *Argh.*

3 . . . 2 . . . 1 . . . *Lip-off.*

My heart shifted up another gear, every bit of me in total panic mode.

I was the only person I knew who still hadn't kissed anyone – and soon, that person would be gone. All of my life till now had been *the before*, and within seconds, it

B____ Garrod is the author of the Super Awkward series. S___ grew up in Worcester, before heading to Leeds U____versity to study biology – which she put to excellent u___ by accidentally starting a career in TV. Since then ____ worked in London, New York and Toronto for ____lcasters including Radio 1, CBBC and MTV, ____hing everything from mental health campaigns, ____ usic TV shows. She now lives in East London and concentrates on social impact campaigns, working with c____ities and broadcasters around the world to make content that can help empower young people.

Find her on Twitter: @bethg

ALSO BY BETH GARROD

SUPER AWKWARD

TRULY MADLY AWKWARD

ACCESS ALL AWKWARD

TAKE A CHANCE ON ME

BETH GARROD

SCHOLASTIC

To Becca, because you can't choose big sisters,
but if you could I'd always choose you.

Scholastic Children's Books
An imprint of Scholastic Ltd
Euston House, 24 Eversholt Street, London, NW1 1DB, UK
Registered office: Westfield Road, Southam, Warwickshire, CV47 0RA
SCHOLASTIC and associated logos are trademarks and/or
registered trademarks of Scholastic Inc.

First published in the UK by Scholastic Ltd, 2019

Text copyright © Beth Garrod, 2019

The right of Beth Garrod to be identified as the
author of this work has been asserted.

Emoji by Madebyoliver, freepik, Dimitry Miroliubov, Yannick,
Vector Stall, Roundicons, Chanut, Katrina Stefanikova,
Gregor Cresnar and Dave Gandy at flaticon.com

ISBN 978 1407 18696 2

A CIP catalogue record for this book
is available from the British Library.

Printed by CPI Group (UK) Ltd, Croydon, CR0 4YY
Papers used by Scholastic Children's Books are made
from wood grown in sustainable forests.

1 3 5 7 9 10 8 6 4 2

This is a work of fiction. Names, characters, places, incidents
and dialogues are products of the author's imagination or are used
fictitiously. Any resemblance to actual people, living or dead,
events or locales is entirely coincidental.

www.scholastic.co.uk

was going to be *the after*.

My head was at an angle I'd only ever attempted in stretches when Anita and I did Joe Wicks videos. Was this normal? Should I lean more, or stay where I was? It was actually quite hard to manoeuvre on a sofa this squidgy ... but if I stayed too still my stomach muscles might start those wobbles they do at the end of sit-ups at swim training.

This was complicated.

No one told me my whole body was going to suddenly feel like it didn't know how to be person-shaped any more. My brain was spinning like it had too many tabs open and might crash any second. Please let it still manage basic mouth movements. And dribbling prevention.

Wasn't kissing meant to be fun, not totally terrifying?!

Anita was watching us from the other sofa. Not at all creepy, Neet?! Through my panic-squint it looked like she was doing fist pumps. She'd been trying to engineer this situation for weeks, determined I should end this term by shaking off my "first kiss curse", as I'd labelled it. She looked like she was one atom of self-restraint away from yelling out motivational phrases. I tried to flap my spare hand to convey that I both appreciated her encouragement, but also ... could she maybe stop?

CONTACT ALERT.

Sean's nose had just touched mine. I downgraded everything else to not important. Even the house party music blurred.

Breathe, Meg. Focus. Remember not to panic.

I was *definitely* panicking.

And now I was panicking that I was panicking.

"Meg." Sean paused. Was pausing a bad sign? Or was he like one of those posh kitchen drawers that you know is going to shut, but just goes extra slow for the moment of impact? I opened both eyes and smiled, even though we were so close everything below the nose was a blur. "Can I just check... Am I thinking what you're thinking?"

How should I reply? Something cute and romantic. Think, *think*.

"Is it something to do with kitchen drawers?"

He definitely flinched.

"No..." He pulled back the tiniest bit. "It's that..." His brown eyes were staring into mine. I think it was meant to be super romantic, but it just made me want to blink. "I'd really like to kiss you."

WOAH. There it was. He'd said it. Just like it wasn't the scariest thing to admit might be about to happen.

I gulped.

As in, an actual comedy gulp that Sean totally heard.

Why couldn't my panic reactions be a toe-twitch or something not so utterly obvious?

"Erm ... that sounds ..." LIKE THE GREATEST IDEA ANYONE HAS EVER HAD. "... nice."

Sean smiled and flipped his long hair to the side. When he did this in class I full-on inward-swooned, so now it was for an audience of just me, it was almost too much. Well, it would have been if ... a massive clump of his hair wasn't now stuck in my lipgloss.

Had he noticed? Should I acknowledge it? Or just let him think I had Sudden Moustache Syndrome?

"Sorry," I mumbled, and tried to brush it away effortlessly. But his hair clump just sort of slid and attached itself to my cheek, smearing my lip-gloss with it. Oh great.

Sean ignored it, and calmly, slowly, put the palm of his hand underneath my jaw, his thumb by my mouth, his fingers behind my ear. It was hot. Worryingly hot. We hadn't even got to the kissing bit yet.

I tried to relax.

Sean closed his eyes again. Yes, good idea, not seeing might make it less terrifying. I shut mine too.

I was now leaning so far forward my right arm was dangling in mid-air like it was lost. What the heck were you meant to do with spare limbs in these situations?

Confused, I put my hand on top of his. Was this a

normal thing to do?

My thumb ring slipped off, but I ignored it. Right now, I *had* to focus on this potentially life-changing event.

It was now or never.

With every bit of me on high alert, I leant in and, finally, we kissed.

...Well, that was the plan.

I definitely *did* lean in. But right where there had once been a Sean was now just an empty space.

Confused, I opened my eyes. Where was he?

And at exactly the wrong moment, I found out. He'd bent down to pick up my ring.

Which meant he was now on his way back up again.

And where there had been empty space was now me. Looking down. Mouth open, lips ready for a kiss that hadn't happened. And as Sean sat back up, the only contact we made was my teeth bashing smack into the bridge of his nose.

It made an actual noise.

The whole thing felt like a horror movie.

It looked like it too, the moment of impact captured in full blood-spurting glory by at least four different phones. Instead of Sean breaking my first-kiss curse, I'd broken his nose.

CHAPTER ONE

"Seriously, though, out of all the tips we've ever read about first kisses, did any of them even *hint* I'd need a first-aider on standby?"

Anita slid her tray down on to the canteen table and laughed — but with a slight pause, as if checking that was the right reaction. I was still fragile, both in teeth and mood.

I pushed my tongue against my front teeth to see if any were wobbling with the aftershock of nearly chipping human bone. Phew. Six days on and still holding firm.

Neet squeezed into the space by the two girls eating beside us. I think they were from the year below. All week, we'd made sure we hadn't sat by anyone from the party, just in case. The comments online had been bad enough – I didn't need them in real life too.

Anita looked deep in thought as she lifted a forkful of jacket potato and peas to her mouth. 50% of the peas fell back on to the plate.

"Am I allowed to say it's not that bad yet?"

I thought back to Saturday – and did an involuntary *mwaaaahhh* shuddery groan like the spirit of the undead was escaping out of me. "Lemme answer that when I'm at least sixty." A vision of Sean clutching his nose as Sasha, the girl whose house it was, yelled, "WHO KNOWS HOW TO GET BLOOD OUT OF A CARPET?!!" popped into my mind. I pulled my ponytail over my eyes as if I could hide from the memory. "Scratch that . . . seventy."

Mum says I exaggerate. She says it about fifty times a day, but I don't think I do. Especially not in this case. What happened at the party had changed *everything*.

I'd always joked I had a kiss curse, but now I knew it was real, and so did everyone who was there, or had access to the internet. So . . . everyone.

I'd thought Sean was hot all term, but had been in serious denial until Neet saw me checking him out during his presentation on fatbergs. She figured if someone could say "congealed oily sewer waste" and

8

I was still grinning like that, then it must be serious.

So with Sasha's party looming, and me racking up more hours as the Great Unkissed, we figured I should just go for it. Get it ticked off. Lose my kiss virginity.

Neet had put me on a heavy training programme of rom-com watching to get my positive vibes up. It was hard to fit in around exams, but ... priorities. By last Friday I'd finally come round to thinking I had nothing to lose (at this stage I hadn't considered the key contenders of "dignity", "respect" and "sensation in my lip/front teeth").

I was petrified, though. I'd had the chance to kiss someone last Bonfire Night, but had totally swerved it, and since then it had officially become A Thing. My First-Kiss Curse. Neet said it was in my head, but I knew it was real.

I'd been kind of happy staying cursed – I hated doing things I was bad at, and there was no way I could be good at something I'd never tried. So maybe kissing wasn't for me? Of course Neet said it'd be fine because I wasn't really into Sean, other than on a deeply visual level, so it wouldn't even be that scary. I just needed to rip the plaster off and go for it.

Ironically, it ended up with him putting a plaster *on*. Multiple, in fact.

Ow.

Neet prodded me in the arm, her mouth screwed up. "Oi. What did we say? No. More. Dwelling."

"Don't know what you mean," I lied – and we both knew it. It was easy for her. She'd snogged loads of people – and maimed zero of them. Not that she liked any of them anyway. She thought I was destined for this great love story. But her? She never let herself like anyone.

"Meg. You've got the same face on as when we tried to watch *Bird Box*."

Second worst night of my life after last Saturday – that film is *terrifying*. But I was too sad to smile and Neet realized tough love didn't work that well on a human marshmallow. She squeezed my hand. "C'mon. . . Life is for the living, not slow replaying of the events of Saturday night." She picked up a chip. "Well . . . that and chips. Want one?"

I didn't know anyone else whose jacket-potato filling of choice was chips. But Neet wasn't like anyone else. I accepted the fried truce offering.

Sean hadn't spoken to me all week, despite people yelling "Look out, Sean, it's Meg-*abite*" when we were anywhere near each other. We'd both been tagged in all the photos from Saturday, although apparently he didn't see them till Sunday as there had been no reception in A&E.

"Can we just agree to pretend the whole thing never happened?" I said. Neet nodded firmly, happy to do whatever it took to stop me moping. "Which includes no talking about it." I had to make sure she knew the severity of this. "No even *looking* like you might even be *thinking* about talking about it. In fact, no acknowledging that Sean even exists – or any boys, for that matter." Yes, that sounded good. "It's easier that way."

Neet looked at me like I might have lost my mind, but also as if, in her role of best friend, the best thing was to just agree. "Whatever works for you." She swiped a veggie nugget from my plate. "You know my silence can always be bought with a nugget. Although next time I need something, it's your turn to help me out, right?"

"Anything for you." I meant it. Neet was more important to me than most food groups.

"Promise?" She held her little finger out.

"Promise." I shook it with mine. In our world, a promise was legally binding. If we promised something was true, it really had to be.

As best mates go, Neet was the best of the best. The Best Best Mate™. Mum and Dad were always on my case about being glued to my phone (sadly not true, as if I was,

I wouldn't have the world's most smashed screen), not being late for swimming practice or why it wasn't OK to send messages that were just question marks. (What was their problem?) (???) Then there was my little sister, Olive, whose main hobby was doing whatever it took to annoy me. But Neet? She was always there no matter what, always knowing what to do to make everything better.

It was time for me to stop being such a selfish sad sack and start being a better friend. After all, it was the last day of term.

"Right, then." I put down the fork I'd been waving about. "Can I take a moment to recognize this monumental last day of the worst term of our lives?" Neet slow-nodded, a seriousness behind her smile. "To say thank you for being my absolute ride or die." For all Neet let me waffle on about my problems 24/7, she never spoke about hers. With her mum being in and out of hospital, this term had been way, way worse for her. "Here's to an awesome summer." I looked round the canteen. "And not seeing this place for almost two whoooolllle months."

I leant over the table and hugged her, trying to ignore that I'd definitely just dunked my right boob in her potato, and she'd activated Awkward Mode. My best mate and emotion went as well together as a heavy eyeliner day and watching *The Fault In Our Stars*.

"For lifey, best friend wifey. Although, wait..." She looked towards the double doors. "Has Mr Finch had a haircut?"

I didn't need to look round to know what she was doing. I wasn't falling for it (although the two girls next to us both spun round to stare – rookie eavesdropping error). Subject-changing was Neet's defence mechanism. "Neet, he's bald."

But she was off the hook as my phone vibrated. A message from Dad. It wasn't like him to text during school hours. He must have had a momentary lapse in rule-breaking protocol.

I squinted at my screen. Reading anything on it was like a form of code breaking. I'd had to cover it with cling film to stop bits of glass ending up in my fingers.

DAD: Don't forget family dinner at 7 😊

As if I could. It was a Friday non-negotiable tradition.

DAD: MUM AND I HAVE GOT SOMETHING TO TELL YOU... 🎉

Well, hello, most terrifying sentence to hear from a parent. Were the caps deliberate, or just another parent-using-phone fail? I showed Neet, too horrified to speak. Her face fell.

"Do you think. . .?"

"Nu-huh. They *can't* be having another baby." I wasn't sure if that was my answer, or me pleading with the universe. "They've already produced one spawn of the devil in Oli. Any more and it could be one of those that eats their way out."

Neet looked like she wasn't 100% sure how to reply. Fair enough. "Well, what else could it be?"

But I never got to reply with a more normal theory, like Mum getting a promotion at work, because someone was standing right beside us. No, not a someone. A some-*two*. A couple of guys from our maths set that I'd last seen at the party.

Please don't let them be here to try and talk to me about last week.

"Oh, hey guys." The tall one slid up into our conversation. Neet and I glanced at each other, both equally as confused.

"Er, hi. . ." Thank goodness I had Neet to reply for the both of us. "How can we, er, help you today?"

She had her "answering unknown phone number"

voice on, but I could hardly criticize when I was on mute.

"Just handing out these." The less tall one pushed a bit of paper on to the table. "Old school, but the more the merrier, right?"

It was a picture of our headmaster, Mr Waterman, with Kim Kardashian's crying face Photoshopped on.

AINT NO HOUSE PARTY LIKE A
KARDASHIAN-WEST HOUSE PARTY.
BUT YOU'RE NEVER GOING TO
GET INVITED TO THAT.
SO COME TO 21 HILLCREST AVE
FOR YEAR TWO OF SAM-FEST.
BRING BEER. OR A FRIEND WITH BEER.

The girls next to us were craning out of their chairs to try and read it, clearly dying to be asked, but even the *thought* of a house party made me want to run away screaming, "What is wrong with you people? I am a human island and I need to be allloonnneeee!" I did what I always do in an emergency: blinked slowly and hoped the moment would pass.

"So, you in?" Tall One nudged Neet's back. He must be Sam. Neet responded with a look that would guarantee he'd never nudge random girls ever again.

"Well . . . um. . ." I fumbled for words. This wasn't a situation we were used to. We weren't the kind of people that just got asked to parties, especially not two in as many weeks. This must be one of those where the only guest list criteria is "breathing".

Could I think of an excellent way of saying no that made us seem interesting and aloof – as opposed to the reality: that I could never be in a social situation that involved boys ever again, and would be much happier at home, with her, our matching glow-in-the-dark pyjamas, popcorn in hand, rewatching *To All The Boys I've Loved Before*?

"Neet, up to you. . ." I'd let her deal with this. She looked at me, trying to read what I was thinking.

"It's a. . ." *Say no, Neet.* ". . .Most probably – right, Megs?"

Not right, Neet?! I kicked her foot under the table. She looked at me all *whaaaaat?* but she knew exactly *whaaaaat.*

Tall One had his head to the side, giving me a weird look. "So, you're Meg, then?" A smile crept over his face. "*The* Meg?"

I knew exactly what he meant. He meant, was I *The Meg* that everyone was still laughing about. I felt the all too familiar kick of embarrassment, and wanted to disappear all over again. Or shout. Or point out to Neet this was a strong argument to support my plan to start going by my middle name. But all I managed was to croak back, "I'm *a* Meg?"

His face lit up even more, delighted to have struck hilarious party guest gold. "In that case, you guys *have* to come." Yup, I was the wild card invite: the person who now got asked to provide the comedy for everyone else. No way was I going to his stupid party.

"We're actually busy..." There was no hiding how over this I was. "*Remember,* Neet?"

Less Tall One looked unconvinced. "Busy doing what?"

"Family funeral."

Quite dark. Must work on my spontaneous lies. Could I make this sound more believable? Details were key.

"...Great ... Aunt ... Matilda?"

Neet was giving me major wide-eyes. Not a great sign.

I tried to look as sad as I could about my fake family member's badly timed death plans. "...Way to start the summer holidays, huh?"

Tall One grinned. "You know when Samfest is then?"

He knew he had me. "Saturday?" I attempted vaguely.

"Nope." He said it like a challenge. "Friday of the bank holiday. Same as last year." I winced, as if this was also a problem.

"Ahhh, shame. I have an, erm..." Must think of something new. "Another family funeral."

Tall One let out a long "Riiiiiight". Less Tall One just laughed.

In solidarity, Neet kept the straightest of faces. "It's been a death-heavy month."

"But that's three weeks away?" Tall One clapped straight back, but Neet didn't miss a beat.

"They're planning ahead... Better deals on venues."

Yup, I'd fooled a total of zero people. I looked around – could I just leave? The girls next to us looked like they couldn't believe someone like me was turning down a party like this. Which gave me an idea...

"These two look like they might be free, though?" I pushed the invite towards them and shrugged at Less Tall One. "The more the merrier, right?"

At least my lack of a life could make someone else's a bit better.

Tall One pulled his bag back up on his shoulder. "Another time then, Megabite." He nodded at Neet. "Megabite's friend." He looked back at me. "Send my regards to your family; sounds like a tough time."

I looked as solemn as I could. "Appreciated." They finally both moved on to the girls next to us. When they were wrapped in conversation, Neet leant forward. "Seriously, Meg." She was whispering. "A funeral?! Next time at least say 'wedding'."

"I was panicking, OK?" I whispered back.

"You could have just said yes, y'know."

"Neet – you KNOW I can't." I stabbed at the food on my plate, guilty that I knew I was being selfish. "You go though, if you want to."

She snorted. "What, without you? Who would I take? My dad?"

I shrugged. "Anyone who's not at my family funeral, obvs."

She folded her arms. "The only thing dying round here is your social life." I mouthed "Ooh, burn" but she carried on. "And think again if you reckon I'm going to stand by and let you say goodbye to every bit of fun this summer."

I instantly felt awful. Neet's mum had gone into hospital before Easter after falling on her way to work and breaking her leg. When they'd operated on it they'd discovered an infection, which had led to sepsis, and ever since then she'd been kept on the ward, on serious meds, slowly getting her strength back. We still had no idea when she'd be home, and it was fair to say this term had been super stressful. So, Neet and I had agreed this would be our summer of saying yes to stuff and seeing where it would take us. My suspicions were to her sofa and YouTube, but I was open to be proved wrong. But my guilt came out as snappiness.

"I don't know what you mean." I knew exactly what she meant.

"Meg, you're *fifteen*, not fifty."

"And your point is?" I knew what it was, but I was buying more time to think up reasons why she should let me be a social recluse.

"My point is" – she was actually hissing – "you need to put this whole first kiss thing behind you and—"

But she didn't get to finish hissing at me as Less Tall One slid his way back over.

"Sorry to interrupt." He clearly wasn't. "But if the funeral gets cancelled for whatever reason. . ." I closed my eyes, wishing we could all just send that moment to *Trash*. "All the details will be on my Snap—"

"We'll be there," Neet called after him as he walked off. I unleashed my full left eyebrow raise at her.

"Sorry, Meg, it had to be done." She sounded totally unapologetic. "Because I have a plan." From Neet this was only ever a worrying statement. Her dog, Barks and

Rec, still hadn't recovered from her attempt to make him Insta-famous. He ran out of the room whenever she even picked up a bottle of hairspray. "I have the perfect way of getting you your Meg-ness back."

"Can we talk about this later?" I slumped forward on to my elbows. Last Saturday had been too awful to risk any kind of repeat.

"No, we can't! Because all the time you're obsessing over what happened with the person who cannot be named – and *yes*, you've got that face on again" – I closed my eyes and tried to reset my face – "you're stuck in a fun rut. It's time to take action."

"But, Neet..." I sat up to protest. "I didn't choose the fun-sponge life – it chose me."

"Nope. Not having it. I'd like to remind you that this is meant to be our summer of saying yes." Oh, hello, guilt trip. "And that *mere minutes* ago you PROMISED me you'd help me with any favour." I groaned. "So I ask again. Are you in?"

She knew I couldn't refuse. In our world, a promise was a promise. "Sure." I already knew this was a bad idea.

Neet looked worryingly pleased with herself. "Excellent. I've got the perfect plan to get you over your party panic..." I braced – her plans were normally terrible and/or illegal. "You, Meg, have got to confront your fears!"

"Pigeons with teeth?"

"No ... although that's rank. You need to prove to yourself that you don't have a kissing curse."

I laughed. "C'mon, we've already established I'm done with boys." Slash all forms of social life. I put my plate back on the tray and began to stand up.

"Too late." Neet stayed sitting, her arms folded in defiance. "You promised."

I stopped mid-stand, fear turning me into an accidental musical statue. "Promised what, exactly?"

She smiled, like this was all just one manageable thing for me to tick off. "To get out of your fun rut."

"And I'm going to do that *how*?"

"Simple." She puffed herself up, excited for her big reveal. "You, Meg, with my help, are going to spend this summer getting the world's best-ever second first kiss."

CHAPTER TWO

"Tests have shown they're bad for your health, you know." Dad leant against the door frame in our lounge. He likes to deliver bad news casually. "Your generation is going to have all sorts of problems we don't even know about yet."

I looked up from scrolling through pictures of everyone celebrating the end of term and smiled.

"On the plus side, the world might end before then, so I might as well not miss out on ..." I looked back down at my screen: a Boomerang of Elliot F pulling a piece of spaghetti out of his eyeball. Maybe not the best example. "... on broadening my networks and cultural understanding with my global community."

I was logged in as Neet. I was staying well away from my accounts and notifications ever since the incident.

Every day someone found a new toothy creature pic to tag me in (although the naked mole-rat had been surprisingly cute). And why had someone thought it was OK to release a shark-attack film called *The Meg*? I'd never seen it but felt I had, I'd been sent so many shark-attack gifs over the last week.

Dad pushed his glasses back up his nose. He liked to do that to appear more serious. "Hmmmm, well the jury's out on that one."

I couldn't help but grin. There was nothing he loved more than some classic dad-ing, because he wasn't just a dad – he was a dad whose actual job was a health and safety risk assessor. That's like being a dad². In the hobbies bit of his CV it probably just says, "gardening, cooking, reading books about wars, and thinking of worst-case scenarios."

But I wanted to be in his good books when he and Mum told us whatever their news was. The fact that he'd been whistling while he cooked made me think it couldn't be anything *that* bad. Although good for him and good for me were *very* different things.

Olive looked up from her slime tutorial vid. "Alexa, tell Dad he needs to give us a break."

Alexa claimed she "didn't know that one", but I think she just didn't want to take sides. Olive had been in a huff with Dad ever since their argument last weekend about whether she could have a phone. Getting one when she turns ten next year wasn't good enough for her, even though I'd only got one two years ago. She'd hoped her presentation on "The Safety Benefits Of Being In Contact For Emergencies" would win him round, but no – and now she was in a full-on week-long mood, and my camera roll was at the limit with all the grumpy selfies she'd taken. Dad was having none of it.

"Hello, Alexa, please also tell Olive that dinner's on the table." My sister was out of the room before he'd finished his sentence. It was like she had two states of being: lounging too close to my personal space, or sprinting to food.

"We walk indoors!" Dad yelled after her. "Slippery floors and socks never end well!"

He huffed in exasperation like she was dicing with death, not dashing for dinner. I followed at normal human speed, hoping I was walking even further into his current favourite daughter position, but as I got to the door he put his hand on my shoulder.

"We don't know where you get it from. . ." He pulled a folded piece of paper out of his pocket. "But your mum and I are very proud."

Ah. A print-out of my school report.

It wasn't just Mum and Dad who had been disappointed with last term's results. I'd been gutted too, and was glad I'd managed to pull them back up. Neet and I had worked really hard to help each other study. It had been a weirdly nice distraction for all those times we were alone at her house, her dad spending every spare second at hospital with her mum. Hopefully her parents would be chuffed too. They were like a second family to me.

"No probs." I shrugged, embarrassed. I did like Mum and Dad being proud of me, I just wished they could do it from far away – and maybe over WhatsApp so I didn't have to hear it directly. "So, er. . ." I paused to try and make my big question sound like an afterthought. "What was that news?"

"Nice try, but my lips." He zipped his mouth with his fingers. "Are. Sealed. Your mum and I want to tell you together." He was grinning, clearly enjoying having a secret. "Come on, last one at the table gets the smallest portion. . ."

I scurried – at a risk-adverse, sock-and-shiny-floor-appropriate pace – towards the kitchen and the amazing smell of veggie moussaka. It was Dad's go-to for special occasions. Maybe the news really *was* something momentous.

"Can I have the burnt bit please, Mum?" I called dibs

before my bum even hit the chair. "Although no peas for the wicked, please."

"I've been your mum for fifteen looong years now," Mum said, splodging a pleasingly massive portion on my plate. Dad cooked, Mum served-up: that was the deal. "Don't you think I know?"

She might well know, but that didn't stop her trying to give us extra vegetables by stealth. I knew her game. I pressed my foot down on to Olive's under the table and smiled sweetly. "You know, Oli was saying how much she loves your veg, Dad."

Olive was still in trouble with Mum after having a tantrum this morning when she was told she couldn't go to some young inventor camp next week, so I knew she had to be polite in front of her – and I intended to exploit that to the full.

"Yes, I love *all* your cooking, Dad," Olive said through gritted teeth, glaring at me as her plate got loaded with green things. "And the way you serve it, Mother."

"So, good last day at school then?" Dad was optimistically trying to make conversation, even though he was competing with cheese and potatoes.

"Uh-huh…" I reached towards the middle of the table. "OK to get some bread?"

Mum nodded. "'Course. But leave some for me. I'll have it for my Santa plate."

We'd always called it that because when we were little, Oli and I used to think Mum was like Santa (albeit less beardy and with a more varied wardrobe), because when she worked night shifts as a firefighter, Dad always left a plate of food out for her when she got home.

Chewing on Dad's home-made bread (his other hobby included weekly themed *Bake Off* bakes), I let Olive chat away about her amazing report (her bribery game for inventor camp was so obvious I almost did her the favour of telling her we all knew what she was up to).

I'd been so distracted by surviving the party aftermath, the reality that this was the start of the summer holidays hadn't properly sunk in. I wondered what kind of curveball Mum and Dad might be about to unleash on it? I looked at them for clues. Nothing. They were happily in love as always. I guess that was nice, but I could do without the high frequency of bum-squeezes and snogs when we were having movie night. No wonder I had a problem with kissing – they'd scarred me for life.

As far as I was concerned, despite what Mr Finch said, Romeo and Juliet had things easy. My mum and dad were the real star-crossed lovers. The *only* thing they had in common was that they loved each other. They'd met when Mum was helping do a safety demo at a health and safety conference Dad was chairing, and somehow that was that. Dad said it was love at first sight, although how Mum could have gone to his flat and not been put off by the "maximum safe volume" marks he puts on his radio volume dial is beyond me. Or maybe he didn't used to be so nerdy? I looked over at him. He'd cut up his entire plate of food before he started so it wouldn't burn his mouth. I guess maybe he was amazing in his own way (although he'd done his salad too, so maybe he was just weird).

"OK, so c'mon, guys. What's up?" Enough was enough. I needed to know. Dad winked at Mum. *Please don't be a baby. Please?!* I looked at Olive, who was dangling a bit of aubergine into her mouth, completely unaware.

Mum sipped her drink slowly. "Jack" – yes, my dad was called Jack Jackson; my grandparents were the Kris Jenners of their time – "do you want to do the honours, or shall I?"

Dad wiggled his eyebrows, a huge smile on his face. "What do you think, Kate?"

I snapped. "Please can someone, *anyone,* put me out of my misery already?!"

Mum put her knife and fork together and cleared her

throat. Here it comes. . .

I held my breath. If it wasn't a baby, we better not be moving. Anything more than a five-minute walk from Neet's would be too far.

"Well, as you guys know . . . Olive, c'mon, this is important." Oli stopped rocking her chair and, after an unnecessarily large eye-roll, started paying attention. "Dad's been having a pretty . . . tough year – that's fair to say, Jack?" He nodded slowly. "But. . ." She gave him a big, proud beamer of a smile. "The news is . . . the job he's been consulting for part-time has come off."

"Woo! Go, Dad!" Yes! This *was* great news. He'd been looking for a new contract for ages, and had been back and forth to interviews for weeks.

(And double yes. They weren't creating more human life!)

Dad grinned. "That's not even the good bit."

Uh-oh. I re-crossed my fingers.

"The job is health-and-safety lead on something quite big. . . For the next four weeks I'm going to be working on . . . a film."

Woah. Olive and I did a double take at each other. That *did* sound good. Much better than his last job overseeing Birmingham's biggest jam-making festival.

"And that film is *where*, Jack?" Mum interrupted

him, so excited she couldn't stop herself answering her own question. "On Skotheos. A Greek island!"

"What?!" My jaw actually dropped. No one in our family *ever* went abroad – and Dad was going for four weeks? That was SO cool! But ... a million questions hit me. Would Mum be OK? How would Dad fit enough suntan lotion in his case to stop him worrying about sunburn? And who was going to cook?

"When are you going?" I needed facts.

"Sunday." The day after tomorrow? "It's happened pretty quickly. And because you two both did so well this term..." Dad drummed his fingers on the table. "I'd love my brilliant daughters to come with me for the first two weeks..."

This time even Olive was speechless.

Our most boring summer ever had just been catapulted into a beach-holiday adventure of dreams.

CHAPTER THREE

To say I was in shock was like saying Ariana Grande has a couple of people following her on Instagram.

My total meltdown had lasted all evening. I'd gone through all stages of surprise holiday shock:

- Assuming it was a joke.
- Being numb with excitement when I realized it wasn't.
- Googling everything there was about Skotheos (IT HAS ACTUAL DOLPHINS?!).
- Happily ignoring Dad's statistics that the back of the plane was the safest place to sit in the event of a crash, as I was too excited about the thought of my first flight.

- Coming to terms with the fact that I was officially the kind of person who found the idea of a plane crash way less scary than the realization that I had nothing to wear.
- Begging Mum and Dad to lend me some money to go shopping tomorrow.

It sucked that Mum couldn't get time off work to join us, but she was really happy we could all go – and we'd promised to ring every day with our news.

Olive and I asked for so many details about the film. *All* the details. Who was in it? What was it about? Would there be people in those chairs with their names on the back?

But Dad was hopeless. All he'd been able to tell us was that the biggest hazard was going to be the treacherous mountain paths, so we needed to pack "sensible shoes with good grip". It was at that exact moment I waved goodbye to any hope of having hot film goss for Neet, unless she was suddenly interested in protective footwear of the rich and famous.

Olive had relentlessly quizzed Dad about which actors might be in it – and if she'd get to meet a real-life famous person. She was *obsessed*. Sadly for her, Dad didn't flinch with any hint of recognition when she reeled off hundreds of potential names, ranging from the world's most in-demand hottie, TJ, through to the *Holby City* cast. So we could only assume the film was one of those obscure indie flicks for old people who like scenery. But who cared? It was still a holiday! On a film set! In actual Greece!

The only thing denting my excitement was how to tell Neet. I didn't want to be halfway around the world from her (well 1879.4 miles, I'd checked) when she was stuck at home on her own.

By the time Olive had gone to bed, and it was just me, Mum and Dad watching TV (they'd let me put on *Mamma Mia* for Greek-island research purposes), I still hadn't told her.

"Megs?" Mum whispered from the other sofa. "You *are* excited, aren't you?"

I realized I'd been staring at the film in a worry trance, so gave her my biggest smile. I didn't want her thinking I was anything other than completely grateful. "Of course!"

But Mum wasn't buying it. She came and sat beside me, stroking my hair like she did when I was little.

"What's up, little sausage?"

"Nothing." I stared at the TV, trying to work out whether to tell her what was on my mind. "It's going to be awesome... Really awesome, thank you SO much."

Hopefully that would convince her.

"But. . .?"

It hadn't. Oh well, I might as well come clean.

"OK, if I tell you you've got to promise that you know I'm COMPLETELY made up to be going."

Mum smiled softly. "Uh-huh. . ."

I shrugged. "I'm just worried about Neet. . . That's all."

Mum nodded – she instantly got it. She saw Neet almost as much as she saw me, and had been in and out of the hospital with Sheila, Neet's mum, ever since the accident.

"That makes sense, Meg. She *is* your best friend."

But there was something else I hadn't shared. Something I'd been thinking about ever since I found out the news.

I'd been working on a plan too – but I had no idea if Mum and Dad would agree to it. I pressed pause on the remote, and with a deep breath to build up my confidence, I talked them through it.

And after lots of questions and a long, long discussion they finally said yes.

It was a long shot, but if there was *any* way on earth I could get Neet out there with us, I knew I had to make it happen.

My hand shaking with nerves, I dialled Neet's landline.

CHAPTER FOUR

A-NITA TELL YOU HOW GREAT BTS ARE:
Sure thing. Want to head here for 10.30? Bring
toast.

I was so glad she was up for a trip to town and
replied instantly.

**MEG: See you there. Marmite, ya? And 👏 👏
👏 on the name.**

Neet was always changing her name on my phone when
I wasn't looking – one of the joys of having the same
password.

I'd already been up for hours, to have my usual

Saturday swim practice. Today was time trials, which were exhausting, but also OK because it meant the biggest breakfast ever when I got back (although Olive got the same, and all she did was sleep). It had felt so good to be back in the water. Pushing myself in the pool helped clear my head after all the drama of yesterday. As suspected, Neet's dad had said no, and now I was dreading telling her about the change in my summer plans. As tough as it would be, I knew it would be better in person.

The worst thing was I knew she'd be lovely and understanding, but that just made me feel even more of a rubbish friend for abandoning her for two weeks. With her dad always at the hospital, and no school, her house was going to feel emptier than ever.

I used the short walk through our estate and across the churchyard to her house to think how to tell her. But when I rang the doorbell, Mr Shah, Neet's dad, answered.

Seeing him in real life made me feel extra awkward that I'd put him on the spot on the phone last night. "Is, er, Neet around?"

He pulled the door semi-closed behind him and lowered his voice. "Sorry I couldn't say yes last night, Megan. I do know you had nothing but Anita's best interests in mind." He looked down the road, as if finding the right words. "Her mum and I were talking on the phone this morning about how happy we are she has a friend like you." He paused. "Especially now."

He sounded deflated, just like he always did when he talked about Sheila.

"S'OK, Mr Shah. I get it." I meant it. It was a big ask, and I shouldn't have added to his worries.

"Well, how about you get yourself inside?" He opened the door again. "Neet's in the lounge. Music way too loud to hear you." He sighed. "As usual."

I found Neet sitting cross-legged in front of the speaker, her arms in the air, her favourite BTS T-shirt on, their album blaring. She had no idea I was there, so I crept up behind her and super-slowly pushed the end of the longest piece of my hair into her ear.

She spun round.

"Whatthehell . . . lloMegan." She fake punched me in the leg and turned down the music. Not a lot, but a bit. "Woah, is it half ten already?"

I sat down beside her. "Want me to come back another time?"

"Oh yeah . . . I've got big plans of sitting here on my own that you can't disturb me from." She laughed, but my stomach sank. Telling her was going to be grim;

better get it done as quickly as possible.

"OK, full disclosure. I have something to tell you."

Her brown eyes popped wide open. "Wah. Your parents' news?" I nodded. "If they need help naming the baby, I'm here for that." She twiddled a rogue piece of her long dark hair that had never made it into her ponytail. "I'm a big fan of Rainbow – think they'll be into it? Or Cliff, if it's a boy?"

"It's . . . it's not that. . ."

"What?" She leant back. "Don't tell me you've completed the challenge already?"

I cocked my head to one side. What was she on about?

"Er, hello?! It's only day one, don't act like you've forgotten. . ." She shook her head, fake disappointed. "MEG'S MISSION TO FIND A HOTTIE, STICK YOUR TONGUE DOWN HIS THROAT AND NAIL YOUR SECOND FIRST KISS!"

Which was the exact moment her dad walked in.

"Erm, is this an, er, bad time?" Was he embarrassed or terrified? I couldn't tell. Thank goodness I had my back to him so I could glare freely at Neet. She wasn't even pretending to hide how much she was enjoying our mega-squirm.

"Nah, Dad, it's all good." Mr Shah took a seat on the

sofa, and I swivelled round, hoping my face had faded from mortified red to something resembling human. "Although Meg and I were just about to chat about the feminist logistics of body hair and whether we were ovulating in sync?"

Mr Shah closed his eyes and breathed in so deeply, it was like he was trying to inhale himself into an outer-body experience somewhere far, far from here.

"So, Megan." He opened his eyes. "Have you told Anita your news?"

Well, thanks for dropping me right in it, Mr Shah.

I shook my head. "Was just about to. . ." Would he take the hint and, well, leave? I waited. Nope. He was here to stay.

"Sorry, best mate, who dis?" Anita stood up just so she could fold her arms and look more annoyed than if she was sitting down. "My dad knows your news before *me*?!"

"I, erm. . ." This was painful. I shuffled on the carpet. "The thing is. . ." I gave Neet a smile we both knew was totally lame. "My dad's got a new job. . . On a film set."

Her face dropped. "Woah."

"On a Greek island."

She whistled an impressed whit-woo. "Go, Mr Jackson!"

"And Ol and I are going to fly out with him... For two weeks... Tomorrow."

Neet stared at me in shock for a moment. Please don't let her be too disappointed?!

But she dropped back on to the floor and knee-shuffled over to me, throwing her arms around me.

"Oh, Megs." She squeezed me so tight. Human-straitjacket-breath-constricting tight. "This is the COOLEST."

Out of all people, Neet knew how envious I was every September when our classmates came back with their holiday stories. She knew I'd ruled out the chance of it ever being me. Up until yesterday, I really thought my only chance of a beach-foot-selfie would be Bognor Regis. Even though she knew this meant all our summer plans would be put on hold, she was still happy for me.

"You da best, Neet." I dropped my voice. "I just wish SO hard you could come."

I didn't need to tell her about asking her dad if she could come too – I didn't want her to be cross or disappointed it hadn't worked out.

She leant back. "Don't be silly. You go have a *ridiculous* time for the both of us. But" – she poked me in the knee – "you'll HAVE to complete that mission now..." She said it like she was being cryptic and her dad didn't know *exactly* what she meant because she'd just said it. My dignity wilted. "For me, and for the sake of our future social life."

Mr Shah coughed. "Megan was so keen for you to go too that she rang last night to ask if you could fly out with them tomorrow."

Wow. I wasn't expecting him to tell her. Neet gave my hand a secret squeeze; she was grateful I'd tried.

"I'm sorry I couldn't say yes, but what with your mum away, I thought it was best."

"No biggie, Dad." Neet knew how stressed her dad had been, and how tight money was for them, and she wasn't the kind of person to make things worse by making her dad feel bad. Thinking about it, maybe I should never have put him in that position? Or dragged my parents into it? But whenever I visited her mum, she always made me promise I was making sure Neet was still having fun, so this had been my way of keeping that promise.

"I've got the excitement of Solihull Splash pool, which can be *deceptively* like crystal-clear tropical shores at times. And did someone say wave machine?!"

Mr Shah smiled at his daughter, clearly thinking the same as me – she was about as ace as people could come.

"You really are something, Anita." He paused. "Which is one of the reasons I'm a little sad too. Because..." He wrung his hands together. "As I said, I had to do what I thought best..." He started to smile. "But after chatting with your mother, we realized that whatever *I* think is best, sometimes she doesn't." He laughed, but it was with nothing but affection. "And, well, although tomorrow's not the right time for you to go, we thought maybe the Sunday after could be."

Sorry, what? Was this actually happening?!

"I'm going to really miss you for a week."

Neet made a noise that definitely wasn't a word. Something like a "nrrhhuuhhgggggeeee?" The same sound I'd have made if all my noise pipes weren't blocked with shock.

Mr Shah grinned. "Mum reserved the flights this morning. She was adamant her being in hospital shouldn't stop you having fun."

Neet looked at me. I looked at Neet.

We erupted into an explosion of singing, whooping, hugging and leaping in circles. Barks and Rec looked less than impressed. But we didn't care. This was a dream come true. Her parents were THE BEST!!! I might have even told Mr Shah I loved him in all the madness.

But as her dad got knocked over by Neet jumping

on him, he laughed – properly laughed, something I hadn't seen for yonks. With Neet's arms wrapped round him, her squealing with happiness, he looked at me and mouthed "Thank you". But he didn't need to thank me.

He'd just launched the best summer of my life.

CHAPTER
FIVE

"Are we nearly there yet?" Olive had joked as Mum pulled off the drive in the pitch black of way-too-early morning. I'd laughed – when she was young, Oli used to say it on the minute, every minute, every single journey. But two hours later, when she'd started to say it for real, on the minute, every minute, somehow managing to be even louder than my noise-cancelling headphones, I was wondering how possible it was to lose a four-and-a-half-foot sister at the airport.

In a bid to shut her up, I'd even resorted to lending her my phone so she could play with the latest filters, meaning I had to swap listening to the 1975 for listening to Mum and Dad chat about the predicted Brussels sprout shortage. Please never let me become that boring.

Or at least please let me care about a more interesting vegetable.

When we finally arrived at the airport, Mum hugged me goodbye while Dad and Olive unloaded the bags on to a trolley in the drop-off area. "Now, remember to FaceTime." I nodded against her shoulder, worried my voice would crack if I answered. I'd never been away from her for so long, and my left eye was reacting by doing a solo-cry. It was definitely the more emotional of my two eyes.

"Sure thing, Mum." Phew, I didn't tip into full-blown sob. Mum kissed my forehead.

"And look after that one." We turned to look at Olive. She was tummy-surfing on the suitcase I'd borrowed from Mum (bright green and said "BRING ME GIN" on one side and "NOW" on the other).

"Just for you," I replied as Olive crashed into an innocent businessy-looking woman – I turned away, pretending not to know her. "Although if she tries to talk to me about slime experiments, I'm out." There are only so many times you can pretend to be interested in the effect of adding shaving foam to a green blob (although, I had squirrelled away a bottle from the bathroom into my suitcase to surprise her with, if things got really desperate).

Mum laughed. "You know I meant your dad, right?" She leant back and held my shoulders, looking me straight in the eye. "He's not always as, er. . ." She looked at him, searching for the right word. He was double-checking the addresses on our suitcases, and shouting at Olive to confirm she'd packed a spare set of clothes in her hand-luggage in case our other bags got lost. "Well, as straightforward as he looks."

I had no idea what Mum meant, but promised her anyway. If she was relying on me to be the sensible one on this holiday, we were *all* in trouble. I'd only just realized I'd forgotten to pack shoes. But a parking attendant was approaching, and you're only allowed to say emotional goodbyes for five minutes, so after another quick round of hugs, it was just Dad, Oli and me.

Being in the airport already felt like being in a film. Standing in the security queue, we were surrounded by people all travelling back home, or going on new adventures. I couldn't help but make up stories in my head about why everyone was here. I grinned to myself. I bet no one would guess that me and my dysfunctional family were on the way to an amazing Greek island to hang out on a film set. My phone vibrated. Uh-oh. I was next in the queue to go through security.

I NEET TO NOT FORGET MY BEST MATE
STUCK AT HOME: Thought – we've never been
in a different time zone before #missyoualready
#Ithink #cosIdontknowwhatIthinkatthistimeona
Sundaymorning

I NEET TO NOT FORGET MY BEST MATE
STUCK AT HOME: Nope. Double-checked. And
I DO miss you.

I looked up. About ten seconds before I was called forward.

Is it too early to eat the rest of that Galaxy from
last night? Asking for a friend.

Well, she moved on quickly. I went to reply, but she got in first.

YOU'VE FORGOTTEN ME ALREADY.

Or not.

"Miss? Any laptops or iPads?"

Oops, time to go. I fired Neet back a picture of me doing the saddest face I could, and chucked my phone down in the plastic tray, along with my tiny case, laptop, two emergency tampons, a hairy Fruit Pastille I'd discovered in my pocket, and my trainers.

"Nice socks," the security guard said, not smiling as he pushed my tray along. Why had I worn the ones that looked like two giant slices of pizza? And why was I the only one who seemed to be leaving sweaty footmarks on the floor?!

"Sorreeee." I looked around to check Olive and Dad were busy in another queue. "I don't-a. Speak-a . . . Eeenglish?" Surprise! I'm too international and exciting to be bothered by unleashing accidental novelty socks! He looked down suspiciously at my tray. Which had my passport in. My very British passport.

Another message from Neet popped up, vibrating my tray. As it lit up, both me and the security guy automatically looked down.

MEGAANNN. Turn that frown upside down!
You're flying off to LOVE ISLAND to GO SNOG
A HOTTIE!!!!!!!

Without waiting to be asked, I stepped forward into the scanner, wishing the weird X-ray things could also block out the soundwaves of the security guard's laugh.

I put my hands up and stood still as it whizzed around, trying to look as self-assured as you can while wearing margherita slices on your feet and knowing Neet's message was slowly cruising past the eyes of three more security staff. I could hear the sniggers rippling down the line.

As I shuffled out, the scanner beeped. A bored-looking security lady felt around the band of my bra, only to loudly declare that, "The wires can sometimes be so chunky they can set them off." Sock-shamed, now bra-shamed. I thought flying was meant to be the scary bit – no one had warned me about getting through security. I ran to grab my shoes and clear the area.

"Miss, is this yours?"

Clutching my trainers, I looked round. A stern old man was holding my overnight case.

What had I accidentally put in there?

I'd been so proud of how much I'd crammed in, but when he flicked open the locks, my stuffing technique meant two pairs of pants projectile-flew out. Like a jack-in-the-box, but a pant-in-the-case. He picked them up with a grabber, as if they were more dangerous than actual explosives.

"Everything OK?" I'd taken so long Dad had caught

me up.

The security guard answered instead. He was still dangling my pants. "Just a double-check, sir. Some irregularities showed up on the scanner."

Dad and Oli watched as he meticulously unpacked *everything*, item by item, making disapproving noises throughout. Highlights included the sample packet of moustache-hair-removal cream I'd snagged from Mum (to attempt to use on my legs), a box of power remove-blackhead strips, enough tampons to last six months (all max flow, of course), some Marmite I'd put into a tiny pot as I could never be too far away from any, and a book on female serial killers. Looking objectively at it, I can't say it made me look the best candidate for air travel.

But eventually, after a lecture about separating liquids from my bags, they let me go, and after whizzing round the duty-free shops – I even talked Dad into letting me get some flip-flops ("Think of all the grip on wet surfaces") – we only just had time to grab food for the plane and go.

"Look, Meg, I've got a chimney!" Olive was squeezing her cup of tea to make little puffs of steam come out the sippy-hole thing. Had I been entertained by such things when I was younger? Probably.

"Cool." I responded generically, looking back at the

loo, where Dad had disappeared to. For someone who didn't like drama, he really was cutting it fine – they'd already called our flight to board. "Don't play with that, though. You don't want to burn yourself."

She smiled and shrugged. "Don't have to do what you say."

If there was anything to pick a fight over, I didn't really think it should be me not wanting her to get first-degree burns. But whatever, it was the principle.

"'Course you do. I'm your BIG SISTER."

We both knew Olive did exactly what Olive wanted, but instead of biting back, she smiled and kept puffing her drink.

Worrying. Very worrying.

I sipped my tea. It was still absolutely boiling, but I didn't want her to know I'd just melted four layers off my tongue.

Olive made another steam puff, grinning to herself. "Wonder if my *big sister* has checked her camera roll recently. . .?"

Argh. I didn't want to show any hint of being interested, but I was dealing with a person who once cut a huge clump of her own fringe hair off just to pretend I'd done it, so I knew I couldn't flat out ignore her threats. Reluctantly, I opened up my album: pictures and pictures of Oli in the car.

Except one.

I zoomed in.

SHE HADN'T?!

Olive nodded slowly, smugly, proud of her handiwork.

We weren't allowed to swear at home. But we weren't *at* home. We were in the middle of hundreds of strangers and small children, which meant I was totally in my right to hurl out every single obscenity I knew (and some I made up to confuse Olive).

"Youuuu—"

But she cut me off before I could get another word out.

"So, this holiday. . ." She folded her arms. "No being mean to me, orrrr I tell Dad what your" – she air-quoted to wind me up even more – "'mission' is."

She'd not just *read* last night's messages from Neet; she'd *screengrabbed* them to prove she'd read them. My little sister, purveyor of misery, bundle of evil topped with a bob, knew about my promise to get my second first kiss on this holiday, and now she was threatening to out me to Dad. Who, without Mum there to make him think like a normal person, would assume I was a boy-hunting maniac and would never let me leave the apartment.

It was official. My sister was the worst.

I lunged to grab her.

"You little. . ." But as I lunged, Olive swerved, and as I stepped left, my foot got caught in my flip-flop carrier bag.

Uh-oh.

Obstruction!

I was going too fast to steady myself. . . I was going down!

Noooooooooooooo.

In what felt like slow motion, in the middle of Birmingham airport, I went full-on flying. But not the plane kind.

Good news – my hands broke my fall.

Bad news – it meant they dropped my cup, and I hit the floor with a massive, tea-soaked splat.

Ow.

I'd always known floors were solid, but this one seemed extra hard.

Ow. Ow.

I lay face down. In shock.

Please let this not be happening.

Could I crawl from here on to the plane?

Life couldn't get any worse.

"DARLING!!!!"

It just got worse. Dad was so loud it sounded like he was being broadcast through the airport speakers.

"WHY ARE YOU ON THE FLOOR?!"

"Oh, it just looked like a comfy place to rest," I mumbled into the ground, although stopped when I tasted what I think was floor-dirt.

"ARE YOU HURT?" Why was he shouting when he was right beside me? Or was it so I could hear over Olive's cackling? I couldn't bring myself to look up. "FIRST AID KIT. WE NEED A FIRST AID KIT."

I sighed into the floor. The tea pool beside my face bubbled. All this for trying to attack my sister. Where was the karma?

"AND WE NEED A 'CAUTIONARY SLIPPERY SURFACE A-FRAME'."

I heard someone say, "A what?!" to which Dad replied, "A-frame," which was not helpful.

Why had I worn white? Lying in a puddle of burning beverage, I already *knew* my top had gone see-through.

And what was that hot, wet, damp feeling in my groin?

Oh yes. I was absorbing groin-tea. Great.

I was SpongeMeg WetPants, the human mop.

A guy's voice cut through the general murmuring of fake concern (that was actually people loving the drama).

"Is she all right?"

Olive didn't miss a beat. "Oh yeah, just my sister being her usual cool self."

But the guy didn't laugh – he sounded worried. "She really went down. I saw it happen."

"Darling," Dad shook my shoulder, finally realizing I'd been motionless for quite a while. "Are you OK?"

There was nothing left but to face the world.

Wiping the floor grime off my face, I pushed myself up. A circle of people had gathered round me. I tried not to focus on any faces, and smiled at Dad to stop him panicking. Maybe it wasn't that bad? Although judging by Olive's fresh burst of howling and pointing it definitely *was* that bad. But Dad seemed reassured I was alive and went back to helping a member of staff flip out warning signs. His priority was definitely spill > daughter.

But there *was* someone whose eye I did catch – the guy who'd sounded worried. He was about my age, had floppy ginger hair, and was kind of cute. Why did he have to be cute?! I smiled, grateful for his concern, but mainly totally mortified – and then even more mortified as I remembered what I looked like. I crossed my arms over my chest, trying to hide my bra, which was now showing through – first it was insulted for being too wiry, and now it was on display.

"Sorry?" I said, scrambling to my feet, although I wasn't sure what for. "Not my finest hour." Now I wasn't bleeding or scarred for life, people had lost interest (sorry to disappoint you, guys!).

"You sure you're OK?" the guy said.

I nodded, entirely sure I wasn't.

"Well, you've certainly brought a whole new meaning to wet T-shirt." He grinned, trying to lighten the mood, but Olive snorted. He immediately slapped his hand on to his forehead. "As in *TEA*. The drink. *Tea*-shirt. Which sounds exactly the same as 'T', now I'm saying it out loud."

Even though I was dripping beverage from all regions, I laughed. "I *am* basically a Digestive right now." Some tea plipped off my elbow. "Consider me dunked."

Olive had gone alarmingly quiet, standing with her arms crossed, the most unsubtle WELL THIS IS INTERESTING smirk on her face.

He thrust a handful of napkins out. I muttered a thanks and dabbed at the most soaked bits (so glam!) as he nodded a goodbye.

"Is anything hurting?" Dad had switched his focus back to me.

"Mainly my pride," I replied honestly, but I was distracted watching Napkin Boy walk off. At least he would never know who I was.

"COULD JACK JACKSON, OLIVE JACKSON AND MEGAN JACKSON MAKE THEIR WAY TO GATE 8B IMMEDIATELY. IF NOT YOUR BAGS WILL BE OFFLOADED FROM THE PLANE."

Et tu, tannoy?!

Maybe if I didn't react, no one would work out it was us.

Olive, however, didn't get the subtlety memo, and started screeching "THAT'S US!" repeatedly, kicking my foot and yelling, "Meg, Meg, Meg."

Napkin Boy looked back and smiled. I did the only thing I could think of – stuck my chin up, pressed some napkins over my soggy bra area, and marched to the gate. Which I realized was in the other direction, so then had to turn and march back again.

But despite everything, I'd soon forgotten all about being a human-biscuit, because I was sitting in my first-ever plane seat, seatbelt clipped on, ready to go. After some bings and bongs, and a safety demonstration with something that looked like a hosepipe (Dad clapped at the end), we were taking off.

My ears popped as we climbed higher. For the first time in my life, instead of looking up and seeing a plane in the sky, wondering who was on it and where they were going, I was looking down at the ground, wondering if anyone was looking up at me. I waved, even though I was about a billion feet too high up for Mum to see – and we were probably over Bournemouth already.

Oli said she wasn't scared, but was suspiciously quiet and had buried her head in my armpit (at least it was tea fragranced) saying she was tired. So I turned off listening to Years & Years and instead we spent the flight playing a Harry Potter quiz game on the family iPad, and munching our way through the miniature snacks they handed out. When the plane started to descend for landing, I was brave enough to look out of the window the whole way down. I was so glad I did.

The view was A. Ma. Zing.

Gorgeous blue sea for miles, rocks, hills, forests filling the islands, and nestled round them, tiny clusters of white buildings, bright swimming pools dotted between them – and we were descending to a tiny strip of land in the middle of it.

Much to Dad's disapproval, Ol and I swapped seats so she could have the window, and we held hands the whole way down. After a bumpy landing, I walked down the wobbly metal plane steps and took it all in. The hustle and bustle of the airport. The signs in a language I couldn't read. The heat that hit me like a punch.

Everyone chatting in Greek.

It was already amazing and I hadn't even set foot on land!

This was the tropical island dream! Time to get to the apartment, get showered and get this holiday started!

Is what I thought – until Dad reminded me we still had to get a cab to the port, then a boat, and then another cab to the apartment. But as Olive and I sat on the open deck of a boat – which was the size of half our street – it was like the warm sea air was blowing away everything that had been stressing me out back home.

Party stress. The kiss. The haters. Yup, they could stay in the UK, thanks. Out here I was new Meg. Meg who had better things to do, like look at the sun glistening off the sea, fish jumping in and out of the water, and, woah – were they the beaches of Skotheos looming into view!? It looked like a postcard.

I messaged Neet a pic of Ol and me.

We're on a boat. #TopDeckLyf

She replied with a gif of an owl doing a sassy neck roll and the words "JELLY MUCH". And then a picture of the empty Galaxy wrapper. And then "Welcome to Love Island 🏳 ♡ 🌴 " which Olive not only saw but then began chanting.

But right now, much to Olive's annoyance, I didn't care. I couldn't care. I walked to the front railing and got my Kate-Winslet-Titanic arms on.

I thought I was going to spend the summer hanging out at home, and now I was here. In this gorgeous, hot paradise.

Un. Real.

But as the boat docked, something equally as gorgeous came in to view on land.

An unreeeeasonably fit, dark-haired, dishevelled boy.

Who, when he saw me, started shouting something.

My name.

CHAPTER SIX

"You *are* Megan, aren't you?" He looked confused at my shock. As if *he* was the one allowed to be confused in this situation.

He turned to his friend and said something in Greek. Probably "Who is this British weirdo?" Name-shouter was super tanned, in shorts, flip-flops and a white T-shirt (zero tea on it), with the sort of body that both filled it, and left it baggy, all at once. If Neet was here, she'd describe him as RIDICULOUS. If she could speak at all.

"I . . . am. . ." I managed to stutter. I *wished* I didn't have dubious brown stains everywhere. And my mascara hadn't totally flaked down my face. And my ponytail wasn't sticking to my neck with sweat. There was SO

MUCH sweat. In places I didn't even know I *could* sweat. And I wasn't pulling a suitcase that said "BRING ME GIN". And I bet any second, Dad was going to march up with an information pack and some facts about deaths from sunburn.

T-shirt Boy looked at me and nodded. I smiled. He didn't. Olive prodded my hand.

"How does he know your name?" She said it loudly, as if he wasn't the third person in this conversation and could totally hear her.

He gave Olive the smallest of smiles.

"Because I was told to meet you here." Which made a lot more sense than "I shout random names at every boat that arrives".

"I'm Olive." She waved, totally unfazed. "Meg's my sister." She loved talking to strangers, which was handy for breaking the socially awkward ice. "She reckons this is some kind of a love island and she's going to meet her dreeeeeeeeam boy." Or not.

T-shirt Boy grinned. Or was it a laugh? Or grimace?! It was hard to tell as I couldn't be staring any harder at the ground than I already was. "Ol!" I whacked her in the arm, as playfully as I could get away with, when really I wanted to maim/potentially kill. But when I looked up, T-shirt Boy was still grinning – and it was all

63

kinds of cute. What was it with boys in transport hubs today?! "Ignore her. She doesn't know what she's talking about."

The conversation instantly stopped as Dad strode over at full "I'm an efficient adult" pelt, dropping his suitcase down with a bang. He stuck his hand out for a shake. "So you must be Vangelis?"

T-shirt Boy nodded and shook Dad's hand. Dad added in a firm pat on the outside of his arm (way too formal considering Vangelis looked like the kind of guy who had never worn a shoe with laces). The pat thing was something Dad did when he wanted to appear cool. It never worked.

"Sorry" – I couldn't bear the awkward pat-shaking any more – "but how *does* everyone know each other?"

Vangelis lifted up his other hand – in it was the sign he'd been holding, that I'd totally not seen as I was far too busy looking at him. In big letters, it said. . .

Καλώς ήρθατε JACK, OLIVE
AND MEGAN JACKSON.
I'M ... Vangelis.

Ahhh, this made a lot more sense.

"Vangelis is here to pick us up," Dad explained. *Two*

minutes too late, padre. "Although, can I just say" – he was going to anyway – "road traffic accidents are the leading cause of death for young people. So on these dangerous mountain roads, Vangelis, we are *very* happy to have a local at the wheel who is no doubt incredibly experienced. Sure you're an absolute pro."

If Dad's arm-slapping hadn't made them instant bro-skis, then this safety lecture would really be a clincher. Parents always complain that we say they're embarrassing, but instead of moaning, maybe they should just not be so embarrassing?

Credit to Vangelis: he didn't look even a bit weirded out.

"Nai." Vangelis noticed our blank stares. "Greek for yes." Without flinching he scooped up both mine and Oli's bags. "Anyway, call me Geli. And follow me..."

Within minutes we were whizzing along a tiny road along the edge of a huge cliff, mountains on one side and a sheer drop to bright blue sea on the other. Much to Dad's alarm, Geli put the roof down. With the wind whipping round us, it was impossible to hear anything, which made me suspect it was a tactical move of Geli's to avoid conversation with my dad. Olive and I went all music video and put our hands in the air. I'm pretty sure I noticed at least four despairing looks from Geli via the rear-view mirror, but I was also pretty sure that despite his accidental Urban Outfitters model brooding looks, I didn't have time to care what he thought. I'd probably never see him again anyway. These views, with the sky looking like an Instagram post filtered up to 100, the sun sparkling across miles and miles of sea, one lone waterskier zipping through the waves, might be normal to him, but the most normal view from our car at home was the rainy A34.

After thirty minutes of gawping at the views, we took a sharp left down a steep hill and rattled along a cobbled road into a village. It was even cuter than I'd imagined: all white and blue buildings jumbled together, bright orange and red flowers tumbling down their walls. Geli briefly stopped to chat to an old man who only had about three teeth, which must make his brushing routine very quick. Once he left Vangelis turned around.

"So, we are almost there... Pretty cool, huh?" We both nodded.

"Is this it?" Olive's eyes were wide with disbelief. I shrugged. Dad had already told me we were staying somewhere basic inland.

"Nah – we must be making a stop." We were parking up on the edge of a huge, empty beach, the waves rolling in on the white sand, the sea so clear it looked like tap water. Along the back of the beach was a white block of apartments, all with balconies and patios that opened out directly on to the sand. This must be where the VIPs were staying.

"Dad – can this be on the visit list?" I *had* to come back here. He leant into the gap between the front seats and twisted to face us.

"No can do, Meg, sorry." Maybe it was too exclusive? He smiled. "Because this is home, sweet home."

WHAT THE HECK?!

This beach paradise was our home?! And Dad had known all along? "For real?!"

He nodded, a big grin on his face, pleased with his surprise.

"Come on then, girls. . ."

He jumped out of the car, but neither Olive nor I could move. How had we got this lucky?

Geli opened my door and held something towards me. Keys. "You'll be needing these. . ."

"Thanks."

But he didn't let go, letting me pull at them slightly. "*Efharisto*, is what we say here."

I repeated it with my best shot, but it came out a bit more like ef-gary-sto. I hope that didn't mean something weird in Greek, like "trifle", or "you're really fit".

"No problem," he said like it was a bit of a problem,

actually. This boy was intense – and intensely hot. He was clearly keeping us firmly at arm's length. Was it because he was trying to work us out? Because if he was, he'd have worked out I'm not very good at talking to mysterious, incredibly good-looking strangers. I pulled myself out of the car and attempted it anyway, as Olive and Dad unloaded the boot.

"Do you know any other Greek phrases? I need to learn!"

"Well, as someone who has lived their whole life on this island, I know a couple of Greek phrases, yes." Oof, burn. "What would you like to know?"

I ran my hands through my ponytail, which, thanks to the wind, was no longer a tail but more of a matted downwards rhinoceros horn with added floof. I tried to pretend my fingers weren't now stuck in my own hair as I tried to untangle them.

"Just whatever you think will come in most useful."

Vangelis thought. "Have you got your phone?"

"That's English, though?"

"No." He laughed under his breath. "I mean, I can write it down. . ." Oh. I yanked my fingers out, opened up Notepad and held out my phone. He typed a long sentence in letters I'd never seen before.

Αστείο γεγονός! Έχω ένα καρότο για κατοικίδιο!

There were some sounds written out in English letters beneath it. "That's how you pronounce it. It should see you through."

"What does it mean?"

"It means you'll be a friend of the locals. Now, shall we take the bags in?"

And with Olive pushing to be first, we headed through a tiny blue wooden gate, along a stone path surrounded by spiky green plants, and up to a huge, white three-storey building.

It was epic.

I don't know why it was called an apartment. It was as big as our entire house. Vangelis unlocked the huge glass patio doors and slid them open. Inside was a lounge and a little modern kitchen. Olive and I dropped our bags and dashed upstairs. There was a double room in the top floor, and a twin and single room on the first floor. The twin had its own balcony overlooking the sea. I threw myself on to one of the beds and yelled, "Shotgun."

Olive wasn't happy but Dad said I could keep it as Neet was coming, and smoothed it over by promising her she could choose her own stuff in the supermarket shop, and I promised she could come in whenever she wanted (after checking the door had a lock).

But with the sea on our doorstep, all Ol and I wanted to do was head to the beach, so after checking it was OK with Dad, I scrambled into my swimsuit – which was much more swim team than sexy beach wear, but *who cared?* – and sprinted downstairs. Only to realize Vangelis was still there. Which made me realize *I* cared. I ran back up, pulled on a T-shirt over the top and ran back down.

Vangelis looked up from his phone. "I'm heading off now. Everything OK with the apartment?"

I nodded. "Everything's amazing. Although..." I hoped it wasn't a stupid question. "Is it OK to swim out there?" It sounded silly but I'd never been properly swimming in any sea.

"'Course." He seemed annoyed I'd even asked, but then spotted the goggles in my hand. "If you enjoy it there are lots of activities you can do here. Kayaking, surfing, many things. We even have marine life you can't see anywhere else in the world."

Wow. The only "marine life" I'd spotted in our local pool were floating plasters. "I'm *totally* going to do some of that."

He picked up a pen and scribbled something down. "Here then. Take this ... and if you're serious, give me a ring."

It was *his* number.

With an awkward thanks, I shoved it into my bag, and with nothing else to say to each other, he left.

"Dad, I'm off for a swim!" I yelled up the stairs.

"I'll be watching from my window!" he yelled down. "Don't go further than the buoys!"

Olive snorted. "That's exactly what Meg's looking for, actually."

But luckily for her, Dad was too far away to hear, and I didn't have time to give her evils, as I was already out the door. The water was even nicer than I'd imagined. Crystal clear, and still warm from the sunny day. And as I swam, fish (sorry, *marine life*) tickling my legs as they darted around me, I couldn't help but wonder. Maybe Neet was right. Things *were* different here. I felt so free. Maybe this really could be my Love Island? Somewhere to meet someone totally new and different from the boys back home. The perfect place to have my second first kiss. Put everything behind me.

Or . . . was I just getting carried away, and the only boy who was going to give me his number was doing it to encourage me to hire a canoe?

CHAPTER SEVEN

When I woke up the next morning, the sunlight was piercing through the gaps in my curtains. It felt like Christmas morning, if December was boiling hot, and you'd pulled your pyjama bottoms off in the night because it felt like sleeping in a furnace.

But who cared? I WAS ON ACTUAL HOLIDAY!

I jumped straight out of bed, pulled open the curtains, and slid open the balcony door. The view was unreal – the beach was picture perfect, the sand all smooth like it had been reset, and it was completely empty except for the three-toothed Random Old Dude and his dog. The sea didn't just look amazing, it sounded amazing – like cars whooshing past my window back home. But sea.

I dragged the little metal chair to the front of my balcony. There were big white walls either side that must be other apartments, but I didn't want to peek over and be nosey in case I got spotted wearing my oversized My Little Pony nightie and people didn't realize it was ironic.

I wanted to ring Neet, but it was only 8:30 a.m. so it'd be half six back home, so instead I messaged Mum, who was one of those weird morning people.

Beats the view from my bedroom. Wish you were here xx

I sent her a video of the insane view. I'd normally post on my story too, but I was still in social media hiding and I wanted this to be a holiday away from everything, especially Megabite comments and discovering what new horrors I'd been tagged into.

Mum replied with a picture of the gym.

Same!

Poor thing. I *must* send her a video every day so she knows I'm thinking of her. I leant back in my chair and took it all in. Live in the moment, *be present*, that's what Mum always said. It was so peaceful – but after twenty minutes I wasn't living in the moment any more, I was melting in it. I was a total sweaty blob, so I headed in, which is when I heard banging noises downstairs. This could mean only one thing: breakfast. I headed down to find Dad pottering away.

"Ooh la la," I whistled. He was heading outside to the garden-patio bit underneath my balcony, three baguettes under his arm.

"We're in Greece, not France." He wiggled, his shorts flapping around his skinny legs. "Although, I did enjoy my little trip to the bakery. Thought we could have breakfast *al fresco*. . ."

Judging by the spread on the table, it wasn't just a bakery he'd been to. There was watermelon, feta cheese, the hugest tomatoes I'd ever seen, yogurt, honey, nuts, butter in paper (melting more than me), and a cucumber as big as Olive's arm.

"Dad, you have outdone yourself!" I grabbed the jug of water to carry out. "On literally everything."

"Glad you like it," he said, laying out the last bit of food. After months of him worrying about work, it was so nice to see him relaxed again. He spotted my stealth attempt at eating a bit of crust. "Shall we wait for your sister?"

Right on cue she appeared. "Chocolate spread! You're

the best!" Without any offer of help, Olive plonked herself at the table and opened a jar of the exact same spread we had back home, ignoring all the amazing stuff around it. "Oh, and good morning!"

Dad raised a toast to Mum and we got stuck in.

"So, Dad," Olive said, chewing her way through a huge hunk of baguette. She was a bottomless pit for food. "Now you're here, you must have more stuff you can tell us about the film...? Ideally the actors' names, pur-lease."

Dad laughed. "Ol, nothing's changed since last night."

"But you went to set last night!"

"And very exciting it was. Excellent rigging, some great systems already in place." He had that wistful look in his eye he got when he looked in a drawer full of sorted cables.

"DAD!" Olive couldn't believe how different their definitions of "exciting" could be – I'd had a couple more years to come to terms with it. Time to help.

"Look," I said, lowering my voice. "Can't you even give us *one* name?" My Googling with Olive had got nowhere. All we had from Dad was that the idea for the film was that the main character lands on a Greek island and picks up the wrong suitcase. He then spends the whole film trying to find out who it belongs to, and falling in love with the mystery girl through the items he finds in her case. Kind of like Cinderella but with a whole wardrobe. Obviously, whoever the girl was, she didn't pack anything normal like comfy pants and razors; it was all perfect dresses, uniquely engraved necklaces, and handwritten poetry. I wasn't even sure it was legal to open someone's stuff, and felt like a simple call to the airline might solve the mystery, but who was I to argue with the magic of Hollywood?

Most of it had already been filmed, but they were doing some last-minute reshoots now, which is what they'd called Dad in for.

Dad took a bite of croissant and chewed thoughtfully. "Hmmm, well it's called ... *Emotional Baggage III* ... yes, three... *The Summer Holiday*." Olive's eyes lit up – finally some intel that could unlock everything. "And I met a lovely man called Thomas. Think he's won an Oscar."

Oli's jaw dropped. "What did he look like? Is he really, really famous? Do you think he'll have a photo with me?"

Dad took another bite. "Definitely." Oli squeaked. "For the famous bit. Not sure about the photo." He chuckled to himself. "If your gran was alive she'd be asking the same..."

Olive scrunched her mouth up. "So . . . he's really old?"

Dad smiled. "What *is* old, Olive?! But maybe, yes, eighties I think, but still at the peak of his game." He gulped some juice. "That's still hashtag-famous, right?"

I laughed, enjoying Dad winding Olive up, but managed to drop a chunk of tomato down my nightie. Great, now I had a big red splodge on my left nip zone. I looked around. I obviously didn't care what I looked like in front of my family, but people had started to stroll along the beach. Maybe I should go and wipe it off. Or put on a bikini top underneath . . . or brush my hair . . . or take off yesterday's make-up? I looked at the uneaten pastries. . . Maybe in a bit.

"OK, Dad." Olive wasn't giving up. "Quiz time. Nod if you recognize any of these names from who you met. . ." Dad continued eating. "TJ?"

Nothing.

TJ was the lead actor in Olive's favourite film series about slime unicorns. He was some sort of slime unicorn prince from LA, and she was ob-sessed with him. In fairness, he *was* so hot he pulled off looking good even as a fluffy confused half-man-half-animal with furry ears and a horn.

"TJ????" Olive shouted, taking Dad's silence for a maybe.

"Sorry, no, Olive. Any more? Or are we done?"

Olive thought for a second. "James Dent? Mollie Myers? Ayesha Simms. . .?"

Dad shook his head. "I think they're shooting a crowd scene with a horse today, so no talent around. But I'm heading down to check some sound leak if you want to come?"

Oli didn't reply and continued with what sounded like a high-speed class register. But as she reeled off names to our confused father, all she got was a shaking of the head. Eventually he cut her off.

"So, would now be a good time for a refresher of the holiday rules?"

Olive and I both said a simultaneous no. Dad ignored us. If there was one thing he loved almost as much as worst-case scenarios, it was rules (which were often related to his worst-case scenarios).

"The number one most important thing is to stay safe. Although it's a beautiful island, I must know where you are at all times." He looked at me like I had a track record of doing unthinkably terrible things. "So no sneaking off, no sneaking about. . ." He looked a bit flustered. "Just no sneaking, OK?"

We both nodded. I could cross the bridge of what

was actually "sneaking" when I came to it (or tried to sneak around it).

"Obviously, all the same house rules as back home."

I sipped some water. "So take coats off in the hall?"

"I'll choose to ignore that, Megan." He nudged my glass nearer to the middle to the table, as I'd forgotten to put it back in the safe zone. "Suntan lotion at ALL TIMES. Nothing below factor fifty." I waved bye to the idea of my first-ever beach glow, as Dad listed more things to stay away from (Jet skis! Sea urchins! Strange people asking us to go in vans!) Olive kicked me, so I sneaked a sideways look at her. She puckered up and blew me a kiss.

"You dare," I mouthed and tapped the iPad on the chair next to us. I could change the passcode any second. If she mentioned boys now, Dad would panic and make some obscure rule like "no venturing out any further than this table", and say something gross about "I know how fifteen-year-old boys think", which was a) inaccurate (he doesn't even know what Fortnite is) and b) absolutely gross.

"...and lastly?" We tuned back in just in time to answer – it was always the same.

"Stick to the rules."

But Dad was distracted, waving over our heads to someone on the beach. Oli and I looked round.

Why was he waving at the three-toothed Random Old Dude? And...

I stopped putting a croissant in my mouth mid-bite.

Because there was something even more confusing. Behind Random Old Dude was something ridiculous.

Someone ridiculous.

A guy, about seventeen, totally tanned, with more abs than I think actually exist in the human body, was jogging at the edge of the water, a surfboard under his arm, his hair bouncing like he had his own perfect wind machine.

How was he moving in what looked like slo-mo?!

Why wasn't he lying in a heap, bright red and sweaty like me, weeping "The heat, the heat, please someone stop this heat!"?

The jug of juice on the table was rippling – Olive had started vibrating.

Then the most confusing thing of all happened. Random Old Dude didn't wave back.

Jogging Guy did.

He was coming over.

To us.

To my family breakfast. And me with my under-boob sweat, hair balanced on my head, and a face 30% covered in croissant flakes.

Dad stood up, his chair squeaking against the ground.

"Trent!" he shouted. "Great to see you again so soon."

I suddenly understood why my sister was doing an impression of an electric toothbrush.

This wasn't OK. It was the exact opposite of OK!

Jogging Guy rested his surfboard against our garden wall. "May I?" He leapt over the little gate as if it wasn't quite high and most people would trip and crash.

This needed to not be happening!

I willed him to not get any closer. He mustn't?!

I edged my chair back, like he was a dangerous animal.

Oli was still vibrating.

Him – magazine cover. Me – meme of the morning after the night before.

"Come on now, Trent, you KNOW I'm not going to like that." Dad waggled his finger at the gate. "No unnecessary jumps, please. Falling is the second-highest cause of accidental death, you know. And please tell me you've got at least factor fifty on?"

Dad swiped his finger across the guy's shoulder, like this Adonis was a piece of furniture he was checking for dust. They both laughed.

What. Was. Happening?

"Sure thing," Trent replied in an American accent. I'd never seen or heard someone so different from my dad standing so close to him.

"Want some brekkie?" Dad nodded at our table. "Although, how rude, these are my daughters, Meg and Olive." Neither of us moved. "Girls? Say hello to Trent."

Finally, Olive stopped squeaking, and hissed in a total monotone.

"He. Is. Not. Trent... HE IS TJ."

Yup. Dad had just invited Hollywood's most in-demand hottie for "brekkie".

TJ smiled at Ol. "Got it, grrrrl!"

Ol looked she might be about to fall off her chair.

"Ahhhh." The penny dropped for Dad. "Trent Jameson. *Of course!*"

"Call me what you want, Big Dog." TJ winked at him. Sorry, did one of the most famous people in the world just call Jack Jackson, 53, with a love of watching *Only Connect* and a passion for cheese tasting, "Big Dog"? TJ opened his arms in Olive's direction. "Wanna hug it out?"

If there was one thing I knew right now, it was that Olive was clinging on to breathing by the tiniest thread. She was about to implode. TJ untucked his T-shirt from the back of his shorts and dabbed himself down. "Swear I'm not too gross."

Pahahahahhaha. As if that was the problem.

But he'd got too near for Oli to control herself any more, and she flung her arms around him. She looked like a koala hanging on to a tree. TJ looked at me while she was limpeted on – she really wasn't letting go. "So, you must be Meg?"

I didn't know what to say – so I held up a banana.

"Do you want a banana?" He looked unnerved. "It's al fresco." I held it out like he might not know what a banana was.

TJ untangled himself from Olive. One of his abs seemed to be twitching. It was very off-putting. "Thanks for the offer, but I'm gonna pass."

Uh-oh. Too late I realized that my arm was no longer protecting the red nipple-like stain on the My Little Pony nightie. And also: I was wearing a My Little Pony nightie?! How could I stop him seeing?! "I dropped tomato on myself."

Not that, Meg. NOT THAT. TJ laughed.

"Think I'm going to not eat that either if that's OK?!" He actually winked. He looked so magazine-perfect that I could almost hear the *ding* sound effect as he did. "I'm only allowed what the on-set dieticians give me."

I nodded as if I could totally identify with this problem.

"I'm heading straight there after this. Protein time, I hope."

"I was just saying to the girls they should come down to the set. . ." Dad walked back to the table. "But I think they wanted a beach da—"

Oli suddenly found her voice, full volume.

"NO WE ARE COMING TO SET TODAY THAT'S WHAT WE SAID DAD THAT WE ARE GOING TO BE THERE. TODAY."

Dad chuckled. "Oh, sorry, my mistake." He looked at TJ, who was now doing some stretches that made me fear for the stitching on his shorts. I downed my water to hide the gulps that would be happening with or without liquid intake. Dad looked at me. "As long as your sister's OK to go with you?"

I looked at Dad, then down at TJ, who was now grinning up from a position that looked like he'd managed to fold himself in half.

"Come on, Meg, we'd love to have you guys down there. . ."

I took a breath to compose myself and sat up. Time to adult, Meg.

"I think I could manage that, yes."

CHAPTER
EIGHT

Beeeeeeep.

"Car's heeeerrrreeee." Olive's yell was louder than any car horn. Someone should patent it. I grabbed my bag off my bed, slid on my flip-flops and clattered downstairs. I'd just finished mine and Oli's nails, and at least 20% of my toe flesh was more glittery than it was an hour ago. But I came to a sudden stop in my tracks at the bottom of the stairs – quite painful in flip-flops. Self-inflicted toe-wedgie. "Dad. Are you really going out in that?!"

My life was the reverse of how the dad/daughter relationship was meant to be.

He smiled happily, clapped, and lit up. Literally.

He was wearing his T-shirt that had a built-in

light-up panel on the front that measured sound levels. He once wore it to one of my birthday parties, which is why everyone in my year now refers to him as Monitor Man.

"Got to look my best for day one with my girls!" He looked down at the panel of lights. "Woooo-OOOOH!" The green blocks went up into the red as he got louder. He chuckled to himself and stamped his foot, repeating, "Best present ever!" Trust Mum to buy him something she didn't have to actually experience him wearing.

Beeep.

Dad's T-shirt flashed fully red. Time to go.

I recognized the car as soon as I saw it. Vangelis. I waved when I saw him behind the wheel, but I don't think he saw me as he didn't wave back. Although, and it was hard to be sure as he was wearing sunglasses, he did seem to be looking straight at me. Oh well. I opened the front door.

"Fancy seeing you here!" I climbed in, and then paused. "You *were* picking us up, right?"

I swear he tried not to laugh.

"That is correct. I've been assigned to your dad and this block."

"Phew."

"No plans to kayak, then?"

I shook my head. "Not yet." Truth was, with the TJ encounter and Olive being on hyper-mode, I hadn't really thought about it since he offered.

I tried to think of something to say, but couldn't. So we both sat in silence, the engine humming away. Was he also thinking of something to say or was this normal for him? Where were the others?!

I rummaged to get my sunglasses out. We sat some more.

If I hadn't been sure before, I was now 100% convinced he'd only given me his number for holiday admin reasons. The only chemistry we had was the kind of chemistry experiment where two substances won't mix, even if you put them in a blender.

As if she felt this awkward silence all the way back home, a message from Neet came through. Since I'd told her about "brekkie-gate", she'd been sending me every picture of TJ ever taken. Which was quite a lot.

NEET (I'd changed her name back): **Sorry. Am still not dealing with you meeting TJ.**

ME: SAME NEET. Same.

NEET: RIDICULOUS x 😑

NEET: I couldn't find an infinity emoji so generic hole will have to do.

Neet liked to give all emojis equal use.

NEET: And am still not dealing with you talking to him about fruit. 😂 🍌

ME: SAME NEET. Same.

NEET: Did Olive say what he smelt of???? I imagine a tree in the rain and muscle rub.

ME: She hasn't managed words yet.

NEET: FYI the most exciting thing that's happened here has been seeing a contestant on The Chase whose name was Dwayne Pipe.

I flicked my phone to vibrate as her messages were coming through so quickly, it sounded like it was malfunctioning.

NEET: Next time you see TJ can you get his personal Snap? Or Insta. Whatever's easiest.

She said this like it was a simple thing to do. Like millions of people all over the world wouldn't pay good money for it. Like I, someone who offered him a banana, would be the person to manage it.

ME: 👀 👀

NEET: FINE. A photo will do. AND NO MORE FRUIT CHAT.

Like I had a choice over the nonsense that came out of my mouth?!

I replied with a thumbs-up, and deliberately didn't clarify that was for the chat bit, not the photo.

NEET: Excellente. And show him that picture of me? Tell him six days till he can appreciate me IRL

I knew exactly the photo she meant. Her go-to profile pic – she's standing by a purple and pink light, looking all mysterious and arty and cool. No one needed to know I took it in Poundland, when Olive was making us look for Troll lights.

ME: I'll drop it into convo . . . when we're next chatting about fruit. 😑

Truth was, I wasn't sure TJ and I would ever actually chat again – and I was fine with that. People like him weren't there to have normal conversations with. They were there to pull casual-yet-sexy poses, wear clothes that would look terrible on normal people and write Instagram captions that were both nonsense and art all at once.

NEET: Wait

NEET: CHANGE OF PLAN. Don't mention me. We don't want to confuse anything!

ME: Again 👀 👀???

NEET: WE NEED TO SECURE HIM AS YOUR SECOND KISS PARTICIPANT. DUH!!!!

This time I actually laughed out loud. *As if* Neet thought these were the two actual options. Him fall in love with Neet from Troll photo, or kiss me. That was a whole new level of not-happening. His face was probably insured. If my kiss curse struck near him I'd probably end up in jail.

Vangelis cleared his throat, reminding me he was still here. Oops. I'd kind of forgotten, lost in a world of my best mate's delusion.

"Sorry, just my best friend being lols." He looked confused. "Sorry – funny."

"What's the joke?" he asked earnestly.

I looked down.

NEET: If not it could be destination tongue fest with hot-but-so-far-a-bit-weird Grumpy Geli???

"Er, nothing." I said, checking there wasn't a single reflective surface in the car that he might have seen that in. I switched on airplane mode in case, which he totally saw.

Vangelis tapped his fingers on the wheel. "Nothing it is."

Did he look annoyed? Or just bored? The silence

returned. It was a real relief when Olive piled on to the back seat.

"Morning, Vangelis, we're going to the set. It's so cool! These are the last scenes they're reshooting...!" She wasn't taking any breaths, and considering English wasn't Vangelis' first language, he was doing well to look interested in the right places. "They're trying to hit a late summer release still and TJ is in it!!!"

At the mention of TJ, Vangelis' semi-smile twitched. Clearly not a fan.

"*Gia, ti kanis?*" Dad said as he climbed in. I knew from his loud practising it meant "Hello, how are you?" He looked a bit too pleased with himself considering this one phrase had taken him an hour of repeating back to a YouTube tutorial.

But it was appreciated, Vangelis turned round actually smiling. Wow. It was good to know what one looked like for reference. "*Kalimera*. And like I said, call me Geli. Now – " he turned to Olive – "shall we go to set?"

Geli waggled his fingers in fake excitement, but as he turned back, I saw him grinning. Maybe it was just me that made him so grumpy. But I hadn't done anything wrong, so I wasn't going to stress about it. Instead, I stayed quiet, and enjoyed the warm air whipping around me, as we made our way up a mountain road, the sparkling sea stretching out below us.

I don't know what I was expecting a film set to be like. Chairs with names on the backs, towering cranes with cameras on, people running about with clipboards, huge lights shining on places that already looked quite bright, people dabbing at other people's faces with tiny brushes while they chatted away as if there wasn't someone millimetres away dabbing at their face with a tiny brush. But if that's what I expected, then I was totally right.

The buzz in the air was undeniable. It was hard to tell who was cast and who was crew, everyone was so glamorous (although I quickly realized the crew were wearing black, and wished Dad had warned me, so I wasn't sticking out in my short denim dungarees and polka-dot red knotted hairband).

"Right then." Dad signed another load of paperwork as more lanyards got put over our heads. "You want to stick with me, or can I trust you to behave if you look around on your own?"

He'd already given Olive and me a briefing about the horrors that lurked on set – tripping on cables (and dying), standing behind people with cameras (and tting squashed as they walked backwards/potentially dying) and making sure our phones were off (so we didn't get murdered by a director, aka, also dying). He didn't seem to realize the biggest horror had already happened: him giving us this lecture in public while his top lit up in sync.

"Think I'll head off if that's OK?" I ate another grape. Geli had given Olive a load – they were the size of eyeballs. "Don't want to cramp your style." I looked at my sister. "Ol?"

But a weird thing had happened. Ever since we'd got out of the car, Olive had been silent. It was like her speech ability was directly linked to proximity to TJ. Judging by her face, he was near.

I looked around, as casually as it was possible to when trying to eye-stalk someone. JACKPOT. TJ was pacing back and forth behind a giant rock, reading through a script to himself.

"Polystyrene," Dad said.

"What?" I never understood what went through his head.

"The rock you're admiring?" Classic Dad. He thought I was admiring the rock, not TJ. "It's made of polystyrene."

"Ohhh." I tried to sound interested – I knew he liked

sharing facts he thought could be cool. But he'd given me an idea. "Soooo lifelike." I got my phone out. Perfect opportunity to grab a photo of the stone/stone-cold hottie for Neet.

Dad raised his eyebrows. There were signs everywhere saying "No Photos".

"I'll be quick! Then I'll turn it off." I swiped open my camera, pretending to use it as a selfie-mirror, and pressed take. Master of disguise!

Which was the exact moment I realized I'd made a terrible mistake.

Olive had turned my flash on.

Instead of pretending to take a discreet selfie, I'd just full-on flashed the rock/TJ. And one of them – not the rock – was now staring right at me.

Neet *better* appreciate this.

"Megggg," Dad scolded me.

"Olivvvvve!?" I scolded my sister, but she was too busy gawping at TJ, who was now walking towards us.

"Meg, you should have said if you wanted a photo." TJ laughed. RIP, dignity – nice knowing you. But he seemed to be immune to awkward and just smiled.

"JJ." He slapped Dad on the back. Dad smoothed his hair and laughed.

"Trent." Was he parent-flirting?! He patted TJ on the

arm. Yes he was. "Good to see you again." Dad nodded at me. "Sorry about that."

Did he mean the photo, or *me*?

TJ was wearing a skin-tight all-black bodysuit with little wires all over it. It left nothing to the imagination – and my imagination was incredibly vivid. TJ clocked me not knowing where to look, but it wasn't my fault everywhere had an inappropriate body part tugging at it. Where was the safe zone?! "Don't mind this. It's a big fight scene day. Swords and everything." I nodded like that made any sense and panic ate another grape. "Ol, long time no see!" TJ held his hand out for a high five.

But Olive was frozen.

"Don't leave me hanging!"

She was *so* leaving him hanging, utterly frozen, like her code had glitched. I had to help her out.

"Grape?"

I could almost hear Neet yelling, "NOOO MORRRREE FRRRRRUIT CHHHHAT." But she had no idea how hard this was – he was so good looking, he made my brain have to relearn English.

TJ grabbed a grape. "Don't mind if I do." He popped it in his mouth, holding eye contact with me. I felt actual sweat stress developing.

96

"Er. . ." I pushed the rest of the bunch into Olive's hand – I had to get out of this situation. "Bye – and good luck. Hope the fight goes well. Eat grapes! Olive, Dad, see you later."

I fled as quickly as I could, to try and stop their alarmed faces burning into my short-term memory. But it didn't work – because as I wandered round the set, instead of admiring all the scenery (polystyrene), and the cool stuff like crew catering where everything was BUFFET SERVICE EVEN THE ICE-CREAM, all I could see was TJ's face.

How dare he take up residence in my brain like this?

When I sent Neet the photo, it only made me feel worse. She replied with messages and messages of things I could say to make him "Think hubba hubba about the Meg magic" (her words). She truly, truly believed, TJ or not (*definitely not*), that I was going to get my second first kiss here and return home a new Meg, a Meg ready to unleash on the world – instead of the Megabite-hermit self I'd left as. I loved her optimism, but so far I'd only met two boys – one who seemed to be permanently annoyed by me, and the other who was ridiculously famous and thought I was a fruit pusher.

Oh, well. I still had six days before she arrived – who knew what could happen? The main thing was I enjoyed my holiday, and Hollywood hotties or not, I didn't want to spend my first-ever day on a film set caught up in my own head, thinking about all the stuff that had happened back home. So, I flicked off my phone and crept over to watch some filming. The scene being shot was something to do with a wild, aggressive horse being tamed, but instead of looking terrifying, the horse kept yawning.

"She's great, isn't she?" a lady in all black whispered to me. She had a make-up brush in hand and a headset round her neck. "Best in the biz."

I nodded. I was a big fan of the horse's work.

"Incredibly cute," I said, trying to sound knowledgeable. "...Very shiny mane."

The lady blinked. "Well, yes... But hair aside, Robyn really is the best director I've ever worked with."

Ah, OK. *The human*. That made more sense. I carried on nodding, as if this was exactly who I meant too. Robyn kept ducking her head under some black material to look at a tiny screen and then popping back to say what to do next (mainly figuring out how to wake up a sleepy horse).

Despite a hundred people trying to get her attention, and a chicken that had gone rogue, she was smiling, keeping totally calm. "Yeah, she seems pretty great."

"Unlike him..." She nodded towards a man with spiked-up brown hair who was yelling at the chicken. "I'm Holly, by the way." She stuck her hand out; I shook it back. "And the man picking a fight with a chicken is Mitch, the assistant director."

I laughed and introduced myself. We quickly got properly chatting, even though we had to do it at a whisper. Holly was part of the glam team. Dad had said the nicest people were in that team. Something to do with being able to put people instantly at ease. They were also the ones who had to wait around in-between takes, just in case they were needed.

It was nice to have someone to talk to, and after admitting that yes, the health and safety lead was my dad, we ended up talking about everything, from how cool it was to have a surprise holiday (me) to how TJ's skin seemed to have natural highlighter in it (Holly) to best tips for underwater mascara (both of us). I even told her about how my best friend was referring to my whole trip as "Love Island" and was trying to matchmake from afar. I think this made her take pity on me as I ended up with handfuls of samples and make-up I would never be able to afford.

"My best friend is going to be OBSESSED with you," I whispered as I stuffed it into my pockets. "Consider this your official warning!"

Holly laughed. "Show me a picture of her and I'll put some bits aside. What's her look?"

She asked this as if it was a question that was easy to answer. I opened up the Troll picture, knowing I was building up some seriously excellent best friend points right now. "Sort of Jameela Jamil on a walk to get a doughnut meets Dua Lipa on a dress-down day... If you can imagine that?"

Holly snorted. "Got it." But she stopped, pressed her finger to the black earpiece she had in and started to giggle.

"Here..." She held it out towards me.

"And you join us at day three of Mitch versus chicken. One of them flaps about, flies off into people's faces and walks, well, like a chicken. And the other? That's the chicken."

I looked over at Mitch. He'd pulled out his earpiece and was chasing around after the chicken, which was squawking so loudly that setting up for the next take had paused as everyone watched.

"What's this?" I asked Holly – I felt like I recognized the voice.

"We all heard Mitch shout at a runner yesterday. I think his words were, 'Do you not have enough brain cells to make a half-decent coffee?' even though he was sipping

on a tea. Well, this one's for you. . . So far it's chicken, 3" – the chicken was hiding under a large bush and Mitch was yelling, "Show yourself coward!" – *"Mitch, 0."*

I laughed and passed Holly the earpiece back. But Holly was smiling at me, a glint in her eye.

"It's talkback. And I don't know why I didn't think of it earlier, but if your best mate really wants you to meet a nice guy . . . I know just the person."

And, picking up her bag of kit, she beckoned me to follow her.

Decision time: stay safe here, or put myself out there and make this mission happen?

CHAPTER NINE

I followed Holly to the sound truck – a massive lorry full of loads of little screens and knobs. The walk had been under a minute, but I'd gone from chilled to terrified.

Holly was convinced I was going to get along with the guy narrating the chicken drama, but now he was nowhere to be seen. Apparently, Mitch had picked up that everyone was laughing at him, so he'd scarpered quicker than the chicken. But I was relieved. Truth was, I was regretting telling Holly about the mission. Talking about it and doing it were two very different things.

But Holly did have a point: yes, I'd met TJ, who was so hot it was probably medically unsafe to look directly at him, but that was *never* going to happen. So, if I wanted to keep my promise to Neet, maybe it was time to get

a bit more proactive about meeting someone I liked . . .
and I did like guys who made me laugh. Like the guy on
the headset.

Annoyingly, I'd had that thought just as Holly asked
if I wanted to stop by a beach party that was happening
outside our apartment that night. So, high on a bad idea,
and before I could think why not, I'd said a confident
yes. But four hours later my party fear had fully crept
back in. Why did I let brave Meg answer questions?!

I'd messaged Neet in a flap, but she'd calmed me
down by saying that it wasn't like anyone here knew me
(her nice way of saying it was a Megabite-free zone) and
if it got too much I could just ring her (and make like a
tree and leave). She thought it was the perfect first step
into social rehab, so I said I'd try and do her proud and
go.

"So. . ." Dad chewed thoughtfully on a mouthful of
leaves. We were eating dinner al fresco again. "It's a
'formal gathering' for the local crew, is that right?"

I nodded, and carried on munching on a delicious
dolmades. If I was eating, I couldn't be saying anything
too incriminating.

"I said to Holly from make-up I'd drop in."

"I see . . . and you don't think Olive would like to go
too?"

She'd probably love it, but it was my first chance to be on holiday and not have anyone related to me cramping my style. Olive leant close to my ear. I could hear her chewing. It was not enjoyable.

"Pleeeease!"

Years of her begging had made me immune.

"How about I take you to the next one, once I know what it's like?"

"How about you tell Dad about your messages with Anita?"

I shot her a look. "You dare..."

Dad put down his knife and fork. "Care to tell me what's going on?"

Nope, I didn't. Not one bit.

"It's nothing ... but if Olive *really* wants to come, I guess she can." I glared at her. "For a bit. A very short bit."

"Yessssssss." Olive punched the air. "Bet all my friends'll be there."

Olive loved that she'd already found a group of mates here – she mentioned it on a sixty-second-rotation basis.

"That's the spirit, Ol!" Dad smiled. "I love it when you girls look out for each other."

Olive and I had two options: point out we weren't looking out for each other, we were simply trapped in a genetically created lifelong cycle of blackmailing each other to get our own way – or smile. We both smiled. Dad nodded to the beach in front of our apartment. "And because the gathering's right here – Olive, you can stay till nine. Megs, 10.15 for you."

He looked like he thought he was about to win an award for Open-Minded Parent of the Year, despite sitting next to three empty bottles of insect repellent he'd doused us in before he'd let us start eating.

"But—" I started to protest.

"10:10. . ." Dad interrupted. This was his thing. Every time you argued, you lost five minutes. I knew when to accept defeat, so I said thanks and shut up. I didn't even know if I'd stick out the party for that long anyway.

After Neet's pep-talk, a secret bit of me, that didn't actually want to admit it, was beginning to look forward to it. As scary as it was, it *was* an actual *beach party*. Would there be firepits like in every American TV show ever? What if someone had a guitar and sang songs?! Did they like the same music over here? Should I wear my swimming stuff underneath just in case? Or would the water be freezing? Did I need to take anything, like proof of being invited, or did you just wander up?

Lost in imagining the party, I finished dinner, without even noticing I'd eaten the last half of it. After a quick family call with Mum (who was *very* excited about the party), I headed up to my room.

Blasting out Twenty One Pilots, and with motivational messages coming through thick and fast from Neet, I started to get ready. I didn't just dance like no one was watching; I sang like the whole world was wearing earplugs. It felt *great* – give or take learning the lesson that shiny tile floors and leaping about *can* cause potential fatal slips. (Dad had been speaking the truth!)

I was on a Greek island! About to go to a beach party! And nobody knew who I was!

I was nobody Meg and I loved it.

What didn't feel as great was that my suitcase had been bursting full of stuff, yet none of it even vaguely resembled the right outfit. What did you even wear to a beach party? Why had I packed two pairs of fluffy slipper socks? It was 30 degrees!

In the end I went for denim cut-offs, black sleeveless T-shirt tucked in, a belt I'd borrowed from Mum, and my favourite "M" necklace Neet got me. I never normally wear much make-up, but as it would be dark and I might see Holly, I risked it with my new eyeliner she'd given me, mascara and coral lip tint. By the time I finished I still had twenty-five minutes before I had to get Olive, so I got my laptop and video-called Neet to see how her trip to see her mum had been. I turned down my music.

She answered immediately.

"HELLLO, GREEEECE!" she shouted, obviously back home alone, as she was sprawled on her couch in PJs.

"Helllllo, Ennnggggeeeerrrrlllland," I shouted back. My laptop bounced around as I waved my other hand.

"Whit-woo, look at you all Kylie Jenner." Neet pouted at me.

"If you mean have I put on the tiniest amount of lip gloss, then yes. Follow me on my socials and call me an influencer."

Neet laughed. "Come on then, show us this dreamy beach..."

"Oh..." I tried to sound casual. "You mean..." I turned my laptop away from me and walked out on to the balcony. "This one?"

The sky was the bright pinks and blues of those amazing mermaid-esque hair dyes.

I was glad I'd turned my screen around, as Neet didn't stop yelling, "Whaaaaaaaat?!" for at least thirty seconds, before starting on an equally as long, "Rid-iiccc-uuu-lllllloouuuuuussss." I ended up sitting down, waiting for her to finish. I did peek round the screen to try to interrupt, but she brought her fingers together to shush me until she was done.

She only stopped when her critical need for breathing kicked in. I turned my laptop back round.

"Uh-huh. I know, right?!"

"Come onnnn, next Sunday." Neet fanned her face with her hand. "There's an Anita-shaped space right there, and I'm ready to fill it!"

"Too right! And down there" – I pointed to a group of people hanging out near the water – "I'd like to draw your attention to what my dad would refer to as a 'gathering', but you and I would call a 'beach party'..."

Neet high-fived her laptop camera. "You got this!" But then her screen went black. "Remind me not to do that again," she said when her face popped back up. "Legit almost snapped my screen."

I sipped my water. "So tell me what news?" I wanted to hear about her hospital visit.

"What news?!" She shook her head. "You being on holiday *is* my news."

"I'm serious. How was your mum?"

"Getting there..." She chewed her lip. "Still no date for her to be home, but..." Neet's smile returned. "I made more progress for her welcome back party! Look..."

She dived down under the sofa – she'd been planning this party for over a month, determined to make it the best surprise ever for her mum and dad.

"HELLOOOOO, SIGNAGE!" She unfolded a banner full of photos of the three of them, massive, "WELCOME HOME, MUM" letters running across it. It was so big she couldn't hold it properly.

"Woooooooaaahhhh. That must have taken for ever!"

"And the rest. But it's worth it, right?"

"Totally." It was an epic effort – her mum was going to love it. "Anything I can help with?"

"Hmmm." She thought for a moment. "When we're back, you can help me practise this lemon-cake thing Mum was going on about today. It has actual layers. And meringue, or something."

"Count me in." Whatever she needed was a yes from me.

"Anyway, enough about home. NEWS, PLEASE."

I scrunched up my nose, trying to think of something to tell her that we hadn't already gone over earlier.

"Did I tell you Holly's putting a load of products together for you?! For free-zy? I didn't even ask?!"

Neet's jaw fell. "Reeedeeeeccculllous."

"That's the kind of thing that seems to happen here! I ended up spending most of the day with her."

"For the record, I would be jealous if she wasn't clearly a total kweeeen." I couldn't imagine Neet being jealous of anyone. Except Jungkook's future girlfriend.

"She really is, Neet, and Ol's made loads of friends too. I'm going to meet them tonight."

"So she's coming with you?" Neet sounded as surprised as she should be.

"Long story." I shook my head. "Well, it's not, actually. She read all our messages about me having a second first kiss out here, and now she's blackmailing me, so I have to do whatever she wants."

"Classic Olive."

"Oh, and she also left the flash on my phone on, so TJ totally saw me taking that photo I sent you."

Neet laughed. "Even more classic Olive. Although..." She put her hand up. "Can we please discuss how fit TJ is again?"

"Neet?!" I didn't want to get dragged back into her dream world of me befriending/more than befriending him. If I gave her an inch, she'd take a mile – and message me about that mile until my data ran out. I stared at her blankly, hoping she would run out of steam – but somehow this just made her more steamy.

She zoomed in on her phone.

"Even half obscured by a rock, he's undeniably fit."

"Neet!"

"*Tell me* he's not as good looking in real life, then."

"I. . ." I paused. "I . . . *cannot* tell you that." I gave up protesting. "It's almost painful to look at him."

"But don't you see?" Neet bounced on the bed, her laptop wobbling. "Isn't it a little bit weird that the Gods of You Having A Great Snog have brought the World's Most-Fancied Boy literally running – in what I imagine were very short shorts – to your door?!"

I decided not to elaborate on the skintight number he'd had on earlier.

"It's not weird, it's just. . ." But I didn't know what it was.

"It's . . . FATE. That's what it is. Which is why" – she leant behind the screen – "TJ is in number-one spot on the list I have made called. . ." She pulled up another bit of huge paper.

"Quite the arts and crafts day," I said nervously.

She straightened it out. Oh no. Please don't let this be what I think it is.

"MEG'S SECOND KISSION," she announced proudly. She'd made an actual list, with a proper straight-lined table. "Kission is kiss mission, btw." She was reading it out as if it wasn't written in giant letters. "In brackets *to undo the total disaster of her first kiss, which ended up in the hospitalization of Sean*."

"Neet!" Even though it was only me seeing it, I was

embarrassed.

"What? I've been bored, OK? Not all of us have beaches and film sets and fruit chat to distract us." She did have a point.

"I thought we'd agreed not to mention you-know-what?" By what, I meant you-know-*who*. Sean.

Neet sat up. "That, young lady, was until I realized you needed tough love. You don't seem to be taking this snogging-a-hottie mission seriously." I could tell her about trying to find that headset dude, but didn't want to encourage her. "You PROMISED you'd try... So I think it's time you got a little kick in the right direction..." She cracked her neck as if about to go through a detailed military plan.

I knew where this was going and no one could hear it. I needed my headphones.

"One sec." Neet froze as if I'd pressed pause. I emptied my bag to see they were in there, but nothing. As a plan B, I peered over the balcony to at least check no one was downstairs. The coast was clear. I plonked myself back in front of the screen. "Continue. Although, do we *have* to do this?"

Neet unfroze herself and smiled supportively. "Well, no. Not at all. It's your call if you want to cheer up your best friend who is stuck at home making banners for her sick mum while you're on holiday." She was grinning, knowing full well I'd cave.

"Fine, get it over with."

She stood up. I could tell from her body language she'd been on a Michelle Obama video-watching spree again. This was dangerous.

"OK then, repeat after me..." She breathed in dramatically. *"I, Meg Jackson, will do everything I can to come back to the UK a new woman."* Here we go. *"One who is not afraid to kiss boys! One who is not scared of parties!"* I pursed my lips, ready to protest that I wasn't freaking out, even though I was. "And don't even *try* and give me that. I can hear Twenty One Pilots. I *KNOW* that's your hype-up album..." I rolled my eyes, but she hadn't finished. *"And I promise to do everything in my power to purge the medical and mental disaster of the world's worst first kiss by rising above"* – she was now flinging her arms around, totally carried away – *"the Megabite nickname"* – ouch – *"by taking on the mission to have the most full-on excellent snog with a total hottie to prove"* – she was now shouting – *"that I, Meg Jackson, AM NOT CURSED AND CAN KISS A BOY WITHOUT THE NEED FOR MEDICAL INTERVENTION!"*

I grinned. "You really expect me to repeat all that in one go!" But Neet had stopped in her tracks, her mouth suddenly hanging open.

And I knew exactly why.

Right behind me, someone had started to howl with laughter.

CHAPTER
TEN

Laughing wasn't the right word. It was more an eruption.
A belly laugh that had been building up for so long it
could no longer come out in an orderly way.

I tiptoed to where it was coming from – the high bit
of the sloping white wall between my balcony and the
one next door. Pushing myself up on to my toes I peered
over, hoping against hope it wasn't what I thought.

Oh no.

It was much, much worse than what I'd thought.

A boy, maybe about sixteen, was crumpled up on
an iron chair right at the back where the wall was the
highest, doubled over in hysterics. There was no one else.
No phone. Which meant, chances were, he was laughing
at me. Please don't let him have heard everything?!

I gripped the wall in sheer panic – a bit of stone dropped down. The boy looked up.

I was busted.

"Sorry..." He tried – and failed – to compose himself, fanning the air in front of his face, but more laughter just spluttered out. "I didn't mean to listen..." So he *had* heard. "I just ... well, no offence, but your friend was literally shouting."

Well, this was mortifying.

"You could have said something!" I snapped.

Balcony Boy realized how seriously not-funny I was finding this.

"Like what?" He had a gentle Manchester accent and was trying his hardest to look more serious. *"Want to borrow my headphones?"*

The corners of his mouth were going against his wishes and trying to twitch into a smile, but I wasn't finding it funny. How could I? This stranger had heard *everything*. My kiss disaster. The mission. MEGABITE?! This was a catastrophe. I'd come on this holiday hoping to get away from that stuff, not bring it next-door.

"OI!!!" A shout came from my laptop on the table. Neet was waving her arms about. *Please don't be about to make this worse.* "STAND UP, CONVERSATION CREEPER! SHOW YOURSELF!!!"

She made it worse.

What were the ethics on closing my laptop and pretending the Wi-Fi had cut out?

Balcony Boy gave an amused shrug, stood up and poked his head over the balcony wall, walking along to where it dropped to waist height. He was tall. Properly tall, over six-foot kind of thing – the kind of person that would always-sit-in-front-of-me-in-the-cinema tall. I felt very exposed, him looking into my personal space, but it gave me my first proper look at him. His afro hair was curly on top and shaved up the sides, and he had that natural swagger of boys in our sixth form. He gave Neet a salute.

"Consider myself shown."

"Ohhhhhh, he's fit!!!" she drooled.

"NEEEET!" I turned and shot her serious daggers.

"Sorry," Neet huffed. "I TAKE THAT BACK. YOU'RE AN EAVESDROPPING LUNATIC WHO NEEDS TO APOLOGIZE TO MEG RIGHT NOW."

"Better," I mumbled, but Balcony Boy was grinning.

"Seeing as you asked so nicely..." He put his hand on the wall and leant forward. "Sorry, Meg. Sorry, shouty girl in pyjamas."

"Other people know me as Anita," Neet said, arms folded.

"And other people know me as Alex." He nodded at the wall. "May I?"

He didn't wait for an answer before he pushed himself up, swinging one leg over and sitting on the wall.

"That's quite far enough." I eyed him suspiciously. Who did he think he was, laughing at me, then straddling what was a very clear boundary? I sat down on the furthest chair away, putting extra distance between us.

"Soooo, Alex." Neet was rolling the words round her mouth like she was doing a vocabulary exam. She'd sat up and pulled her hair into a ponytail. "Tell us what you heard."

Alex smiled. "You really want to know?"

I said "no" as Neet said "yes". Neet was louder – Alex carried on.

"I know that you've got Meg on 'MEG'S MISSION'," he air quoted, "to get rid of some kiss curse?" He was trying so hard to keep a straight face. "And 'become a new woman'." A snort popped out. "...Or some kind of Little Mix lyric like that?"

I stopped pretending I wasn't dying on the inside, and died on the outside too. My head dropped on the table with a bang.

"You all right?" Alex sounded concerned. I raised one hand up without lifting my head at all. "Oh, phew."

He paused, a thought coming to him. "What about that poor lad you had your first kiss with? Tell me he didn't need stitches!"

I would have clarified that the nurse said it was only "superficial damage", but couldn't get a word in over him cracking up all over again.

"Oi," Neet shouted out from the screen. "Not funny!"

"I beg to disagree." Alex shook his head. "I just hope your next random victim – SORRY, *hottie* – has better luck."

I hauled myself up. "It won't be some randomer, Judgey McJudgington. Not that it would matter if it was..." Neet heckled "Yes, grrrrl" in the background. "The idea is to find someone I actually like. And, y'know, take it from there."

"Ahhh ... so you're a romantic?" He smiled. "Cute."

"No!" I didn't know what I was so defensive about; why I cared what this total stranger thought. "I just want it to be ..." Not injury inducing. "... right."

"So ..." Alex was grinning – he knew he was winding me up. "... will you tell him how you got the Megabite nickname before ... or after?"

Right. That was ENOUGH.

"Please return all limbs to your side of the wall." I folded my arms. "Now."

Alex laughed playfully, and swung his leg back over, just as a girl walked out on to his side of the balcony.

"Sorry, Al, am I really hearing this right?" She stood beside him – she was almost as tall as him, and was in a floaty maxi dress, billowing in the breeze, looking like a modern day goddess. Next to her, Alex visibly shrank, as if his confidence had suddenly been zoomed out.

Balcony Girl leant over the wall and waved at me and Neet. "I'm Phoebe, by the way. Alex's sister. Is my brother giving you grief?"

I think I liked Phoebe already. I shrugged non-committally, but Neet yelled, "HELL, YES."

Alex shook his head. "Just saying hi to our new neighbours."

Phoebe poked him in the shoulder. "It sounded like you were giving our neighbour your hot take on her love life. . ." She looked at me. "That right?"

It was, but I also didn't want to call him out on it. Neet, however, didn't care, and yelled, "Exacto!"

"Ladies. Before Al takes the moral high ground, lemme fill you in." She smiled, but in a Disney villain way.

Alex sloped back to the chair he'd been sitting in. "Here we go again."

But Phoebe was on a roll. "Before my brother was

coupled up, he used to be the *definition* of a serial snogger."

"Literally not true." Alex shook his head. "Just my sister believing everyone else over me, as per."

"Disagree." She looked back at me. "It didn't even used to be a thank you. Just next." Well, this had got interesting. Alex was now the one with his head in his hands.

"Fake news."

Phoebe shook her head. "Whatever, Al." She turned back to me and Neet. "Anyway, that all changed when he met Lucy. Who is a total dreamboat of a woman. An all-round excellent human – and, incidentally: My. Best. Mate."

Wow. The plot thickened even more! Phoebe nodded. "I *know*! *He* knows. We've had *maaaaaaaaany* discussions about it."

"*Many*," Alex agreed.

"Obviously I think she's had a temporary bypass of sanity, but . . . if it's what she wants? And they're super loved-up now. Which is just as well because if he hurts her. . ." She ran her fingers over her throat, making a comedy *krk* noise. "No punishment will be too harsh. But. . ." she smiled. "It's been almost six months and I think, *think*, I might almost be ready to approve."

"Why, thank you." Al sighed, clearly having had this conversation many times before, but Phoebe hadn't finished. "And after a tearful airport goodbye, Mr No Romance here has been messaging Lucy every second of every day..." She put her fingers up into a heart shape. "Even if he pretends not to."

"*Cuuuuuute*," Neet heckled, in the same way he'd said it to me. Alex exhaled slowly, his cheeks puffed out, not enjoying his love life being the one scrutinized, and as Phoebe chatted away, telling us all about how if they got married she'd upgrade her best mate from friend to sister, Alex gave me a look I totally understood.

We both wished our worlds had never collided.

CHAPTER
ELEVEN

I'd only met him an hour ago, but already I knew my holiday would be much simpler if I stuck to one golden rule: avoid Alex at all costs.

Which is why I was trying to pretend he wasn't right beside me as we walked down the beach. Quite hard as navigating pebbles and sand made me wobble like I was learning to walk. When I'd said yes to heading to the party with Phoebe, I didn't realize he'd be part of the package, but from his expression, I think he felt the same.

"So, you said she was nine..." Phoebe was watching Oli, who had already ditched us for her new mates, who were now cheering as she shimmied under a limbo bar.

"Going on twenty. Honestly, her social life is way

better than mine." She was wearing a neon T-shirt with a glittery sea on that said "GIVE ME A WAVE", so surely it should be me that was embarrassed by her and not the other way round.

A cheer went up as Oli easily cleared the bar. Her new mates had no idea how competitive she was – I almost wanted to wish them good luck, but they were too busy whooping as she did the fastest celebratory floss this island has ever seen.

Alex laughed. "Little sisters are the worst, right?"

"Oi!" Phoebe prodded him right in the ribs. "How many times? Being twelve minutes younger doesn't count!" I couldn't help but smile – it was nice having people nearer my own age to hang out with, and, despite me wanting to avoid Alex, them being neighbours meant Dad had been more chilled about me heading to the party. Even if it had meant him knocking to meet their mum – who was also working on the film crew doing script continuity, so I got a free pass to hang out with her kids. Result.

"So what have you seen on the island so far?" Phoebe was scanning the party, working out where we should stroll to. "The set's cool, right?" They'd already been out for a week.

"Un-huh." I kicked the sand as I walked. I liked the

way it sprayed up. "But the best bit's been the swimming. Have you been in the water? It's like a lovely warm bath... Well, a bath with fish in it."

"Disagree." Al scrunched his nose. "I saw something weird in there yesterday... Sort of odd and scaly and flapping about scaring people." He made a thinking noise. "Oh no. *Wait*. That was Phoebe."

I rolled my eyes. Being with these two was a lot like being at home with Ol. "Good one, Alex."

Phoebe crossed her arms, fake indignant. "Yeah, Al. Pipe down. There's two of us now..."

We reached the proper main crowd of the party and stopped. I stood staring at this bunch of strangers, who all looked like they were having the time of their lives, and I wondered if this whole thing had been a mistake. Parties and me were not a good idea. Especially without Neet here to be my safety net.

Phoebe leant close to me so Alex couldn't hear. When Alex had gone inside to grab food earlier, I'd told her the full story of Neet's "kission" for me, and how I felt a bit out of my depth putting myself back out there. "We might only have met an hour ago, but in holiday time that's years. We've got this, OK?"

She was awesome. Despite the incident on the balcony spreading the snog humiliation story from the

UK to an international audience, I was the tiniest bit glad it had happened, as at least it meant I'd met Phoebe. I took a deep breath and surveyed the party.

It was as amazing as I'd imagined, but with added great music. Speakers the size of Olive were blaring, three fires had already been lit, there was a queue for the most delicious-smelling BBQ, and everyone was smiling, dancing or running about. Where had all these people come from?! Did they ship them in on a boat destined for actual Love Island? It was like being on a beach made up of the ASOS website – it's just I felt like the only one from the sale section.

"Checking the scene for 'hotties'?" Alex asked, trying and failing to sound serious. I hated that this was the main thing he thought about me.

I forced myself to stand my ground.

"We don't all think like single Alex did," I said imperiously.

"Ohhhh, burn. . ." he replied, but he was laughing.

"Yes, Al. Meg actually has stuff going on in her life. . ." Phoebe looked totally relaxed, but I felt even more out of place with every step we took. The more chilled everyone around me was, the more I was panicking. "Swimming's your thing, right?"

I nodded; it was Olive who had told her about my

medals when she'd joined us on the balcony. She had no filter over what people wanted to know about. "It's not really a thing. It's just something I do, I guess."

Phoebe waved over at a group of girls. She was totally at ease, ready to see where the night would go. Me, I already had palm sweat, sand rubbing underneath my flip-flops, and was wondering where everyone went to have a wee. "Well, when you're at the Olympics, remember us, right?"

"Sorry, who's going to be at the Olympics?!"

Just from the expression on Phoebe's face, I didn't need to look to know who'd joined us. I bet she was the exact reason he'd come over – and I wasn't equipped for any of this?! How was I meant to say words that made an actual sentence around him?

"Err, no one... Except Olympic people." More commonly known as Olympians. "Phoebe, Alex ... this is TJ." Alex's standard grin had swapped for something altogether less impressed. TJ gave him his trademark dazzling smile anyway. He was wearing head-to-toe designer clothes, and had a camera slung over his shoulder that looked like it was worth more than my house. Olive was going to freak when she saw him.

Phoebe stuck her hand out. "I would ask if Meg means *THE* TJ, but judging by the people taking totally indiscreet photos of you right now, Imma go with yes."

TJ laughed and shook her hand back. Phoebe didn't need to know I'd been one of those people earlier. "Well, I'd heard you're *THE* Phoebe and assumed those photos were all for you. . .?"

Phoebe laughed extra hard and their hand-hold went on at least a second longer than felt normal. TJ turned to Alex. "You must be Alex."

Alex didn't put his hand out. "Uh-huh."

TJ's confidence was like reinforced bulletproof glass and any attempt to ruffle him bounced right off. "Sweeeeet party, right?"

Alex grunted.

"Sweeeet," I agreed, not able to deal with the awkward. Must remember how bad that sounds in my English accent and never say it again. But everyone was looking at me expecting some kind of actual conversation. "So er. . ." Words were hard when all I could think was "WHAT IS LIFE WHAT IS LIFE WHAT IS LIFE." "Do you . . . come here often?"

TJ flicked his hand through his hair, leant back and laughed. "You crack me up."

I fake joined in with too much enthusiasm. Yes, TJ. That was *clearly* a joke. I am *hilarious*.

He waited for me to finish. "So, you guys up for the

same as me?" Attempting social rehabilitation? I very much doubted it. TJ did gun fingers and swivelled his hips. Do NOT look down, Meg. Phoebe caught my eye, trying to do the same. "Getting our party ON."

Alex did a little cough-laugh, before getting evils from Phoebe and composing himself. "Totally. . . So I'm going to head and do just that. Megan, hope you meet lots of people. Non-*random* people. . ." My nostrils flared at him reminding me about the mission in front of TJ, but with a quick bye to Phoebe, Alex was already off, swallowed up by the crowd within moments. I instantly felt more relaxed. Until I remembered I was talking to a movie star and a super-cool girl and freaked out all over again.

TJ swigged on a can of Diet Coke. He drank it in the way people drink in adverts, all slow pour and satisfied gulp. I didn't know there was a celeb way of drinking a drink until now. I had *so* much to learn. He wiped his mouth with the back of his hand. "You two here for the long haul?"

He was definitely someone who would not know what a protective parent curfew was. Luckily Phoebe answered.

"Guess we'll see where the night takes us." She had a mischievous look in her eye (I already knew my night was taking me to a 10.10 p.m. check-in with my dad).

"Nice... I've got a big scene early tomorrow." TJ cracked his neck. "Stunt day. A high-speed chase – on jet skis, would you believe."

I would believe – Dad had been lecturing me on the dangers of them this afternoon. Now I knew why.

"Good luck," I said, trying not to stare too intently at his cheekbones. Had they been surgically chiselled or had he been 3D printed instead of the standard birthing process?

TJ took another choreographed swig of his drink. "Oh, I've got the easy bit. Those guys and gals have the hard job." He waved his finger towards the big location filming trucks parked on the road for the evening. "Making me look good."

I mean, he was doing a pretty good job of that just standing there, but I should keep that thought in my Meg-only brain file.

Stuck for anything to say again – my A-list anecdotes were unsurprisingly not that extensive – I looked out across the beach and spotted Geli. Another person at the party I wasn't expecting. With a quick nod of acknowledgement he headed over. Wow. Was this an out-of-character display of friendliness?

Geli said a "hey" to TJ and Phoebe, but walked

straight to me. "Your dad let you come, then?"

It had only been 1.5 days, but he already knew the score.

"Just. Not until I'd promised to stay away from jet skis, though." Which made no sense at all. I kicked at the sand waiting for my next great line of conversation to come. "Soooo, this is way cooler than parties back home." Well, the two I'd been to.

Geli shrugged, jingling something in his pocket. Car keys. "Is that correct?"

I laughed. "You really need to experience spending an evening eating crisps in someone's kitchen while their brother keeps hijacking the speakers and playing 'Baby Shark' on repeat."

He smiled. "I have no idea what that is, but it sounds like fun?"

"Trust me. The beach wins." I looked out to the horizon – the moon was bouncing off the water. "It doesn't look real, does it?"

Geli nodded. "Sunset from the sea is even better. You have to let me take you out. Sometimes the seals come and say hello." Well, that sounded like something I couldn't say no to. Plus kayaking meant not having to converse, so we'd both be way happier. "Beats this hands down."

Finally – we had something in common.

"Deal." I smiled at him. "Although we might need to take her too..." I pointed over at Olive, who was doing handstands where the sea lapped on to the beach.

"No problem. Bring who you want." The coolest idea hit me. We could take Neet when she arrived next week. Perfect plan.

"Be prepared to run Dad through plans for any emergency though. Freak storms. Shark attack. Oh, and kidnaps. Always kidnaps. They're his fave."

Geli nodded. "Understood."

But our conversation got interrupted by TJ and Phoebe heading over.

"You guys want to play volleyball?" Phoebe knotted up her top. She had actual abs. TJ definitely noticed. "This dude," she pointed at TJ, "reckons he's some kind of pro."

TJ rolled his head back. "Not what I said, Phoebe." He grinned. "It's not *my* fault my last role was playing an icon of the sport." Oh yes – his slime unicorn character had also been a volleyball champ in the daytime. As you do.

"Well I laugh in the face of Hollywood training." Phoebe was so relaxed around everyone. She was amazing. "It's time to show you what us Brits are made of, right, Meg?"

I nodded, hiding my panic. As the only other British person here, I thought we were mainly about tea drinking and getting too involved in *Bake Off*. "Er, well if you're stuck for players, guess I could."

TJ whooped and whipped his T-shirt off, spinning it round his head. *My poor, brave eyes!* When they woke up, they thought today was any other normal day, but in twelve hours they'd been confronted with close-hand TJ semi-nakedness TWICE and not had to pop out. "Let'ssssdoooothhhiiiissss." Even though TJ was the one stripping off, I was the one turning red. I cleared my throat and concentrated as hard as I could on the sand. Lovely, safe, not naked-TJ sand.

"Geli, what about you?"

He was staring at TJ like he'd just discovered a new species.

"Maybe another time, yes?" And despite my attempts to persuade him, he headed off. Which turned out to be his loss. He missed an awesome game. After waiting our turn (which seemed to come about a lot more quickly when it involved people making way for a Hollywood star), me, Phoebe, TJ and some other people I'd never met launched into my first-ever game of beach volleyball. With the edges marked out in sand, and everyone laughing and whooping, it was a million times more awesome than anything that happened in my school hall (although the ball did whack me in the face at least three times when I accidentally slipped into forgetting not to gawp at TJ).

Even though a crowd gathered, I managed to eventually relax into it, and ended up leaping and diving about. Mr Dennington, our games teacher, would have been so proud. And, much to TJ's annoyance, it was me who managed to slam down the winning shot for the whole game, beating his team. Phoebe ran straight over to give me a hug.

"Yesss, you smashed it!" As she squeezed me, she whispered something no one else could hear. "See? Fun things happen when you let them."

And, as everyone else bundled on us, TJ jokingly shouting it was a fix, I thought maybe, just *maybe*, she and Neet could have a point.

CHAPTER TWELVE

Most people ended the match gently glowing. I, however, had fully committed and finished a big sweaty mess. Grabbing a water, I told Phoebe I needed to check on Oli and headed off on my own. Olive's new mates had seen me playing volleyball with TJ and, when I found them, they treated me like a celeb-by-proxy. But after they'd asked me a billion questions about it, and Olive had filled me in on her limbo victory, it was time for her to head back. The more she protested the firmer I was, which was quite fun (I can totally see why Dad does it now). Total parent power trip. I even got to give withering looks to her friends when they said it was a lame curfew. Turns out, I do definitely feel braver with people who are at least a foot smaller than me.

I wanted to explore, so once she was on her way back, I carried on down the beach. I couldn't find Holly anywhere, so I was all alone – the perfect chance to catch-up with Neet. I'd had a zillion messages from her while I'd been playing volleyball.

> NEET: Please tell me you are ignoring my live commentary of Holby City because you are still at the party and doing something way more fun? 😬

I almost couldn't bring myself to tell her the truth. But I also absolutely could.

> ME: YOU MEAN LIKE PLAYING BEACH VOLLEYBALL WITH TJ?

> NEET: FOR REAL????????

> ME: ✅

Her reply took a while.

> NEET: Sorry. Just died there. You can thank me later for making you go 🏁 ♡ 🌴 🏐

She was right, I did need to. She'd talked me into it and now, whatever happened in my life, I could always casually tell the story of when I beat TJ – *yes, the world's hottest movie star TJ* – at beach volleyball. I know I shouldn't care what all those idiots who called me Megabite thought about me, but I was pretty sure none of them could beat that.

NEET: Want to know something else amazing?

ME: 🥺🥺🥺

NEET: 555552 SECONDS TIL I'M THERE WITH YOUUUUUUUUUUUU!

ME: BEST THING EVER.

ME: 555537 now

Neet: Still CAN. NOT believe Dad's letting me go?!

ME: 😊 😊 😊. How is he?

The typing dots came up. And went. And came back up again.

NEET: You know. . .

I did. Tough. Although her mum was the one in hospital, he'd been the one keeping it together – and Neet had been the one keeping him together. So it was *my* job to keep *her* together.

NEET: But we'll get there 😊😊

I wanted to tell her to be more honest with me. To let me help more. To know it was OK to let other people prop *her* up for a change. But I knew she'd hate that, so instead I sent her a heart emoji and hoped she'd know what it meant.

NEET: Love you too you sxc volleyball beast!

I put my phone away, as the path I'd started to walk up had trailed off, and it was getting darker by the second. The moon only partly lit the ground, and as I wound my way up the rocks, it became a bit of a scramble. I used my hands to help steady myself. It was so steep I wasn't sure whether to turn back.

But when I looked down at the beach, and how cool

it already looked from up here, I *knew* I had to get to the top. So, pushing what Dad would think to the back of my mind (THAT I WOULD ALMOST CERTAINLY SLIP TO MY DEATH/WOULD BE LOOKING AT MY PHONE AND WALK OUT IN FRONT OF A CAR (even if there were no cars)/GET KIDNAPPED), I carried on.

Suddenly I heard laughter above me: I wasn't alone. I froze. What was happening up there in the dark?

I squinted up. I could just make out the flicker of a flame over the top of the rocks. My heart sank. As much as I wanted to get to the top, I wasn't about to gate-crash someone's party. But as I went to turn back I stopped. I recognized a voice. It was Geli, chatting away in Greek with his friends.

I didn't know what to do. Say hi? Or try and make my way back down without him knowing I was ever here? I definitely didn't want him to think I'd followed him, so I reached my foot down in the dark to creep away, undetected.

But instead of finding rock I found something else. Something long. And thin. And snake-like.

ARGHHHHHEEEEE.

I full-on screeched. An actual "argh". I didn't even know I could make a noise like that. The thing under my foot darted away. Did it howl?! I couldn't see anything as there was now a light shining on my face.

"*Pios ine aftos?*" Geli pointed the torch away from me. "Megan? What are you doing here?"

A couple of his mates ran up behind him, probably to protect him from the wailing banshee that they were now discovering was a sweaty British girl. CRINGE.

"Erm, not dealing with treading on a potential snake?"

"Round here we call them tails." Geli shone his torch near my foot. There was a very annoyed, very furry-looking dog looking at me. The one that had been with the Random Old Dude.

"Ah. . . Sorry." I wasn't sure if I was apologizing to Geli or the dog.

"Trevor says not to worry."

I looked at the dog. "*Signomi*, Trevor." *Thank you.* I'd finally remembered the first Greek word Geli had taught me. Geli smiled. "You want to join us?" His mates had gone back to chatting round the fire. "Not many of you guys make it up here."

"Us guys?"

This time it was Geli who looked caught out.

"Ahhh, yes. . ." He looked down at the beach. "You know. . . *Tourists*." He was trying to be polite, but I could hear the disdain behind his words.

So that's how he saw us? Not as friends, or individuals, or people to get to know. Just a bunch of people who dropped in and out of his life, while he waited for us to leave? I stepped up on to the rock where he was standing. It was a stretch, but I didn't flinch. "Well, this *tourist* loves a challenge."

Geli grinned. "In that case ... *Kalosirthes*. Welcome."

I held his eye contact. "*Efharisto.*" His mates around the fire were cracking up over something. "What's so funny, anyway?"

Geli dug his hands in the pockets of his shorts, and stretched back. "Just Hollywood Boy doing what he does best. . ."

I looked out to where they were all staring. TJ at the edge of the calm water, standing on the rocks below us pouting, posing, taking topless selfies, leaning on a surfboard perfectly aligned with the point the moonlight hit the water. Geli shook his head. "Be careful around him."

He said it quietly, but before I could ask what he meant, his friend with the bandana interrupted.

"As if there's any surf tonight." He sniggered. "His feet are totally touching the bottom."

He clinked cans with the girl next to him as they laughed and moved for a better look. I felt a bit mean, considering TJ had been the only person except Geli to come and say hi to me at the party. But ... well ... he did look like a bit of an idiot.

"You not into Instagram, then?" I asked Geli.

He ruffled his hand through Trevor's shaggy coat. "I think you know the answer to that."

I think I did. He was the only person I'd met who had a phone like one of the old ones Mum and Dad had discarded in our kitchen drawer.

"Here." Geli took a step to the edge of the cliff. "Can I show you something?"

"Options for a new profile pic?" I joked. He looked at me like I was speaking a foreign language. Which I guess I was.

"No, the best view on Skotheos."

Deciding that keeping quiet was better than making bad jokes, I followed him to the far edge of the cliff. Geli might be moody, but I did trust him, and didn't feel at all worried going into the dark with him. One of his mates had started playing the guitar, and as the light flickered the whole place felt kind of magical. But that was nothing compared to when I saw where he was pointing. A dramatic cliff jutted out into the water, a huge hole in the rock making a massive arch with what look like a lightning bolt cut out of it.

Geli shrugged. "It's known as *Yria's Point*. We like to call it Potter's Peak."

The flash did look just like the one on Harry's head. It was amazing.

"So you're into Harry Potter?!"

"Meg. We're a Greek island, not a planet from outer space." Geli lifted his scruffy backwards cap up and shook out his tangled black hair before putting it back on. "But that's not the point."

We stood in silence, listening to the waves (until his mate started to sing, which sounded a bit like Ed Sheeran being murdered, which took the edge off the magic a bit).

"Ten out of ten view. Seriously." I'd never seen anything like it. We stood some more. His mate attempted some high notes that had a real distressed cat vibe. "The soundtrack not so much." Geli laughed. He seemed a different person to earlier. I spotted something in the trees at the edge of the cliff – it looked like a piece of thick wood tied up round a huge tree branch. "What's that?"

"Oh, that..." Geli scrunched his mouth. "Just something I made."

"What, you *made* it?!" He was like the Greek Bear Grylls.

"I wish I hadn't. I thought it would be a cool place to sit on nights like this, but. . ." Oh yeah – if it was undone it'd be a swing dangling over the cliff edge. He paused. "Well, it's tied up now."

"But it looks amazing." Why was he being so moody about it?

"Apparently so. For the second it takes to sit on it and take a photo."

Ahhh. I got what was annoying him. He'd made it to show off his island – and everyone else had used it to show off themselves.

"Well, maybe one night we could check it out?"

Too late, his guard had gone back up. "Maybe. . ."

I didn't have time to try and talk him into it – maybe best, as Dad would freak – because my phone alarm started buzzing. Ten o'clock. Which meant ten minutes to curfew – and I was a good twenty-five-minute walk away.

"Geli – that's me done. Dad's expecting me back at ten past."

He nodded. "You'll be OK walking by yourself?"

"Obvs," I snapped, offended he'd think I needed help, but he looked blank. "As in obviously. . . As in yes."

I realized that I'd been a bit harsh. "As in thanks for asking, though."

He pointed towards a small patch of trees. "It's quicker if you head that way. Past the public toilet and down the path. Every second counts, right?"

"Uh-huh." I laughed and started to walk off.

"*Kalinihta*, Meg."

I shouted the same back to him and his mates, and spent the next minute doing the fastest walk I could, panicking I'd just assumed that meant goodbye and hadn't yelled something way weirder like "Don't trip over a tree root".

When I got my phone out to use as a torch, I had the urge to do something I hadn't done since the party of doom back in the UK. Maybe it was because I'd had a way better time at the beach party than I'd thought, or maybe it was because out here, in the dark, real life felt extra far away. Whatever the reason, I logged in as me and opened my feed. As expected, my notifications were lit up, unchecked for almost two weeks. With one eye squinting, I clicked on the heart – and immediately saw enough *Megabite*s and shark and teeth emojis for me to swipe straight back out. But I saw Neet's name too. I *had* to remember not everyone was laughing at me.

Eurgh.

Pretending it didn't happen was so much harder when the internet was determined to remind me it did. But I thought back to what Neet had said at school. If I never faced up to what had happened then I could never move on. I'd passed the first big step of opening my account, so now I had to do what I'd gone there to do. Head to TJ's page to do something that, before the Megabite thing, I wouldn't have thought twice about. I'd been following TJ for years. Credit to him, that boy knows his angles. His pouting selfie from a few minutes ago had over 50k likes already. Oh. No. 500k. *Half a million people*. Which was half a million (minus about 200) more people than I even knew. Insanity.

As I hurried down the path, I clicked *like* – and chuckled to myself. Not a manic giggle. Just a satisfied snort of happiness. How bonkers was life that, one week ago, Neet was showing me his attempt at the #EmuChallenge, and now here I was liking a photo I'd seen him take?

Phoebe was right. I was so glad those losers back home hadn't stopped me having fun out here. In fact. . . I searched through my camera roll and, with my thumb shaking a little, I posted the picture of the beach party I'd taken from the cliff.

One small click for me, one big leap back into my old

life. Haters could hate – but I had breakfast feta to look forward to, and a morning swim, and reliving volleyball with TJ, so for one evening they could say what they wanted. I wasn't going to hide. Not tonight.

But as I hurried down the path, I got a weird feeling, and it wasn't just doubt about posting that was creeping up on me. It was something else.

I wasn't alone. Someone, or something, was behind me.

I was in a pitch-black forest, only Geli knew I was here, and I was being followed.

I was an idiot.

I stopped and listened as best I could.

My fingers tightened on the alarm Dad always made me carry. Or maybe it was my lip balm. I couldn't tell.

There was a sudden screech – was someone being attacked?!

Oh no. That was just Geli's mate's singing going up a notch.

But there *were* definitely footsteps, and they were getting nearer.

If I sprinted it'd still take a few minutes to get back – but on the other side was the sheer drop of the cliff. I only had one option: I ducked down behind a tree, hoping they might not spot me and walk past.

But as the footsteps got nearer I realized I'd watched too many murder shows on Netflix. Or was too genetically linked to Dad.

I *wasn't* being followed. They were just two people walking, chatting quietly and laughing as they went.

What a dweeb. I took a some deep breaths to shake out the adrenalin, waited for the coast to clear, and stepped out to run back.

And instantly wished I hadn't.

Because in the dark, although it had gone quiet, I wasn't alone. And instead of stepping on to a path I'd stepped straight on to a *someone*. The foot of a girl – a girl I hadn't heard because she was in the most-fullest of full-on snogs.

She yelped and stepped back, and I said a truly mortified sorry, but it wasn't either of us that was the most shocked. It was the boy who looked like his nightmares had just come true.

"Meg?!"

It was all I could do not to laugh.

"Alex. Fancy seeing you here."

CHAPTER
THIRTEEN

Maybe I'm just allergic to kissing? When I try and do it I maim people, and when other people do it near me I stand on them.

It's like natural selection in action – and nature is telling me it's Game Over. I'm not even cut out for the most basic stage of passing on my DNA.

I rolled over in my bed, the sheet scrunched at the bottom. Do people who live in hot places never get to experience the joy of a duvet? Sure, they may look happy and healthy, but what do they use when they want to feel sorry for themselves with a Netflix binge? I'd had to put my My Little Pony nightie in the wash, so was sleeping in Dad's David Attenborough T-shirt. He was a total fanboy. I hadn't helped overheating matters by going to bed in a sheet mask, but my sunburn was on the verge of turning from bad-tourist red, to full-on Rudolph glow, and it was desperate times.

I picked up the handheld fan Mum had bought us. It was a giraffe whose nose span round. It wasn't cool but it was *cool*. I was a fan. Of the fan.

As it whizzed away, my face mask crisping up in its breeze, I thought about how hectic today had been. I'd met TJ?! And Phoebe. And Holly and Alex. I felt so bad for his girlfriend. Cheating was the worst. I really hoped he'd already told Phoebe – or was I going to have to? *Eurgh*. Liking people could suck.

I looked at my phone. Almost midnight. Dad had been FaceTiming Mum when I got back, and they were both drinking wine and eating cheese. Apparently it was a date night. I didn't really see the appeal of watching someone eat Stilton, but each to their own. But I was happy – glad I'd gone to the party. It had been nice to be just Meg again instead of Megabite. Not Meg who most of my year had decided was a total loser. Just Meg, like I used to be two short weeks ago.

Which is why on my walk/run/snog-sabotage back, I'd made up my mind. If Neet had been right about the party, maybe she was also right that out here, where life already felt different, it really was the perfect place to attempt kiss number two. Properly put the last one behind me. Move on.

Argh.

Even thinking it was scary.

But how could I make sure it wouldn't be as disastrous as the first one? I was going to have to do it differently. This time I needed rules.

1) I had to like the guy. *Really* like the guy. And he had to like me too. This wasn't about ticking a box, this was about really wanting to share a kiss with someone. It had to be special and worth it.

2) I had to look up the Greek equivalent of 999 beforehand, just in case.

Could I really do this? And even if I could, was I even going to meet someone to do it with?

In the morning I'd clear my head with a swim – although waking up would mean getting to sleep first. I flipped my pillow over to press my face against its cold side. But like everything out here, there was no cold side. It was hot hot hot.

PIP.

What. Was. That?

PIP PIP.

I sat up. Something was hitting my window.

PIP.

Surely it couldn't be a bird? Or did Greece have freaky insects that were big enough to make an actual bang?

I swung my legs out of bed and armed myself with the nearest weapon I could find. The giraffe fan. Sure, it might just waft any intruder/mutant insect with a nice breeze, but at least it had the element of surprise. I held it out in front of me, fencer style, and shuffled sideways towards the window.

PIP.

OK, Meg. Don't panic. There's probably a reasonable explanation.

PIP BANG.

Or not.

There was only one thing for it. I had to be scarier than whatever was out there.

Taking a deep breath, I pinched the bottom corner of the long curtain, and with my fan held in front of my face, I mustered the scariest-yet-non-Dad-wakingly-loud "warghhhhh!" I could and flapped the curtain back.

"ARRRRRGGGGGGHHHHH!"

"Arghhhhhhh."

152

I couldn't tell who was more terrified. Me or the person leaning over on to my balcony.

Giraffe fan still raised, I slid my door open ever so slightly. "You know this is 100% not OK?!"

A shocked Alex put his finger to his lips. "And wearing a psycho killer mask is?!"

I put my fingers up to my face. Oh, the sheet mask. I'd forgotten about that.

"I don't need to justify my facial moisture needs to you. What are you doing?!"

"Can I?" He was asking to climb over the wall. I hesitated, then nodded. Alex swung his other leg over and dropped down on to my balcony.

"First up. Sorry. . ." His voice was low, but urgent. "I needed to speak to you."

"And waiting for the morning wasn't an option because. . .?"

He looked back at his side of the wall. "Because I needed to speak to you before you saw Pheebs."

Ahhh. I knew where this was going – and I didn't like it. "You scared me to death."

"Ditto. Have you seen *Texas Chainsaw Massacre*?"

I crossed my arms. "Have you seen *Random Man Throws Stuff at Window Then Horrifically Murders Holidaymaker*?"

He stuck his lip out as if really racking his brains. "No, but it sounds like a corker."

I raised an eyebrow – not that he could see underneath the mask. I peeled it back. Didn't want him missing out on my disapproving looks. Alex stared at me like I was actually regenerating.

"So...?" What was he going to have to say for himself?

"So..." He shifted awkwardly. I wasn't going to help by filling the silence. He'd made this mess. "I'm sorry you saw what you did." He looked embarrassed, checking back at the window, terrified Phoebe might hear something going on.

"Are you sorry I saw, or sorry you did it?"

He squirmed. "Both. I *really* need my sister not to find out about it."

As I suspected – so he wasn't just a cheat, he wanted to be a liar too.

"Maybe you should have thought of that before you did it." Zero sympathy given.

"I know, I know." He put his hands in his pockets and kicked the tiled floor. "I hoped if I could explain, maybe you'd hear me out?"

"And you thought turning up on my balcony at midnight would get me onside how?"

"I dunno. . ." He paused. "I just didn't know what else to do."

"Not cheat on your girlfriend would be a strong start."

He rubbed his face hard with his hands. "I know. Honest, I do. It's just . . . complicated."

I folded my arms. "Not from where I'm standing." I couldn't believe he'd gone from being so cocky earlier, to looking so meek now. "Phoebe is going to *kill* you."

Turns out a boy in leopard-print trainers couldn't change his spots.

"Don't I know it." Alex properly sighed. "So, can I explain?"

"I want to get back to bed." I crumpled up my face mask. "So if you getting on with it will make that happen sooner, then yes."

He cracked his knuckles, stressed. "Look, I know I messed up. *Big* time. But I also know if Phoebe finds out, she's going to spend the whole holiday worrying about Lucy."

"So?" My loyalties lay with Phoebe, not him.

"So, I need you to not tell her."

I shook my head. I wasn't going to be part of his cover-up. Lucy and Phoebe deserved to know. "Alex, that's not fair."

"I know – and I will tell her. *Them*." He sounded desperate. "The day we get back. I just need you to not say anything before then." He looked at me, begging me to help him. "Please, Meg. I know it sucks, and I know it's my mistake. Things haven't been right with Lucy for ages, and I don't want this to hurt Phoebe even more than it will."

I couldn't see how lying could be the right thing, especially when Phoebe had no idea things weren't as loved-up as she thought . . . but I could see how stressed I'd be if the situation was me and Neet, and she was miles away getting heartbroken – by my imaginary brother.

"How can I trust you'll tell them?" Honesty didn't seem to be his strong suit.

"I thought you'd say that. Here." He held out his phone. "Phoebe's number, so you can ring, message, whatever you need to do to check I've kept my word." He didn't need to know we'd already swapped numbers earlier.

We stood in silence, the only noise the sea crashing behind us.

I didn't know what was the right thing to do.

It was too much for my half-asleep brain.

"OK, fine." I'd never seen anyone look so relieved.

"On one condition. . . I won't bring it up, but if Phoebe asks, I'm not going to lie to her. I can't, OK?"

Alex nodded, a grim look on his face. "I get it. I hate this too."

"And you took the mick out of *my* kiss curse?" We both laughed, but not in a way that was funny, just sad. There wasn't anything left to say. "OK, well, I'm going back to bed now." I walked to the door, but as I went to slide it shut, Alex turned back.

"Look. This may be off key. *Waaay* off key. But, maybe there is something I can do to say thanks."

Reluctantly I turned back. I was tired. I didn't need this. "I don't want to be paid off, Alex. Like I said, if she asks, I'm going to tell her."

"I know. I get it. But it doesn't mean *I* don't want to say thanks. For doing it for me."

"I'm doing it for Phoebe. So you don't ruin her holiday – or her friendship." He needed to be clear about that.

"I know. But I figured if I'm going to be keeping my head down to survive this holiday, why not use that time to help you?"

"Because I don't want you to?"

"Not even if it helps with your mission?" It was the first time he'd said it gently, not mocking me, not laughing. "I could be your island wingman! No interfering, just here if you need a guy on the inside..."

"You do know my love life isn't a criminal operation, right?"

"Yeah," he laughed. "It's much more risky than that. Last time someone almost died." He realized I wasn't laughing. "Too soon... Sorry." He wasn't funny. Well, maybe a bit, but I didn't want to give him the satisfaction of thinking it. "Look. No pressure. But the offer's here if you want it."

I didn't want it. I slid my door shut.

But as I stood in the moonlight, I caught my reflection in the mirror, and thought for a second. I *did* want to go back to the UK a new Meg. A Meg who wasn't scared of a kiss. A Meg who wasn't scared of anything. And I wanted to prove to Neet I was trying.

I pulled the door open. Alex was halfway over the wall.

"Wait..." I was still whispering but he stopped in his tracks. I couldn't believe what I was about to say. "I'm up for giving it a try."

Shocked, he jumped back down and walked over. "Seriously?"

"Uh-huh. But there are rules."

"First rule of kiss club is no one talks about kiss club?"

I gagged. "No, first rule of kiss club is you never say the phrase 'kiss club' ever again."

"Fair."

"Second is it's got to be with the right person. For the right reason."

Alex nodded. "I know. I get it. It's got to mean something." He sounded sincere. "And three?"

"The big one. No one, as in NO ONE, can find out about the mission. About me."

He looked at me, his head slightly tilted. "Is that a big deal?"

I couldn't believe he'd ask. "The biggest. Out here no one knows anything about me, and I want to keep it that way." But it was more than that. No one knowing about the whole Megabite thing was the only way I could be my old self, and be in the kind of situations where I might ever like anyone. "I'm going to need you to promise." I knew how lame it sounded, but he had to take me seriously.

"Sure." He put his hand out. "Let's do it. Let's make it official." He cleared his throat. "From this point onwards, I, Alex, Next-Door Neighbour Who You Now Know the Deepest, Darkest Secret About, promise you, Meg, Fan of David Attenborough and Believer in True Love, that I won't tell anyone about your mission. And behind the scenes I will help you find – and get to know, as in *really* get to know – the guy of your Greek dreams… and I'm not going to quit until it happens."

Without stopping to think if I'd just made a huge mistake, I shook his hand.

"Deal."

As petrifying as it was, there was no going back now.

CHAPTER FOURTEEN

First things first. What's your type?

Last night I'd given Alex my number, but I didn't think I'd wake up to a WhatsApp from him.

I immediately sent a message. Not to him, but to Neet.

Neet, what's my type?

We were years past the point of needing hellos or explanation. I expected her to reply in a few hours, but she replied immediately.

Funny. Smart. Or looking like TJ in those volleyball pics 👅👅👅

I decided to only send Alex the first two. He replied with an *On it*, although I had no idea what exactly he was on, apart from the other side of the wall. I felt so weird about everything that had happened last night, and urgently needed to get my head straight. So I left a note for Ol and Dad and sneaked out to the beach. It wasn't even eight a.m. and I'd never in my life got out of bed at this time without it being physically painful. But here, with the sun already shining brightly, and the sea outside my window, I couldn't get up quick enough.

The sand was already warm under my feet.

No one was around except Random Old Dude and his dog Trevor (whose tail looked fine, phew). He gave me a big wave and a whoop as I ran into the water – which helpfully covered my massive shriek of "WHATTT'SSSTHATTTT?" when something that felt like a long piece of wet bacon brushed against my leg. I'd almost splashed my way into the middle of a swarm of jellyfish. Even though they were the harmless ones, I stood on the spot flapping, malfunctioning between being grossed out and amazed. But once they floated by I properly took the plunge, and soon was speeding through the gentle waves, my front crawl whizzing me back and forth to the buoys. I felt calm here, like life was simple.

When I got back to the shore Dad was waiting,

holding open my towel for me. He wrapped me up in it like when I was young after my Sunday night bath. He'd laid out a plate of croissants and melon down by my clothes.

"Thanks, Dad." When he wasn't being totally uncool he could be pretty cool.

He kissed me on the head. "My pleasure. But can you do me a favour?" He held my chin so I had to look him in the eye. "Only go in the sea when there's someone to make sure you get out safely?"

The only time I would ever worry about Dad is if he wasn't worrying about something.

"But, Dad, that's what *I'm* here for. To make sure *I* get out OK!"

He looked up just as a speedboat came in to view from round the cliff. "And no boats."

"Can I have this croissant if I say yes?"

He picked up the plate. "Or night swimming. Or jet skis. Or those deathtrap banana boats."

"Fine." I accepted the legally binding pastry and, in a contented truce, we sat on the sand and munched them together, the two of us quietly looking out to sea.

"Would have been cool if Mum was here, wouldn't it?"

Our family already felt lopsided without her. I couldn't imagine what it was like for Neet.

Dad put his arm around me. "The coolest, Megs."

We carried on in our happy silence until the local church bell rang nine and Dad decided it was time for him to go check Olive was alive. I was going to join them later – Dad had arranged for Geli to take us down to set again, which was fine by me as "hanging out with Hollywood people" had a slightly cooler ring to it than "hanging out with me, myself and I". My phone rang.

"Please tell me that's not legit." It was Neet, in her parents' room wearing full Ivy Park power tracksuit, which meant only one thing. She'd taken on a home DIY project. "First your message wakes me up at five-thirty, and now you're on an actual paradise beach while I'm stuck here constructing a bookshelf?"

I wiped off any croissant flake evidence that could make her even more jealous.

"Sorry about the waking up – I thought you'd be on silent." She normally was – it was only since her mum had been in hospital she'd switched. "So do you want the honest answer or the one that will make you feel better?"

"That one," she said, pointing furiously. "And I'm only doing this to say thanks to Mum and Dad." She moved so I could see her creation – an empty oblong. She saw my face. "Yup, *sure,* currently a book non-shelf, but YOU JUST WAIT. My way of paying them back for the holiday – it's been leaning up against their wall for *months*."

"Yas, Neet!" There was no challenge she couldn't take on. I was so glad she was coming out here – she deserved a break more than anyone.

"Earth to Meg??!" Neet pushed her finger down on the drill, which made an aggressive *WRRRRRR*. "Are you thinking of TJ's RIDICULOUS bod again?"

I knew she'd prefer a tiny lie than me being emotional at her. "I can't not not say that."

"Perv."

"Says you."

Neet scrunched her lips all the way up to her nose. "Fair." She leant back, put the drill down, and fanned her face. "But those beach pictures?! C'mon. No wonder people are freaking out you're there."

She stopped suddenly. Too suddenly.

I raised my right eyebrow. "*Who* exactly is 'people'?"

"...Me?" We both knew she'd been rumbled.

"What do you know?" I put on my teacher voice and folded my arms. "And FYI, withholding info WILL be seen as a crime punishable by absolutely no more TJ gossip."

"Fiiiine. Fiiiiine." She sighed. "Have you, er, checked Instagram today?"

My stomach lurched. What with everything that

had happened, I'd forgotten I'd broken my posting ban. Somehow the whole Balcony Boy thing had parked in the brain space where that stress should be. "Should I?"

She shook her head. "Maybe give it a while."

Too late. What was it about bad news that stopped procrastinating in its tracks? I opened it up.

"I know what you're doing!" Neet was shouting. "It's muted the video." I carried on anyway. "MEG. STOP RIGHT NOW."

But it was too late. I'd already seen my notifications and DMs. Seems the guys from the party back home had had some time on their hands last night, and that time had been spent telling me that I was "BRITISH GIRL ON THE LOOSE", "MEGABITE ON TOUR" and "INTERNATIONAL SAFETY ALERT NEEDED".

"MEG, STEP AWAY FROM THE INTERNET!" Neet was yelling, and the drill was joining in too. But my finger had gone rogue, scrolling up and down – what I saw made me feel sick. There was no way I was posting again. "OR I'LL TAG YOU IN THAT PHOTO WHEN WE DRESSED UP AS A POTATO SALAD."

This time my finger understood what was at stake. I swiped away. Neet didn't look happy. "I *told you* it was a bad idea."

"You also said they'd forget about it?"

"They *will*." Her voice softened. "But it takes two to move on. Or tango. Or whatever."

She walked to her room. "So, progress report. And remember, more progress *here*" – she picked up the list – "means less time worrying about stupid comments *there*."

I wanted her to know I was trying – for her – so I tried not to dwell on what I'd just seen.

"Well, first up, the party *was* a good idea. So thank you for that." I twiddled my hair. "Second up, I *maaaaay* have come round to the idea that I need to make this second kiss happen."

Neet's eyes almost popped out. "Did. I. Hear. That. Right?"

I rolled my eyes. "You *know* you did." She didn't move. "Don't make me say it again." She was completely still. "C'mon, Neet. I know the screen hasn't frozen cos a bird just flew past your window."

Caught out, she sprang back into life. "Was it my pep talk?" She was all excited. "I've been reading Michelle Obama!"

I knew it. "That definitely helped." I laughed at how happy this was making her. Her hands were now in the air, twirling as she chanted, "MEG'S GONNA SNOG, MEG'S GONNA SNOG."

"So what's the plan?" She flicked the paper to straighten it out. "Who's the lucky dude going to be?"

"To be decided," I laughed, but remembered I hadn't told her what happened after I went to bed – she knew about discovering the kiss, but had no idea about Balcony Boy's midnight visit. Would she think I'd made the right choice? Before I could tell her, she carried on.

"What if you've already met them?" She waved the list around.

"What if I haven't?" She pointed at the name at the bottom of the list. Geli.

"Nah, I can't work him out. Sometimes he's nice and sometimes he's ... well ... weird. He seems to love slash hate me all in the same convo."

"I will focus on the *love* there."

"And *I* will focus on keeping a grip on reality."

"Talking of keeping a grip." She smiled in a most creepy way. "A tight, tight grip. What about TJ?"

"Never going to happen. . ." I shook my head. "There's punching. And there's *punching*."

Neet shuffled on her bed and crossed her legs. "Megan Jackson. NO ONE is out of your league. That's just an outdated societal contract to make us doubt ourselves." She paused dramatically, before grinning a little. "And hypothetically, if there were leagues, you'd be in the top one anyway."

I blinked, calmly. "Thank you, extremely biased best friend... But the evidence does point to the fact he normally goes for girls on magazine covers, so I'm not sure why he'd suddenly be interested in normals?"

Neet spluttered. "SHUSH WITH THAT?! You are equally as desirable."

"Not sure all the people calling me Megabite would agree..."

"They're just jealous."

"OF WHAT?"

"The fact you're amazing and are on some sort of #ad holiday."

"Such a mum comment. Let's be real. They're calling me Megabite cos I bit their friend – and I want them to stop."

Neet put down the pen, serious. "Megs, you *can't* stop them. The only thing you *can* control is how it makes you feel. So maybe focus on the you-not-caring bit instead?"

I sighed. She was right, as always. But the "what to care about" bit of me played by its own rules. Time for a subject change to prove I wasn't just being negative. "I *guess* there is that funny guy from set..."

Neet waved a pen, clicking the nib in and out. "NEW ENTRY ALERT."

She was something else. "Stand down. He could be a seventy-year-old man who just sounds young."

"Well, let's find out! And while you're there, find out why Geli seems to have a split personality." Bit harsh. "And remember, you're the one currently writing off TJ, not the other way round." I guess I was, if I looked at it like that. "And we need to. . ." But she stopped talking. "Shhhh." She put her finger in the air, and spun round. "Yup. Phone's ringing. Catch up later, yessssss?"

I didn't have time to reply before she ended the call. She knew my answer was yes anyway – these days whenever their phone rang, she always sprinted to it in case it was her mum. But I also heard *my* name being called. I looked along the beach. Dad was waving. "Five minutes till we set off. Or shall we leave you here?"

A part of me wanted to stay. The weather was amazing, and my first-ever beach day was just what I'd been dreaming of. But Phoebe was going to be on set, and I could hang out with her and plan a beach day together for tomorrow. I just needed to bury the whole situation with Alex as deep down as I could. I felt horrible about it already.

I dashed back and changed into some shorts and a

Billie Eilish T-shirt (I think it was a fake, but I still loved it), and soon I was back in Geli's car, Olive wriggling around beside me. Today was clearly a monumental day. He'd greeted me with a wave AND a smiley hello, and even asked if I'd managed to not tread on any snake-dogs this morning.

Olive talked the whole way about her new mates – they didn't have access to set so were meeting at crew catering. She'd worn her new favourite T-shirt (bright yellow with "AIRPLANE MODE" on it) so I knew she was out to impress. Everyone goes on about what to wear for dates, but no one ever talks about the pressure of wanting new friends to like you. That's the *real* test.

As Dad, Oli and I flashed our passes and walked on to set, I got the same nervous feeling as yesterday, like I had a big sign above my head saying, "My normal life is at school in Solihull. I don't belong here." Everyone was busy doing something – all I was doing was watching them do it. I looked around, grateful I at least had Dad and Olive. Safety in numbers.

"Jack." A man in a headset and a top that probably fitted five years ago ran up. "Can I borrow you for a sec? Got a pyrotechnic issue."

Reluctantly, Dad had to rush off, and with him gone, Olive couldn't get rid of me quick enough. So within seconds, it was just me. Dumped by my own family, and not meeting Phoebe for half an hour. I wandered up the steps of the tiny, winding street that cut through the middle of the main filming area, to have a nosey around. The whole village had been cordoned off for filming. The bright blue sky was full of cables stretching across the jumble of roofs, and there were cameras and giant silver bits of fabric everywhere. They weren't using this bit of the street today which is why I could walk through it. I peered in the windows of the perfect white houses. Had they just been painted or were they always like this? Inside, crew were doing all sorts of weird things, like spraying a glass with deodorant and putting hairspray on to a strawberry cupcake. At school they always told us about how to be doctors and lawyers, but no one ever said how to become a world-travelling cupcake-sprayer – finally a job I'd truly be interested in.

"Helps them look frosty on camera." Glass woman looked up. She'd caught me staring. "Or cake fresh. Keeps it glistening take after take." She nodded to the front door. "You can come in if you want."

I pointed at the sign. "Is this TJ's house, then?"

She shook her head. "Nah... Well. Kind of. The front's their house, but they've already shot the interior scenes on a lot back in the States. All this" – she gestured to all the people working away – "is just for if they catch anything through the window." Wow. All that effort and it might not even be seen. Like Neet and I doing make-up tutorials just to stay in and watch films on the sofa.

"That's bonkers."

"Magic of Hollywood, right?" The lady smiled as I looked around, impressed. "But if you want the biggest crew secret ... it's the amazing rooftop up there." She looked towards the stairs. "The perfect place to get away from it all."

Wow. Cake sprayer *and* mind reader. She let me in and as I headed up my phone vibrated.

PHOEBE: Change of plan. Family trip to some monument aka driving hours to look at bricks. 😔 Crew catering at 3?

I *should* have stayed at the beach after all – then I wouldn't be here feeling like such a Billy No-Mates. Sunbathing was one of those things no one questioned if you did it on your own.

I pushed open the wooden door at the top of the stairs and stepped out. Ouch. I winced. The sun was blinding. But, once I'd got my sunglasses on and could see, it was beautiful. A jigsaw of rooftops stretching down towards the sea, a cat sauntering across them, and the most gorgeous view of the clear sky hitting the deep blue ocean. Cake-spray lady was right – up here, it was like the commotion of downstairs was a million miles away. It was the perfect place to wait it out.

I looked around for somewhere shaded, but heard something weird coming from the shadow by the far wall.

Squinting, I stepped closer.

Bipidy bumpidy ripidy rumpidy.

Was instant heatstroke a thing?! I crept forward, making sure whatever it was didn't hear me.

There was *something* there. A black silhouette. For the second time in twenty-four hours I could hear Dad's nags about letting people know where you were.

Bumzidy rumzidy dumzely clumzely.

Was hallucinating a growling monster the first sign of madness?

C'mon, Meg. Get a grip. There *had* to be a logical explanation. Maybe it was a malfunctioning prop?

"*WOOOAAAAARRRRRGGGGGGHHHHH*," the silhouette thing bellowed.

Nope. Time to get out of here, and *fast*, before it noticed me.

But my foot had other ideas – instead of being stealthy it stomped straight on to a twig.

SNAP.

Shadow monster thing turned round.

I screamed. Loudly.

I'd seen too much *Doctor Who* to think this was OK.

Although ... full frontal it looked less monster and more rubber statue with a towel on its head.

"Meg?!" The towel was whipped off, revealing...

"TJ?!"

He grinned. "Did I scare you?"

I took a second to compose myself, my fear morphing into fury.

"No. In Britain we scream as a friendly way of saying hello."

"Really?" He flicked the towel down by his leg. Now he was facing me I could clearly see he was just wearing a wetsuit. Did he even own clothes that he didn't have to peel off? He was the wardrobe equivalent of a banana.

"No." He looked embarrassed – I hadn't meant to be mean; it was just my kneejerk response and better than saying, "I thought you were a creature from the undead."

"Yeah, of course. Right." He ruffled his hair as if resetting his TJ-ness. "So what brings you round these parts?" He had a glint in his eyes. "Or did you know I was here?"

Was he implying I was a groupie? When actually I was here trying to be a solo-ie?

"I think the fact I screamed shows I clearly didn't." I sounded even more offended than I felt. "I was looking for somewhere to chill out."

TJ breezed right over my snappiness. "Well, now you know where I run through my vocal warm-ups." So *they* were the weird noises. "Get my head in the zone for stunts." He twanged his wetsuit. I tried not to look down. "Spoiler alert, though. No posting any pics!"

He laughed, but I could tell he meant it. It must be so weird living a life where people constantly waited for new photos of you. I was bothered enough what my school year were saying – he had to deal with the world.

"Maybe a stupid question, but, er, why the towel on the head?"

He picked it up and threw it at me. "Nice catch." It wasn't. It was a totally standard catch. "Blocking the light and sound really helps channel inner focus." Wasn't that what eyelids were for? "Try it."

He was staring at me so earnestly that I put it over my head to be polite. Yup, it felt like having a towel on my head. But worse – it felt like having a towel on my head while TJ from the movies stared at me wearing a towel on my head.

"Er, yeah, great..." I mumbled. "So ... er, focused." The only thing I was focusing on was that I looked like a total idiot.

"Told you." TJ started to lift it back slowly, sort of like a furry wedding veil. The two of us suddenly face to face, closer than felt normal.

The two of us suddenly in a weird, close silence.

The two of us—

BANG!

The door flew open and a breathless Geli rushed out.

"Meg, are you OK?!" He sounded panicked. "I thought I heard you scream..."

When he saw us, he immediately stopped and composed himself. I brushed the towel off me, and stepped away from TJ, embarrassed, although I didn't know what about.

"Sorry, Geli. I just got a fright." I must have a very distinctive "oh God, there's a monster" yell. "Thanks, though."

But Geli wasn't looking at me – he was looking at TJ. "Rubin told me you might be up here." He looked around. "Nice spot."

Geli said it like there was hidden meaning – but it

was so far hidden from me, I just replied with, "Yes? The sea looks amazing."

Then no one said anything. For definitely too long. So long that I found it funny – and then back to painful. Eventually, I folded TJ's towel and put it on a chair.

"Well, this is *lovely*. But I'm going to go check on Olive."

Geli gave me a nod. "I'll walk you down."

But I didn't need to be protected – the only people who had made me feel weird today were these two.

"It's fine, thanks."

"Don't forget your towel." Geli picked it up. TJ snatched it out of his hands.

"That's mine, *bro*." He then turned to me, his face totally changing. "Meg, don't go. Stay and chill up here?" He patted one of the wooden sunloungers.

I didn't know what was going on between these two, but I did know I didn't want to be part of it. They might not like each other, but I wasn't going to choose a side.

I wasn't a point to be scored. "See you both later."

CHAPTER FIFTEEN

So I was back to where I started: wandering aimlessly around set, trying to smile at people in a way that meant "I am definitely having a well-planned day and am definitely not passing time feeling completely awkward." But after peering in all the windows I could, and doing three laps of the empty streets, I still had another half an hour until I was meeting Phoebe. I was hot, sweaty, and my hair was at least 50% heat fluff.

At loner rock-bottom, I messaged Olive, who had borrowed a phone from Dad for the day.

ME: How you getting on? Don't forget that sun spray.

She'd been having a hissy fit about putting it on earlier.

DEMON CHILD: Chill out, Mum.

I wanted to reply with an eye-roll, but I was on the hunt for someone to hang out with and Emergency Little Sister Desperation levels had been reached.

ME: What you up to?

DEMON CHILD: Busy right now. Putting on sun cream. See you later.

She then sent a selfie of her mates, Ol in the middle, the sun cream on her face spelling out "Meg is a loser", four people around her cracking up.

"Can't she read?!" someone yelled. He sounded furious.

I looked up to see what the drama was. Right in front of me was a line of track with a camera on, leading up to a scene that had paused filming, people bunched around holding weird objects, like giant clips, and huge bits of what looked like tracing paper. In the middle of them was Mitch, the shouty chicken-chasing assistant director. He was puce with rage – poor whoever it was on the receiving end.

Uh-oh.

Why was he staring at me?

Uh-uh-oh.

Was the *she* he was yelling about me?!

"NO PHONES." Spit missiles flew out of his mouth in my direction. "Or are YOU more important than everyone else on set?"

Ground, swallow me up.

It wasn't just Mitch staring at me. EVERYONE was.

"I. . ." my voice was wobbling. "I. . ."

"Don't stutter. PUT. IT. AWAY."

So I did. As fast as I physically could. "Sorry," I mumbled. I couldn't look up. Everyone must think I was such a wally. Staring at the floor, I shuffle-jogged towards an alley as fast as I could. But due to only looking at my feet, I ran slap-bang into something else.

"Careful there, honey!" Phew. A friendly face. Holly. She held out a bottle of water. "Need this?"

I wasn't sure if she meant because of the heat, or because I looked like I was going to faint with shame.

"Thanks." I took a swig, grateful for a second to compose myself. "Don't suppose you could fix my make-up so no one recognizes me ever again?"

She put her arm around me. She had a shaved head, but still smelt of Neet's mum's hairspray – safe and warm and sweet. "Why would we want to cover up your beautiful face? Just because of that silly little man?"

She was like a mirage. "Why are you so nice?"

"Pish. Most people are, it's just. . ." But she didn't get to finish, because there was an unmistakable roar of a Mitch in full flow.

"WHOSE IS IT?!"

Everything fell silent – except a phone ringing. Loudly. It wasn't even a normal ring, it was a tinny version of the *Star Wars* theme tune.

"OFF THE SET, NOW." Mitch was bellowing. "WHOEVER IT IS – OFF. SET . . . NOW!!!"

No one spoke up.

I peeked round the corner. The phone was still ringing. Whoever's it was must be terrified.

Mitch threw his headphones to the ground.

"CAN'T YOU EVEN BE MAN ENOUGH TO OWN UP???"

Holly muttered, "Or woman?"

"I PERSONALLY WILL BOOK YOUR FLIGHTS HOME MYSELF!!! FOR TODAY!!!"

A small, scared runner shuffled towards Mitch. Oh no. Please let him be OK! He looked petrified.

But instead of apologizing, he lifted up the cushion on Mitch's chair. Underneath was a phone, lit up and ringing. Shaking, he held it out to Mitch, who grabbed it and turned it off.

It was Mitch's phone.

Suddenly, instead of tense silence, there was laughter – *so* much laughter – and with safety in numbers, no one even *tried* to hold in it. Mitch was so furious even his hands went red. Spluttering, he tried to regain some control and respect.

"CAMERAS READY TO ROLL IN FIVE..." But he was the only one paying attention, so he yelled something about a "script break" and marched off.

It was joyous.

Holly tapped me on the arm. "'Scuse me, love, I need to go say congrats."

She squeezed past me and walked straight up to the chair. In all the commotion I hadn't noticed someone had sat down in it. I could only see his back – he had a backwards cap and a Patagonia T-shirt on, sleeves rolled up. People were slapping him on the back.

Holly grabbed his cheeks. "Well done on the most perfectly executed stunt of the whole shoot!" The group around cheered. "It was *you*, wasn't it. You rang him, didn't you?"

Patagonia boy shrugged, then laughed and held up his phone. "Withheld number, OF COURSE." I instantly recognized his voice. It was the funny guy from the talkback the other day. Interesting.

The clapping started again. And with his arms up in fake grandeur, he spun round, everyone whooping.

That's when I realized we weren't strangers.

I *had* recognized his voice. We *had* met before.

It wasn't the first time he'd come to my rescue.

He was the boy from the airport.

CHAPTER SIXTEEN

For the second time today, I froze.

He, however, strode over, big grin on his face, leaving the rest of the crew to celebrate without him.

"So we meet again, tea girl."

I nodded. He really must think I was the epitome of cool. First falling over with a hot beverage, now shutting down a film set. I needed to try and show him I could also be a normal human.

"It's you, isn't it?" Yup, nice one, Meg. Grade-A conversation skills right there.

"Yeah, it is. Although ... that would be the right answer for anyone." He smiled – woah. I'd remembered right. He *was* cute. His dimples could rival Ariana's – although his hair was more ginger pom-pom than one-metre ponytail. I could almost feel Neet moving him to the top of her Kission chart. "Nice T-shirt, by the way. Her album is. . ." He put his clenched fists in the air and did a little shimmy.

"Too right." It was weird feeling both like I knew him, and like he was a total stranger all at once. "What are you doing here?"

"I could ask the same about you." He stuck his hands in his pocket. "Been back and forth for the last few weeks helping my brother out with whatever needs to be done. Which mainly seems to be taking the mick out of that egomaniac." He gestured towards where Mitch had stormed off. "Although. . ." He discreetly pointed to where TJ was chatting to Random Old Dude. He was everywhere! "There are *too* many easy targets here. That one keeps moaning about getting hounded for autographs. He doesn't seem to have figured out the things he signs every day are our petty cash forms."

I laughed and tried to ignore how easily I'd gone along with making laughing at TJ our common ground. Again. There didn't seem to be many people who were on his side, even though he'd only ever been nice to me.

"So does that dude work here?" I nodded towards the old man.

"TJ? Yeah. He's the one who says the lines and flexes muscles that us mere mortals can only dream of."

He kissed his biceps. They were as flat as a pancake. But who doesn't like pancakes?

"You know what I meant."

I tried to think of a way of saying "Random Old Dude with his dog" without sounding offensive.

". . .That Random Old Dude with his dog."

He laughed. "I'm not sure that's his birth name, but yeah, he does." He paused. "I *think*. I don't know what his real name is." He turned back to me. "Or yours. No, wait . . . that's a lie." He took a moment to think. "Is it Meg?"

I gawped. "How did you know?"

"Besides the airport announcement?"

Cringe. "Oh yes. So glad you remembered."

He looked to the side, as if it was awkward that he did. "Yeah, it was . . . that. Anyway." He cleared his throat, getting his flow back, and stuck his hand out. "I'm Billy. Too late for formal introductions?"

"Never." I shook his hand back. "I'm . . . exactly who you thought I was."

"Well, lovely to meet you, 'exactly who you thought I was'."

Dad joke, but I laughed. Again. It was becoming

a habit when he was around. We stood, neither of us knowing which conversational crossroad to take – commit this chat into something more, or let us stay as two people just bumping into each other.

But the decision was made for me. The bell rang. Three o'clock. Time to meet Phoebe.

I tucked my loose bits of hair repeatedly behind my ears, something I did in times of stress. "Look, I've gotta go. I'm meeting someone for lunch." Did Billy's smile drop? Just a bit. "Unless..." C'mon, me. This was the perfect opportunity to put new, non-hermit Meg into practice. "Unless" – deep breath – "you want to come with?" Oh gawd. As soon as the words were out of my mouth I regretted them. He was going to say no. What was I thinking?! "It'sjustcrewcatering. AndmyfriendwillbethereandmaybemysisterOliveit'snot abigdeal."

The words couldn't come out of my mouth fast enough.

Billy stepped back. Had I scared him off?

"Oh. I've got to head back to—"

I didn't let him finish his sentence; this was *exactly* why I shouldn't put myself out there. "Of course. See you around."

He scrunched his face, confused. "I was going to say

I have to head back to get my bag. But then I'm up for coming with you, if that's OK?"

Five minutes later, despite what I'd thought, we were winding our way down to the catering tent, chatting about nothing in particular. I found out he lived in Glasgow, was obsessed with Wes Anderson and was an ice-creamgan (a word he'd made up to describe a vegan who couldn't say no to ice-cream on Skotheos). He found out that this was my first-ever holiday abroad, that Neet was arriving in five days, and that I'd never had a nosebleed. Or tried an olive, which was now a matter of principle, as it had started to really bug my sister. She said it was a personal attack.

When we finally got to catering, there was no sign of Olive, but Phoebe was already there, sitting on one of the white plastic chairs overlooking the little wall at the edge of the cliff. She had tiny round yellow lens sunglasses on, her braids piled on her head, and looked intimidatingly cool. As soon as she saw me she broke into a massive smile and waved us over. I gestured that Billy and I were joining the queue for food and would be a sec. It was amazing. You didn't have to pay for any of it – just show a lanyard, and the people serving it seemed to want you to have as much as could fit on a plate. Food heaven.

"So, Phoebe." I put my plate down on the table; it was a mountain of bright tomatoes, feta, green leaves, tuna, olive oil, balsamic vinegar, and some amazing twisted pastry things. "This is Billy... Long story, so go with it, but he's the guy I told you about who saved me in the airport."

"Ohhhh." I could see Phoebe's brain putting it all together. "I like you already!" She stood up and went in for a casual hug. "I'm Phoebe."

Billy tried to hug her back, but hadn't had time to put down his plate. When he stepped back, he was blushing. "I, er ... think I just got ice-cream on your top."

"No stress, it needs a wash anyway." She was always so quick to make everyone feel relaxed – I wished so hard that I hadn't been lumbered with a massive secret that was going to devastate her. It wasn't fair. On either of us. She looked down at what Billy was holding and did a double-take.

"Yes." He slow nodded, a confident smile on his face. "A plate of ice-cream." Phoebe snorted. "They'd run out of bowls, so what's a guy to do? Other than wipe it on strangers, of course."

I leant back in my chair. "You calling my friend strange?"

Billy slapped the table, "Geez Louise. Tough crowd!

I'm the one about to eat ice-cream with a fork. Cut me a break here?"

Phoebe and I laughed, both of us already knowing we'd found a three to our two. It seemed on holiday, because time was limited, all the making friends stuff was on warp speed. But I could feel another thought nagging at me. Neet's list flapping round my brain.

Did I like Billy as a new friend ... or something more?

I sneaked a look at him. He was slurping from the curved bit of his fork – it was a lot more cute than it logically should be.

But it was like a seesaw. I was so relaxed with Billy that I thought about Neet's list, but thinking about the list then made me totally un-relax. Eurgh.

I pushed it all to the back of my brain. I wanted to enjoy this for what it was.

"So, Pheebs." I prodded at my salad. "What was the day trip like?"

I was hoping to keep conversation away from the party last night. My face couldn't be trusted to not give away that I had something to tell.

"Far away. And full of bricks. Old bricks. And my brother" – *Megs, don't react* – "snoring the whole way like he hadn't slept a bit. But the view on the drive was onnnne hundred."

Billy scooped up a forkful of green melting goop. His plate was beginning to look like a bath bomb. "Pretty cool, right? You should check out Skotheos Ruins. It's this crazy castle thing on a rock in the sea."

"Sounds dope." Phoebe was impressed.

"Yeah, like twooooo hundred." Billy paused. "Is that a thing?"

I was going to tell him we all knew it wasn't, but got distracted by my phone vibrating. I'd switched it back on during the walk. When I saw who it was I got a shock.

Alex.

Had Phoebe spotted?! No, luckily she was busy stirring Billy's ice cream soup with a straw, about to have a slurp. Braver woman than me. Taking the opportunity, I opened the message.

What's your type? Funny. You seem to be laughing a lot rn ✓

What? He was spying on me? I looked up, and discreetly scanned the area. There he was, leaning against a wall, a little smile on his face.

When we made eye contact he did a slow wave. I spun back to the table and flat out ignored him – and flat out ignored the thought he'd re-filed to the front of my brain. Was it that obvious? Did I *like*-like Billy?

Meet later for a debrief?

I shoved my phone in my pocket. I couldn't deal with him now. I threw myself back into the conversation.

"Anyone fancy a beach day tomorrow? I'm heading down if you want to join?"

Phoebe pushed her sunglasses back up her nose. "You know *I'm* in." Whoop! "Ice-cream boy – what about you?"

"Sounds great. I'll check if my brother needs me, and if not ... see you there." Sweet. "Although..." He put his hands on his face either side of his mouth like that Scream painting. "Pray for me and my sun-allergic skin. I might have to go full balaclava."

"Don't worry." Phoebe rummaged in her bag and pulled out sun cream. "We got you."

My dad was going to love her. "So ... numbers?" She pulled her phone out, unlocking it. She had this amazing knack of making everything sound not a big deal. Bet no one ever said no to her. I watched Billy punch in "ICE CREAM INNOVATOR" and then his number. Phoebe looked at me. If I hadn't guessed before, it was obvious from the way she was biting the insides of her cheeks to not give away her grin that she was trying to set me up. "Megs, your turn." She looked at my hand, which was clutching my phone. My knuckles were actually white. But I couldn't give my handset over. I hadn't closed my messages from Alex. What if he sent another message while they were looking at my screen?

This. Was. Terrible. I *had* to think of something.

"It's OK." Billy broke the confused stand-off. "I've got yours, Phoebe. We can sort stuff, right?" He shrugged as if it was no big deal.

Was I relieved? Or a little bit gutted?

"Well, if you're sure?" Phoebe sounded put out on my behalf.

Billy laughed feebly. "Don't want to fill my phone up with too many new numbers." Phoebe and I glanced at each other. As *if* that was a thing. Especially for the most chilled-out guy on the island. "It's not like I'm here to, y'know . . ." He was sounding clunky, like his words were suddenly the wrong shape for his sentence. ". . . hook-up or anything."

Where did that come from? My nostrils flared more than Phoebe's. Was he implying that Phoebe was cracking on to him? Or worse, that I was?!

None of us knew what to say.

Billy slurped his ice-cream while we all tried to think of something to kick-start the conversation with. Luckily, Phoebe managed to conjure up some generic chat, like how long we were all here for, and who in our families were working on the crew, and eventually, much like his ice-cream, the atmosphere thawed.

But the thing with words is that they're like bad haircuts: once they're out there, however much you want to, you can't pretend they never happened. So, it was a relief when I saw my sister – I made my excuses and headed off.

"You all right, Ol?" She was with the people from the photo earlier. I walked straight into their conversation. Normally I'd loiter until someone invited me in, but it was an older sister privilege. Olive didn't exactly look delighted to see me.

"Sure am, Megan." She turned to her mates. They were a mix of girls and boys all about her age, including a few I recognized from the party last night. "This is my sister. The one I was telling you about."

There are two ways for someone to say that. One way where their voice goes up, and you know it's all good, and one where they're totally monotone, and clearly don't want you to know what they are saying. This was very much the second one.

Two could play that game.

"All good, I hope. Like how I don't shout when she borrows my phone all the time." I smiled sweetly. "And I don't mind walking her to the shops so she can work on her slime unicorn collection." Olive glared at me. If looks could kill, I would have spontaneously combusted.

I ruffled her hair. Her friends just stared at me blankly, except one with long blonde hair who looked me up and down. "Sounds kind of lame tbh."

Just like that I regretted saying what I'd said. It was fine for me to be mean about my sister, but no one else was allowed.

"*Tbh.*" I mimicked how she'd just said it. She might be cooler, more opinionated and better dressed than me, but she was still about six years younger and there was *nada* she could do about *that*. "It's actually more to keep our next-door neighbours' kid happy." Olive was looking at me like I'd lost my mind. Our neighbours were in their seventies and their children were older than Mum and Dad. But what her new mates didn't know wouldn't hurt them. I breezed on. "Soooo, what have you guys been up to today?"

A boy with headphones on put his arm around the blonde girl. "You know. Hanging out. Kicking back. Doing stuff you don't need to know about."

My face was notoriously bad at hiding my thoughts, which right now were, "How can someone who doesn't even come up to my shoulder be so annoying?" Olive was awkwardly staring at her feet – so she wasn't loving this either. I knew I'd done my bit, but if they were her new mates, why were they making her feel this uncomfortable?

Big sister mode engaged. I'd caused this whole situation – and it was going to be me that got her out of it.

"Sounds loads of fun. I mean with your total lack of access on set, and ..." I wasn't sure where I was going with this "... inability to reach cupboards, I bet the options were *limitless*." I'd never been this rude to anyone. I sort of liked it. "Anyway." Time for my killer blow. "Ol, I came over to ask you something." I reached into my brain to grab a good enough lie. I had to go big or go home. I knew just the route to go. "I was just talking to TJ." I said his name extra deliberately.

Jackpot. THIS certainly got their attention.

Blonde hair girl put a hand on her hip. "What, *the* TJ?"

I nodded as if the thought of there being other TJs had never occurred to me. "Yeah? Course."

The girl next to her whispered, "She played volleyball

with him last night!" Blonde Hair tried not to look impressed as she continued to stare me down.

"Anyway, he was wondering . . ." But I didn't know what to say next. I looked round in panic.

Quick, Meg. THINK. I needed something to make Olive seem super cool. Something so big they couldn't question it. But what?!

As I looked behind her, I saw something. A bunch of people dressed as sailors eating lunch. And that's when it fell into place. ". . . if you wanted to be an extra?"

Blondie's mouth fell fully open. "Noooooo."

Headphone boy gasped.

I smiled, happy I'd struck gold. "Yes, he wants you to be in the film."

Goodbye, smug faces! Hello, extreme jealousy.

I could explain to Olive later what had happened. The film wasn't out until the end of summer, and they'd have forgotten about trying to spot my sister in a crowd scene by then.

Well done, me.

Or not. Because when I saw Olive's face, I knew I'd made a mistake. A *massive* one.

My sister had actual tears in her eye, she was that happy. She threw her arms around me.

"TELL HIM YES PLEASE!!!!! This is the best thing

EVER EVER EVER!" And even though the others didn't hear what she whispered in my ear, the words hit me like a sucker punch. "Meg, you're the best sister in the WORLD."

CHAPTER SEVENTEEN

By the time we were back home having another amazing al fresco dinner, I still hadn't figured out a way to fix things. Just after I'd dropped my bombshell to Olive and her friends, Dad had materialized and herded us in to a people carrier that was doing a trip back to our apartment block.

Luckily, I'd managed to tell Olive to keep the whole extra thing a secret for now. She was so excited I knew that telling her the truth – that I'd completely made it up – wasn't an option. Which meant two things: I had to make it happen, and then get Dad to agree to it.

I wasn't sure which was going to be harder.

Neet's advice had been to beg TJ to pull some strings to get Olive a cameo role. But she didn't seem to understand I couldn't string together a normal sentence around him, let alone calmly explain I'd name-dropped him to get one up on some nine year olds.

"So, girls." Dad took a slow slip of his white wine. We'd chatted to Mum before we started, so she could feel like she was at family dinner. "Any exciting young-people things to tell your old father here?"

I tore off a piece of bread. "Just the usual. Wild parties. Talking only in emoji. Netflix and chilling. Avocados."

He took another sip, not reacting in any way. "Good to hear it. Beats my day of trying to rope in volunteers for my safety refresher demo on Thursday." He wiped his mouth. "What about you, Ol?"

I nudged her foot under the table. She was chewing at twice her normal speed and staring at her plate. For my sister, who was normally all chat and confidence, this was odd.

"Just having a great cool time, thanks, Dad." She seemed to be actually trembling at the strain of stopping her news popping out. "Nothing really much to tell you that could be an important thing to tell you."

She glugged her Appletiser. Well, at least I knew now she was *terrible* at keeping secrets.

Dad looked at me and lowered his eyebrows. *Did*

I know what was going on? I stuffed some bread in my mouth and shrugged innocently.

"Olive. . ." He put his knife and fork down. "Is there something you need to tell me?"

She shook her heard, and then *kept* shaking it. Concerned, Dad put his hand on her arm. "Ol, you know you can always tell me *anything*. I might not agree with everything you two do, but as your sister can confirm, I will always, always try to understand."

Oh, God. I felt sick. If he found out about my lie, I'd be in so deep, there was no way I'd be able to explain or find a plan b. I'd somehow have to make it happen.

"THIS FOOD IS NICE." I waved a forkful of fish in the air. "IS THIS BREAM?"

Dad looked at me, unimpressed. He was after solidarity not fish waving. "Meg. . ."

He wanted me to shut up, but if I didn't talk then Olive might. The way she was squirming right now made me think she was on the edge of a mega blab.

"SO HOW WAS WORK? YOU HAVEN'T SAID MUCH ABOUT WORK? DID THAT CRISIS GET SORTED? YOU SHOULD TELL US. TELL US! WE ARE HERE FOR YOU TOO, DAD. WE LOVE YOU."

"MEG!" I'd pushed it too far. "One sec, OK? Something is very clearly up with your sister."

Gah. My heart was pounding. But hopefully, hopefully Olive could hold out. I channelled as many positive, calming thoughts her way as possible.

Weirdly, it seemed to work. The trembling stopped. Her breathing slowed to something nearer intense panic, rather than police-dog sniff. I smiled at her reassuringly. She could do this!

"MEG SPOKE TO TJ AND I'M GOING TO BE AN EXTRA!"

Or not.

"I'M GOING TO BE IN THE FILM, DAD!"

"Olive!" I blurted, but it was trumped by Dad shouting my name way louder.

My sister mouthed a "sorry". But it was too late – the damage was done.

"Megan – do you want to explain what's going on?" Dad sounded not happy. Not happy at all.

"Erm..." I pushed my food around my plate. I *could* get him to say no to my fake plan and make my life a whole heap easier, but then Olive wouldn't speak to him for the rest of his holiday/life. Or, I could get him to say yes to my fake news, and then not be able to pull it off and risk Olive not speaking to *me* for the rest of my holiday/life.

"Well, I, erm." Whatever happened, I had to make

it sound like not a big deal. "Well, I was chatting to TJ." True. "And he was talking about crowd scenes." Veering slightly off the truth path. "And one thing lead to another" – definitely true –"and he asked if Olive" – I grasped around for something to make it sound more legit – "*and I* . . . wanted to be extras."

Yup. BING-BING-BING. I'd hit the all-out-lie jackpot.

Dad didn't say anything, he just looked over my shoulder out to the beach. The only sound was the rhythmical whooshing of the sea. Olive and I looked at each other, both panicked. She was worried he'd say no. I was worried he'd say yes. Or no. Or anything, really.

"I'm not going to say this hasn't come as a bit of surprise." Dad turned his attention to me. "And it would have been helpful if you'd spoken to me before telling your sister." The annoying thing was, I totally would have done if it hadn't been a massive on-the-spot lie. "Buuuut, I understand what a once-in-a-lifetime opportunity this is for you both. So. . ." I crossed my fingers – although I wasn't sure what for. "I'll give your mum a quick ring after dinner and let you know our decision."

"Pleeeeeeeeeeeeeeeeeeeease!" Olive looked like she was squeezing the word out. "Pleeeeeeasse *pleeeeeeasssssse* say yes."

What a lucky escape it would be if our parents ended up being the bad guys instead of me! Although, did that thought already make me the bad guy?

Eurgh.

I'd only been trying to help.

I finished dinner as fast as I could, and after helping clear up, headed out to the beach, taking Olive with me.

It was my favourite time of the day. Still really warm, but with an orange glow in the sky as the sun went down. In the distance a little boat was cutting its way through the sea, a white line trailing behind it. Olive and I sat on the beach chatting, trying to see any signs of seals or dolphins and watching tiny crabs pop out of the sand and scurry about. The more excited she got about the whole being-an-extra thing, the worse I felt. I suggested going for a swim – it was harder for her to talk to me about it if my head was underwater. The sea was still warm and we did handstands, spotted fish, and competed to see who could float the longest (me). When we were drying off I tried to steer the convo to work out whether I'd seen a bad side to her new mates, or if I was missing what made them so cool. But she didn't want to talk about it. She only wanted to talk about seeing herself in the film.

It was a relief when Neet rang. Olive had a quick

chat with her, but soon got bored of our conversation (mainly Neet being overwhelmed with my new freckles, and me showing her how one of the mosquito bites on my leg was oozing something that looked like precious amber) and headed off to build a sand unicorn. Which meant I could officially start the crisis meeting.

"So how's it going with the extra sitch?" Neet was out walking Barks and Rec.

I lay back on the towel, kicking up sand with my feet. "Bad to worse. Olive told Dad. And, in a panic, I said I was asked as well. Aka my total idea of hell. Me, in a film?!" Neet's eyes couldn't have gone any wider. "And now Dad's going to speak to Mum, and if it's a yes, well . . . not to be blunt, but I'm screwed." I looked up to check Olive couldn't hear me. "She is going to *hate* me."

Neet sighed. "No, she's not. Because this is going to get sorted." She tapped the screen. "Even if you don't fix it, I'll be there in five days and we'll figure something out."

I sighed. "Promise?"

"When have I ever let you down. . .?"

She never had. "Thanks, Neet. You da best." It was weird to feel this bleurgh while sitting somewhere so amazing. But I was fed up of talking about me. As much as Neet hadn't replied to my questions today, I wanted her news.

"So what's up with you?"

"Same old, same old." Classic no-details Neet, but this time I wasn't going to let it go.

"Did you go to your gran's?"

"Yup. I showed her Facetune. MIND. BLOWN."

"Please tell me you saved the pics?"

"Obvs. Sending your way after this."

"Did you finish the bookshelf?"

She nodded proudly. "Yup, and it's a triumph. Although..." She grimaced. "Not sure they're going to love the yellow paint. It was a last-minute idea."

"Sure they'll LOVE IT. Has your dad seen it yet?"

"Nuh-uh. He's at the hospital."

"Well, it can be a nice surprise when he gets back." Neet smiled, but I could feel her sadness. "Any news on when your mum might be home?"

Neet shrugged. "They're still saying another two weeks before she's out. I can't WAIT for things to be back to normal. I just..." Her voice dropped. "I just want her home."

"I know, Neet. Everyone does..." I so wished I was there to give her a hug. But she perked up almost immediately. "Think I've finished planning the party, though. Gran and I ordered some see-through balloons and I'm going to put petals inside them, and then I'm going to hoover like I've never hoovered before." *Had* she hoovered before? "Gran reminded me Mum's into stuff like that."

"Consider me reporting for Hoover duty." Neet smiled. "You've put so much effort in – she's going to LOVE it. Your dad too. Can. Not. Wait!"

Neet grinned. "Thanks. Anyway. . ." She sat up on her bed. "That's not what I was ringing for. You checked Insta stories since this morning?"

I shook my head. "Do I want to?"

"Sam posted." Nope. The name meant nothing. "You know, the Tall One from the canteen?" Oh yeah. Him and Neet ended up swapping details. "He put up details of the party. . ." Neet looked excited. I did not. "C'mon, Meg. We HAVE to go."

"Do we?" I was liking my bubble of a world out here. Finding my feet with new people, where no one who knew who I was.

Neet nodded firmly. "Yes, we do." I kicked some more sand. "Meg. Listen. You're already doing so great. By the end of the holiday you'll have put all that Sean stuff behind you." She did a little wiggle. "You might even have found looovvvvveeeeeee." I gagged. "Maybe you can bring someone with you! That would shut them up!"

Forever the fantasist. "What, the movie star, the boy from Glasgow, or the one who lives in Greece? Hahahahaha."

But instead of stopping her daydream in its tracks, Neet put the camera right up to her face so all I could see was one big eye. "PRAY TELL ME WHO IS THIS BOY FROM GLASGOW?"

Oops. I'd put my sandy foot in my mouth.

Where should I start? That he was Napkin Guy from the airport? That he was the funny guy from the set? Or that he was the guy who'd had us laughing all afternoon until he'd gone all weird? I kept it to the facts. But the more facts I seemed to say, the more Neet's eyebrows went up.

"Soooo . . . do we have a new prime target?"

"Can we not say *target*, please?"

"Soz."

"Maybe when you're here you can help me figure it out." Because in-between worrying about my lies to Olive and Dad and trying to not feel guilty about keeping Alex's snogging secret from Phoebe, I'd been trying to unpick how I felt about the boys I'd met so far, and the answer was: a big confused mess.

But now was the perfect time to tell Neet what had happened last night with Balcony Boy. I was nervous about what she'd think, but to my relief, she totally understood my dilemma, and reckoned she'd have done the same. She even seemed excited that he was helping me, as it was proof I was really trying, which was how I'd hoped she'd feel. But we didn't chat for long, as her dad came back with fish and chips, and she had to go.

I checked Olive was still OK and lay back down, slowly letting myself relax in the last of the sun.

"Thought it was you!" I squinted my eyes open to see Phoebe looking like an actual celeb in her bright blue lycra shorts and matching crop top. I was a total scruffpot next to her – the baggy T-shirt I'd thrown over my swimsuit already had a chocolate stain on and was now also soggy with two big round wet patches seeping through from my chest. As I looked up at her, she got hoisted in the air.

"PUT ME DOWN," she yelled, kicking out at the person behind her.

"My pleasure." I recognized Alex's voice instantly. Phoebe yelped as he half-dropped her on to the sand.

"Oh, hi, Meg." I nodded a hello. I wasn't sure I was ready for an in-person conversation with him. Especially not with his sister here.

"Phoeeeeebbbeeee!" Olive yelled from the sea.

"Come look at this!!" She pointed to the rocks at the side of the beach. "Jellyfish!"

"Coming!" Phoebe jumped back up and looked at Alex. "I *will* get my revenge. When you least expect it."

He grinned. "Looking forward to it."

He sat down next to me. "I hoped you'd be out here. I haven't had any updates. How's our mission going?"

Wow. "Our" mission. He really was taking it seriously. I ran my fingers through the sand, little bits of shell bubbling up to the surface.

"Bit of a non-starter, really." Billy's comment was still whirring in my head.

He nudged me. "Don't be like that. You're only a few hours in!"

"Not to be rude" – which meant I was going to be – "but what's it to you anyway?"

He pulled his knees up to his chest. "I dunno... Is it wrong for me to want to see things work out for you? Besides, it gives me something to think about that isn't my mess of a life."

"Glad I can be a *distraction*..." I sounded cross with him, but really I was cross I'd ever accepted his offer of help. It was already too awkward.

"Come on, Meg. How am I meant to help if you won't tell me anything?"

"There's nothing to report. Other than what you saw earlier."

"So. . ." He held his hand up. "Nothing to report actually means there's . . . *one*" – he lifted up a finger – "TJ, who is, well. . . TJ. *Two*" – another finger went up – "the mysterious, 'get me I'm so brooding' Geli. And all girls like mysterious, right?"

"We're not a hive mind, you know."

"Fine. So girls don't like handsome bilingual guys who drive cool cars and can surf like they're off the TV? I'll remember that. . ." I didn't react. I certainly wasn't going to admit that one of the best bits from last night was when I bumped into Geli. "And *three,* the guy who, *hours* after you telling me you wanted someone to make you laugh, turned up and spent the whole afternoon – you guessed it – making you laugh."

I glared at him. When he said it like that, keeping my promise to Neet sounded like it could actually be on track, that I'd already met some amazing people. But did I actually *like* any of them? And did they like me?

"So, what do you suggest I do?" I bet he was one of those gross lads that always had a strategy, and techniques to hook girls in.

Alex chewed on his bottom lip, thinking. "If you really want to know, I think you need to stop

212

overthinking everything. Not put the brakes on before you've seen where it could go with any of them."

"What do you mean?"

"Well, you clearly have your guard up. . ."

"I don't have my guard up!" I snapped.

"Which is exactly what someone with their guard up would say." He was so annoying.

"Go on then, what would someone *like you* do?"

He tried not to look offended – and failed. "Like I said, *someone like me* would get to know them better." Yeah, right.

"I bet you don't even know the names of half the girls you've snogged."

"This isn't about me." Which clearly meant I was right. "Let's start simple. What about Billy? You obviously like him." I felt a blush coming on.

"Yeah, but do I *like*-like him?" The million-dollar question. "And did Phoebe tell you? After you saw us, he went all weird and said he wasn't looking for a 'hook-up'."

"What?" Alex's smile dropped. "Who would say that to someone they'd just met?"

"Exactly." I paused, waiting for him to jump in with something useful. He didn't. "So. . . Mr Lover Lover. Now what?"

Alex leant back and closed his eyes. "Guess you just need some one-on-one time with them."

"But I never know what to say?"

He kicked some sand on to my foot. "You seem fine with me…"

"But that's because I already know you're a deeply flawed human."

He snorted. "Thanks a lot."

"Any time." But I was smiling too. "So what *do* I talk about?"

"Easy. People love talking about themselves, so ask them questions." Sounded OK so far. "Make yourself sound … I dunno." He scrunched his nose. "Cool and interesting?" Nope. This plan sucked. "And … maybe don't rock up looking like the grubby before photo in a washing-powder advert?"

"Oi!?" This time he got a fistful of sand right over his head. A challenge I could do – insults I wasn't going to stand for.

Hearing our laughs, Phoebe headed back over, followed by Olive, who seemed to be an even bigger fan of her than I was. Soon the four of us were running about, playing our own version of tag/rugby – Alex called it *tugby* – laughing so much Dad messaged to ask us to keep it down. When I looked at my phone, I also had a voicemail from Mum. I pressed play, and tried to listen to her message over Olive's shrieks.

But I instantly wished I hadn't.

I stood motionless on the beach.

My up-and-down day had taken a full nosedive.

My nightmare had gone global.

CHAPTER EIGHTEEN

Mum always had our backs. Which in this case had proved to be a disaster. She'd thought of the perfect solution to the extra situation. I'd help Dad with his safety demonstration, to show I was a reliable adult, and in return I could chaperone Olive on set so we could both be extras. Our day on set that currently DID NOT EXIST, but which Mum had apparently proudly announced to the world on Facebook. Luckily I didn't have to witness it, as I was back in social media hiding.

I spent the next day with Phoebe on the beach, but as laid back as I was trying to come across, on the inside my brain was playing worry ping-pong, lurching between stress about the demo and total stress of getting Olive and me a role in *Emotional Baggage III*. And now it was

D-day. Demonstration day.

I rolled over in bed and checked the time. 10:03 a.m. Despite the sun streaming in, I must have hit snooze at least five times.

I'd dreamt that all my toenails had fallen off. I wasn't 100% sure what that meant, but I was pretty sure if I googled it would say that it means "you've told a massive lie that's spiralling out of control and now you're faced with blagging you and your sister a part in a major movie."

"Ten mins, Meg! Quick quick..." Dad was shouting up the stairs. "Geli's picking us up. Don't forget I need you to look ... presentable!"

Erm, I hadn't been awake long enough to be this insulted.

A familiar sound wafted through the wall – "7 Rings". I normally loved that song, but Alex's terrible singing was really ruining it. I recorded an audio note of his caterwauling, and sent it straight through to him.

The music paused. *"Oi!"* he shouted through the wall.

A second or two passed before a different song came on: "Mantra" by Bring Me. Another great choice – or not, as seconds later he started warbling along even louder. I cracked up all over again.

> BB: I'm making it my own, OK????? Now. Shall
> we meet up to talk the mission today? 4.30?

I hadn't seen him since the evening before last, but didn't have any updates. Billy hadn't joined us yesterday, so it had just been a great day on the beach reading and listening to music with Phoebe. So as much as I didn't want to talk about it, could meeting up be a good idea to help get things moving? I paused to see if I could think of somewhere no one would see us.

> ME: Bench on the top of the hill by that
> mermaid-goblin statue thing?

"Knock knock..." Dad poked his head around the door. Instinctively I hid my phone, no idea why. "Five mins ... and pyjamas weren't *exactly* what I meant by presentable."

With a "sorry", I grabbed my towel, had a two-minute power shower and pulled on a black denim skirt and a strappy vest from yesterday. Which I immediately dropped toothpaste down. Not ideal considering the whole crew were going to be watching the demo, but I hadn't properly unpacked and time wasn't on my side.

The others were all in the car when I got there. I

tried to style out my tardiness by giving them all a big "*Gia!*", hello in Greek. All Geli gave me was a grunt.

Olive shrugged at me. "He was fine till you got here." She put her headphones back in. I remembered Alex's advice. And Neet's. *Find out more about them! Ask questions!* Who cared about his mood, I had a job to do.

"Hey, Geli..." Did my voice sound as forced to everyone else as it did to me? "Seen any seals recently?"

Even though it was morning, he already had sand in his hair. "Not this morning, and yesterday I had to help my friend take his horse out for run." He made it sound like they'd been jogging together. "Why do you ask?"

I shrugged. Maybe I'd been too obvious. "No reason."

He nodded as if that's what he'd suspected and turned back round. I messaged Neet.

ME: FYI Geli is total mystery to me. GET HIM OFF THE LIST.

She replied instantly, even though it was 8:42 a.m. back home.

NEET: Snooze you lose Gel-ster.

I wasn't exactly sure what she thought he'd lost, other

than another awkward conversation with me (and some might think that was winning). It was such a shame he was so up and down – all the stuff he did in his spare time was my idea of heaven. Adventuring round the island on a horse, seal spotting, paddling out on his own? Which reminded me, I still needed to ask Dad if he'd let Neet and I go on that kayak trip with him.

NEET: In 70 hours I will be in the skkkkkkyyyyyy

NEET: On my way to youuuuuuuuu

I replied with a gif of an iguana in a Hawaiian shirt nodding, along with the words **YES AND YES**.

Having Neet here was going to be awesome. As I stood at the front of the marquee, the venue filling up with alarming speed, I wished so hard I could see her smiley face in the audience for this demo.

Why had Mum thought I could do this? I hated people staring at me.

All the seats were now filled, but people were still coming in, standing in bunches around the sides and back. There were hundreds of them. Even Billy and Phoebe were here. Please don't let Alex be here too. If I'd laughed at him for singing, what was he going to say about *this*?

The more people turned up, the more my stomach cramped with nerves, but the more delighted Dad looked. I could see the familiar glint of "yes, I'm about to deliver excellent safety advice whilst simultaneously frightening everyone about all the disasters that can happen" in his eyes. His happy place.

He saw me looking around in panic.

"Your mum and I wouldn't have asked you if we didn't think you could handle it." He put his hand on my arm and gave it a squeeze. "Super Meg, remember?" It's what he used to call me when I was younger and he would lie on his back, feet in the air, so I could lie across them and pretend to fly.

I tried to smile. As much as I was freaking out, I wanted to do a good job for him – and I needed to prove I could so I could take Olive to the fake shoot day I hadn't yet figured out how to wangle. "So what exactly do you need me to do?"

He picked up a pile of notes. "Just lie completely still, all we need. . ."

But I got distracted by a fresh horror waving at me in the background: *why was TJ here?* Along with all of his glamorous, amazing castmates? And me standing in front of them all in a toothpaste-stained top, about to take part in a dorky safety demonstration?

TJ mouthed "good luck". I stared at him. I HAD to think of a viable reason to flee. Immediately.

Dad was still talking to me.

". . .and that's it. Just think, Meg. You could literally save someone's life." He patted the tabletop, showing me where to lie. It was very high. And very visible. "CPR can more than double chances of survival."

C.

P.

R.

Wasn't that . . . the one . . . where you had to check people for breathing and, I dunno, pump their chest!? This did not sound safe to demonstrate. It sounded like it may result in death by embarrassment. I didn't feel right. Things were spinning. I was going to have to make a run for it.

"WELCOME." Oh no. Dad was going for it. "I'M DELIGHTED WITH THE TURNOUT." Everyone shut up immediately. Wow. This *never* happened at home. "I even have my lovely daughter Megan here to help out."

Billy and Phoebe whooped. I tried to give them a smile. Billy was wearing a *Broad City* cap. He saw me notice it and mouthed "yas, queen!", and for the tiniest split second I forgot the impending doom, forgot his weird comment about hook-ups, and felt the same burst of excitement I'd had when we'd met yesterday. Which instantly popped like a bubble as Olive shouted, "Go, Smeg!"

Dad was in full health-and-safety flow. "No time like the present to refresh our knowledge of some potentially life-saving safety basics."

Correction: literally any time would be better than now.

"What do I always say?" Dad paused. No one filled in the blanks. "BETTER SAFE THAN..."

TJ and his mates yelled, "SORRY!"

Dad waggled his finger at them. "Nice try! But it's actually ... UN-SAFE. So, let's crack on. Meg." He pointed to the table. "Up you pop."

Neet had once told me she had a technique for not being scared: to remember everything was temporary. But as I clambered on the table, this already felt like something I would remember for ever.

But what were my options? I didn't want Dad to look bad. This job was important to him. So, as calmly as possible, I sat on the table, my feet on the chair underneath it. Olive was mouthing something at me from the front row.

"What?" I mouthed back. Dad was going on about

something to do with early-warning signs of cardiac arrest. My phone vibrated in my pocket.

PHOEBE: Nice pants. 😶

That's what Olive was saying. I closed my knees – had everyone seen them?

"So, does everyone remember those seven steps?" There was mumbling. "I know, I know... *Boring* isn't it?" Dad took a deep, slow breath and stepped forward. "Well, excuuuuuse me. What could POSSIBLY be LESS boring than all the lives you could be saving?" With his arms waving about, he both looked and sounded like he was auditioning for a part in the *Greatest Showman* sequel. "Buying crucial seconds of time for medical professionals to arrive!" He turned to me. "Maybe you all need to think about this as people, not process. Meg, can you lie flat, please? And close your eyes."

I lay down, happy to shut my eyes and block out the audience. I crossed my fingers this would be over quickly. As in nanosecond quickly.

Dad turned back to the room. "Volunteer, please?" I wasn't doing this alone?! He hadn't mentioned *that*. I heard the rustling of a hand go up. "Thanks very much – I'm sure Meg will be happy you stepped up."

A ripple of quiet laughter went round. Olive must have volunteered – she hated me getting all the attention. "Come on up, please..." The volunteer stepped beside me. "Now, first things first— Meg, keep your eyes shut. You're the victim remember?" I certainly was. "Is the subject breathing? You've got to lean right in and look for vital signs. Is there any breath on your hand, or face?"

I felt something close. Very close. And it smelt nice, like trees in the rain ... and not at all like Olive.

WHO WAS IT?

I let my eyelid creep up a tiny, tiny bit.

Approximately three millimetres from my face was ... TJ.

Argggghhh! I full-on yelped. Why had HE volunteered? And why had Dad thought it was OK to pick him?! I automatically recoiled back, which would have worked if I wasn't lying down, and didn't just full body spasm on to the table instead. Someone in the audience sniggered loudly. I did the only thing I could think to do: tried to pretend I was in the throes of death. Which felt like a much more appealing option than my current reality.

Everyone cracked up as I thrashed around. Someone even shouted, "She's a better actor than some of these lot!" which amused them even more.

Underneath all the laughter I heard TJ's voice. "Thought you'd prefer a friendly face?"

Friendly face?! Did he honestly not know that that was about the hundredth word I thought of when I thought of his face?!

Without thinking I sat up.

CRACK.

Owwwww. My head hit something hard. Very hard.

The audience gasped. My eyes sprang open. Oh no. No no no.

I didn't realize TJ had leant in to whisper to me. And from the way he was clutching his head, I'd just headbutted him very, very hard. "Oh my God, I'm so sorry!"

TJ tried to smile like it was OK, but he wasn't a good enough actor to make me believe I hadn't just really hurt him.

As the audience settled back down, Dad took me to one side for a word. "Meg, what's going on?"

I smiled feebly. "Sorry, I just ..." I tried to find a polite way of saying, *am in complete shock you'd think this was OK*. "... thought you'd picked Olive."

"She didn't put her hand up." Figures. "And in an emergency you don't get to choose *who* is involved. I thought you were *adult* enough to handle this?"

Eurgh. I hated it when parents threw your own arguments back in your face. *Unreasonable*.

"I am, Dad, I promise." Like it or not, I *had* to get through this.

TJ walked over and put his hand on Dad's arm. "Hey, I've got an idea, JJ – how about Meg and I swap?" Wow. He must really be scared of what I could do next. "Be nice to work my corpse skills!"

GREAT idea. Then I could make sure I didn't go *anywhere* near him.

Dad didn't look happy. "Not *corpse*, TJ. We're saving lives here – that's the whole point!"

"Exactly, Dad! It's a great idea. TJ's the actor. I should be the clueless one doing the saving!"

And before Dad could stop him, TJ climbed on to the table, while I stood next to him, smiling enthusiastically. Dad had nothing to do but to carry on.

"S ... sorry about that. As you can see, we are doing a bit of a role swap. So where were we? Oh yes. Breathing's been checked. Now it's time to check out the victim's chest."

Olive actually screeched. Her blonde hair friend next to her seemed at real risk of wetting herself from laughing too hard. I was only in this blimmin' situation to prove a point to them. My upper hand over them suddenly felt decidedly lower.

Swallowing my pride, I took my instruction, and looked at TJ's chest in the most medical way I could, definitely not noticing anything attractive about it at all. Nope, nothing at all. For a change he was wearing something not skin-tight – a sleeveless T-shirt cut ridiculously low at the sides. I concentrated on plastering my face with my most "I am not a pervert, I am purely concerned about my victim" look. Which was quite hard, as terrible T-shirt or not, TJ was something else. And his nipple kept popping out to say hello whenever he did an in-breath.

As Olive continued to snigger, Dad made me put a loo roll beside TJ's chest and pump it as he talked through chest compressions. At least I didn't have to make physical contact with TJ. I wasn't sure my limbs would cope. It was so long before Dad finally got me to stop pumping, I'd worked up an actual sweat. Saving lives was hard work.

"So, has everyone got that?" The audience gave a strong, "Yes." Relieved, I went to step off stage.

"Great." Dad sounded pleased. "In that case part two." There was a part two?! Please no. "Time to check the airways. TJ. . ." Dad dropped his voice. "Let me know if you're not comfortable with this."

This did NOT sound good. But TJ didn't budge.

"Meg, time to tilt the patient's head back and check his airways..." Was it possible to somehow do that without any touching? I looked down at his perfect face, looking all peaceful. Was it even *legal* to touch a face when it looked this perfect? TJ opened his eyes just to wink.

"I'm all yours," he whispered.

Oh. My. God. I didn't know exactly what that meant, but I did know it took all I had not to splutter in his face.

With Dad directing me, I slowly put one hand under TJ's chin (I WAS TOUCHING HIS CHIN) and one under his head (I WAS TOUCHING HIS HEAD). I was literally *handling* TJ – doing it with all the confidence of someone touching the *Mona Lisa*.

"Great!" Dad was so pumped. Did he not know this was the worst-best moment of my life? "Now tilt the head." I did, ever so gently. One of my hands was in TJ's hair. Neet was never going to believe this. Could he feel my hands shaking? From this angle, directly above him, I could see he was trying not to laugh.

"Good job. Now, take a normal breath" – already a fail as my breathing had been faster than a hamster's this whole time – "put your mouth on to the patient's" – SORRY, WHAT? – "and blow firmly but calmly until his chest begins to rise."

I looked at Dad. Was he really expecting me to do this? In front of everyone?

Put my mouth . . . on TJ's mouth?!

STATE OF EMERGENCY.

I didn't even listen to what Dad said next. I'd heard all I needed. He basically wanted me to snog TJ in front of everyone. In front of him!

What was he thinking? This was Megabite times one million.

"Go on then, Meg. . . We're waiting." Dad looked out at the audience and then back to me, his voice lower. "I thought you said you could do this?"

"But, Dad. . ." I hissed, looking down at TJ's perfectly stubbly, perfectly perfect, tanned American face.

TJ licked his lips.

He knew how awkward this was, and was *loving* it.

Someone started a quiet chant of *snog snog snog!*

I breathed in.

Leant in.

And, with every bit of me on highest alert, I made lip-to-lip contact.

"MEG!" Dad actually roared. I leapt straight up. "I said to stop before you made contact!"

Olive exploded with laughter. I staggered back. *That* was what I missed?! *That* key detail?

Oh, God.

Had I just unauthorized mouth-planted myself on TJ?!

I'd probably broken about a hundred laws.

And *everyone* had seen.

"TJ, I . . . I am SO sorry!" Not to mention completely mortified.

He sat up and grinned at me, a glint in his eye. "Any time."

TJ raised his voice for the room to hear. "So am I now officially saved?"

Dad looked flustered. "Well, yes, but you'd have a much better survival rate if Meg repeated the cycle of compressions and breaths until medical help arrived, but I'll spare you that." He looked at me, unimpressed. Yup, my own dad thought I was a snog-fiend. "I've left leaflets for you all to take away, and it's probably worth mentioning that some guidelines now say that if you're not properly trained then skip the whole mouth-to-mouth bit."

SO WHY HAD HE MADE ME ENDURE THAT?!

TJ jumped down off the table and stood beside me. I don't think I'd blinked for a minute. This was horrific.

"It's all good, Meg." But I had no response other than repeating "sorry" and staring at the floor wanting it to swallow me up. I stayed that way until everyone, except Dad and Olive, had left.

Dad gave me a hug.

"Good job, Meg. I haven't had applause like that in ages." I wonder why. This was surely one of his more memorable demos. "A few hiccups, but I'm proud of you."

All well and good, but being proud isn't going to help me get over what just happened, is what I thought. Instead I just mumbled a depressed, "Thanks."

"C'mon, don't look like that. You can say yes to that day's filming now!" If anything was going to cheer me up, it wasn't being reminded of that disaster.

"Oh, wonderful," I sulked.

"What was that?"

"Nothing." I needed to get away from here.

I made my way to the rooftop I'd found the other day and lay out on a lounger, squinting up at the sun. There wasn't a cloud in the sky.

Could the memories of what just happened please get melted away? How could life be so simple and so complicated all at once?

And it was about to get worse. Neet messaged me in

a flap. A TJ fan account had just posted a Boomerang of the actual moment of headbutt impact, and Sean's best mate had somehow found it and already tagged me into it. It was like Megabite all over again. Just this time with the world's biggest movie star. I just had to hope no one had any footage of our one-way kiss. What would everyone say then?!

With my heart in my mouth, and Neet sending me motivational messages, I logged in to my account just to switch my profile to private. If there was one thing today had taught me – other than how to restart a heart – it was that when it came to other people I was still a walking disaster. And that no one seemed to take the on-set phone ban seriously. I thought the demo was a safe space?! There was no way I could go to that party back home. Not now. I had proved yet again I wasn't qualified to deal with real people, and I'd had more than enough of people laughing at me. At this rate I didn't even feel brave enough to go home at all.

How had that one kiss with Sean managed to do so much damage? It was seeping into everything.

I lay. And thought. And sweated. And thought. . .

"Hey there, stranger." Phoebe plonked herself down beside me, Billy following behind her. I sat up with a start – I must have dozed off. "We figured you were hiding. You OK?"

I nodded and stretched out my arms. "You know..."

Which meant no, but I didn't want to talk about it. Billy put the wodge of papers he'd been holding on the floor and sat down on the next lounger over.

He pointed to his cap. "Well, if it helps, Abbi, Ilana and everyone standing by us thought you did a sterling job." Bless him for trying to cheer me up. He reached into his bag and pulled out three cans of Fanta Limon that he passed round. "If I ever get to save someone's life it will all be down to you."

One thing was for sure: however I felt about him, however he felt about me, he had my back, just like Phoebe.

"C'mon, Megs..." Phoebe was wearing a neon-pink wrap that she'd tied up behind her neck, looking total *fashun*. "Not many people can say they've snogged TJ."

Billy chuckled. "Last count was probably over a thousand, but yeah, sure."

Despite my bad mood, I laughed too. Might as well do what Neet was always telling me, and face up to it. I guess it *was* a much bigger deal to me than anyone else.

Phoebe took a sip from her can. "Seriously, if there's anything we can do to cheer you up, just name it."

But I had had an idea. I'd had it a second ago when I'd realized what Billy's papers were. And with no dignity left to lose, I went for it.

CHAPTER NINETEEN

Flip-flops weren't exactly ideal mountaineering footwear, but I managed to make good progress along the rough path at the top of the cliffs. The walk on my own was calming me down. I'd never seen views like it – and although I still didn't see the seals Geli had mentioned, or the infamous Skotheos dolphins, I saw loads of fish jumping out of the water.

The TJ headbutt situation had gone semi-viral and Neet had been trying to cheer me up with a photo series of my favourite things from back home (Marmite! Barks and Rec! Chocolate lip scrub from Lush!) but it hadn't worked. I felt humiliated – and knew Neet couldn't quite get over the fact I'd had lip-to-lip contact with TJ, which she thought was so good it trumped any horror. But she hadn't been there.

I sat down on a sandy white secluded beach and stared out to sea. Everything felt more dramatic when you were staring out to sea. I turned up my "Don't Worry, Everything Will Be OK" playlist. I needed to get a grip. I was on this amazing holiday, and was super lucky. I'd just been hanging out on a film set, for goodness' sake. And Neet was right – this morning, accident or not, I'd semi-snogged one of the most famous people in the world. Luckily he'd found it funny, and now I had a story to tell people for the rest of my life.

But maybe that was the problem?

Always being bothered what everyone else thought. I just couldn't shake it. And if I was really honest, was this actually what the whole stupid mission was about? Not how I felt, but what I thought others felt about me?

GAH.

My head went round and round in circles until Mum rang to "have a chat". She said she was loving my daily vids, but I knew if a parent didn't ring with a specific question, it meant they were worried about something. I still felt bad she wasn't here, so tried as hard as I could to sound happy and breezy and talk about all the good things, like Dad's new obsession with eating al fresco, and how many friends Ol had made.

But eventually, after a long pause, Mum brought up the safety demo. So *that* was why she was ringing. As I filled her in, she kept sighing in that way she does when she disapproves of a decision Dad's made, but doesn't want to undermine him. When it got to the TJ volunteering news, she broke her calm and said, "Well, he didn't tell me THAT bit!" But it was nice hearing her voice, and chatting just the two of us. So, after our call, I took her advice, and even though we both agreed Dad would kill me, did the best thing in the world for me to chill out – a solo swim. I explored all around the little bay I was in, even going into this cool cave with rock pools all around it. When I dived down I was surrounded by plants and fish all colours of the rainbow, and by the time I emerged, I felt miles better. With a spring back in my step, I dried off and trekked up to the bench to meet Alex. When he saw me he stood up.

"Walk and talk?"

I nodded. "Sure."

We strolled in silence, but it didn't feel as awkward as I thought it would. I think we both enjoyed having someone we could say anything to, no secrets, no pretence, no judgement as we both already knew each other's worst stuff.

"So ... does you kissing TJ mean my services are no

longer required?

I couldn't help but snort. "If that was your definition of a successful kiss, I feel sorry for all the girls you've worked your way through."

"I haven't had any complaints so far."

"Ewwww." He could be so gross.

"Not to be pedantic, but so you know..." He paused. "Headbutting wasn't exactly what I had in mind for 'cool and interesting'."

I shoved him in the ribs. "Oh, cool, thanks for clearing that up." The silence returned until he offered me some chewing gum.

"So..." It was time to tell him what I was thinking about. "I think it's time I called a day on this whole, you know ... mission thing."

"Am I allowed to disagree?" He said it so quickly, like he already knew what I was going to say.

"Sure – as long as I can disagree right back?"

He took a swig of his water. "First things first. I see where you're coming from. Today was ... maybe a setback, yes." That was one way of putting it. "But I thought this was about facing those fears? Not giving up at the first hurdle."

"Tenth hurdle." I shook my head. "I'm just not sure it's working. Whenever I face something, it headbutts me. Literally."

Silence again. Alex looked out to the sea and raised his hand at someone. "That boy. I just don't get him."

I looked out. Geli was out on the waves, kayaking. He gave the shortest dismissive salute back.

I nodded towards him. "That is kind of what I mean. I feel like I've met all these boys, like I promised Neet I would, but instead of it being fun, or making me feel better, it just feels really pressured. Like all I have is a constant stream of stress. And to be honest, I think I feel worse than ever?!"

Alex smiled. "Liking someone *is* stressful!" He pushed his sunglasses back up his nose with his little finger and laughed. "I mean, look at me and Lucy. Not exactly unstressful right now."

I fiddled with my water bottle top.

"Still not telling them till you get home?" I kind of hoped he would change his mind as I hated Phoebe not knowing. But I didn't exactly want to see her upset and have her holiday ruined either.

He shook his head. "Phoebe told me this morning that her birthday present to Lucy is surprise tickets to Leeds festival ... camping ... for all three of us."

"Ouch."

"Exactly."

"Does she have any idea that ..."

"... that Lucy and I aren't a happy, picture-perfect couple?" He looked down. "Nah."

"What about Lucy?" It was the killer question I'd been trying to work out. How much did she know about the state of her own relationship?

"I think she thinks the same as me." He shook his head again, almost in disbelief. "Like I said, I 100% shouldn't have done what I did. But ... well, it's complicated." I got the feeling there was something he wasn't telling me, and despite what he'd done, I felt the tiniest bit sorry for him – I couldn't imagine going through something like this with no one to speak to. He sighed. "But what can you do? Block everyone out just so you don't risk ever hurting anyone? Or vice versa?"

"That's exactly what I always say to Neet!"

Alex raised an eyebrow at me. "Weird, cos some might say that's exactly what you do, too."

He deserved another jab for that. And got one. "Not *everyone*. Just the ones who make everything more complicated."

"Lemme guess. Like TJ, Billy and Geli?"

I shrugged, not wanting to admit he'd hit the nail on the head. "M'bee."

"So what? Even though you've had fun with all of

them, that's *it*? Game over?" He waited for me to react. I deliberately didn't. "I mean, I've got eyes. Your dad literally told us to check out TJ's chest, and even lying down he looked like the cover of *Men's Health*..." He still wasn't getting a reaction from me. "Or is his name-dropping chat too much?"

This time I had to speak up. "Well, he's always been nice to *me*. Maybe people should give him a break?"

Alex looked at me knowingly. Point proven – to him *and* me. Somewhere, deep down, when niggled, I did like TJ. I guess I just didn't want to be that clichéd girl falling head-over-heels for a hot celebrity. He waited a while before he said anything. "Phoebe tells me Billy's a good bloke." I kicked at some stones and shrugged, non-plussed. Billy was great to hang out with, but something had felt off ever since his weird reaction when I met him. And wasn't something going on with Phoebe? "And, well." Alex looked out to Geli, who had his back to us, powering his way round the coast. "Jury's out on that one. But whatever floats your boat . . . or kayak."

I laughed, but it was just surface level. I was done. I knew Alex was trying to help, but I didn't want to talk about it.

"GUYS!" A voice shouted from the main road. I looked round. Billy was running towards us. "Meg. . ." He was out of breath. "I've been trying to find you *everywhere*."

Alex side-eyed me. He was relentless. "You OK?"

"Uh-huh." Billy slung his canvas tote off his shoulder. "Hi, Alex. Phoebe gave me a message for you…" He looked up, trying to remember. "Something to do with … she's had to go and buy a melon … or was it that she needed you to get one? Or don't buy one?!" He looked totally confused.

Alex put him out of his misery. "I'll message her. Don't worry."

Billy looked relieved. "Probably best." I couldn't quite put my finger on it, but whenever they were together I felt like there was some kind of atmosphere between them. A bit like TJ and Geli.

"Anyway." Billy turned his attention back to me, and opened his bag to dig around. "Meg, do you want the good news or the good news?"

This sounded promising. "Erm, the good?" He thrust out a handful of thick cards. "Take one. Take two!" They were black with gold embossed writing on. "TJ told me to hand them out." He wiggled his eyebrows. "To *select* people, obvs…"

Intrigued, we both took one.

TJ'S BEEN NOMINATED FOR A

TEEN CHOICE AWARD!
COME CELEBRATE AT HIS BEACH PARTY!
FRIDAY NIGHT FROM 6 – ARINAS BEACH.

That was tomorrow night at a beach near us.

"Cool, huh?" Billy was grinning from ear to ear. "He's got security to make sure it's invite only. Word is, he's flying in one of Diplo's mates to DJ, and there's a drone to film it, like the Fyre festival … before it all went wrong. He's made all the runners become his personal party planners."

Alex looked unconvinced. "Was the dress code his idea?"

I looked again. In tiny letters at the bottom it said:

Dress code: as little as possible.

Billy laughed. "Probably."

Neither of them had noticed I hadn't said anything.

Alex was turning the invite over. "So this is all for some award? Best actor?"

"Ahhh, I think he's keeping it on the d-low, but…" Billy looked around to check no one was listening. There wasn't a soul for miles. "Best Liplock."

Alex tried – and failed – not to laugh. "Wow." He let

the info sink in. "Can see why he needs a party."

Billy nudged me. "If only we had footage of you two in action this morning to help swing the votes, huh?"

I looked at him in a way that made it quite clear this was not OK.

Alex shook his head. "Too soon, too soon."

"Can I make it up by letting you know I got one for Olive?" Billy passed me another card. And then another. "And your dad. But only if he wears that light-up T-shirt."

"Thanks, Billy." I took the invites. "Olive will love it. Dad? He'll probably be happier staying in and planning how to avoid all the accidents that could be happening." I took a breath. Might as well just come out with it. "I'm... I'm not gonna make it either."

Billy did a comedy freeze. "Say what?" He shook his head disapprovingly. "Phoebe *said* you'd say that. She said to find out what else you had planned that was better than an epic night with us..."

Phoebe was so wise. Neet was going to love her. She *knew* the answer would be playing Uno with my dad – but after today, I was officially done with putting myself out there.

"Erm..." I tried to think of a cover-up. Nothing came.

"Billy." Alex sounded serious. "Meg *has* to go, right? I mean, how often do you get invited to a celebratory liplock-nomination party?"

Billy nodded. "Exactly."

Alex was trying to force me out of my comfort zone, but I wasn't having it. "What if I don't want to?"

Alex looked me dead in the eye, challenging me to say yes. "Other than Olive not being able to go?" Ouch. He thought some more. "Other than you not being able to show TJ that swing thing? *Imagine* the pics for his 'gram. . ."

"Oi, that was meant to be secret." I shot Alex a look – I'd told him about it when I'd been explaining how I'd ended up behind that tree when he was kissing that girl.

Billy laughed. "Obvs show me then . . . but seriously, if you don't go then you don't get to hear part two of the good news." He prodded my arm. "And you're going to want to hear it."

Did I even have an option? "Fine. Fine!" I couldn't believe I was doing this. "I'll *go*. For a bit. A quick bit. But this had better be good."

Billy grinned. "It's all sorted." It took me a second to catch up. But when I noticed how hard he was smiling, I knew *exactly* what he was talking about. "If you attend the party, the morning after. . ." He shimmied in celebration. "You and your sister will be required on set by midday. Don't be late."

And before I could worry if it was the right thing to do, I made my second unannounced attack on a boy that day. But this time it was the biggest, happiest hug.

After seeing Billy's pile of TJ's scripts earlier, I'd begged him to see if they could talk TJ into pulling some strings with the crew to get Olive and me a part. And he'd done it?!

Olive was going to be an extra.

Thanks to him, somehow I hadn't let her down. I'd managed to stick to my word.

As I hugged Billy, him making fake cries for air, I realized something else. In all this worry about kissing and boys and missions, I'd missed something way more important. Because I finally understood that I didn't fancy Billy. It was something way more.

I'd met an amazing person I could properly call a friend.

CHAPTER TWENTY

I sat in my room staring at the mirror, not sure if I was ready for tonight.

To say Neet was jealous of missing out on this party and the filming tomorrow would be an understatement. She'd just messaged saying she'd looked up chartering a boat from the UK, but it would take 17 days and cost £50,000 – which was £49,996 more than she had.

> **ME: You know I wish one billion times over you were with me.** ♡♡♡♡♡♡ 🦡

I pressed send. The good news was that in two days she would be here, so I was just going to have to be brave and do tonight on my own. Well, not on my own. I had

Phoebe. And Billy. And even Olive and Alex, I guess.

Olive burst into my room, ignoring my lifelong request for her to at least knock. She threw her hands in the air and spun round, showing off her sequin top with matching shorts.

"AMAZING, HUH?" Sometimes I wished everyone could be a bit more Olive. "I'm like a human disco ballllll!" She spun quicker and quicker until she got so dizzy she had to steady herself on my bed.

"You look INCREDS, Ol." I held my arms out to hug her. She smelt of coconut and honey. Occasionally, I quite liked her. "Your friends are going LOVE it." She smiled. I'd been trying to be nicer about them – they clearly mattered to her, even if I thought they were absolute gremlins. Billy had sorted invites for them, getting me even more best sister points. "And whaddya think about me?"

I stood up. Alex and Phoebe had been hanging out on my balcony last night, and Alex had made the totally unsubtle hint that maybe my usual approach of brushing my hair and adding lip gloss might not be quite glam enough for the party. I'd known what he was really saying, though. If I wanted to keep this mission alive, I really should make an effort. Phoebe hadn't clocked the subtext, and like the star she was, ran to grab some things to lend me. I was now wearing a bright blue dress with thin crossover straps, fitted down to the knee, with a yellowy gold lightning print on it. After seeing me struggle earlier, she'd even scrambled over the balcony wall to help pile my hair up into this sort of messy bun, carefully pulling out individual bits to hang down, one by one, like every strand mattered.

The whole time, I hoped so hard I was making the right choice about Alex's secret, as I really wanted to be a good friend back to her.

"Two words, Megs." Olive leant back like she was a judge on *The X Factor*. Wit and woo."

I wasn't sure either of those were actually words, but who cared? I replied with my version of a shimmy – the dress definitely felt too tight, but Phoebe had promised that was how it was meant to feel. I'd worn a full bikini underneath just in case it did have any #slips.

KNOCK KNOCK.

The front door.

Olive pelted downstairs – I followed more calmly (it was the only way I could really walk in this thing). I got down just as she managed to unbolt it.

Standing on our doorstep were Phoebe and Alex.

Phoebe put her hands up to her face, in a super-cute reaction I knew was for Olive's benefit. "Wow, Olive, you look like a. . ." She was jiggling on the spot. "A human disco ball!"

Ol stuck her hand up for a high five. "Exactly!!" She started spinning on the spot again.

Dad leant over to me. "Good luck tonight!"

We'd been talking about the party after she went to bed last night. He hadn't wanted Olive to go, but she was *so* excited. I mean, rotating-with-excitement levels. Alex, who wasn't planning on going, had heard, and had suggested to Dad that he could pop down for an hour to be her "date" and get her back safe.

Olive was now chanting, "I'M GOING TO TJ'S PARTY!"

Dad whispered again. "Try and stop her eating more sweets if you can."

"You guys ready? And, Megs. . ." Phoebe looked me up and down. "You look WAY better in that dress than I ever could!"

This was a woman who looked iconic in a towel – I'd seen it – so I very much doubted it, but tried to take the compliment. She always made it her business to constantly lift up other people. A true perfect human. And with her beside me, as nervous as I was about this whole thing, I was glad I'd said yes. Phoebe took a selfie of the four of us and posted it. She tagged me, not seeing me flinch as she did, but I didn't want to admit to someone like her that I was a social hermit, so I shut up and tried not to worry. As we headed out, even though the party was on the next beach along, we could already see the huge bonfire and the music was getting louder every second.

Olive had my phone and kept running off to take night-time photos, which I knew would just look like a black screen with a small orange blob (fire) or small white blob (moon). Phoebe smiled at her dashing about. "You make sure you take care of that one." She was talking to her brother. "Lucy is making a very special exception loaning you out."

Phoebe laughed, and Alex and I did our best to join in. SO AWKS. Thank goodness it was dark and Phoebe didn't see me grimace. I hated it. I wished so much this wasn't happening – or at least that I didn't know. Luckily, Alex was better practised at carrying on like everything was normal.

"She'll be looked after, watched over, and escorted home. OK?" I couldn't help it. I jumped in with a new topic.

"Did you guys hear there are going to be fireworks?"

Phoebe linked arms with me, the conversation from a second ago already forgotten. "Yeah, apparently TJ flew in this badass woman who did the Olympic opening ceremony."

That guy was extra.

Alex elbowed me on the other side. "Bet they'd look amazing from that swing. . ."

I elbow-shoved him right back. Ever since I'd said I'd go, he'd made it clear that tonight was the night I had to try and see if the TJ headbutt kiss could be upgraded into something more. He thought there had been something between us in that safety demo, and him letting me accidentally kiss him proved it. "You know who'd love to see it? TJ."

Sometimes I wondered if Alex had ever been introduced to the concept of subtlety. I braced for the reaction.

Phoebe whistled. "Whaaaat? Am I late to the party? As in metaphorically, not literally, as we're five minutes early."

Alex nodded. "Uh-huh."

I was so glad Oli was skipping ahead of us.

"Is there a little something-something between you and TJ, Megs?" She made an "mmmmhhh".

I snorted. "Erm, Pheebs, back to reality please." The idea was ridiculous.

She shook her head. "Nah. Don't give me that." She

was as bad as her brother. "Time for some truth." She thought for a second. "*He* volunteered to get up close and personal with you in that demo." I went to interrupt but she held up her finger. "NO ARGUMENTS. We all saw it. His hand *shot* up. Then there's all the morning jogs. He doesn't come say hi to us, does he, Al?"

"Nope."

"*Exactly*. And then he sorted you and Ol out with parts in the film. And. . ." She took a deep breath. "As if we need anything else, he said yes to Billy getting party tickets for all your sister's mates. That is *true love* right there."

Phoebe and Alex high-fived.

"You should go into law, Phoebe. Or politics. Or anything where you have to bend the truth a lot."

"So you're saying we're wrong?"

"I'm saying. . ." But I didn't know what I was saying. I mean, TJ *was* all kinds of hot. The entire world thought so. And I had said yes to the party. And taken Alex's advice and worn this dress. But. . . "Look, I don't know what I'm saying. Other than I'm sure there's nothing."

"Make us a promise." Alex put an arm round Phoebe. "In fact, not just to us, Neet too. That if you at least like TJ in any way *at all*, you'll stop with all this self-doubt stuff. Give it a go?" Was I that obvious? It was nice they thought I had a chance. "What's the worst that could happen? A headbutt? You've already done that."

"Thanks . . . I think?"

Phoebe was excited. "You said you wanted to like someone and now look. The most eligible bachelor IN THE WORLD is gagging for you." She realized she'd come on a bit strong. "Probably."

But as we arrived at the party, one person made a beeline straight for us.

TJ.

Even I noticed that he headed straight to me. I felt the familiar wave of excited nerves that pumped through me whenever he was near. He still didn't seem real.

"Meg. Yes!" I felt him looking me up and down, which I wasn't sure I liked. "Now you guys are here the party can really start!" He spun Olive round – it was sweet he always made such an effort with her. He was wearing a Gucci polo shirt with a perfect amount of buttons undone – forearms had never looked so good. He held his arms out, looking at the party he'd created. "You likey?"

"It's unreal!" The party was *insane*. There were lights strung from trees, firepits, a make-your-own smoothie stand, even a neon sign that said TJ in huge letters. Understated was not his style. "Nice, er. . ." Help. I was suddenly lost for words. Was it because Phoebe and Alex were staring at me, trying not to look all "I told you so"? Or because TJ was blasting me with a beam of pure smoulder? C'mon, Meg, I thought you were better than this?! "Nice, er, food stations."

Food stations?! What kind of phrase was that? But TJ didn't pick up on it. "Sushi, BBQ. You name your fave – we got it."

I fought the urge to say "Pot Noodle".

TJ leant closer to me. "And tell me you've got some time to hang out with me tonight?" He winked, but I was distracted by Alex elbowing Phoebe repeatedly behind him. They could totally hear. "We might even get to put some of that advice from your dad into practice. And, y'know. . ." I didn't. "Find out what happens next. . ."

The world stopped around me.

Was TJ predicting a medical emergency?

Or was my kissing curse about to change in the most unbelievable way?

CHAPTER
TWENTY-ONE

It was happening! Here I was. A new woman! One who wasn't scared of things like parties! Or putting myself out there with someone I might like! Who might happen to be a global superstar!

On the outside.

On the inside I was more terrified than ever, and didn't know how to handle this in any way, shape or form. So as soon as TJ paused to take a photo with a fan, I mumbled something about needing to rinse my hands in the sea, and ran off, weaving between people so that even Alex and Phoebe couldn't keep up.

Talking about getting a second first kiss had been sort of fun. A quick, easy fix for what had happened with Sean. But now it was looming, there was nothing easy about it at all. If I'd got it wrong first time, why wouldn't I get it wrong every time?

And in what world was attempting to find this out with TJ, TJ FROM THE ACTUAL MOVIES, a good idea?

With one click, he could tell his millions of followers what a kisstastrophe I was.

And that's if I didn't scar him for life and end up with a legal bill that I'd be working to pay off till I was ninety-five.

Perhaps disappearing home early (and staying there for ever) was the best option. How long did I have to stay to have kept my promise to everyone that I was trying?

I sat down on a log by one of the fires and smiled politely at the people doing beach massages. They were working their way through Olive and her mates. Sometimes she lived the life of a lady who lunched, not a nine-year-old annoying sister.

My phone vibrated.

NEET: Any gossip yet? 🏳️ ♡ 🌴

My finger hovered over the reply button. But what could I say to sum this up? I could hardly think it, let alone type it.

NEET: Also I just ate this baked bean and it reminded me of you.

A picture of some beans, one with black marks that looked like a smiley face, came through.

I sent her an audio note of me making a generic overwhelmed *waaaah* noise, which worked for both my life, and the bean.

"Mind if I join you?" I looked up. It was Billy wearing a retro *Wizards of Waverly Place* top. His merch game was strong.

"For that T-shirt alone, it's a yes."

He smiled and shuffled next to me. "Sooooo, you look like you're having the *best time*."

"Am I that obvious?"

"Well, I'd expect a little more from someone who was celebrating their friend's Best Liplock nomination." At the mention of TJ I felt awkward all over again. I started picking my nail varnish off. Billy cocked his head on one side. "Ahhhh . . . is that it?"

"*What* it?"

"*He* it."

"Do you know where I can get some water round here?" Hello, totally obvious subject change.

Billy smiled with one side of his mouth. "...And that's the best you've got?"

I laughed. He was on to me. "Maybe. I just feel... I dunno." I threw my fists down on to my legs. "Well, that's just *it*. I don't know what I feel." I didn't even *look* like myself right now, and I'd just spotted TJ in the middle of a group of girls who were all laughing a lot. "I bet none of them have ever headbutted him or yelled in his face. Twice, if you include the towel thing."

"OK, I only half know what that means, BUT, I think that if you like him..." He shrugged. "Just see what happens. He's harmless."

"Disagree – I saw a member of crew walk into a wall while trying not to stare as he showered off after a scene."

"Fair point. But you do know guys, even famous ones, are just people too."

"Ones that make no sense."

"Says the girl who's at an insane free beach party looking like she's at a funeral."

Ouch.

"Says the guy who 'can't have too many numbers on his phone'." Oops.

Billy leant away from me. "It's like that, is it?" But I didn't know what to say; I hadn't meant to bring it up at all, but it had obviously been lurking a lot nearer to the brain-surface than I'd realized. He rolled his eyes. "It's a long story, OK?"

"Well, I've got a long time. . ." But I'd had an idea. "Has it got something to do with a girl back home?"

He tutted. "Girl. Or guy. Miss Assumptions."

"Sorry." Wow. My party-guest skills were on point today. But Billy was smiling.

"No biggie. Just saying. Not that there's a significant other right now." He got his phone out. "But, it's a fair comment. I *was* being weird. So let's sort it out. . . Number, please. And Anita's. . ."

I typed them both in; I knew Neet wouldn't mind. Pulling me towards him, he took a selfie of us, his fingers up in a peace sign, tongue out, and sent it straight to Anita.

> Yo. It's Billy. You don't know me, but I like
> Selena Gomez and can't wait for you to arrive
> and make this one smile like she means it.

Within seconds Neet replied with a picture of her doing the exact same pose.

> Yas Billy. Challenge accepted T-2.

Billy clapped. "I like this one!"

"Warning. She's my best mate and you're not having her."

That couldn't be further from the truth – I couldn't *wait* for us all to be together.

NEET: I love him already!!!!

I showed it to Billy and he laughed.

"Don't tell me she's on a mission too. . ." Erm, what?

I hadn't told him about the mission?! Had Phoebe said something – she promised me wouldn't tell a soul!

Billy stuttered "To . . . er . . . befriend a guy from Glasgow?" Was he was covering something up, or was I being paranoid?

"Befriend if you're lucky." Hmmmm, I think it was just a coincidence. "Nothing more, sadly for you. She never likes anyone like that."

"Weird." He sounded intrigued. "Wonder why?"

But despite thinking about it a lot, I didn't have the answer. Maybe it was a protection thing like Alex and I had been talking about. It was hard to know when she wouldn't admit to it.

OOOMPH.

TJ leapt over the log and landed on the sand in front

of us with an unconvincing forward roll. He stood up with a flourish.

"Stunt training!" he said to no one in particular. "Meg! Just who I was looking for..." He held out his hand. "Firework time. Wanna come?"

"Errr..." I looked up at TJ.

All eyes were on me, people curious as to who the most famous person on the island was inviting up.

Billy pushed his foot into mine. A reminder it was now or never.

C'mon, Meg. You can do this.

Shaking, I put my hand in TJ's. My palm was totally clammy. But OMG. Not the point.

I. Was. Holding. Hands. With. TJ.

Before I could process this ridiculous life development, he pulled me up.

"Hurry! It's about to start." And without being able to say anything more than a "byyeeeee" to Billy, we were both running. He was fast, but so was I. People stared as we raced through the party – the DJ even yelled, "Shout-out to TJ and his finnnneeee ladyyyy." I wasn't sure if I was the "finnnneeee ladyyyy" in question, especially as one hand was constantly hoiking down Phoebe's dress to prevent my second pants exposure of the day. I thought we might be going up the hill to Geli's spot, but

TJ stopped when he got to the rocks at the end of the beach. There was a rug laid out.

He gestured at it. "Have a seat." I lowered myself down. TJ didn't move, he was just sort of peering at me. "Can I just say you look a million bucks in that dress."

His compliments were sweet, but they made me slightly uncomfortable and I couldn't work out why. TJ sat down beside me. RIGHT beside me, so close his right arm was touching all of my left arm. How was I meant to concentrate on fireworks when I was having my own internal display with this level of TJ contact?

"Having a good night?" He was his usual confident self.

"Uh-huh." I made it sound as normal as watching *SAS: Who Dares Wins* on a Sunday. "Congrats on the nomination. . ."

He put his arms out and locked his fingers, cracking his knuckles. "Thanks. No biggie." His nonchalance didn't really add up with the lavish party happening around us.

"And, er, thanks for getting me and Olive parts as extras."

He shrugged. "Any time."

"And thanks for volunteering at the demo earlier. Sorry about the headbutt."

"No damage done." He ruffled his hair. "Rather me than someone else." He looked down – I suspected just so he could look back up from under his long eyelashes. "Ten out of ten technique, I must say."

How could he honestly say things like this and expect me not to disintegrate with awkwardness?

"And thanks for being nice to Olive." WHY WAS I STILL SAYING THANK YOU?! "She's obsessed with you."

TJ laughed. Were his teeth glow-in-the-dark?! "She's a dream."

The kind of dream where your toenails are falling out, sure.

I looked up at the hill in the distance again.

"Why'd you keep looking up there?" TJ seemed put out that I was distracted. Truth was I was trying to work out if Geli was there – or if he'd even been invited. I hadn't spoken to him properly for days. "Do you want to climb up? It looks kinda steep."

"It's not that bad." TJ waited for more, but I didn't want to tell him about Geli's swing. But then Geli hadn't exactly been that great to me recently, and Alex said cool and interesting was a good thing. "At the top is this awesome swing thing. You can see for miles."

"Would your dad disapprove?"

"Totally."

TJ swigged his Coke. "Might check it out, then."

I felt a tiny bit guilty that I'd mentioned it, but also pretty sure TJ was just bluffing.

"So, Meg. I wanted to tell you something." TJ turned to me, suddenly intense. I tried to keep calm. "Ever since I met you. . ." He paused. I think I stopped breathing. What was he going to say?! "I wanted to tell you that—"

PFFFFFFFTTTTT.

A shower of stars flew up in the night sky, bursting into life at the exact wrong time.

BANG.

But who cared?! What did he want to tell me?!

I tried to look like I was enjoying the display, not resenting every single explosion.

TJ grabbed my hand again. And took a breath like he was about to speak.

Phew. Here we go. . .

BANG BANG PFFFTTT BANG WEEEEEEE.

This time the explosion of colour was so huge, light splattered across the whole horizon. I could almost picture Dad running out on to his balcony to measure the sound. I'd categorise it as "deafening".

But what was he going to tell me?!

The millisecond I detected a vague lull, I went in, trying to sound casual.

"Sorry . . . er, what were you saying?"

TJ turned to look at me again. We were almost as close as during the demo. And this time there was no Dad. No audience.

He squeezed my hand. My sweaty, sweaty hand. He leant towards me, his lips almost touching my hair.

"I was saying, I wanted to tell you that your eyes are like—"

BANG.

Wait. Did he just say poo? *My eyes are like poo?!* Or pools? I stared up at the sky, trying to figure it out.

BANG. POP. BANG. BANG.

CUT ME A BREAK HERE, FIREWORKS! I smiled at TJ, hoping it was an appropriate response for whatever he was saying.

"And that ever since I met you, I've been feeling—"

BANG. POP. CRASH. BANG.

Oh c'mon, Catherine wheel. This wasn't funny.

"Sorry, what—" *BANG* "did—" *SCREEEECCCCH* "you—" *BANG* "say?"

But the banging carried on for another five minutes solid.

Was it possible to feel personally wronged by a Roman candle?

I clenched my teeth, willing this beautiful, expensive display to end IMMEDIATELY.

When we finally got a second's peace, TJ turned to me.

I was SO ready for the big reveal.

He leant in again.

"They're being set off from boats."

"*That's* what you wanted to say to me?"

He laughed. "No, what I wanted to say was—"

BANGBANGBANGANANGANGANG.

Right. This was hopeless. The most romantic moment of my life – maybe – and it sounded like I was in Call of Duty.

The fireworks then went on for another twenty minutes. A long, long, uninterrupted twenty minutes. How dare they?

And through it all TJ held my hand. Every time I sneaked a look at him he was totally absorbed in them, loving it. I, however, hated each and every one. On a very deep level.

At one point they spelt out "VOTE TJ", to which he clapped and punched the air. But I'd stopped noticing them long ago, trapped in a circle of my own thoughts:

Could he feel the same full-on hand sweat I could?

Was it all mine?

Why did hands sweat, anyway? They didn't do any exercise.

What *was* he going to say!?

What was he thinking?

Was he thinking?

Did all Americans pump the air and whoop as much as him?

Did Geli's seals like fireworks, or did they think the world was ending?

Did my eyes look like poo?!

Did TJ bring me here to kiss me?!

Or was it because he thought I liked fireworks?

And if he did try and kiss me, what on earth was I going to do?

When the fireworks finally finished, a huge cheer went up from everyone on the beach (I managed a slow clap, so the fireworks knew I wasn't happy). TJ stood up, stretched out and crouched back down beside me.

I was more of a mess than ever. Emotionally and physically.

"What did you think?"

Where to start? "Pretty epic."

"You like my fireworks?" TJ grinned. "Gee, thanks. Just bought them."

I clapped. "Ariana fan in the house."

He suddenly looked serious. "I'm a fan of someone else too."

OK. Right. Something was happening. Unless he was about to say Cardi B or something.

But, by the look in his eye, that's not what he meant. *HELP.*

He moved from a crouch to sitting again, leaning right into me.

I laughed nervously. And looked down.

I think I hated this.

Did I hate this?

So many things that could go wrong. What if I was misinterpreting everything? And what if I wasn't? Well, then I was in even more trouble.

But as I looked down, something brushed under my chin. TJ's other non-sweaty, perfectly poised hand. He lightly held the side of my face. Probably best as I think I might be about to pass out. "I don't normally do this, but. . ." He gently pulled on my face, turning it towards his.

I couldn't hold his eye contact, it was all too intense.

My mouth felt like sandpaper.

I needed to buy some time. "Safety demo part two, huh, TJ?" Bad joke.

TJ didn't smile, he just stared at me. Sort of *into*

me. "Call me Trent. . ." He bit his lip. "And that's not something I say to a lot of people."

Breathe, Meg. ". . .OK." Stop being weird and making unnecessary conversation. "Is this part two of the safety demo, Trent?"

What was wrong with me?! Why couldn't I stop sabotaging this moment?

"We both know that's not what's happening here. . ." TJ paused. "Meg – I want to kiss you."

Oh no he didn't?!

Those six words made my world spin. It was all too much. "So. . ." He leant towards me. "Can I? Kiss you?"

I felt like I was starring in one of his movies. Him, the beach, the fireworks, the bright moon, the sea, the smell of TJ, his hand on my face.

Moments like this didn't happen for people like me.

He was waiting for an answer.

All I had to say was yes.

And then I, Meg Jackson, aka Megabite, would be officially kissing TJ. Trent actual Jameson. And hopefully not causing him injury.

I thought of Neet cheering me on.

Took a deep breath.

And replied.

"Yes."

CHAPTER
TWENTY-TWO

"So then what happened?"

I'd rung Neet as soon as I got home. I still couldn't believe what had happened, and nor could she. She'd gone through the seven stages of shock. Then grief. Then shock again. And now she was making me go through it again for the third time.

"Well, I closed my eyes."

"Andddd..."

But this is where it got tricky. Because when I'd closed my eyes, instead of relaxing, and finally letting whatever was going to happen happen, I saw Sean's face.

And I saw all the people calling me Megabite.

And all the comments on social.

And TJ's face when I'd headbutted him.

And then I saw it happening all over again.

"And that's. . ." I pulled the bedsheet over my head, even though my phone arm was still outside. It somehow made it easier to say if she couldn't see me. "And that's when I said stop."

Neet took a slow breath like I was explaining the theory of quantum relativity. "So let me get this straight." I heard her get out of bed and start pacing. "You've already made contact with TJ's actual lips in the demo, in front of your dad, yet, when you're in some sort of romantic paradise, and it's just the two of you, and he's clearly into you, and you're most *definitely* into him, you suddenly can't?!"

I nodded.

"I'm going to assume that sheet moving is you saying yes."

"Uh-huh. . ."

"Sorry. I'm going to need a second here." She hung up. And two seconds later rang back.

"OK, I'm back in the room. Just needed to deal with the fact MY BEST MATE JUST PIED TRENT 'I DON'T LET MANY PEOPLE CALL ME THAT' JAMESON."

"Shhhh!" I pulled the sheet back. "I don't want to wake up . . . I dunno, everyone."

It was almost one a.m.

"You do know Chrissy Teigen once described him as the closest thing to airbrushing a human could get?"

"I am aware, yes." I might need Neet to reassess her "is this making a situation worse" sympathy settings.

"So then what?"

"I explained it was all a bit too public."

"And he said?"

"Ummmmhhhh."

"Meg?! Tell me what he said!" She was flapping her arms.

"No, that's what he said. '*Ummmmhhhh.*' I even tried to say it in my best male American accent."

"Probably not used to people not wanting to snog his face off. Then what?"

"He said, 'Don't you wanna kiss me?'"

"Cringe."

"EXACTLY. But what could I do?"

"Say you'd made a massive mistake and snog his little face off?"

"Neet?!" I sat up. I was fed up with all this heat on me. "When was the last time you snogged someone?"

"This isn't about me. I just thought you were into him, that's all." She sounded huffy, but she was right. I hadn't been sure at first – I didn't just want to be taken in by all the obvious stuff. The way he looked. That confidence he oozed. The fact that when he walked into a room, or on to a beach, everyone wanted to talk to him.

But the last few days, I'd seen a different side to him. A real side. Someone who helped me with my extra dilemma. Looked out for my sister. Made me feel less awkward in safety demos (or at least, tried to). It wasn't the fireworks or stunts I liked – it was the Trent who secretly psyched himself up with a towel on his head.

"I did." I sighed. "I *do*. . ."

"So? Now what?" We hadn't got to this point of the story before.

"He suggested we meet up again tomorrow night. After filming. Just the two of us."

Neet's mouth dropped open. "So, a *date*?"

"Neither of us used that word."

"OH MY GOODNESS, YOU'RE GOING ON DATE WITH TJ." She exhaled with a whistle. "After starring in his film."

"Being a background supporting artist."

"After starring in his film. And then the next day I'm going to be there ready to third wheel." She flicked her long hair from side to side. "I can't waaaaait!"

Neither could I – I was dying to see her. I just had the most stressful thirty-two hours of my life to get through first. Which is probably why after we said bye, no matter what I did, I couldn't sleep.

I should have been stressing about filming tomorrow. One wrong move and my terrible thinking face was going to be captured in a movie for ever.

I was one nostril flare from being a meme. I could be Left Shark!

But none of that felt half as scary as what was happening after.

I'd found someone I liked. He seemed to like me too. And we were going on a not-date.

But could I really go through with my second first kiss?

And could I really do it with TJ?

CHAPTER TWENTY-THREE

If there was one day you want to go to bed early, a moisturizing face mask soaking in as you experience the greatest sleep of your life, it's the day before you make your Hollywood debut.

I, however, woke up at seven a.m. due to Olive accidentally spilling a surprise tea on my arm while shouting "IT'S THE DAY WE'RE GOING TO BE FAMOUS!" in my face.

Nothing could have made me want to stay in bed more.

I'd had about twenty-seven minutes sleep in total, and my eyes were so puffy I looked like I had two pink macarons on my face.

I said thanks to Olive and tried to muster

enthusiasm. I knew how important today was to her. She wasn't to know that at five a.m. I'd woken in a full body sweat imagining there were more pictures of me and TJ together on the internet, only to check and discover there *were*.

Luckily, it was me and Phoebe and some other people too, but it hadn't stopped people saying confidence-boosting things like, "Why does he hang around with uggers when he could hang out with me?????" Sean's best mate must have some sort of TJ alert set up, as he'd been commenting away, telling anyone who wanted to know that I was Megabite who had "chewed my mate's nose like an apple". None of it exactly stuff I needed to see before I was going to be in TJ's film, then in some sort of date situation with him.

I was so freaked out, even Olive asked me if I was OK, and she didn't even pick up something was wrong the day my appendix burst (she'd continued to offer me crisps as I was being sick into a plant pot).

In a panic I messaged Alex and asked if he'd be around after filming. I needed a pre-non-date pep talk. He'd replied with a 👍. And then a less helpful 😛 😛 😖 😖 😖.

But whether I liked it or not, today was going to happen.

We weren't needed on set till midday, so I went for an early morning swim. Most people were staying away as the waves were full on, but after reassuring Dad I'd be OK, I ran straight in. The waves felt like they were knocking some of the panic out of me, and I loved it.

While I was drying off, Phoebe replied to my message suggesting we meet for some #selfcare to say she was on her way and had a plan.

"Erm. . ." I saw what was in her arms. "Is that a plan, or the contents of your bathroom?"

She laughed and dropped a bunch of towels. "I googled self-care, and seeing as we don't have any bathbombs or charcoal smoothies, I thought this would do." She threw a tealight on the sand. It was already thirty-two degrees and blazing sunshine. "Beach yoga! Are you hashtag ready to hashtag self-care yourself to hashtag ultimate goals?"

"Hashtag of course. Have you ... ever done it before?"

She shook her head. "Nope. And I'm as flexible as a piece of uncooked spaghetti. But I watched ten seconds of a yoga class for babies and reckon we can figure it out as we go. You in?"

"Abs-so-freaking-lutely." I picked up the towels. "I know just the spot." It was the place where I'd gone with

TJ last night. A little covered place where no one would see us.

So we headed there and wobbled about, making lots of ummmms and ahhhhs. I was pretty proud of my invention of "pose of balcony earwigger" in honour of Alex's day one balcony straddle. I'm pretty sure we didn't do anything vaguely classed as exercise (Phoebe said we'd invented No-ga), but we laughed so much I definitely felt miles more relaxed.

"Phoebe, you are a genius." We began packing up. "Although your fam are deffo going to wonder why there is sand on every single towel in your apartment."

She flicked them out for the hundredth time. "I'll remind them that people pay good money for exfoliation."

I laughed, but secretly there was something I'd been building up to ask her.

"Pheebs..." I paid an undue amount of attention to making sure every edge of the towel matched perfectly as I folded it. "Can I ask you something?"

She looked at me. "Go on..."

I'd hoped to drop it casually into conversation, but had failed miserably.

"I totally think the answer's no..." *C'mon, Meg.* "But did you... Oh, never mind."

"Spit it out, you've got a film to shoot."

"OK... Did you tell Billy about the whole kissing mission thing?"

Her smile dropped. I instantly knew I shouldn't have asked. Of *course* she hadn't.

"Sorry, Phoebe. Forget I asked." What had I been thinking?! "Just me reading too much into something he said."

She didn't look that impressed, so it was a massive relief when she accepted my apology. I could be such an idiot.

"No biggie, but you should remember Billy has a habit of saying weird stuff." She picked up the tealight. "You and me have each other's backs, right?" I smiled, and tried to hide my panic that I was worrying more every day that not telling her about Alex was the right thing.

"Hey, look." She was pointing to a bunch of people doing the world's slowest synchronized dance on a little boat. "What's that?"

I had no clue, but as the boat got nearer I began to make out what it was. Onboard were six old people, Random Old Dude at the front, Trevor beside him, his paw hanging over like he was the captain. Music was playing from a speaker tied up to the mast, and they were slowly moving their arms like they were passing an imaginary beach ball between them, all following a man standing on a box.

I couldn't believe my eyes. "Is that Geli?!"

Phoebe nodded slowly. After a long, long, pause she finally spoke. "That boy is like an onion."

"He makes you cry?"

"No ... he just has layers ... and then even more layers underneath."

They started doing some kind of tai-chi and were nailing it way harder than our yoga. Those oldies had flex! "You want to wait at the jetty? I need to hear about this!"

Phoebe looked at her phone. "Argh, no can do. Got to get back to help the bro with lunch." She rolled her eyes. "He could literally cook a salad wrong."

I laughed, although it was mainly to cover up my mega awkwardness whenever his name came up. Guess I should just be brave and wait for Geli alone. We'd hardly spoken in days, but I wanted to ask him about that kayak trip. I'd been saving it till when Neet was here and this time tomorrow she'd have landed. Could. Not. Wait.

It took ages for everyone to file off the boat. I sat quietly as the old people walked past, chattering away. They'd obviously had a great time. Even Trevor looked super chilled. Geli took yonks tying up the boat, sweeping the deck and checking the mast. He took everything so seriously. When he finally stepped up on the rickety wooden jetty and began to walk towards me, I thought I'd at least get a smile. But nothing.

"Well, that looked amazing. . ." I was so enthusiastic it sounded fake. "Who knew you did that?"

He stopped reluctantly. "Anyone who ever asked?"

So it was like that.

I didn't know what I'd done wrong – and why was it always up to him to decide whether we were being nice to each other. Well, this time I wasn't going to let him choose.

"It looked amazing. All your. . ." I couldn't think of the word. "Students? Looked super happy as they walked past."

Still no smile. "They are an excellent group."

"How long have you been teaching them?"

He coiled up the cord in his hands and tied a firm knot. "I wouldn't call it teaching. But a few years now. I started it for my *papou* to get him back out on the water." His *papous* was his grandad – he'd talked about him before. He looked back at the boat. "*Alesandro*. It's named after him now."

"You really are an onion." Well, I hadn't meant *that* to come out my mouth.

He looked at me suspiciously. "A what?" His dark brown eyes always seemed to have loads going on – his mouth had the opposite problem.

I shook my head. "Nothing ... it's just ... well." Where was I going to start? "It's just cool that you do this, that's all."

He nodded, but still no smile. He'd never been this cold with me before. "Should I be surprised you showed TJ the place I didn't want anyone to know about?"

"Pardon?" How did he know?!

"I told you ... and now three million people know."

Oh no. Please tell me he didn't mean what I think he meant? I got my phone out, and went straight to TJ's feed. There it was. His latest grid post, him on Geli's swing, location tagged. The video automatically started to play.

"Guys, you have to get yourselves here! Like now!"

OH NO. I closed my phone.

"I'm so sorry – I just..." What? Hadn't thought? That was a lie. Truth was I'd been stuck for conversation and trying to impress TJ, and figured I could get away with it. I was wrong. "... I made a mistake."

Geli shook his head in disbelief. "Credit to the guy, there's been a queue all morning. Even my little sister."

Geli had let me into his secret and I'd betrayed him. Ruined it.

I felt awful.

"I'll get him to take it down." But we both knew the damage was done. "I'm SO sorry. Is there anything I can do to put it right?!"

Geli shook his head. "No, no." He seemed weary. "Guess it will all die down again when you guys go." *You guys.* He still thought we were all the same – people who turned up, gatecrashed his home, took what we wanted and disappeared. But I hadn't exactly done much to make him think otherwise. He'd told me loads about his home, and I hadn't taken the time to find out anything. All I'd done was hang out on the beach or the set.

"I wanted to talk to you, actually..." I hoped this might help. "My best friend arrives tomorrow, and I wondered if you could give me some tips? I want to show her the island, do some of the stuff you were talking about ... kayak and maybe even see the seals, if we're lucky?" It was ever so slight but his face softened just the tiniest bit at me remembering what he'd told me. "*Parakalo.*" Please.

He walked me back to the apartment, talking the whole way about ideas, tips and things he'd recommend. For the first time in ages, I was seeing the same Geli that I'd seen that night by his bonfire – funny, friendly and willing to let me into his world. A Geli I liked. When the time came to say goodbye, I wasn't sure he'd forgiven me, but hopefully he didn't still think every single one of us visitors were the same. That was something, but was it enough? Because when he was being like this, I wanted to get to know him more and more.

But I couldn't shake another thought. One Phoebe had started. Onions may have layers – but get too close and didn't they always end up making you cry?

CHAPTER TWENTY-FOUR

"You're going to look gorgeous, my dear..." Holly looked at my reflection in the mirror. "Proper Stefanie Giesinger."

If only?! But, as I looked at Holly's handiwork, I hardly recognized myself. Olive and I had been in make-up for two hours each – we were playing merpeople in a scene where TJ's character, Ashton, becomes convinced the girl he's looking for has to be a figment of his imagination. That night he has a nightmare which slowly turns into a dream of friendly merpeople who tell him to keep looking, and he wakes up to discover the girl was real and is out catching crabs. I found that funny when TJ told me. He didn't.

Olive was all shimmery, and Holly had made my hair

all wavy and five times as thick as normal. I was dying to see our costumes.

Dad had even ducked out of his day-long meeting to quickly pop by, but all he'd done was stand, hand over his mouth, repeating, "If only your mum could see you." Weird, but lovely. Neet's reaction to our picture had been to send a video of her pointing to what she claimed was a tear in her eye.

It was one of the last scenes to be shot, so we were extra lucky TJ had wangled us a role in it. I was SO glad his character wasn't going to be there when we shot it. It was scary enough seeing him later.

"Megs, on a scale of one to ten, how mer-mazing do I look?" Olive waved her hands in a silent fishy dance. It was a serious mood.

"Scale is the right word." She had gold ones all around her hairline. "Although please leave enough room on my phone for me to take some pictures too."

She posed again without looking up. She'd been sending them to Lindsi, the blonde hair girl, but Lindsi hadn't bothered to reply. "Sure. Oh, and Neet says 'Geli is now back to joint first', if that makes any sense."

"PHONE!" I stuck out my hand. She could NOT find out about Neet's list. I couldn't have the mission back on her radar. Olive looked pleased with herself. Damn. I'd reacted and given her clues. "Is this your mission, then?"

"PHONE!" I repeated, until she begrudgingly gave it back. "And no. She was talking about ... people she wanted to meet."

Holly snorted behind me. Even she knew that was a lie.

Olive jumped up on the ledge in front of the mirror. "More than TJ? I think not." She picked up a copy of the day's shooting script. "Can't believe he sorted this out for us."

Holly waited till Olive had wandered off to look through the rails of wigs before leaning in to talk to me. "Did Ol just say TJ sorted it out?"

"Uh-huh."

She stopped curling and held the tongs up. "It wasn't TJ, Megs. It was Billy and that Vangelis lad."

"Geli?"

She nodded. "Yeah – Billy told him. . ." She stopped, realizing Olive was too close by to say the full thing. "You know, your *situation*. He asked his mate to put in a word with one of the production assistants, and the rest, as they say, is history."

I didn't know what to say. TJ had seemed happy enough to take credit. And if Holly was right, why hadn't Billy told me? Or. . . I thought back, and didn't feel so great. Had I just assumed it was TJ and not bothered to check?

"Olive Jackson?" A man I didn't recognize put his head round the corner.

"Meeeeeeee." Olive ran towards him with such speed he stepped back in alarm. "Is it time?!"

He held up his clipboard as if to protect him from impact, and scanned his list. "Olive ... yes. Merperson seven?" She nodded and stood up extra straight. "Yup, come with me to wardrobe. We're on camera in under an hour."

"Coooooool!" She looked back at me. "And my sister, Meg?"

I swivelled my chair round and went to stand up. I had only got involved to keep an eye on Olive, but she seemed to already be in charge.

The man looked down his clipboard. "Nope, sorry ... although, one sec." He lifted up the wire clipped to his shirt and spoke into the mic. There was a lot of nodding.

Eventually he looked back up. "Has no one told you about the change in plan?"

I shook my head. This didn't sound good.

"Fine. Sorry, Holly, Water Dream Girl Four just dropped out, so we're going to need Meg for that instead. In just over two hours – that doable?" He looked at me

hovering out of the chair. "Yup, she's going to be great."
Wow. Me – a *Dream Girl*?! I had no idea what part that
was, but it sounded like a real upgrade. I couldn't *wait*
for everyone to see this!

Holly raised her eyebrows at the man, but he just
flashed a smile and marched out, Olive bouncing after
him.

I got my phone out. "Better text Dad and let him
know I can't supervize Ol any more..."

Holly put her hand on my shoulder. "Don't you worry
about her – I'll make sure there's a runner with her." She
grabbed my beautiful boofy hair and pulled it up into a
ponytail. "It's you I'm worried about."

I didn't know what she meant.

But two hours, and a whole heap of latex later, and I
fully understood.

Goodbye, glitter and music-video hair – hello, Meg
the swamp creature.

Credit to Holly, the half a pot of prosthetic pus she'd
used *did* look very realistic. I kind of wanted to squeeze
one of my many face pustules, even though it was hard
to see from my right eye, as it was covered with what
looked like melted gangrenous flesh. Turns out the
Water Dream Girls were the only thing in the film that
weren't perfect and gorgeous. In fact they were the exact

opposite – the most nightmarish creatures from the deep you could ever imagine, that crawl out of rocks in Ashton's nightmares, to represent his ultimate low point. And I'd been cast as one of them.

Holly had promised me all the make-up would come off in time for tonight, but I had also noticed her hide the pot which clearly said *Takes three hours to fully dissolve*.

I put my fingers up to my face – I felt like bubblewrap filled with custard – and did a mental cry.

My one and only time in a film, and I looked like I should be the star of *Dr Pimple Popper: Marine Life Special*. I wanted to think of an excuse to drop out, but Holly rightly pointed out it could land Geli and Billy in trouble as they'd talked the crew into giving me a role.

So here I was, following clipboard man on to set, fake pus dripping on to the floor as I stepped up on to a large polystyrene rock.

I looked around for a familiar face – but the only thing I saw in the distance was Billy, putting on a prosthetic fish head and walking in the opposite direction. I'd have to track him down and say thanks later.

"Do you know how long this will take?" I asked the runner who was directing us into position.

She turned round and jumped when she saw me.

"Probably only an hour or two." She pulled out a napkin. "Your chin's leaking by the way."

We'd never met, but she dabbed at the ooze coming from me. At that moment I decided no one could *ever* be told I was in this film.

"Marks please, everyone!" Mitch yelled, as the lights got adjusted, an eerie green shining on to the fake rocks, a rolling fog being blown in. Marks were the little crosses that showed where we had to stand. "When we say action, let's do it as discussed. Rocking, twitching, and you" – he pointed at me – "as you're SO vile, we'd love a bit extra." He really needed to work on his motivational chat. "Maybe a growl? A dribble? Just give us what you've got. . ."

"The overwhelming desire to run away?" I muttered, but he heard and gave me an intensely disapproving look.

Note to self – now was not the time for jokes. "So, let's run the action through, and then we'll go for a take."

They counted us down. I had no idea what to do.

5 . . . 4 . . . 3 . . . 2 . . . 1 . . . clap!

I'd never realized that the 3, 2 and 1 were done silently, just with fingers counting down to the clap of the clapperboard.

"CUT!! DREAM GIRL FOUR, you're not playing a

293

corpse, you know. ACT."

I winced and apologized. They counted down again.
5 . . . 4 . . . 3 . . . 2 . . . 1 . . . clap!

This time I went for the growl, but Mitch said it was too fake. We restarted, and I tried a twitch. He asked if I'd trodden on something. We restarted. This time I ran out of options, so stood gormless, thinking what to do. Mitch said it was "perfect – both haunting and grotesque".

Soon it was time to go for an actual take. Holly ran over and topped up my pus. "You've got this. When you're done, come find me, and I'll make you look all hot and not at all diseased for your date tonight."

At the mention of the date, I felt even more sick. Maybe that's what I should channel for the action. I hadn't told Holly it was with TJ – I'd just fudged something about a guy from the island. I did *want* to tell her, but I also knew what she'd think – that I was just another smitten fan who had fallen for him – and I didn't want to have to explain that I'd got to know a different TJ. That I'd got to know *Trent*.

But then things took an even worse turn. Walking over to my mark, in a pair of tiny shorts, one piece of seaweed draped strategically over his left nipple, was TJ. There was NO WAY he could see me looking like this. I even smelt of gone-off milk.

Too late. He winked. "Looking good, Meg."

"Errrr. . ." was all I could say. I swear even he, a professional actor who had worked on a film called *World's Most Revolting Mutant Monsters*, looked repulsed as he got nearer. What was I was going to look like in HD?!

I tried not to think about Olive shimmering away somewhere, living her best life.

"Ready for your big moment?" He twitched a pec as he said it, which triggered a woman to run over and start brushing one of his many abs with what looked like a mouse's toothbrush covered in shoe polish. TJ was totally unfazed. "Helps me 'get more definition'."

I didn't know where to look. Or how the lady explained to her parents what her job was.

As I tried not to look, an irritating pustule rubbed my non-flesh-melted eye. I tried to discreetly nudge it away, but as I touched it fake pus squirted out, right on to the make-up artist's hair.

TJ shook his head in a "let's not mention it" way, but all I could look at was the blob slowly trailing down his cheek.

"Erm, I seem to have squirted something on your face." I went to dab it away with my finger, but that had a fake dead nail hanging off it, which TJ recoiled from in horror, so I stopped. "I'm so sorry."

"What's a little pus between friends, huh?" Answer – the most mortifying thing that could happen, especially as the make-up artist was now dabbing it away. "It's not like there are any paps around." Just a billion cameras to film this from multiple angles. But hello, new terrifying thought. Paps. What if they were there tonight and got a picture of me and TJ together? I'd be internet famous. And – I actually shuddered – what if he really did go for a kiss and another Megabite situation happened and then I was internet famous for biting TJ's face?

"Meg?" TJ shook my arm. "You ready?"

I shook my head. He laughed, but I wasn't ready – for *any* of it. Because he was so perfect, and so confident, and I was just *me*. When I was with him, I didn't even feel like me. I felt like I had to be a Meg that lived up to his normal, A-list life.

Mitch stepped forward. "ASHTON'S NIGHTMARE. SCENE 53, TAKE ONE. Camera's speed..."

5 ... 4 ... 3 ... 2 ... 1 ... clap.

For the next two hours TJ, the boy I wanted to kiss more than anyone in the world, had to stand less than an arm's length away from me, having water sprayed on him as he ran his hands through his hair and generally writhed about looking tortured and sexy, while I yelled in his face, bits of pus and fake dead skin flying at him. I even got praised for the "genuine spittle" flying out of my mouth, which was definitely up there with the worst compliments I'd ever received.

It wasn't the most perfect start to a date I could have imagined. But in fairness, it probably wouldn't be my worst.

When they finally, *finally* yelled, "It's a wrap," TJ put his arms round me and hugged me in front of everyone.

"Nice job Meg." At least two other sea creatures raised what were either eyebrows or rotting bits of flesh. But for the first time today, maybe even this holiday, I didn't care what anyone thought.

I snorted into his shoulder. "Don't get too close, I might ooze on you."

"You sure know how to win a guy over." He stepped back and held my eye contact for longer than needed. "Still on for tonight?" It was all I could do to nod. "Good, because I think it's going to be really special ... half eight by that swing?"

"Perfect. Although..." Well, this was awkward. "Weird thing, but could you take that picture of it down?"

But I never got the chance to hear his answer,

because a man walked up, threw a towel over his shoulders and whisked TJ away. In film world, I was just a prop they didn't need to bother with.

CHAPTER TWENTY-FIVE

Holly was right – all the silicone *did* come off my face. What neither of us had predicted was how bright red my skin would go in the process. I'd swapped fake pus for a real rash – and I wasn't sure which was worse, especially when it clashed with my existing sunburn. I'd been hoping to seriously upgrade on my mutant sea creature look, not match it.

I only had almost three hours before I was seeing TJ, so Holly advised me the best thing to do was stay out of the sun. And cross my fingers.

I messaged Alex to ask him if we could make our meeting a phone one, but he told me he wanted to witness my facial disaster in person. What a guy. But I was so stressed about seeing TJ, and so desperate for any help I could get, I said yes. So after Holly had slathered almost an entire tub of aloe vera on my face, I headed to the sound truck to find Billy and say thanks for sorting this whole thing out. But when I got there, he was nowhere to be seen. It was just people I didn't know wearing headphones and sitting in the dark not speaking. Perfect. I sat down and let myself go unnoticed as I ran all the scenarios for tonight round in my head.

My phone rang. Neet. I ducked out of the booth. The signal wasn't good so it was audio only.

"NEEEET!"

"Dream Girl FOUR!!!! How you doing?"

Under pain of death, I'd sent her a picture of me in my new make-up. She'd told me I was the sexiest Water Dream Girl Four she'd ever seen, and that the lady in the background staring at me in horror was probably just mid-sneeze.

"You know. . . Still in shock about earlier, and weeing myself about later."

"Standard."

"Neet." I lowered my voice. "Going on a date with someone like TJ is not standard."

"It will be once you become Hollywood's hottest couple."

"Which will happen exactly never."

She paused. "Guess what I'm doing right now?"

"Projecting celebrity fantasies on to your best friend?"

"Yes, and. . ." She gave me no time to reply. "Packing my case to come and see youuuuuu!"

"Whoop-whoop! I cannot wait. I asked Dad to get some of this amazing cheese pie thing that you're going to love."

"Don't, it's too much!" I heard her feet shuffling round with excitement. "*Love Island*, here I come."

"Honestly. Dad and Oli and me and Phoebe and Billy and Trevor the dog – probably – are all so excited." I even think Geli was looking forward to our day trip, but I'd leave that as a surprise. I spotted Olive in the distance. She was on her own walking back up the same path I'd just seen her walk down. She told me she was meeting her friends, so I wondered if there had been a change of plan.

"And TJ?"

"Weirdly, I didn't get to check in-between popping pustules in his face. But his answer would definitely be yes."

"You do realize your life is ridiculous, right?"

"*I'm* ridiculous."

"No – you're amazing." She said it firmly. "Which is one of the many reasons I need to check that you're dealing with tonight."

"Imagine *dealing.*.." I paused. "And then imagine the opposite. I'm that."

She tutted. "Which is why *I'm* here. So, talk to me. What's freaking you out?"

"Other than everything?" I looked around again, checking no one was nearby. "Oh ... I don't know. The fittest lad in the world – who I've spent the day spot oozing on – maybe trying to kiss me?" My heart raced just thinking about it. Wasn't it meant to be exciting, not deeply disturbing? "Which would only be maximum level scary if the 'me' in question was a normal, functioning person, but I'm not, am I?! I'm the girl who can't kiss."

"*Can't* is a state of mind."

"Ask Sean that."

"Can't." Exactly.

"And we already know TJ is a good kisser – we saw it in Star City cinema last year." Little did I know then how weird my life was going to get. "What if I do a repeat of last time?"

Neet sounded sad for my stress. "Meg, that was a one off."

"But this time there could be ... photographers! What if we're papped?"

"Stand behind a tree. A really big tree."

I kicked the ground.

"What if he's changed his mind after seeing me today?"

"Then you don't need to worry about kissing him, duh."

"You're right. Win win. Anyway..." I sat down on a tiny wall, pulling my knees up to my chin. There was way more important stuff to talk about. "What about you? How's your mum?"

She hesitated. "Good... Excited about me flying out." I was so happy that it was making her mum happy too. "She sends her love."

"I send it back."

"And asked me to get a big jar of local honey for her. Don't let me forget."

"Would I?" She laughed. We both knew I was so forgetful I often forgot how forgetful I was.

"Look, I'm going to have to go. I was just ringing to say good luck. But I've got me some packing to do – at the moment all I have is vintage cameras, glitter and books, and I feel like I should at least add a toothbrush into the mix."

"Clothes too?"

"Yeah, yeah. You sound like my dad."

We laughed. It was going to be SO good having her

here in person.

When I headed back into the sound truck I was still smiling, but everyone inside was properly cracking up. Holly was in the middle of them laughing the loudest.

"Meg, you're going to *love* this." She held out a headset. "It's a stone-cold classic."

A man next to her flicked a button, and one of the little TV screens switched feed to a new camera. It was skew-whiff, but I could see the back of a guy's head, and a really pretty girl looking at him, all big eyes, and cute-but-coy smile. I pulled the headset on. Was this a rehearsal?

"So how come I haven't seen you before?"

Oh. The voice was unmistakably TJ's. I suddenly felt very uncomfortable. But everyone around me was still listening in, laughing.

"What are we, er, listening to?" I tried to hide the wobble in my voice.

A guy with grey hair leant back in his chair. "Don't think he understands the concept of recording wildtrack."

"Wildtrack?" I hadn't got a clue what it meant.

"Yeah, we like to record natural background noise, and this bozo has only gone and plonked himself right in front of the camera we left rolling."

I looked at Holly. This didn't feel right, but she was loving it. "Honestly, brace yourself, Meg. The way this is heading it's going to be gold."

But I didn't want to listen. It felt like spying. I took the headset off and handed it back to Holly.

"Isn't it working?" Grey-haired man had seen me take it off. "Not to worry." He pressed a big green button. Suddenly TJ's conversation wasn't on headsets, it was blaring out full volume through the speakers.

Holly munched on a biscuit like she was watching a soap opera. "Gorgeous, isn't she? She's one of the wardrobe assistants, apparently."

Would it be too obvious if I made an excuse to go? What was I so scared of seeing? Was I being protective of TJ, or myself?

The girl stepped back. TJ put his hand gently on her right arm.

"Honestly, you look a million bucks." The exact same thing he'd said to me last night. He looked over his shoulder and back. "And, Cara... Can you call me Trent?'" He laughed. "Which is not something I say to a lot of people..."

Ouch. He might not say it to a lot of people, but he'd said to me.

Holly slapped my elbow. "Call me Trent? How many

305

times has he wheeled that line out?"

I didn't mean to, but I snapped back, "Maybe they know each other well!"

Holly cocked her head to one side, confused by my outburst. "Erm, yeah, sure. I mean, she's literally someone they drafted in today to help with your scene, but sure . . . they probably go way back."

Thank goodness it was dark and my face was already red, because I knew I was becoming redder. I felt all hot, and my stomach had started cramping.

Had I been wrong about TJ?

Had everyone else been right?

I tried to keep calm and not let my mind run away. C'mon, Meg. Remember all the time you'd spent together. The effort he'd made at the fireworks. The chat we'd had on the roof. The way he looked out for Olive. The compliments he'd given me . . . when I was in Phoebe's dress. When I hadn't felt like me.

I turned back to the screen.

And felt another wave of sickness.

She was smiling.

"'Call me Trent'? What is that?" She looked down, even the top of her head was drop dead gorgeous. "Your go-to line?"

TJ looked offended. Holly and the grey-haired man

high-fived through their laughter. I wanted to scream at Cara, "YES! YES IT IS."

But TJ looked calmly at her, in his classic up-from-under-his-eyelashes way. The exact same way he'd looked at me last night.

"As if I would do that to you. . ." He gently stroked the side of her face. It was like he was acting in his own scene he could star in again and again. "Can I ask you something?"

She nodded. TJ stared into her eyes. "Cara . . . can I kiss you?"

The *exact* same line he'd used on me.

And just like that, he kissed her.

And just like that, I knew I'd got him totally wrong.

And just like that, I knew I wasn't letting anyone fool me ever again.

CHAPTER
TWENTY-SIX

I thought I might cry. But I managed to fake laugh enough to not be suspicious, and made an excuse about needing to go see Dad. I couldn't get away from set fast enough. I wanted to get home, and shower this day, that stupid person, off me.

But as I turned to walk past the wardrobe truck I saw a familiar face. Well, it wasn't familiar as such, but it was the prosthetic head that Billy had pulled on earlier. His giant fish head and blue jeans were sitting on a low wall. I strode over.

I might be terrible at choosing people for my love life, but my friends were rock solid.

"All right, fish boy?" Billy nodded, which was hard as his head was rigged to his shoulders. "Aren't you hot in there?"

He laughed, and it sounded all echoey. "Yeeesss!" He poked a straw through his mouth hole, sipping his usual Fanta Limon.

"I found out it was you who got Ol and I the parts. . ." Now wasn't the time to go into what had happened. "And I just wanted to say, you are the literal best."

He waved his hand in the air. "No problemo." He sounded so throaty in his costume.

"Warning, I'm totally going to hug you when you're out of that fish thing, which I must say you are really rocking." He slurped again. I sighed. My head was spinning with way too many things. Not least, how did Billy get a helmet for filming when I had to show grotesque-actual face?

But something about talking to a big fish made me feel safe.

"Can I tell you something? That no one knows?"

He nodded. Maybe if I turned on my brain tap and let everything out, my head would feel less hectic.

Without pausing for breath, my words tumbled out. "I'm sorry if I was weird when I first met you. Long story short, but I'd just had the worst party where I'd kissed this boy I liked."

I was going all in.

"Except I *didn't* really like him, and I definitely didn't

309

kiss him. I actually bit his nose, and he bled everywhere and had to go to hospital. Don't tell anyone, but back home everyone calls me Megabite."

Billy dropped his head to one side. Was he confused or being comforting?

"It was mortifying, so I decided that I needed to get my head down and not risk anything even worse happening. But Neet said I was being ridiculous."

Everything was spilling out and I couldn't seem to stop it.

"She said I needed to get that kiss out of my system. So I kind of promised her I'd kiss someone out here, but then everyone I met suddenly became an option, rather than a person. She even made a list..."

I paused. Should I say the next bit?

"You were even on it for a while. I know?! Sorry, gross, sorry."

I slapped his arm to show I was chill but a bit of fish flesh plopped to the floor. But Billy being Billy just chuckled. Maybe all good confessionals should happen when one of you is wearing a giant fish head.

"I even lost my mind and thought maybe I had something with TJ. But everyone was right – he only cares about TJ. And wearing confusingly tight clothes. And telling us about all the amazing stunts he can do."

I finally took a breath. "So now no kiss is happening, I'm still as freaked out about facing life as I was – maybe even more – and I've broken my promise to Neet. If I wasn't in hiding from all my social accounts, I'd post and say '15 going on 50, please come back in 35 years'."

I didn't know where all this was coming from. I was figuring it out at the same time the words were coming out.

"But I'm done trying to fix things. Fix myself. I'm done trying to shake off being Megabite. I just make things worse. All I want is to be me, and not have to worry about all this stupid stuff. Even if it means avoiding everyone."

I inhaled, suddenly self-conscious. "So, er, yes. Thank you for coming to my TED Talk." Oh, God. Was I going to cry?! And by the sympathetic groan coming from the fish head, was Billy?

I hadn't really thought about it all like that before – all added up, I felt a bit hopeless. I'd been running away from what had happened instead of facing it, and now I'd run so far I had no idea how to fix anything, and if I'd ever get back to my old self. I was going to have to tell Neet there was no way I was going to that party back home.

"Hi, Meg, how'd the shoot go?" I looked up.

The person walking over looked a lot like Billy and *sounded* a lot like Billy. I squinted. Yup. It *was* Billy.

A freshly showered, very real Billy.

I leapt up.

"WHAT ARE YOU DOING HERE?"

I looked back at Billy-fish. And back to Billy-not-fish.

Billy-not-fish looked at me, confused.

"HOW ARE THERE TWO OF YOU?"

Billy-not-fish stared at me, worry on his face. "Megs, are you OK? Are you having a reaction to the silicone?"

No more words would come. All I could do was point at Billy-fish, who was slowly flicking off the clasps underneath his costume.

CHAPTER TWENTY-SEVEN

"Honestly, Random Old Dude was almost as confused as Billy." I dropped my head into my hands as I sat next to Alex under the trees. It was early evening, but it was still hotter than any summer's day back home. Or was that just the intense shame-heat of discovering it was Random Old Dude in the fish helmet? Why hadn't I checked? Or said Billy's name at any point?!

I heard yet another stuttered attempt at breathing from Alex. He was still laughing, then. I swear I'd seen a tear roll down from under his sunglasses.

"So *then* what?" As if he needed more from this story – but I'd started so I might as well finish.

"Well, as Billy stood looking at me like I'd lost my mind, Random Old Dude put his hand on my shoulder..." I paused before I could relive the horror. "He said that if I was really stuck he could ask one of his grandkids if they would kiss me, but he'd really rather not." Alex full-on spluttered. "You should have seen the fear in his eyes. Or maybe it was disgust? I'm trying not to think about it."

Alex tried to stop laughing long enough to get words out. "So ... so he ... does ... sp ... speak English ... then?"

"Sadly for me, yes. Which reminds me." I'd forgotten this bit. "To try and redeem myself I remembered that Greek phrase Geli had given me on day one to 'get in with the locals'. So I pulled my phone out and showed it to him. Αστείο γεγονός! Έχω ένα καρότο για κατοικίδιο!"

"Did it work?" I shook my head.

"Apparently it means – and I discovered this as Random Old Dude repeated it back to me – 'Fun fact! I keep a carrot as a pet!'."

Not the best time to discover Geli's little joke.

"Credit where it's due. That's funny."

"Not the point, Al. And not even the worst bit," I sighed. "Because after the comment about kissing one of his grandkids, I then had to persuade Billy that he hadn't walked in on me cracking on to Random Old Dude."

"Well he does tick the 'mature, kind and offers out his own grandsons as sacrificial lambs to help you' box." Alex paused. "That was a box, right?" I didn't reply. Not verbally. I just looked at him with the kind of contempt that I hoped was burning its way into his soul. He knew *exactly* what my boxes had been. "Did you explain?"

"In-between dying of embarrassment and trying not to be accused of sexually harassing an old man dressed as a fish, I didn't get much chance."

Today really wasn't going the way I'd hoped.

"Look on the bright side, Megs." Alex had finally got his laughing under control. Couldn't wait to see what he came up with. "At least you weren't oozing fake pus on him."

"You're right – my life is so bad, I do now consider that a plus. A pus plus." I pulled my hair out of its elastic band and shook it down my back. I was meant to be getting ready for my TJ date right now, but I'd left a message with a runner to tell him I couldn't make it any more. I couldn't be bothered to explain to TJ what I'd heard, and how I'd been the last one to realize that he was an even better actor than I'd thought.

I was *such* an idiot.

"Phoebe and I are having a beach BBQ tonight if you fancy it? Totally al fresco, your dad will love it. He's invited. Olive, too." As much as he'd laughed at the whole story of what had happened, I knew this was Al's way of trying to cheer me up about my evening plans majorly heading south.

It did sound good. "Are you cooking?" Alex nodded. "In that case . . . nah."

"Oi!" He nudged me in the arm, but I smiled. It was nice to be asked.

"Thanks, but I'm going to have a quiet one with Dad and Ol. Ring Mum, tidy up for Neet getting here tomorrow. . ."

"Put on a face mask that makes you look like a serial killer?"

"You know the drill."

Alex grinned. "Going to be nice to meet the famous Neet."

"You are very honoured."

I meant it. My best friend blew all the others out of the water.

CHAPTER
TWENTY-EIGHT

"YOU MADE A SIGN!!!!!" Neet shrieked with the hugest smile as she walked out of arrivals at the airport, making me instantly drop the sign I had made (which said, in big sparkly letters, "JUNGKOOK'S GIRLFRIEND").

It. Was. So. Good. To. See. Her!!! I ran straight for her, ducking under the barrier to give her a hug. *In your face, retractable tensile barrier.*

"You're here!" One of the most obvious things I'd ever said, but I was too happy to be clever.

Neet was grinning so hard, looking amazing in a T-shirt she'd designed herself and some high-waisted shorts, her super shiny hair pulled up into space buns. Totally awesome and totally Neet. "Your freckles are even better in real life."

"And real life is even better with you. Now give me your bag. You're" – I looked at my watch – "three minutes late, and we have a strict schedule. Oh. . ." I rummaged in my bag. "I got you these." I passed her a Fanta Limon and a bar of white Toblerone. "Not necessarily Greek, but definitely holiday."

She gave me another hug and looked around. "Can I just say, this holiday is already RIDICULOUS and we haven't even left the airport."

"That's what I love about you: easily pleased." The arrivals hall didn't even have any windows. I turned towards the exit. "Your carriage awaits."

As we stepped outside, Geli's white Mini pulled to a stop next to us. We'd bumped into each other when I went for an evening swim yesterday and he'd offered to come and pick Neet up today. It probably helped that TJ had deleted the swing picture – but what clinched it was how funny he found it when I told him I'd shown Random Old Dude the carrot thing.

Olive leant across Geli and beeped the horn wildly. "NEEEEETTTTTT!!!"

It was fair to say everyone turned round – and that included the pigeons.

Olive jumped out. She was almost as pleased to see Neet as me. "How are you? How was your flight? Did you get any plane food? I had one of the special ones and it was basically curry. And it had a tiny chocolate pudding with it. Can I show you around the set later? And introduce you to TJ? And my new friends? We can have dinner *al fresco*! Look at my arm!" She held up her arm. "I've got 23 bites! And if I take off my watch, I've got the coolest white patch!"

Neet gave her a cuddle – she was a lot nicer to my sister than I was – and took a deep breath.

"Bumpy but fine, tomato pasta with lemon cheesecake – delish – yes please, love to, love to, count me in, and woah and woah." Neet did her thing of making whoever she was talking to feel like the most important person in the world. "And can I say you are ROCKING that T-shirt."

Olive beamed at the compliment. She'd been saving her "Yay! Vay! Cay!" top especially to impress her. Yes, I'd given Neet a heads up, but she probably would have said something perfect anyway.

I flung Neet's bag in the tiny boot as Olive opened the back door.

"I shotgunned the front seat, but you two can have the back, right, Geli?"

Geli turned around. "I have no idea what shotgunned means, but Olive is very persuasive." When he saw Neet, he did a double take. Ever so slightly, but enough for me to notice. "You must be Anita?" He held his hand out. *"Herome poli pou se gnorizo."*

Neet looked at me in a totally unsubtle SO THIS IS GELI way. He totally saw. Great, now I had no option but to try and pass it off as something else.

"Neet – this is Geli, who I was telling you . . . knows about seals." Anita looked at me all innocently, not jumping in to save me. "And he likes cooking. . ." This was getting weird. "WITH. ONIONS."

She acted as if the penny had dropped. "Ahh, of course." She put her hand out to Geli. I was about to explain that he'd just said "pleased to meet you", but before I could she replied, *"Telia! Herome ke ego poli pou se gnorizo. Anipomono na do tin Skotheos."*

Geli whistled. "And I cannot wait for you to see it!"

As we leant into the middle to clip our seatbelts in, I whispered so the others couldn't hear. "Erm, what was that?"

She smiled sweetly. "I've been practising for your new number one."

As if. I prodded her so hard in the ribs she actually squeaked. I slid nearer to her, my bare legs making a fart sound on the hot fabric. "Erm, that wasn't me, guys. Well, it *was*, but you know. Not *that*."

Neet grinned. "It's OK, Megs, we're all friends here." Olive cackled. But what Neet didn't see was Geli's grin getting even bigger. Interesting.

"So. . ." I put my sunglasses back on. "I thought we could go straight to set if you're up for it?"

Neet grinned. "YES. I am SO up for it!" She stretched her arms up and out. "I just want to see this amazing islllaaaaannd! SHOW ME THE ISLAND! GIVE ME ALL THE HOLIDAY!!!"

Geli turned the keys in the ignition, luckily not seeing Neet mouth to me "LOVE ISLAND" and me mouthing back "I HATE YOU".

Soon we were winding our way along the mountain road, Olive talking non-stop about everything that had happened so far, which I couldn't hear as the top was down and the wind was whipping my hair like I was headbanging. But Neet still managed to reply to everything, while also pointing out a zillion cool things I'd never spotted, like a tiny little lighthouse, and how the sea looked about five different colours of blue all at one time. It was so surreal her being here.

When we walked through security on to set I thought she was going to pop with excitement.

But it was contagious. If someone like her was this overwhelmed, then it made it OK that I felt so excited too. As I walked her round the dressing rooms, the houses being used for locations, and the backstage areas, all she said was a combo of "OMG", "Oh, my actual God", and "Ridiculous". For the big finish I took her up to my secret rooftop. I was kind of hoping to see TJ with a towel on his head, but he wasn't there. I was still mad at him – not that he knew – but thought he could make up some karma points by serving as a trophy-hello to Neet without him knowing. It wasn't exactly nice of me, but I didn't really care after what had happened.

Neet stood at the edge of the rooftop balcony, looking down the hill at all the crew and scenery being moved on trucks and cranes. She was clutching the bag of make-up Holly had left for her, her eyelids all gold and sparkly after Holly couldn't resist demonstrating it in action. "You do know this is totally insane, right?"

I stood next to her. "Yes. I can confirm it is."

"We are literally living the dream." She filmed her billionth clip of the day. "Megs, you should definitely be posting more. People are not going to believe it when we tell them."

I shrugged. We both knew she didn't care about likes. What she cared about was the fact that I hadn't posted since the last round of Megabite comments. She was trying to get me out of social media hiding, and I wasn't having any of it.

"I'll tell you what you are not going to believe..." I paused. Nothing. Good, she was letting me get away with my subject change. "The catering. Imagine everything you've ever wanted to eat..."

"Pizza all day, every day."

"Yup, that. And everything. All. For. Free."

"Forget the scenery!" She put down her phone. "What are we waiting for?"

But when we got to catering it wasn't the world's biggest arctic roll that shocked me, it was the couple sitting at the middle table.

Neet grabbed my arm. "Is that...?"

I nodded. "Uh-huh. And he's having lunch with ... Olive."

I let Neet stand and stare long enough for her brain to catch up with her eyes. "Sorry." She shook her head. "Back in the room. Sure, he might be Trent Jameson, but to me, Anita Shah, he is the dude who messed my best mate around."

I winced. I was suddenly mega nervous about seeing him again, but I knew I had to put that behind me and introduce him to Neet, get that box ticked.

I grabbed her hand and, trying not to panic about

what I was going to say, walked us towards him. "Sorry to interrupt. TJ, this is Neet." I sounded so formal. "Neet, this is TJ. And, well . . . you know Olive."

TJ stood up, a little confused. "If you're the amazing Neet I've heard about" – he pushed past the hand Neet had put out – "then a shake's not going to cut it, I'm afraid." He went in for a hug.

Neet didn't move her arms. Her best-friend solidarity was award-winning. TJ stepped back away confused. Neet wasn't smiling. "Non-consensual hugging is not OK. Famous or not."

TJ looked horrified. "Right. Of course. I'm . . . I'm so sorry. . ." He jammed his hands in his pockets. I'd never seen him this uncomfortable in his own skin. "I just thought. . ."

Neet folded her arms. "Well, you thought wrong."

Olive's forkful of sweetcorn was hanging in front of her face as she froze, dealing with the shock of someone declining a TJ hug.

With another apology, he sat down. Even though it was me who was mad at him, and Neet was punishing him on my behalf, I felt bad.

"Corn in mouth, Ol." I pulled up some chairs as she rebooted into life. "Have you guys been here long?"

Olive smiled creepily. "Yeah." She waggled her

eyebrows. "Just the *two* of us." I couldn't help but wonder what TJ was getting out of this arrangement, other than an ego boost. TJ reinserted himself into the chat, trying to smooth over the bad beginning.

"Neet, did Meg tell you she nailed her film debut?" Olive coughed. "As did Olive."

Neet nodded slowly, her head turned, so she could fully side-eye him. "This does *not* surprise me. Megan is in the top three of all humans." Olive coughed again. "As is Ol."

TJ clearly had no idea why my best mate was being weird with him, and I wasn't about to explain.

We made some more clunky small talk, before I couldn't bear it any more and said Neet and I had to go.

Neet grabbed her bag. "See you around, then. . ."

TJ stood up to be polite. "Hopefully soon."

"We'll see, TJ. . . Or should I call you Trent as 'not many people call you that'?" And, with a flick of her hair, she sass-walked off via a haul at the pizza counter, me scurrying after her, wishing she was maybe just a touch less loyal sometimes.

When we were out of hearing distance, which was quite soon as she really could stride, we slowed down and chomped on our slices of margherita.

"Sorry about that, it just sort of popped out. Please

remember, I am sleep deprived." She used her napkin to wipe some of the sweat off her forehead. "And intensely sun over-prived."

"Don't worry about it." I meant it. "I mean, I was probably going to let it slide cos I'm a wimp, but it was nice to have someone not treat him like TJ the film star, like everyone else does."

Neet looked puzzled. "Everyone?"

"Uh-huh. Half of them laugh at him for being too Hollywood, and the other half..." I thought of Cara yesterday, and the people at the party trying to get photos of him, like me on day one. "The other half love him."

She raised an eyebrow. "*Love* him? Is that why he was having lunch with your little sister?"

I stopped walking. I'd never thought about that. She had a point. Because while all those people had been trying to get him in their Insta stories, or in their selfies, I'd never really seen him hanging out with *anyone*. Even I'd only spoken to him just now to parade him in front of Neet to make a cool story to tell people when we were back home. Was I as bad as all of them?

I assumed he had everything. But who was *his* Neet? Or Phoebe, or Billy, or Alex?

Eurgh.

My brain didn't know what to do with the concept that, right now, I might be feeling sorry for major Hollywood star, and girl-slimer-on-er, Trent Jameson. But Neet had finished her pizza, and it was time for the next part of the plan.

"So, options. You want to head back . . . or get straight on Meg's mystery tour of Skotheos surprises?"

"No brainer. Mystery tour it is. Showers and sleep are for wimps."

I laughed. "Panic not – swimming in the sea is basically a shower, and activity one is kayaking. You've got your swimming stuff on underneath?"

She nodded. "You know I follow your instructions to the letter."

So, gulping down my last mouthfuls, we strolled back along the cliffs, across the tiny beaches, and along to the other side of the rocks by our apartment, where Geli was waiting with kayaks. The three of us spent the next few hours paddling and splashing about along the coastline, taking in the amazing clear water, the gazillion fish that Geli seemed to know all the names of (as in the species, not that they were called Stuart and Dave), and – like they knew Neet was here – we even finally got to see the famous seals he'd told me about. They were the coolest – like giant cute, furry slugs with big eyes, but in a good way. As they splashed around, yelping and playing (although, full disclosure, their fish breath was baaaad), an actual dolphin popped up to join the fun. Marine life jackpot! With our paddles in hand, we managed to track them round the coast. Geli kept repeating, "Let the water guide you! Don't fight it! Work with it!" With his advice we made really good progress, and soon we were at the most beautiful spot I'd seen all holiday, at the edge of a cove, huge rocks all around us.

Neet lay back flat on her kayak, taking in the peace of no sound except the waves lapping, and the seals flapping their fins on the rocks at the shore. "Can I just say that I may have to fly home tonight, as *nothing* can top this."

"Not going to let that happen." I slid out of my kayak and into the water. "You guys going to join me?"

"Is Beyoncé a queen?" Neet said straight back.

I looked at Geli. "That means yes." Neet went to stand up, but instead of doing what Geli had showed us, she wobbled from side to side, and with a massive "wuuu-aaaaa-arggggggh", plopped into the water next to me, arms and legs flailing. When she emerged from the water, her gold eyeshadow was all down her face, and her hair was slapped against her forehead. "Just wanted to dazzle you with my aquatic skills there. Prove Meg wasn't the only talented one." She spat out a stream of water. "Mmm, salty. Geli? Care to join us?"

He shook his head. "Someone needs to look after the kayaks."

Neet did a quick burst of front crawl towards him. "And *that's* an excuse I'm not buying." She grabbed on to the tip of his kayak, and pulled it with everything she had. "Let the water guide you! Don't fight it!"

Despite Geli using everything he had to try and stay upright, he crashed down into the water, the paddles flying as he threw them in the air.

I thought he'd be mad, but when he came up he was smiling. Straight at Neet.

As big as the ocean was, I suddenly felt I'd managed to make it very crowded.

Maybe I'd got it all wrong.

This *was* a Love Island after all.

I'd just been getting the coupling up all wrong.

CHAPTER
TWENTY-NINE

"Meg, should we ask your dad if this is a symptom of heatstroke?" Neet rolled over in her bed.

"Don't think cos the light's out I'm not giving you a dirty look." It had taken me all evening to properly broach the subject of her and Geli, and she was having none of it. It had been an eventful first evening as well. Neet and I had gone on a banana-boat ride after dinner with Billy, Phoebe and Alex. Neet was 100% down with my plan to keep hanging out with Phoebe, as we didn't think it was cool if I just disappeared now Neet was here. Plus she was awesome and, just like I thought they would, everyone got along really well. Olive had spotted us from the apartment and because she is evil-in-unicorn-pyjamas (/in a strop we didn't ask her), went and dobbed us in to

Dad. Which meant when we got back to shore we were greeted with him giving me an almighty bollocking. Apparently, banana boats were "Darwin's theory of natural selection in action" especially "in the evening, when the sea should be out of bounds". It was just the kind of conversation you want on your best friend's first night of holiday, especially in front of your new friends (topped with your little sister waving smugly from the apartment balcony throughout). I'd had to promise him I wouldn't do anything like it again. All pretty serious, considering I'd just been bouncing about the sea on a giant inflatable banana.

"You're ignoring the facts here. Geli took us on the tour because *you* asked him. He picked me up from the airport cos *you* suggested it. If he likes anyone, it's YOU. Talking of which..." Neet turned the bedside light on and got out of bed.

"What are you doing?"

She rummaged in her case and made an "A-ha!" My heart sank as I realized what she was waving.

"Please don't."

"Please *do*, more like." She flicked on the bedside light. "List time."

"Oi!" I flicked the light back off. "Not now." Truth was I really meant not *ever*. I was done with the mission

– I just needed to break it to Neet.

She jumped back into bed, list in hand. "I can't belieeeve I didn't get this out sooner." I could: I'd been avoiding telling her. "So. . ." She shone her torch on to it. "TJ's a no, right? Well, he is." She crossed out his name. "That wasn't even a question. Which leaves Billy and Geli. Billy's obviously ace." Neet had got on with everyone earlier, just like I knew she would. "But he's a proper mate." She put a dotted line through him. "So that leaves the one and only Geli . . . who you keep. On. Talking. About."

Her pen hovered in the air.

"Yes, because YOU clearly like each other."

She tapped me on the head. "As discussed, he likes you. And as you know, I don't do liking anyone." She tapped me again. "Well, except you, but you know what I mean."

I did. Neet had snogged loads of boys, but she never, ever *liked* them. It was as if liking someone would be some sort of weakness. As if it meant she wasn't just fine on her own.

But despite what she said, I'd never seen her act around anyone the way she had with Geli this afternoon. And I'd never seen Geli act like he did around her either.

"We're going to have to agree to disagree here." I said

it like I was going to move on, never bring it up again. However, my secret strategy was to wait until I had more evidence and then never stop bringing it up until she caved and admitted it.

"Fine, then. What's your plan? You promised me you'd try to finish this mission and there are five days left."

Eurgh, she sounded like Alex. "I *have been* trying." I was going to have to come clean about it being over. "But you're here now, and that's the priority."

"Well, now *I* agree to disagree. The main thing to me is getting the old Meg back. . ." We both lay in silence. "Is there really no one?" She wasn't giving up.

"*Really.*" I didn't want to talk about it now. "What do you think of Skotheos?"

"Actual paradise." She sighed. "Whyyyyy don't we live here?"

"Because then we'd have to take holidays to the UK and pretend to be excited about drizzle and trains. . ." Neet laughed at my terrible logic, but she had a point. Everything was nicer here – the food, the weather, the people. Life was just more chill on every level. It was only missing one thing – our families. "Did your mum like the pictures?"

"Loved them. I think I broke the hospital Wi-Fi, but

I had to send them ALL. We saw dolphins. With our own eyes! Mum was SO jealous!" I smiled in the dark. Kayaking had been even better than I'd hoped. At least my mission to help Neet switch off from all the drama and responsibility back home was working – she already looked more relaxed than I'd seen her in weeks. Which would cheer her mum up, too.

"We can print some of them for your welcome-home banner! Maybe make some kind of dolphin-themed welcome home area?"

"Awesome idea." She went quiet. "What's a dolphin's favourite Justin Bieber album?" I tried to work it out but couldn't. "Pur-poise."

Yup, her home-made jokes were the worst. I groaned. "So, wanna hear the plan for tomorrow?" I'd worked out every hour to make sure we maxed out every moment.

"Tell me everything!"

"Well, in the evening, I was thinking maybe – DRUM ROLL – beach BBQ? Dad's already agreed to it."

She made an excited "yee-haw".

"In the day I thought we could explore the town, maybe take in some culture? And by culture I mean ice-cream."

"I appreciate culture very much."

We chatted until I drifted off, happy to be making

plans, happy to be on holiday, and even happier to be back together.

I was woken up by an excited Neet flinging open the curtains at seven a.m.

"Meg, you HAVE to see this." Feeling like I'd had my head filled with wet sand, I dragged myself up and followed her out on to the balcony to look. Despite only having four hours sleep, Neet was so vibed about our first al fresco breakfast feast that she'd gone from asleep to wide awake in 0.5 seconds.

It was another amazing morning. The bright blue sky didn't have a single cloud, the sea was super calm, and like me, Neet was in love with it.

She was still so excited that after breakfast – which apparently "lived up to all her cheese and bread fantasies" – I took the opportunity to admit I wasn't ready to face the party back home. But her excitement over mini pastries had its limits, and she was properly disappointed. She said it wasn't really about the party, more that I was still letting the Sean stuff get to me, especially as I'd successfully been to parties out here. I didn't have the heart to admit the mission was over too. That I couldn't see any way out of feeling like this. And after two days of the most holiday fun it was possible to have – wandering round the village (convincing ourselves three ice-creams was a legitimate lunch), choreographing and performing surprisingly excellent synchronized swimming routines with Phoebe, and making a jellyfish friend called Barry, I still hadn't been able to be totally honest with her, and she was still trying to talk me round about the party.

"I just need one reason, Meg." She flicked a tiny shell at me as I lay next to her on a lounger on the beach. "You know I'll be there, right?"

I did, but that wasn't it. Life was just simpler when I was in control, with no parties, no boys, no kissing involved. "I'm not saying it's for ever."

Neet snorted. "Just as well."

I ignored her. "I'm just not ready *yet*."

She sat up and leant forward, flicking her sunglasses up on to her head.

"Ready for *what*, exactly?"

"Y'know?" But how could she, when I wasn't even sure myself? "Just facing everyone, I guess."

By the time the sun set, even though I desperately wanted to please Neet, I still hadn't changed my mind. But the interregoation had waned a bit as Billy, Phoebe and Alex had joined us on the beach, and together we'd managed to pull off the BBQ. Dad and Olive even joined for a bit, and despite Dad remarking "It's edible!" every thirty seconds, in the same shocked way you'd normally say something was delicious, it was a success. Even Geli rocked up. He said he usually walked along this beach at night, as it had an amazing view, but it was the first time I'd seen him do it. I couldn't help but think that the amazing view he liked so much was my best mate.

After Dad and Ol went home, in an epic-battle, Neet, Phoebe and I smashed the boys in some beach volleyball and in trademark me style, I really over-committed. Afterwards, as the fire died down, so did I, and I slumped down in an exhausted heap next to the flames. But I was distracted. Neet had got a call, and I could tell from the way she was walking in circles something was up.

Neet didn't cry. That was one of her things. So why did it look like she was pushing at her eyes like she was fighting a losing battle with a tear?

Alex came over and ducked down beside me, his voice low. "Is your friend all right?"

He'd noticed too. Not a good sign. "I was just thinking the same..."

I walked away from the fire, trying to look inconspicuous. Billy, Geli and Phoebe were attempting handstands by the water – Geli and Phoebe a lot more successfully than Billy, whose T-shirt kept flipping down over his head, making him look like a human tube. Neet was now sitting on a rock, her head in her hands. I wished I could see her face,

I got nearer, and began to really panic.

There were *definitely* tears.

Had something happened with her mum?

It was no good me trying to watch her out of the side of my eye; I wanted to be with her in case she needed me.

I turned towards her, but she was already running straight for me. "It was Mum..." She flung her arms around me, full-on sobbing. Time felt like it was blurring around us.

"What's happened, Neet?" I hugged her so hard. "Tell me."

But when she took a breath, she didn't look sad. She looked the exact opposite. "She's coming home, Meg! The doctor says the infection has cleared, and she's coming home – this Saturday!"

"YYYYYYYEEEEEESSSSSSSS!!!!!!" Without even thinking I picked Neet up and spun her round again and again. "Yessss, Neet!!!! This is the best news. Ever EVER!"

She was my own personal ray of sunshine, and it was more than time she got some good news of her own.

"I know, right?" We spun some more, both of us yelling. This was the news we'd been waiting for for months! I couldn't believe it was actually happening.

But when I eventually put her down, Neet looked less happy than I thought she would be. "I just wish I could be there when she gets home..."

Oof.

If I hadn't talked everyone into letting Neet come on holiday, she *would* have been there. I knew how much this moment meant to her – what a big deal she wanted to make of it for her mum, how much preparation she'd already put in – and now she was going to miss it. I put my arm round her. "Sorry if it wasn't the right thing coming out here."

"As if." She smiled. "It's just a bit of a surprise, that's all. The main thing is, she's coming home."

"Totally."

Neet laughed. "All that planning – she's never going to have a clue... That banner took me *for ever*. And those balloons I'd spent the whole morning filling with petals. I'd even been practising that cake – y'know..." She laughed. "All the normal, 'my mum's been in hospital for three months' stuff?" She gave me a squeeze. "But I need to get over it, right? When I get home, I'm going to have my mum back."

Before I could answer, Billy and Geli ran over.

"So was that screaming and spinning thing normal behaviour, orrrr..." Billy nudged me. "Has someone got news?"

I looked at Neet. It wasn't mine to say – she never normally told anyone about her mum. "Just standard best-mate stuff, Billy." Classic Neet.

Geli looked at me, then at Neet. "As long as you are both OK?"

"Very OK..." She paused, but then broke into an uncontrollable smile, giving up on trying to play it cool. "Just got some good news about my mum. No, not good. *Awesome.*"

"Well, in that case..." Geli looked at Billy, and without warning picked him up, spinning him in a circle, Billy's legs flying out behind him. Together they yelled, "Yeeeeessssss!" just like we'd done seconds earlier.

Neet clapped. "Very *Strictly Come Dancing*, guys. It's a ten from me!"

Soon Alex and Phoebe were doing the same, all of us celebrating Neet's news, which quickly turned into music being played on portable speakers, as we danced and laughed around the dwindling fire.

Good news was the best – celebrating it with these friends, right here, right now was even better. Well, except Alex's singing, which was even more painful at close proximity.

Slipping away from the action, I lay back on the sand, watching everyone having fun together. Neet had made something brilliant, my first-ever holiday abroad, even better. I was so lucky.

I just couldn't believe we were going home in four days. I wished we never had to. Back home to everything I wanted to avoid. I bet all this would seem like it never happened. Would we even keep in touch?

"Megs." A breathless Neet ran over. "Geli was telling me about this place up on the hill." Ahh, his swing. I gave Geli a knowing look. *I thought it was top secret, but now he wanted to show it off to Neet?* English might not be his first language, but the sheepish look he gave me confirmed he knew I was on to him. "We're all gonna head up. Fancy it?"

I did, but I wanted Neet and Geli to get a head start. "Sure, I'll catch you up. I need to go get my battery pack."

Neet shot me a dirty look, knowing *exactly* what I was up to. "So you need all that phone battery to. . .?"

But I was one step ahead. "Use the torch. It gets dark up there, right, Geli?" He shrugged, clearly wanting to spend time with Neet, but also not wanting to take sides. "And you know. . ." I thought of the one thing no one could argue with. "My dad."

I sprinted towards home before anyone could stop me. When I got there Olive and Dad were outside playing rummy, a citronella candle burning, lighting them up in an eerie yellow glow.

"All OK?" Dad looked worried.

"Stand down. Just here to get something." I took the stairs two by two, grabbing my battery off my bed. But I shouldn't rush – I had to kill time to make sure Neet and Geli had set off. So when I went back down, I grabbed a chair next to Olive. "Good game?"

Olive nodded. "Sure."

Dad sipped his water. "She still hasn't forgiven you for not inviting you to the 'after party'."

The harsh truth was I wanted this one night without her. "But then who would keep Dad company?"

"Trump." She slammed down a queen of diamonds, then looked back at me. "Leaving me out like always. Just cos Neet's here..." *As if.* It was because she was acting like a brat. But I couldn't exactly say that in front of Dad.

"Olive, it's 9:30 p.m. Too late for you to be going out." Dad peered up over his reading glasses. "And you and Neet need to be back by quarter to eleven. I promised her parents half ten, so this can be our secret."

Sometimes Neet and I felt like we had four parents we shared collectively. They messaged each other almost as much as us. He was going to be so happy to know Neet's mum was coming home, but I'd leave it to Neet to share the good news. "I'll be waiting up."

I agreed and started the walk back to the others. Curfew was only an hour and a bit away, so I needed to make the most of it. I could see their wobbling lights up in front of me as they slowly made their way up the steep hill. Behind me the light from our apartment block was disappearing.

The beach felt huge in the blackness, and the sea so loud, so rhythmical. It was hypnotic . . . and also a bit scary when it was this dark.

"Meg!" Footsteps ran up from the water. I almost jumped out of my skin.

"Al?!" I threw my hands up. "Have you not learned the 'don't give Meg surprises in the middle of the night' rule yet?"

He winced. "Sorry. Still working on it. . ."

"How come you're not with the others?"

"Dunno. . ." He shrugged, sheepishly.

"Al. . .?"

"Just thought maybe you might need some company."

"I'm quite all right on my own, thanks," I snapped.

"My mistake. I didn't mean 'need', I meant 'want'." He grinned. "I've hardly seen you on your own since Neet got here. And maybe I wanted to chat to you. . ."

"About?" I played dumb, but I knew where it was going – and I knew I was going to have to come clean. I could tell him as a practice for telling Neet.

"About you know what." He rubbed his hands together. "Time's ticking. What can I be doing to help?"

We picked our way up the first bit of the path on the rocks, as I figured out how to answer. "Well, that's the thing. I don't need any help."

Alex's eyes popped wide. "What? Is the deed done?" He held his hand up for a high five.

"Nope. I've made up my mind the deed won't be done. Here. Or probably anywhere. . ."

He dropped his hand down. It was hard to balance on a rocky path when you were holding an unrequited high five. "Explain?"

"Simple, really. I haven't found anyone I like enough. And I'm not going to leap on a randomer. Like I told you, it has to be special." I was being matter-of-fact, like the decision was made for me, rather than me wimping out.

"So, despite my amazing advice, there hasn't been anyone you even vaguely like?" He looked disappointed.

Great. Another person I'd let down.

"No, Alex. There wasn't. Not even close. Once I took your advice and got to know everyone they were all totally out of the question. So, do you want to drop it? Or would you like it if I grilled you on your love life?" I hated how quickly I got defensive when I felt uncomfortable, but I couldn't stop. "Have you told Phoebe there's trouble in paradise?" He shook his head, embarrassed.

But the conversation stopped there. Was there a noise coming from the sea?

A voice?

Was someone shouting, "Help!"?

I looked at Alex. He looked at me.

And without saying another word, we both ran.

CHAPTER THIRTY

I'd always wondered how I'd react in an emergency. But the truth was I didn't make any decisions. I went full autopilot.

As the person screamed louder, I swam faster, barely noticing the weight of my wet clothes pulling me down, or the waves getting bigger and bigger.

There was no doubt what was happening.

Their shouts were cutting through the dark night and the cold water.

Someone was drowning.

And if Alex or I didn't get there in time to save them, no one would.

I took the deepest breath I could, pushed my head back into the water, and swam like my life depended on it.

But when I stopped, the shouting had gone. The silence it left was more terrifying.

Was I too late?

No. With a splash, a hand flapped up out of the water and a head popped up, gasping for air – but that was enough. I dived down and locked my arms round their body. I'd got them.

Kicking with all the power I had, I pushed us both up to the surface.

"I've got them, Al!" I yelled, relief surging through me.

But as they sucked in their first breath, I got a shock of my own. It wasn't a *they*. It was a *he*. Someone I knew.

I put my hand under his arm and supported his body on my legs under the water. "Breathe. TJ, it's going to be OK."

His face was pale, his breaths were huge and irregular, and despite me holding him tight, he was frightened, his arms flailing around in panic.

"One ... two ... three ... breathe. Do it with me. One ... two ... three ... breathe." My mum told me that focusing on breathing was the best way to calm someone down. "One ... two ... three ... breathe." I tried to do it myself. All around me the water was so cold, so deep, so black, which meant we were a long way from shore – adrenalin must have powered me further than I thought.

"Meg! You OK?" Alex splashed up beside us. "TJ?!"

"He's all right." There was no time to talk about it. "We just need to get him to land." I pulled myself in front of TJ. Some colour was returning to his face, but his eyes were still wild. "One . . . two . . . three . . . one . . . two . . . three . . . TJ. Just like that. Are you with us?"

He nodded. Good. But my clothes were feeling heavier with every second. We needed to get back to land. And fast.

"What can I do?" Alex was treading water next to me, sounding calm, but his face looked as scared as I felt. In the panic I hadn't thought about how dangerous it was going in without raising an alarm. Alex spotted something in the water a short way off. "One sec." He swam over to it and returned a few seconds later pushing something towards TJ.

"Surfboard. Grab on." TJ nodded and flopped an arm over. I didn't let go of him just in case. "Is it yours?"

TJ grunted a yes, but we didn't have time to go into what happened, we had to get him back. None of us were safe out here.

"OK, TJ, I've still got you, but you need to get your other arm on." He looked at me, frightened. But putting his trust in me, he did as I said. Phew. We'd got him stable on the board.

"OK, let's go. . . We've got this." Alex said it with so much determination, I couldn't help but believe in him. In us. And with one arm around TJ, the other pulling us through the water, Alex doing the same on the other side, we slowly, slowly made it towards shore.

But as we got nearer I heard something that was almost as scary as TJ's first scream.

"MEEEEGGGGGG!"

My dad. And he was yelling.

This was Not Good.

But . . . if I could see his silhouette, it must mean we were near the beach? I felt for the seabed with my feet. Phew. We could finally stand up.

"MEGGGGG."

That one was Neet.

Were they all there? They must have heard the shouting. I stood up – my legs were like jelly.

"It's OK!" I shouted back. "We're fine!" Their torches weren't reaching us yet, so they didn't know what was happening.

"Almost there." Alex stood up and put TJ's arm across his shoulders, tucking the surfboard on his side. "I've got you, man."

My dad yelled again. I really wasn't ready to face him; not here, not in front of everyone.

But TJ wasn't moving. "Meg, please. . ." He spoke for the first time and he sounded petrified. "Your dad can't know."

"What?" He'd nearly died. How did what my dad thought matter?

"You don't understand. . ." TJ shook his head, his voice breaking up. Was he going to cry?! "I'm not allowed. . ."

"MEEEGGGGGG!"

"Allowed what?" I didn't get it, and by the look on Al's face neither did he.

"To be in the water." TJ was frantic. "I'm not insured. I can't swim that well. It's part of my contract. You CAN'T tell him or I could get sued."

Suddenly it clicked – it was his surfboard that gave it away.

"More pictures?" He must have been back out posing on the rocks like the other night.

TJ nodded, mortified. "I was only meant to sit on it, but the waves got big, and well . . . you can guess the rest."

Alex didn't look any less confused. "But if you can't really swim why even have a surfboard?"

TJ tried to laugh. "Got to do it for the 'gram, right?"

Neither Alex or I found it funny.

"MEEEEEGGGGG!"

Dad was now apoplectic.

All TJ's bragging about his stunts. All those photos. Was it all a lie? To get likes, online and in life. How tragic. His real life was even more made up than his characters.

But we'd run out of time to talk. Dad had waded out to meet us.

"THE LOT OF YOU, GET ON SHORE, NOW."

By the look on his face, I wondered whether I'd rather have been lost at sea.

CHAPTER
THIRTY-ONE

Everyone was SO happy to see us. Neet bundled me in a massive cuddle, and Phoebe did the same to Alex. They'd picked up our shoes and stuff that we'd dropped on the way in. No wonder they'd been scared. Even Billy looked freaked out, and he normally saw the funny side of everything.

Olive had come down in a dressing gown, taking photos on her camera like this was the most exciting night of her life. Geli was beside her, his arm protectively round her.

"Megs, what happened?! I thought you were meeting us there?" Neet's voice was shaking.

"EVERYONE, QUIET." I'd never heard Dad so furious. "Geli, please can you go with Olive to get towels and water. And, you three. . ." I felt like a soggy rabbit in the headlights. "First things first. Are you all OK?" We all mumbled yes. "This is serious. I'm going to need you to SPEAK UP!"

This time we all replied with a loud "Yes". TJ sounded a different person to the one he was two minutes ago, his normal, confident self back on show. Dad looked the tiniest bit relieved, grabbed my head and kissed me on the forehead, his breathing all raspy. Once that was done, he returned to his shouty self.

"Meg, I was quite clear there was to be NO night swimming. I couldn't have BEEN any clearer." How could I explain and not get TJ in huge proper legal trouble?

Alex took a step forward. "Blame me, Mr Jackson. These guys came in to save me." What was he doing?! "They heard me yelling. . ." He bent down and rubbed at his thigh. "Cramp."

"You *idiot*, Al." Phoebe was seething. Was Alex really going to take the fall for this? "You could have died. So could they!"

"Megan." Dad did the scary use of my full name. "Is this true?"

What a choice.

I wasn't worried about TJ – he'd known the risks.

Alex, though? He could get in serious trouble all for nothing. I looked at him – he gave me a secret nod of encouragement. He wanted me to say yes.

This didn't feel right – I could only manage an "Uh-huh".

Dad exhaled through his nose, processing it all.

"TJ, you know you're not allowed in the water. IN ANY CIRCUMSTANCE. You can't even swim!"

Phoebe and Billy looked stunned at the revelation. A night of surprises, huh?

TJ nodded. "Sorry, Big Dawg. I only waded in a bit..." He was totally drenched, so not sure my dad would buy it, but the pitch black was on his side. "I was just keeping an eye on Meg."

Woah! Way to make me sound like the needy one? Maybe he really *was* a good actor?!

Alex really didn't deserve to take the fall for him. I had to say something.

But at that exact moment Neet squeezed my hand, letting me know she was there for me, and I remembered what she'd said the other day. I had her. Alex had Phoebe, and yet again, TJ was on his own. Despite having just risked my life for him, I felt sorry for him. I might regret it but, like Alex wanted, like TJ wanted, I kept quiet.

Dad looked disappointed. "Let's be clear. Let's ALL be clear. Alex, that was a foolish thing to do and you put people's lives at risk. For what? Ten minutes of fun?" Alex nodded, his face sombre, even though in reality he'd done nothing but help. I couldn't believe he'd do that for TJ. "Meg, of course I'm proud of you going to help. But I am *incredibly* disappointed you didn't use more sense. You should have raised the alarm."

I apologized again, and then we all stood awkwardly, cold and shivering, no one knowing what to say. After a few seconds Geli sprinted out of the dark towards us with Olive on his back. She threw the towels right at us, one hitting me slap in the face, which broke the mood.

"Look." Dad was cross, but was calming down a tiny bit as we dried ourselves off. "We've all had a shock. So let's go back to ours, warm up, and we can talk about this in the morning."

As we made a subdued walk back, Billy saying his goodbyes and heading home, Alex and I hung behind to talk to TJ alone. The others knew something was up, and gave us space.

"Guys, I can't thank you enough." He sounded shaken. "I mean, you legit saved my life." He laughed, like he couldn't believe what he was saying. "Twice. What with what you said to Meg's dad. . ." He trailed off. "I mean the saving I get, but. . ." He stopped again. "Why'd you do that, Alex?"

Alex clicked the side of his mouth. "Just seemed like the right thing to do."

"But *why*?" TJ was confused. Alex just shrugged, so I answered for him.

"That's what friends are for, TJ."

By the time we went to bed I was shattered. I filled Neet in on what had really gone down, but reliving it all meant I couldn't sleep. But as I lay in the dark, the lie that I'd told Dad wasn't the one that was running through my mind. It was one I'd told Alex. The same one I'd told Neet.

I'd thought it was true.

But tonight had made me realize I'd been kidding them – and kidding myself.

There *was* someone I'd met this holiday who I liked. *Really* liked.

Someone who I'd been myself around. Someone I'd been real Meg with – in my stained T-shirts, telling my worst stories, not trying to impress them in any way. Someone who made me laugh, made me look forward to seeing them, and made time for me, my friends and my family.

But that person had a girlfriend, which meant I needed to keep my feelings to myself.

And even if he didn't, I already knew he couldn't be trusted with people's feelings.

Why, oh why, had I let myself fall for Alex?

CHAPTER
THIRTY-TWO

I'd told Neet that breakfasts out here were something special. Something to really remember. But this one was so bad I'd label it "please delete".

Dad hadn't smiled the entire way through his baguette, or said the words "al fresco" once. "To be clear, Meg – and I'm very sorry you're going to be affected by this too, Neet, but there's really no one to blame here except my eldest daughter – your mother and I are in agreement that you're grounded for the rest of the holiday."

I'd guessed it was coming. Two days and three nights of being stuck in the apartment. Two days and three nights of ruining Neet's holiday.

I'd never been grounded before, but even if I had, it wasn't like there was a lot to do outside my house.

This? With the beach and sea and friends outside my window – some I may never get the chance to see again? This would be hell. Neet rubbed my leg under the table. We'd chatted about it last night and she said if this happened, she would stay in with me. I'd told her no way was that an option.

"But, Dad. . ." I protested.

"But nothing, Meg. I've explained my reasons." He picked up the paper on the table. It was entirely Greek and he definitely couldn't read a word.

Olive swiped another croissant. My appetite had gone, and she was maximizing on the extra food. "No more night swimming for you-*hooo!*"

How *dare* she smile? I wanted to leap on the table, squeeze the grapefruit in her eye and yell, "BUT I WAS SAVING TJ'S LIFE, YOU DWEEEEEB!"

But I didn't. I just chewed on a grape like it had personally wronged me. I was due some serious karma credit right now – Neet too. Her probably more, as this morning I'd had a major wobble over whether to fess up, but she said we were in so deep, we might as well stick by TJ. Dad was freaking out about me going into the water – not who it was I'd gone in to help.

But what did he think I should have done? Let him drown?

"It's not fair on Neet, you know." The words just popped out.

Neet studied her croissant intensely – I felt bad, dragging her into it, but it was true.

"As you're always telling me, Meg, you're an adult, you can make your own decisions." Dad sounded like he'd rehearsed it. "And this is one you made." Eurgh, why couldn't he see it my way? Wouldn't any normal parent just be proud?

"You wouldn't ground Olive." I pushed my plate away. I was done. "Especially if Esther was here." Esther was her best mate.

"Wrong there." Even after a sleep he was still fuming. "Surprisingly I would like both of my daughters to outlive me, if that's OK?"

"There's staying alive, and there's wrapping us up in cotton wool."

"This isn't up for discussion, Megan."

"Just saying." I knew how awkward this was for Neet, but I hoped she'd understand. "I'm almost sixteen. You *have* to let me start doing stuff."

"And what stuff would that be, I wonder?"

"Oh, I dunno. Banana boats. Walking places on my own without you texting to check I haven't been kidnapped. Jet skis..." I could go for hours. "Letting me sleep with my phone on charge as it's actually very unlikely it will combust." Dad had stopped eating and was giving me a very distinct "ENOUGH" look. "Not letting someone drown, when I know I can handle it."

"Enough." His voice was a whole lot louder.

"If you said yes to more stuff you'd realize the world wasn't out to get you."

"Enough, Meg!" He was boiling over, ready to blow – but I couldn't find my mouth-brakes.

"No wonder Mum always says you should live a bit more. . ." Yup. Too far, and everyone around the table knew it.

"MEGAN, I SAID ENOUGH." Dad took a deep breath. "When we've all finished breakfast I would like a private word with you."

It didn't sound optional, and despite it being a perfect morning, the breeze taking the edge off the sweltering heat, we all finished our food as quickly as we could. Dad had to take a work call so, while I waited for my impending yelling, Neet and I headed up to our balcony to ring her dad.

"I'm so sorry, Neet – this is the exact opposite of what I wanted."

I'd wanted a stress-free time for her. I couldn't believe Dad would take the second half of our time together away from her – even if he was blaming me.

"Stop apologizing! What was the alternative? Risk TJ drowning? Then who would star in *Look Who's Singing and Dancing Now IV*?!" TJ's next film. She looked me dead in the eye. "By saving TJ, you, Meg, have martyred your holiday for the sake of all cheesy musicals for the next five years. The world thanks you."

I laughed. Trust Neet to find a positive spin. "Fine..." But I wasn't really bothered about the world. I was bothered about her. "But you *have* to promise you won't babysit me." I got my phone out. "I'm going to make you some plans with the others that you *have* to say yes to. No argument."

She raised her eyebrows and she slid our balcony door open. "Errr, earth to Meg! We have this view, each other, AND a freezer full of Maxibons, so this situation MORE than works for me."

I smiled, but was already secretly planning things I could set up that she couldn't say no to. I would enjoy my holiday prison a lot more if I knew she was having the best time – especially if some of it was with Geli. I felt like I was letting Phoebe down too.

Neet's phone started vibrating on the bed. "It's my dad," she said, running to answer it. When the video flicked on, all we could see was ceiling and the top of his head.

"HELLO, ANITA? HELLO?" he shouted. And kept repeating.

Neet rolled her eyes. "Every time..." She yelled, her mouth pattern overexaggerated: "PLUG YOUR HEADPHONES IN." She pointed to her feet. "MOVE YOUR CAMERA DOWN."

After some fumbling, the camera lurched him into view (still only his head, not even any neck, but we'd take it). He plugged his white headphones into the socket, and sat very straight at their kitchen table, as if it was an interview, not a chat. "Ah, that's better." He looked up as if noticing us for the first time. "What would I do without you?"

Neet brushed her shoulder. "Any time... All OK?"

He nodded. "All good. Very good, actually. The house seems so much tidier all of a sudden... How are you two?" We looked at each other – where to start?

"Good, thanks," I answered for us. "Obviously best thing ever having Neet here."

Mr Shah smiled. "That is good news indeed. And, Anita – are you staying out of trouble?"

She grinned. "Always..." Shame the same couldn't be said about me. "Dad, we saw seals. And dolphins. With our own eyes!"

He beamed. "*Ridiculous*. Is that what you would say?"

Neet laughed. "Nailed it."

"So what do you have lined up for today?"

My stomach clenched. He was going to be so disappointed if he found out I'd ruined our holiday.

"Loads," Neet answered, "and check out this view." She switched to the back camera.

"Beautiful." He exhaled. "Nature can be such a blessing. Make sure you make the most of it."

Wow, being on his own was making him more philosophical than normal. We began to chat about how amazing it was going to be having Anita's mum home, so after telling him how made up Dad, Olive and I all were, I left them to properly catch up.

Despite being grounded, and about to get another mega yelling-at from my dad, as I lay on the balcony, music playing through my speaker, Neet chatting in the background about her mum coming home, the world felt pretty all right.

A day later and we were still on a high over the news about her mum. Neet was still refusing to go anywhere without me, but as we were flying back home in forty-eight hours, I covertly messaged the others to see if they wanted to come and see her in case it helped change her mind. Until they arrived, I wanted to make the most of being together, so we got comfortable on the sunloungers, put a BTS/1975 double-whammy playlist on, and lay out in the sun, starting the same book at the same time so we could read it in sync.

Five minutes in and I was already fidgeting. Doing nothing was exhausting in this heat. I picked up my phone and opened up Instagram. Yesterday Neet had logged in as me and taken me off private. Minx. How bad was it though? I clicked into my notifications. The tagging me into images of extra-toothy animals was dying down, which was good, but thanks to Sean's mate @ing me in the comments, I had loads of TJ fan spam. Especially since he'd just started following me. I was surprised how un-freaked I was at seeing his name in my followers, but maybe that was because I really had seen a whole new, way less appealing side of him. I skim-read some comments, but they were mainly about him, so I deleted, moved on, and out of habit began to scroll. Could there *be* any more pictures of people posing on giant inflatable flamingoes?

"NEET." I spotted something outrageous. "You did NOT tell me about this. . ."

I rolled over on the sunbed and held my phone out. She put her hand up so she could see through the sun bouncing off the screen. When she realized what it was, she smiled, all innocent. "*What?*"

"Don't play *what* with me!" I pinched and zoomed. Was she actually sitting on Geli's knee? On his swing? They must have taken it when I was busy saving a life/ getting grounded. "I can't BELIEVE what I'm seeing here!"

Had she morphed him into a new person?! One who worked his angles for the likes?!

She turned back to her book.

"I know – bad quality, huh? But it was so dark it was a total light-mare."

"That's not what I meant." And she knew it. "Time to admit what's going on."

"Nothing, that's what." But I could see the hint of a smile.

"I've known you since, what? Birth?" I sat up. This was serious. "And I have NEVER seen you look like this about a dude." I pushed the picture towards her again.

"This face" – she pointed at her big grin – "is alllll about the swing. It was most excellent . . . until I heard screaming and thought you were dying. Which was not."

"Minor matter. The important thing is you. And Geli. I need the truth."

Neet didn't say anything. Which was the same as

admitting there was something to say.

"O. M. Actual. G." I dragged myself up. "Budge up. . ." I sat down on her lounger. "So what are we going to do?"

Neet was trying not to smile. "Nothing, is what." She closed her eyes as if she was calmly soaking up more rays, despite her being in total shade.

I felt more giddy than when TJ had asked me on a date. This was EPIC.

"FINE. I'm going to text him." I had his number from day one. "Arrange a—"

"No way." She grabbed my phone. "Not happening."

I tried to wrestle it back. "Neet, c'mon. You can't just pretend you don't like him."

"I DO like him." She put her book down. "As a friend."

I didn't believe her – and neither did she.

"I don't get why you're being so cagey about it . . . it's OK to like someone!" How could I help her let her guard down? She'd had such a tough year that a holiday romance could be a perfect, tiny burst of fun in the middle of all her stress. I had an idea. "It would make up for me being grounded if you and him hung out. . ."

"Not going to happen, Meg. We're going back in two days. Let's keep stuff simple."

I spluttered. Could she hear herself?

"Simple?! You're the one who packed an actual flipchart of potential boy options for me!"

She huffed. "Only because you were obsessing over that Sean kiss, and what everyone thought." I hated her being snappy – she really didn't like me talking about her love life for a change. "I couldn't think of any other way of helping you get over it. Get you to say yes to normal things like that party. . . But if you can, I'm all ears."

I didn't know what to say. I still hadn't confessed my weird, inappropriate Alex feelings. I walked over to the table and squirted on more sun cream. I hated being cooped up here when the beach was so lovely and empty, and below, Olive was bouncing a ball on a wooden bat. Sometimes old school stuff was perfect – not that she was smiling.

Neet sat up and slurped her drink. "Sorry, Megs. . ." She sounded calmer. "It's just always easier to give advice rather than take it, right?"

"Totally."

But there was some advice I *did* want. It had been playing on my mind. Was I wrong for liking Alex? Shouldn't I be able to stop myself liking him because he has a girlfriend? Or maybe that's why I liked him, because I knew it could never work.

I needed to know what Neet thought about him. I checked we were alone on the balcony and went for it.

"Just quickly. . ." I sat down on one of the chairs, and leapt back up – the plastic had heated it near melting temperature. "Hypothetically, if you HAD to. Snog, marry, avoid: Billy, Geli, and er. . ." I tried to make it sound like a random thought. "BB." I was using our secret Balcony Boy name for him just in case.

"I like it. . ." She hardly took a second to answer. "Snog Billy. He makes me laugh. Marry BB." My heart stopped a bit. "He just seems like a really solid bloke. A good life choice. If we ignore *you know what*." She balanced her hands like scales. "But walking you back from the party that night?" She laughed. "And the whole saving an international movie star and not taking the credit?"

When she said it like that, he was kind of lovely as a friend. Still a terrible boyfriend though – and either way, there was no point me dwelling on it. Noah Centineo was also lovely and that also wasn't going to happen.

"But that means. . ." I'd been slow off the mark.

She smiled. "Yup, avoid Geli." She flicked a bit of ice from her drink at me. "The only way I can avoid you nagging me. . ."

I flicked the ice back, but it was now just cold water.

"Like you haven't been nagging me!"

"And still should be, since you've totally given up!" So she knew without me having to tell her. Of course she did – she always did.

I laughed. I figured I might as well tell her the rest of the truth. A problem shared and all that. "You know . . . if BB was single, and not a massive dirty cheat, he could have been number one on the mission list. . ."

Neet sat up, suddenly serious. "In what way, Meg?!"

And just like that I wished I hadn't said it – because no good could come of this. I already felt guilty on his girlfriend's behalf, and Phoebe's too, for letting the thought go further than my own head, even if it was to the one person I trusted most in the world.

It had been a slow realization. He'd really annoyed me at first, but him helping me had slowly become me telling him everything, properly trusting him. Despite what I thought when I first met him, that he didn't care about anyone, he'd always looked out for me. But it was the TJ thing that sealed it – how Alex always did things, big or small, to look out for people, never needing anyone to notice or say thank you. That and the overenthusiastic morning singing. Yup. There were the inappropriate fireworks again. I wiped some sweat off my top lip. Was it from guilt, stress or the sun?

"Oh, I dunno. Just..." But what did I mean? That my most fun times before Neet arrived were with him playing tugby, or laughing about my terrible face rash after the filming, or even that night in the sea, knowing that we would both do whatever it took to make sure nothing bad happened to each other. "I just wish he wasn't who he was."

"And what does that mean, exactly?!"

"Beside the whole girlfriend thing...?" I laughed at the ridiculousness of it. "He's just one of those people. Breaks hearts. Snogs around." Phoebe had said it and I'd seen it in action at the party on my first day. Plus his advice about glamming up for TJ hadn't made me feel good – it had made me feel like a fake. "You know the drill."

Neet was looking at me, her head tilted. "I don't though, Meg." She paused. "Obviously this stays between us, because his girlfriend needs our support, not more problems." Agreed. I couldn't help how I felt, but I could help what I did about it. "But all I know about BB is what I've seen, and he's done nothing but stick his neck out for other people. Especially when you're involved."

Eurgh. As usual on this holiday I had no idea what to think. What to feel. But it didn't matter anyway – he was flying back tomorrow night at midnight, and life would return to normal. Horrible normal.

"Thanks. That's good to know. I guess. Classic me to feel this way about the one guy who's so off-limits it's untrue." Yup, there goes another terrible choice by me. "And who mainly talks to me about how he can help me meet other guys."

Neet grinned. "Semantics."

KNOCK KNOCK.

Someone was at the front door.

Olive was always making me let her in rather than dig out her keys. I turned to Neet – she looked as comfy as me. In this heat, it took a surprising amount of time to find the perfect relaxing position, and I wasn't giving it up without a fight.

"Shall we?" I put my headphones back in, and got back to enjoying not moving. The music helped me think. How was I going to persuade Neet to go out with the others later? And how had I not figured out sooner how I felt about Alex? It was like once I'd discovered these feelings all hidden away, they instantly seemed so obvious I couldn't imagine how I hadn't noticed them before.

But there was no way I was causing more trouble with him and his girlfriend, so I had to be firm and go cold turkey on the thought, or I wouldn't even enjoy hanging out with him and Phoebe as friends.

Splat.

Something cold hit my legs. I looked at Neet. Her head was buried in a book. Had I imagined it?

Splat.

Where was it coming from?

SPLAT. *Splat.*

Drops of water were being flicked at me from behind the wall.

"OI!" I stood up, giving myself a head rush. "Phoebe?" I peered over, but it was a combination I didn't expect. Geli and Alex.

Geli smiled. "Well, if you won't answer the door. . ."

It had been *Geli*?! He normally just sat in his car and beeped.

Alex leant on the wall, grinning in a way that was distractingly cute. COLD TURKEY, MEG. "Desperate times, desperate measures. . ."

Neet put her fingers in the glass of water on our table, walked over to me and flicked them back. "And what *exactly* was so desperate?"

Geli grinned. "I wondered if you guys fancied doing something? Meg, I thought maybe your dad might be OK with another kayak trip if I told him it was an educational experience?"

I pressed my knee into the back of Neet's. I knew

exactly what kind of *educational experience* he was after. She pushed my knee straight back, not a single muscle in her face moving. Did boys do this stuff? Neet and I were like ducks – all normal face above the balcony wall, all coded foot signals beneath.

"Geli, that's *genius* . . . but he's on set with his phone off." I also knew he'd say no – I'd already tried every trick in the book. "You should go though, Neet!"

If those two got together, I would happily be grounded for life. Anything would be worth it.

Neet linked her arm through mine. "It's wifey for lifey, I'm afraid." Geli tried (and failed) to not look too disappointed. "Sorry, though. That one the other day was *amazing.*"

Oh, God, they were now both smiling at each other like, despite having literally just put her arm in mine, they'd forgotten anyone was here. I tried to lean out of their intense gaze.

"Orr. . ." Alex gave me a wide-eyed look that meant he was also feeling like a spare part. "Or you could always climb over to the dark side if you fancy a change of scenery?" He gestured to his balcony. "To two metres left of the scenery you've been looking at for the last day and a half. . ."

"I better stay here, in case Olive forgets her keys

again."

The truth was, I didn't want to get even more grounded – if that was possible. Yes, I'd been ground down a lot, but I felt like Dad still had tricks to grind me down even further into some kind of human dust.

"One sec. . ." Neet tugged at my arm. "Will you give us a moment?" She dragged me inside, her eyes lit up – worrying. "Idea," she whispered. Yup, I was right to be concerned.

I couldn't help but groan.

"Oi, hear me out. . ."

My suspicious right eyebrow went up. "Go on, then. . ."

"I'll say yes to Geli. Go on this kayak. . ."

"OMG why don't you just adddmiiiit you like him?!"

She buried her face in her hands. "Fine. . . Maybe I do!"

This was TOO BIG not to acknowledge. I forced a conversation interlude as I hugged her, ran on the spot, and generally squeaked about.

"So?" I tried to compose myself. "What's the idea . . . other than snog his face off?"

"We'll see. . ." She bit the insides of her cheeks until she got a straight face back. "You never let me finish. What I was saying was. . ." I waited. "I'll go with Geli ifff . . . you say you'll go to the party back home."

"But—" I started to protest but she cut me straight off.

"But nothing." She crossed her arms, a look of nothing but mischief in her eyes. "So, are you in?"

Hello, rock. Hello, hard place. Nice to be stuck between you.

CHAPTER
THIRTY-THREE

When it comes to making Neet happy, there could only be one answer. So she and Geli headed off, and Alex had stayed out with me, hopping over to my balcony. Just what my head didn't need. It seemed the more I realized how much I liked him, the more I couldn't string a sentence together. Right now I was limited mainly to noises involving "o", "u" and "h". Alex, however, was being his normal self. His normal, really cute, really understated self.

STOP THAT, MEG. Not cool.

"I bought snacks..." *He brings snacks?* Argh. What was my head playing at?! I tried to get a serious grip, as he emptied his bag on the table. Cans of drink, a huge bag of salty, oily crisps that I always stole whenever he was eating them, and a wafer thing called "Knopper". "I got that cos it made me laugh."

"Thanks." I laughed – it sounded so forced, but nothing was coming naturally. I wish Neet hadn't run straight out, leaving me alone with Alex and yet another big, stupid secret. I opened the crisps and put so many in my mouth it was physically impossible to talk.

"So how's balcony life?" Alex plonked down on to a chair, unaware I was in my own personal hell.

Chew. Swallow. Speak.

"It's actually been great cos of Neet. I just feel mega guilty for us being stuck here." Alex's parents had reacted in a more normal way – even though they thought he was out swimming, all he'd got was a "don't do it again". "Have your parents calmed down?"

He wrinkled his nose "This isn't going to help, but they've moved on already. To be honest, it was Pheebs who gave me both barrels."

I reached for some more crisps; they were next to his phone, which had lit up.

LUCY: I owe you big time

Alex flipped it over.
Eurgh. Double guilt thump. For Phoebe and Lucy.

What I felt, and what I knew.

I looked out at the sea – a group of boats were out fishing, like a perfect old school painting. Everything here felt slightly unreal, including the situation with the person sitting next to me.

Eurgh. I stuffed some more crisps in. Was I working my way through them so quickly from nerves, or because they were delicious? I messaged Phoebe to let her know we were up here, in case she was around.

"So." Alex smiled. "Don't be mad, but when I got out the shower just before Geli arrived I heard you and Neet whispering about some dude, or something?" I stopped mid-chew. WHAT HAD HE HEARD?! Why had I forgotten their bathroom window was right above us?! "Obviously I tuned right out, but tell me . . . is the mission back on?"

I studied his face for clues. What did he know?

"I'll take your weird staring as a yes." Alex laughed. He wasn't acting like he knew anything. Pheeeew. "So, go on then. What's he like?"

My thoughts were screaming so loudly, I couldn't find actual words to say.

YOU, ALEX. HE'S LIKE YOU. BECAUSE HE *IS* YOU.

All I could do was gawp. Neet should never have left

379

me alone!

Should I tell him he'd got it wrong? Misheard? I was the world's *worst* liar. Maybe I could just vague my way through it. He could NEVER know BB was him.

"Is he..." Uh-oh, he was starting with questions. "I dunno ... tall?" I nodded. "Taller than me?"

Well, this was awkward. "Erm ... I don't think so?"

"OK, any other details...?" He didn't seem as excited as I thought he'd be.

"Ermmmmm..." How could I describe Alex? *To* Alex. "Funny?" Vague, good.

"Tick!"

"Kind... Most of the time." Except when he was cheating on his girlfriend.

"Just as well... It's underrated, right?"

This was killing me. "And just, er, well, someone I wasn't expecting..."

"He sounds like a catch..." Alex's phone vibrated again. "Sorry." He picked it up. "Can I?"

It was Lucy.

"Course." I was happy for any extra time to try and figure out how to get out of this conversation, but Alex fired off a reply and put his phone straight back down.

"All OK?"

"Uh-huh..." He clearly didn't want me to know

what was going on between them. He puffed out his cheeks and exhaled. "Just one of those days. ANY. WAY." His smile was back. "I said I'd help you finish your mission, so. . ." He put his arms out. "Hit me with it."

"With what?"

"Whatever reason you'll find to say you can't hook up with this dude."

IF ONLY HE KNEW.

"Well, the thing is, Alex. . ." He leant back, already suspicious of whatever excuse I was about to come out with. How could I explain? "He's one of those guys who sort of . . . y'know."

Please, Olive, ring the doorbell. Or a seagull attack me. Anything?!

"Well, he's the kind of guy that's kissed a lot of people. Like a lot-lot."

He shrugged. "And?" Trust him to say that.

"And, well, I don't think it's a good idea."

"So what – no one's allowed to change?"

"It's not just that."

He snorted. "Surprise, surprise. . ." I did sound like a total wimp about it. But what could I do? I felt like I was having an out-of-body experience, seeing myself heading towards a moment potentially even more embarrassing than the Sean kiss. "Meg?" He sounded intrigued. I looked at him, willing him to stop. "What? Do I know him? Is it weird or something?"

Definitely *or something*.

This was way too close for comfort. I had to get out of this conversation. Now.

"Sorry, you've got it all wrong... Forget I ever said anything. In fact..." I looked at my watch. "I need to go. I, uh ... said I'd call my mum."

But Alex stood up too. "No!" He sounded urgent. "Stay?" He breathed deeply and steadied himself on the table. "Please, Meg – sit down..." He looked serious. Defeated, maybe? "There's something I need to tell you."

Uh-oh. This didn't sound good.

"It's not just my sister I've been keeping something from. I haven't been totally honest with you either..."

CHAPTER THIRTY-FOUR

"So this is where you've been hiding!" Phoebe couldn't have chosen a worse moment to climb over the balcony. "Can I?" I nodded, but as she swung her leg over the wall, Alex and I looked at each other, acknowledging we'd just swerved something major. But what? Phoebe gave me a hug. I still felt mega awkward being around them at the same time, knowing I knew something she didn't, but I hadn't wanted to leave her out either.

"Good to see how you are are you?" Yup. I'd officially stopped making sense. Phoebe looked at me like I'd lost my mind. She put the back of her hand to my forehead. "Earth to Meg?! All OK?"

"Sure." I forced it out. "How are you. . .?"

"Goooooood. Cos I just saw two people holding hands

in the sea where they thought I wouldn't notice." She grinned. "But in your honour, I had eyes like a hawk." Phoebe looked disappointed at my inability to react. "Neet and Geli? Isn't that like MASSIVE news?"

I nodded. It *was*, and I loved it. I just needed to remember how to use my face and voice muscles to show it. "NO, THAT IS GREAT." I actually shouted. I still had work to do.

Phoebe studied me. Then Alex. "Sorry – have I interrupted something?"

Great. Her suspicions were up. We probably didn't help by both shouting, "NO."

"Righttttt..." She pulled up a chair and sat down between us.

I looked at Alex. How was he coping with this? And what was he about to say?

"Crisp?" He held the bag out for his sister. She took a handful, munching on them happily. "Going to miss these. I'm considering swapping clothes out of my case to pack some of these instead." But she stopped mid-sentence, distracted by Alex's phone which had lit up again.

LUCY: Please don't ignore me. We need to talk.

Phoebe grabbed it to read what we'd all just seen. Alex tried to swipe it away but she was too quick.

"What's this?"

He must have confessed to Lucy about the kiss! Is that what he was going to tell me?

Phoebe looked furious. "Tell me you haven't done something stupid, Al." She was speaking slowly, calmly, like one wrong word and she might be about to explode.

Alex shoved it out of sight on to his lap. "Can we talk about this another time?"

Phoebe sat up straight, her body looking tense, as if ready to attack. "Embarrassed in front of Meg, are you?" She shook her head. "If you've done something to hurt Lucy . . . I'm going to actually. Kill. You."

Alex still didn't look up. Why wasn't he saying anything? Was he finally learning that you don't mess with best mates? Blood might be thicker than water, but best mates help each other out with tampons, and tears – and that's both.

"Meg." Oh, God. Phoebe turned to me. "Do you know what's going on?"

Another good thing about being on a really hot holiday is no one could tell I was suffering from intense panic sweats. Thanks, sun.

"Meg. . .?" Phoebe was still glaring at me.

What could I do? Tell Phoebe about the kiss? Or lie to her, when I already felt bad enough about all the secrets?

"Oh, is that Olive?" I looked at the beach. Neither Phoebe or Alex looked round.

"MEG?" Phoebe was determined to get an answer out of me. "Tell me what you know."

She sat down – this interrogation was here for the long haul. This was awful.

I was stuck between Phoebe, who I loved, and Alex, who half of me adored, and the other, more logical half knew had dragged me into some bad, bad stuff with his girlfriend and his sister.

I took a step backwards. Would they notice if I slow walked out of here? I took another one. They were totally noticing.

What could I do? I'd never lied to Phoebe, I just hadn't told her. But Alex was desperate to tell them only after they got home. Who was I going to let down?

I looked at Alex and the way he looked at me, just like that night when we rescued TJ, made me know what I had to do.

"OK." I took a deep breath. I had to do what I thought was right.

I couldn't look at Alex as I told Phoebe about what

I'd seen that first night. He was going to go home hating me, but that was the way it was. It was his mistake not mine, so I just had to hope that he'd understand why I couldn't stand here and lie to his sister.

If this balcony had a roof, it would be fair to say Phoebe hit it. And then went way above it just so she could yell at Alex even more loudly. I apologized so much for not saying anything sooner, but even though I explained why, I still felt totally awful.

She was apoplectic – and I didn't blame her.

But luckily for me, all her rage was directed firmly at Alex.

She was walking around, waving her arms, yelling things like, "She didn't deserve this!" and "I should never have told her you'd changed!" and "Now I'm going to have to clear up another mess of yours!". She only stopped to tell me she was grateful I'd told her, and understood I'd been in a no-win situation, which was the biggest relief.

And the whole time Alex just sat there.

And Phoebe yelled more.

And I stood there wanting to disappear.

And Phoebe yelled more.

And Alex kept sitting quietly – was he not going to explain himself at all?

He waited for Phoebe to get everything out before he

eventually spoke up.

"OK." He sounded weirdly calm. "Thanks for that, Pheebs. But—" She went to interrupt him, but he didn't let her. "If you'll let me finish, I think it's time I also come clean. . ." He looked right at me. "To both of you."

Woah. Why was he bringing me into this?

"I was going to tell Meg as you arrived, but, well, you might as well both hear it at once." Phoebe looked at me, not understanding what was happening, how I fitted in – but neither did I.

Phoebe raised an eyebrow.

Alex sipped his drink. I swear he said "OK" under his breath as if giving himself a pep-talk.

He began to speak, and as he did, I realized that whatever I was expecting, I'd misjudged him totally.

If I thought he was a good liar before, now I realized he was an actual mastermind.

CHAPTER THIRTY-FIVE

"Phoebe, I wanted you to hear this from Lucy, but to be honest, I can't deal with another day-and-a-half of this." He tried to put his hand on her arm, but she pulled away. "You've got to *promise* not to be mad." Too late for that. "At Lucy." Woah – what did he mean? Somehow I felt that there was only one person she was going to be cross with, and he was sitting right in front of her. But he wouldn't continue till Phoebe promised.

"OK, then." He breathed out and swallowed. "Lucy and I . . . we're not together."

Oh. My. God.

Phoebe looked shell-shocked. "You *what*?"

"Yup. We haven't been for a few weeks. It happened just before we came out here ... Lucy broke up with me." Alex sighed, looking almost relieved that the truth was finally out. "That's why she was emotional at the airport. She knew I wanted to come on this holiday to try and get my head together and wanted to check I was OK." He smiled at Phoebe. "She was looking out for me."

Phoebe looked like she wanted to say everything, but somehow couldn't say anything.

I knew how she felt. All that time I thought he'd been a terrible boyfriend, he'd actually just been dumped?!

"Is that true?" Phoebe's voice was shaking. Alex nodded, a grim look on his face. His sister asked exactly what I was thinking. "Why didn't you just say something?"

He leant back. "Because Lucy asked me, *begged me*, not to. She wanted to tell you herself, as soon as we got back from the holiday." Ahhh, so *that's* why he said it was complicated, and why he didn't want me telling Phoebe about the kiss! He put his hand on Phoebe's arm. This time she didn't flinch. "She is SO worried you'll hate her."

Phoebe shook her head, struggling to take it all in, trying to make sense of it all. "I could never hate her. It's just ... I mean ... she had her reasons, right?"

He nodded. "That's what I keep telling her. I think we both knew it wasn't right from day one, but, well, it was a weird situation..." I thought of all the times Phoebe had talked up their relationship – it must have been impossible for either of them to admit things weren't what she thought they were.

"Riiiiight." Phoebe was nodding slowly, as if this news jigsaw was slowly, slowly slotting together. "So what? You're heartbroken?"

Well, here we go. I prepared to hear about how the boy I liked was still in love with a girl who I'd been worried about all holiday, but who actually didn't like him after all.

The world was weird.

"I don't think so..." He looked at me, embarrassed. "I guess I kissed that girl, the one that Meg saw, because I was trying to get everything out of my system."

"Did it work?" Was Phoebe cross or confused? I was in actual shock – Neet was going to freak when I told her.

"Nope." Alex laughed.

"So why are you so calm about it all?"

"Because this holiday has made me realize Lucy definitely did us both a favour." Phoebe looked at her brother, trying to understand him. He'd definitely usurped Geli as Chief Island Onion.

"In what way?"

Alex grinned like a little kid. "Because I finally met someone who makes me feel the way I think it *should* feel. The way I think I want it to feel. All the time."

Oh, great, just when I thought he was happily single, I was going to hear about the amazing new girl he'd moved on to. What a day. I took a handful of crisps and tried to engage my "I'm so happy for you" face.

"Go on, then." Phoebe grinned at me, already up for some gossip and assuming I was too. "It's not like my head isn't exploding enough already?!" I couldn't have said it better myself.

Alex smiled to himself. "Well, it's someone who makes me laugh..."

Good for her. I picked some sunburn off my forehead to try and distract myself from the gloom.

"Someone who I feel totally myself around." He sounded almost giddy. Was it the girl from the party? "Someone who makes me say yes to stuff I'd normally run a mile from, including letting myself properly like someone." He laughed, but then wrinkled his nose, suddenly self-conscious. "Sorry, am I being too cringe?"

Phoebe shook her head, but I was trying not to vom at how cute this was – for this girl who I was trying not to hate.

"In that case I'll say she's also total flames..." He bit

his lip. "Not that that's the best thing about her. Not by like a million miles. That's just an added bonus, right?"

She sounded amazing. I WAS SO HAPPY FOR HER. I wiped my greasy hand on my top, leaving a big finger stain. I bet Flames Girl didn't rock this kind of hotness.

"Well, she sounds..." I just wanted to run away. Maybe do a silent cry. "Wonderful." I started to gather my stuff up from the table, ready to make my move out of here. "I'd love to meet her." Total lie.

"Me too," Phoebe piped in.

"But, guys..." Alex laughed – sort of at himself. "You have!"

So it *was* the party girl. Unless it was Neet. *What would I do if it was Neet?!*

"And I know this is THE worst timing, but I figured for once, honesty might actually be the way forward."

But then he smiled.

At me.

"...It's you, Meg."

CHAPTER THIRTY-SIX

We all sat there.

Him smiling nervously, fiddling with his can.

Me having an internal meltdown, which I think resulted in a panicked stare back.

Which just made him grin more.

Phoebe looking like she was still processing everything. She stood up. "And I think that's my cue to pretend I've got somewhere else to be." She smiled at me – phew. "Anyways, I think I've got a best mate to ring. . ." So she really wasn't freaking out.

Unlike me.

Especially now it was just the two of us.

Did I really hear Alex right?! I didn't know where to start.

"But I thought you said to be cool and not be covered in crisp stains?"

He laughed. "I pour my heart out and *that's* your response?"

I shrugged. I had no idea what my response was other than *eeeermmmeeeeggggeeehhhhddd*.

I carried on staring.

He dropped his head into his hand. "I am SUCH a loser, aren't I?!" I wanted to say no, but still couldn't manage controlled reactions. He looked up, embarrassed. "Sorry, I know I've weirded you out, but I couldn't *not* tell you."

Still. No. Words.

He started twisting the ring pull on his can. "I mean, you were just telling me you've met this BeeBee dude, and I had to ask questions and pretend it didn't totally suck." So *that's* what he'd been doing! "And I know it's all too late, and you don't even like me that way anyway, but, well. I guess I just wanted, *needed* you to know." He smiled. "And fair play to him."

"But, Alex." Uh-oh. There were words. And I wasn't in full control of them. "Don't you get it?"

I couldn't believe I was doing this. But it was like Neet said – you could either let things happen at you, or make things happen.

"*BB*... Balcony Boy... He's you!"

Alex looked like I'd dropped an even bigger bombshell than his.

Well, Neet couldn't say I hadn't put myself out there. I was so out there, I didn't know where in was any more.

"For real?"

"Don't act so shocked when *you're* the one who's spent the whole holiday giving me advice on getting other guys!"

He rubbed his hands quickly over his face. "Meg, don't you get it? I had *no* idea what to say to you when you asked me what to do!" He snorted. "Ask questions? Make an effort? That's just what Phoebe used to say I should do with Lucy. I mean, I've got NO idea how a guy like TJ thinks! *If* he thinks..."

"But you offered?" I didn't understand.

Alex rocked in his chair. "Yeah. I was trying to say thanks. But then you kept asking me all these questions, thinking I knew the answers, and all I knew was my love life was a total disaster." He chuckled to himself. "I mean, what kind of idiot spends a holiday trying to fake a relationship with the girl who dumped him?" Wow. I'd really got some things wrong.

Alex sat forward, his voice suddenly softer, more serious. "And the whole time, the only thing I did know was, this girl in front of me ... the one who seemed to only speak to me to tell me what a douche I am, or to get advice on finding a guy. This girl who laughs at my singing, uses her clothes as a napkin and keeps asking me how she needs to be different..." He looked down again. "Well, the only advice I ever really had was..." He paused. "Was that she seemed pretty perfect just as she was." He fell forward, laughing and shaking his head. "Yup, look at me with the cool lines..."

But they *did* sound cool to me. So, so cool. Way better than TJ's random brags.

"Alex. Not gonna lie. I wasn't expecting this."

He grinned. "Ditto." He picked up his can. "Did Neet put something in our Fanta?"

"Genuinely wouldn't put it past her." I took a big sip just in case.

"I really thought if I told you, you might not want to see me again." Wow – he really didn't know anything about anything. "I thought TJ was going to sweep you off your feet and that was that."

And he'd still been helping me to prepare – not sure I could have been so nice.

"Don't remind me. That was *naaat* a high point." I sighed. "Although..." I mean – was this a high point? Finding out the guy you like likes you back when you're grounded and hours away from flying home and probably never seeing each other again. "I'm not entirely sure what to do about this either."

By *this*, I think I meant *us,* and from the way Alex grinned, I think he knew exactly what I meant. But before he could reply, Olive ran out on to the balcony and plonked herself beside me. What was it with sisters today? Chatting away like nothing happened, we tried to carry on as normal. Which was hard when I kept sneaking looks at Alex only to find he was already looking at me.

This was the worst best secret ever.

Unable to shake Olive off, we ended up all heading back to our own apartments. I flopped on my bed, struggling to comprehend that on the other side of the wall was the one boy I liked. And he liked me back.

This really *was* Love Island.

I immediately picked up my phone to message Neet, but as I went to press send, I stopped. Knowing Neet, she'd probably rush straight back to get full details, and I wanted her to enjoy her day out as long as possible. I could tell her in person.

But as I looked at my phone, it lit up with someone else's name, and as I read what they said, I wanted to whoop so loudly the whole island could hear.

CHAPTER THIRTY-SEVEN

Neet got back around sunset and reacted in the same way many people would react if you told them you'd been proposed to by Harry Styles. Shock, delight, bouncing, freezing, screaming. I knew Alex could hear the whole thing, as our bedroom walls were made of paper, but I didn't care.

Happily, the excitement was a two-way thing, as when Neet told me about her day (at a slightly lower volume in case Dad or Olive heard), doing boat stuff with Geli, her taking controls of *Alesandro*, I had the same reaction. They hadn't kissed, but I was holding out for a happy, romantic ending – and by the grin on her face, she wasn't *not* up for that plan either.

I showed her Alex's message, which I still hadn't

replied to, despite looking at it at least 237 times.

ALEX: You + Me + 🏖️ + 🕯️ + 🐬 (maybe).
Tomorrow night at 7 🌴?

"Does he want to burn a dolphin with me?"

"Yup, that's definitely it." She waited a beat. "Or he wants to take you on a candlelit beach date, you idiot."

Ahhhh, that made more sense. Although. . .

Waaaaaaaah! A proper date?! I'd never been on a date!

And even more warrrggghhhh, if I was stuck in this apartment, I never would.

"Sorry. Nope. Can't compute." I looked at the message again. "Are you sure that's what he means?"

"Trust me. If there's one thing I know, it's obscure emojis. Credit to Alex, he knows his date trees too."

"But I want to spend my last night with you!" Why was I even stressing when Dad was never going to let me out? Neet shrugged.

"And I want to see you too . . . after you've snogged Alex." She got a dreamy look in her eye. "The perfect end to the holiday."

I spluttered. "One step at a time!?" I also was more than a bit stressed I hadn't heard from Phoebe again.

Was she really OK with all of this?

"Oh no – it's ALL happening. Out of nowhere you're going to complete the mission after all. Put everything behind you!" Neet put her hands in the air. "Unleash your inner Meg!"

I laughed. I panicked. I sat down. I stood up.

"OK. Look ... if I do manage to get Dad to say yes, I will *think* about saying yes to Alex, for the world's quickest date, IF you promise to see Geli?"

She'd already told me that as well as going for lunch on set tomorrow with him and Billy, he'd asked to meet up, just the two of them, for some of her final night. She hadn't given him an answer yet.

Neet grinned. "Let me get back to you on that."

She was impossible! So I did the only thing I could do: started chasing after her, pillow in hand, until she promised she would.

When we woke up on our final full day of holiday, despite Dad still not changing his mind about ungrounding me yet, life was good. Neet's mum was coming out of hospital in a matter of hours, Neet and I were going to do balcony No-ga (the yoga Phoebe and I invented), and I was still optimistic I could win Dad round. These last few weeks had been a rollercoaster, but suddenly it finally felt like everything was taking a turn for the better.

And that was before Phoebe's message came through. I'd invited her for No-ga too but hadn't got a reply.

PHOEBE: See you on the balcony in ten?

Phew. She wasn't avoiding me. That was a start. What she thought mattered to me SO much.

But there was more.

PHOEBE: BTW, I spoke to Lucy and everything Al said was legit.

PHOEBE: So just so we're all clear... I APPROVE!

YESSSS! This was THE BEST news! I actually punched the air.

ME: And just so we're clear... YOU ARE A GODDESS

What a relief she didn't think I was a revolting human for liking her brother. If anyone ever ended up fancying Olive I'd assume they were recovering from a life-changing head trauma. Phoebe was a better sister than me – again.

Now if I could just talk Dad into letting me out the house, I could be going on my first-ever date with Alex. Alex from next door, who made me feel happy-sick when I thought about him.

"Meg, I can't believe it." Neet was jumping on my bed, old-school style. "After all this. . ." She waved the paper list she'd brought. It really *was* everywhere "The answer was staring us in the face all along."

But Alex wasn't my answer. He wasn't the solution to a problem. The end to a mission. He was someone I had truly, totally, and accidentally fallen for.

"Mum always says a watched kettle doesn't boil." I scrunched my mouth. "Which is nonsense and has no relation to this situation at all, but basically, WHAT IS MY LIFE RIGHT NOW?!"

We did another celebratory dance.

Neet sat down, breathless. "So, what's the plan?"

I shrugged. There wasn't much I *could* do, other than continue to try and make Dad change his mind by being the dream housework-doing, joke-laughing-at, safety-conscious daughter I'd been for the last day and a half.

I was desperate to see everyone one last time.

They'd promised they'd all swing by here, but it wasn't the same. Alex and Phoebe were setting off around half nine tonight. If I couldn't talk Dad round, then all we'd have was one more conversation on our balcony and that would be that.

So, after messaging Alex to say I'd try my hardest to be there tonight, Phoebe, Neet and I zenned our way through No-ga, and then I left Neet to get ready for lunch with Geli while I went on another charm offensive with Dad. I found him playing cards with Olive on the beach in front of the apartment. He hadn't fully rubbed in his sun cream, and Olive hadn't told him, so neither would I. She grinned at me, our secret.

"Soooooo..." I tried to sound as casual as I could. "How you guys doing? Need any drinks?"

Dad looked at me as if I was speaking fluent Greek. "What do you want?"

I looked offended. "Nothing!" I pulled out what was behind my back. "I sliced this watermelon. Was worried it might go off."

Truth was I'd scoured the kitchen for whatever Dad would think was the most ideal mid-morning snack. Olive immediately started gnawing her way through some slices, juice flying everywhere. Dad took a piece cautiously with a hesitant "Thanks" as if it might be poisonous. I smiled sweetly.

"Who's winning?"

Olive looked up from her melon, her face covered. "Me. Obvs." She got stuck back in. "Eurgh, pips?!" There was no pleasing some people.

"Sooo, what's the plan for today?"

Dad was still looking at me funny. "Olive's off her to say goodbye to her friends." She interrupted with a "whoop-whoop", or at least that's what I think it was, as her mouth was so full. "And I'm going to use the rest of my morning off to walk a geotourism trail of the island. Apparently the obsidian quarry is something else." He adjusted the massive shade above him, then walked over to the table to top up his sun cream. "Once the heat dies down, of course."

Each to their own. "Sounds like a bit of a mission. Make sure you take lots of water."

He smiled at me. I *knew* health and safety could bring us together again.

"I was thinking about whether, after you're back, whether maybe ..." I was definitely taking the scenic route to my question. "... I'd be able to pop out for an hour? To say goodbye to everyone?" Dad didn't say anything. I needed to lay it on thicker. "It is mine and Ol's last night." Still nothing. "To finish the best-ever holiday in the best-ever way."

Cheeeeseeeeeefest.

Olive snorted as she played her next card.

"To finish *your* mission, you mean."

She said *what?!*

Olive was busy staring at her Uno cards, working out whether to play a blue, or red zero. Had she forgotten Dad was here?!

Dad picked up the sun cream. "What do you mean, Ol?"

She looked up. "Oh, I thought you'd gone?" She looked genuinely surprised. Who did she think I'd been talking to?

"No, Olive," I hissed. "He's literally, quite clearly, one metre away."

She gave me a slightly apologetic look.

"What mission is this, Olive?" Dad had his Responsible Parent voice on. She had two options: lie, or tell the truth. I had to depend on all things sisterly and sacred she'd lie.

"Meg's holiday mission to kiss a boy."

That was IT.

I was done. From this moment on I would consider myself an only child.

"Is this true, Megan?" Dad walked back over. I held out the watermelon lamely.

The only way forward now was denial. "When is anything Olive says ever true?" All rules were off. "Have you checked her for heatstroke?"

He didn't seem convinced. "Olive?"

She shrugged as if it didn't matter to her who he believed. "Uno, by the way."

But the damage was done. Dad sat down. "I think it would be best if we had a family night tonight."

It'd almost been a yes. I *knew* it had.

I retreated back inside thinking of ways I could accidently engineer Olive getting packed into a suitcase and rerouted to somewhere with no phone or internet. How could she be so selfish? Everything was just a game to her.

But maybe this game had two players. If she was going to trap me here, I was going to spend my time wisely, collecting a dossier of material to embarrass her with, ready to ruin her life when she was older. It might take six years, but revenge would be so worth it.

Eurgh.

To cheer myself up, I fired off a text to tell Mum how much I was looking forward to seeing her. She didn't need to know it was because Dad was driving me insane. In a rage I marched off to find Neet. I really hoped this didn't mean she'd give up on her plans. I'd escape off the balcony if I had to.

When I found her, she was already outside, Geli parked up at the front, ready to take her to lunch. The two of them were chatting to Random Old Dude, Neet patting Trevor.

Geli gave me a massive smile. "Surviving?"

"Don't ask."

"How did it go?" asked Neet. "I'm guessing the clenched fists aren't a good sign?"

"Olive's an idiot. And now I'm stuck here for my last night." I actually made a "grrrr", I was SO angry.

"Your last night?!" Random Old Dude threw his hands up. "We must say goodbye." He awkwardly came in for a hug, kissing me on either cheek as he did. Very continental. I kissed him back.

"Ahhh." Geli clapped his hands together. "So Meg got her kiss after all."

I stepped back. "What did you say?" I stared at Geli.

His smile had totally disappeared, replaced by something that resembled a giant foot in his mouth.

"Nothing. I meant nothing." But we'd all heard. I looked at Random Old Dude. He shrugged, as if he too was confused. So he can't have told him.

"Who told you?" But I didn't let Geli say the answer, as I saw the shock on my best friend's face. "Neet?! You promised."

"Meg!" She shouted right back. "As if!"

But there was no one else. "Who else could it be?"

"Don't ask me!"

Telling Geli was bad. Denying it was worse.

"Well, I am," I spat back. Geli was still trying to talk, but I didn't need him to confirm it, I needed Neet to take responsibility for what she'd done. "I thought our promises meant something." Random Old Dude interrupted to say goodbye, aka, flee. Neet and I both waved a polite goodbye but then turned straight back to each other. Our first ever argument.

"Are you really saying what I think you're saying?" She'd never spoken to me like this in her life. But it was a two-way thing. I was SO cross with her.

"You know *exactly* what I'm saying." That she'd come out here, and instead of keeping my secrets had shared them with the first boy she'd opened up to. "Nice to know I can trust you – right up until some guy comes along."

Neet shook her head at me. "I'm done with this." She opened the car door. "Geli, shall we?"

She jumped in, not giving me a second look. Geli looked like he wanted to explain, but I was mortified. Had she told him *he* was on the list? That there *was* a list. How tragic would he think I was? I wished she'd never come.

I marched back into the house, slamming the door and stomping upstairs, fuming at the world. So this was it, my last day of the holiday. Grounded. Inside. Not going on a date with the one boy I'd ever really liked, and with a best mate who'd betrayed me. Brilliant.

This whole thing had been a disaster.

I was a disaster.

I walked out to my balcony, pulled on my sunglasses and plonked myself into a chair. I was going to miss this view. How could somewhere that looked so perfect cause so many problems?

"Meg?" I jumped out of my skin. I hadn't realized Alex was on his side. "What's up?"

My rage was so extreme he was picking up on it from across a wall.

"Don't ask," I huffed. I was going to have to tell him I couldn't make the date as well.

"That's exactly what I'm doing."

"Geli knows about the mission." Alex's mouth dropped ever so slightly. "And, not that she'll admit it, but Neet totally told him."

Alex looked away, but when he looked back he didn't look like his normal self. He looked a million miles from it. Serious. Worried.

"Meg." He paused. "Don't blame Neet." Wherever this

was going, it didn't sound good. "I . . . I think it was me?"

I sat bolt upright. "Are you being serious?!" Or was he trying to help Neet – being classic nice-guy Al again? I searched his eyes for a clue.

"Serious, I'm afraid." It took a few seconds for it to sink in.

"But you promised?" He really was a world-class liar after all. And instead of even *thinking* he could be an option, I'd blamed my best mate and ruined everything.

Well done, me.

It seemed the only choices I'd made all holiday were the wrong ones.

"I can explain. . ." Alex sounded desperate, but I was done.

"No need." I stood up, fed up with him. Fed up with me. Fed up with everything. "Nice knowing you." And without letting him say another word, I picked up my water bottle and walked back inside.

As I lay on my bed, the curtains drawn, the room as cold and dark as my mood, my final day of holiday slipping away, there was only one thing I could think about. Alex had proved my suspicions right. I didn't want to be anywhere near someone I couldn't trust. But the one person I did want to be near wasn't speaking to me.

How could I make it up to Neet?

CHAPTER THIRTY-EIGHT

Two hours and a billion messages later, I still hadn't heard from Neet. Geli had replied to the ones I'd sent him apologizing to say he was sorry but Neet had asked to stay out all day. Apparently, he'd being trying to tell us about Alex the whole time.

The betrayal by Alex was bad, but falling out with Neet felt like the world had shifted beneath my feet. I'd been so annoyed about Olive telling Dad that when I thought someone else had blabbed too, I'd jumped to all the wrong conclusions.

Alex had been messaging ever since I stormed off. He'd apologized a million times. But he'd also explained. Apparently he'd told a couple of people at the party on the first night, before I'd caught him snogging that girl. Before he'd made the promise not to tell anyone.

At the time we didn't really know each other, and he thought all I wanted to do was kiss someone, so letting some single guys know was his idea of helping.

But those guys had included Billy, TJ and Geli. Which explained a lot. Billy's weirdness with me, probably thinking I was a manhunter. TJ assuming I'd be into him – although he probably did that with all girls. And guys. And anyone with a pulse. And Geli being distant and judgemental, until I'd actually taken the time to get to know him and his home.

The whole thing made me cringe so hard.

I made me cringe so hard.

All the people back home were right. I was one big Megabiting loser.

Eurgh. It all sucked so much.

I guess I could see why Alex had done it – I just wished he'd told me.

Thirty minutes ago, with me still ignoring his messages, he'd dropped a package of Fanta Limon, salted crisps and a mint Cornetto over the balcony wall. But I was so muddled about everything that I'd let the Cornetto melt – no bigger declaration that things were not OK.

Another hour later and I still had no idea how to fix things, so when I heard some shuffling next door, I peeked out. Phoebe.

Regardless of my imploding mess of a life, I did want to say thank you and bye to her more than anyone else.

I dragged the curtains open and shuffled out.

"Hiyer."

She was unclipping the bikinis she'd put out to dry, and looked surprised to see someone.

"I had no idea anyone was in!" Probably not best to admit I was in a motionless slump on my bed. I nudged the packet of melted ice cream out of view with my foot and pulled on my best game face. I didn't want to catch her up in another one of my problems.

"Oh yeah, just reading, taking a break from the sun. Anyway. . ." I held out what I had in my hand. "I wanted to give you this."

It was a postcard I'd written to her, and some shells I'd picked up from the beach, when I'd been strolling with Neet a few days ago. I was going to post it as a surprise, but figured after everything going down with Al, maybe in person was best. On the front was a picture of a dog looking confused on a banana boat.

Dear Phoebe,

Wish you here! OH THAT'S RIGHT. You are!

Thanks for making my holiday extra sunny. No-ga 4eva.

Please stay in touch – I need to keep up with your taking over the world/Olympic beach volleyball dreams.

Then there was a squiggly drawing I'd tried and failed.

(That was meant to be a fist bump).
Love Meg xxxx
PS the doggo on the front – it me.

Phoebe smiled as she read it. When I'd met her, I would have thought she was too cool, too beautiful, too everything to be nice to someone like me, but she'd been a proper friend since day one.

"The holiday wouldn't have been the same without you." I felt suddenly embarrassed. "That's all."

She gave me a massive smile, put down her washing, and leant over the wall.

"I'm going to miss you too." She hugged me, hard. "You and Neet are goals."

I flinched, but luckily she didn't notice, as we were still caught up in the hug.

"Well you are The Goal." I wasn't going to let her argue. "End of."

"Look..." She chewed her lip. "I'm not going to interfere – look where that got me – but for what it's worth, I've really never seen Al like this. I've got no idea what's going on, but I do know he just watched *The Notebook*. For *fun*."

Woah. That was bad times. And also exactly what I might do if worrying about Neet hadn't propelled me into a new realm.

But she didn't have time to speak, as her mum was yelling for her to get a move on as I'd caught her mid-packing. So, with a final goodbye I left her to it.

I sat on a sunlounger, and tried to let the sun thaw out some of my worry, but the more Neet wasn't replying, the more knotted up I felt. It had just gone two-thirty, and in my dream situation we'd be together planning something amazing for her last night. But here, I was alone, wondering if she'd forgive me.

Although... I heard a bang from the back of the house. *Was I alone?*

I sat up to listen. Dad should have finished his walk and be back at work, and Olive was out with her mates.

But I could definitely hear banging.

"*Hellllo?*" I called. The banging didn't stop. What was it?! Slowly I made my way to Olive's door. *Thump, thump, thump.* It was definitely coming from in there.

I put my hand on the door handle. My heart was racing. With a one-two-three, I pushed it open.

My former sister spun round, shocked. She pulled her headphones off.

"What do you want?" She was recording herself on our iPad, practising a video for TikTok.

"I thought you were meant to be out?"

She shrugged. "Change of plans." I didn't get it. It was her last day too, and if I wasn't trapped here, there's no *way* I would be inside.

"Are you seeing your friends later then?" If Olive went out, maybe that would give me a bit more room to try a final bargain with Dad.

She shrugged again. There was something she wasn't telling me. Did it have something to do with why she'd had that outburst earlier? I needed to find out. I sat down on her bed. She gave me a grumpy "Oi", but it was too half-hearted to take seriously, so I didn't move.

"Everything OK, Ol?" I picked up the picture she'd put on her bedside table. It was one we'd taken in the garden, Mum smiling as she took the selfie, me, Dad and

Oli running and laughing behind her.

"Why wouldn't it be?" Hmmm. Suspicious. Being snappy when we were feeling defensive was a family trait. So what was she hiding? I thought about her friends. Had they been making her feel rubbish again?

"No reason." How I could get more information when she so clearly wasn't up for chatting? "You going down to set later?" Another shrug. "I thought you might get that photo with TJ?" He'd promised her one before she left.

At the mention of TJ she looked even more stern. "Don't think so." She put her headphones down and flicked off the iPad. The way she was fiddling about, I knew if I waited, she'd say something more. I pretended to be looking at my new freckles in her bedside mirror for an unnecessarily long amount of time.

Finally, the silence killed her – she cracked. "Lindsi thinks he's overrated."

Ahhhh. So that was it. Annoying Blonde Girl was putting thoughts in Ol's head, undermining her. As annoyed as I was about earlier, big sister defensive mode kicked in.

"And do you agree?"

Olive twisted her mouth to one side. "Dunno." Which meant no.

"So what happened today?"

"Think they decided to go to a different beach or something." She was mumbling, exactly what I do when I'm lying.

Hold up. *They?* So this wasn't a Lindsi thing. This was a *whole group* leaving-Olive-out-thing? How dare they?

And then it clicked. Ever since Neet had arrived I hadn't seen her with them. In fact, ever since the filming, I'd only ever seen Olive on her own.

"Ol. Can I ask you something?" She looked at me, with the full realization it was coming anyway. "And be honest... If we temporarily forget about the whole you-telling-Dad-about-the-mission thing, which I promise WILL come back to haunt you..." She didn't even look vaguely guilty – she was made of stern stuff. "Will you promise to answer me truthfully?"

"S'pose," she said, with zero enthusiasm.

"Have your friends been leaving you out?"

She didn't say anything, but she didn't have to. I could tell by the look on her face. I knew exactly how she was feeling: like an outsider, lonely, and like you've done something wrong. It was nothing but awful.

I shuffled along on the bed. "Come here." I held my arms out for a hug. She looked at me, working out what to do – and despite her hobby of trying to pretend nothing bothered her, crumpled straight into them.

I hadn't liked those guys from day one. She'd been so excited to meet them, so proud to have found her group. How dare they make themselves feel big by making her feel small?

As I held her I realized I should have seen it sooner. The snapping at me, the overreaction to being left out, which I guess I had done since Neet got here, and all those times I'd spotted her hanging out on her own. I stroked her hair like Mum always does.

"Ol, listen. You and me? We might be bad at showing it, but we'll always have each other's backs, OK? No matter what." I felt a tiny nod from within my big cuddle. "And those guys, they're just jealous." Me getting her that part as an extra must have been the final straw for them – so much for my trying to impress them on her behalf; I'd just made things a million times worse. "You had something they didn't, and they didn't like it."

"That's not true, Meg." Her words were muffled, going straight into a mixture of my T-shirt and elbow. "They literally have the *best* lives."

"They *literally* don't." I hated seeing her like this and feeling I'd been a part of the cause. "Trust me ... they don't have you for a kick-off." She made a *duhh* of disbelief at my cheesiness. Oh good, if her snark was returning, she was cheering up. "And" – I leant back so I could look her in the eye – "they certainly aren't going to see themselves as the best merperson the world has ever seen in *Emotional Baggage III: The Summer Holiday.* Coming soon to a cinema near you..." I used my best movie voice.

"Thanksmeg," she said all in one word, her smile slowly coming back. She liked to say that so Mum and Dad couldn't tell her off for calling me "Smeg", as she argued it was just the way her words came out.

"Do you want to know another secret?" Her eyes lit up. She loved nothing more than knowing something she shouldn't, especially if she thought it was a grown-up thing. "But you *really* have to not tell anyone." She nodded. "OK ... well, you know how sometimes someone's life seems perfect? It doesn't mean that behind the scenes it is..." And with her listening like I was telling her the hottest gossip to ever drop, I told her the truth about that night with TJ and the rescue – and by the end, she'd returned to her normal, fully charged-up, excited self. Job done. Now all I had to do was think of a way we could make her last day better. And get Neet to forgive me. And work out if I wanted to say goodbye to Alex before he left.

Woah. Brain overload.

One thing at a time.

"OK, Ol, enough of this. It's our last day, and we need to make the most of it." Oh goodness, was I about to sign myself up to a whole afternoon of balcony Uno? But Olive didn't exactly look excited about getting back out and facing the world. I knew how she felt. "Look, I'm not having this. I'll level with you. I've messed up a bit. A lot. But you've got to promise me that whatever happens, you won't let some annoying, self-obsessed losers stop you doing what you want." If there was one thing I'd realized from the last few weeks, it was that if I hadn't been so busy worrying about what everyone thought about me and that first kiss, I wouldn't have made everything ten times worse. Neet would have never come up with the stupid second first kiss plan, and none of this would ever have happened.

"What do you mean?"

"If you want to get a picture with TJ, you go get one." Ol looked unconvinced. "Seriously. If you don't put yourself out there for what you want, you'll only end up regretting it." I exhaled, realizing how much of my own advice I needed to take.

And as I looked at the picture by her bed again I got an idea.

I had two options.

Sit here and wait for the world to rumble on. Or do what I was telling Olive. Step up and try to fix stuff, regardless of how scary it might feel.

It might not work, and time was tight, but finally I knew what I had to do to make it up to Neet.

CHAPTER
THIRTY-NINE

The first call had been to Mum. She'd been weirded out, but said yes.

The next thing had been to ring Billy and ask if he had Holly's number, and whether his brother would be up for a big favour. And, like the saint he was, he got on it straight away. He was with Neet and Geli having lunch, so had been extra cryptic on the phone.

Then I got in touch with the person this all depended on – Geli. When I told him the plan, he promised to do all he could.

Mr Shah had been a bit confused when he'd picked up the phone. His first reaction was to assume there had been a disaster, but I told him he'd been hanging out with my dad too much. I then explained everything;

how much her mum coming home meant to Neet, and what I needed to do.

I even messaged Alex. I told him I'd forgiven him, but there was no way I'd be able to go on the date. It was bittersweet as he told me what he'd been working on – candles on the beach at his favourite sunset spot, accompanied by a feast of crisps and a final instalment of terrible singing.

But I didn't have time to think about what could have been. The only person I could focus on today was Neet. I messaged her.

> ME: I hope you know how sorry I am. But actions speak louder than words. If you forgive me at all, EVEN THE TINIEST BIT, please let Geli take you to set at 6:15. You don't need to reply, just please please go with him. #alfresco
>
> ME: 🐾 🐻 🍙 🎽 📁 ⚠️ 🕐 (They were the weirdest I could find) xxxxx

By the time it hit six p.m., I was a bag of nerves. During the afternoon, my bedroom had become a control room – and now I was pacing round it, waiting to hear from Holly or Geli to know if my plan had any hope of working.

I'd arranged the surprise welcome-home party for Neet's mum that she'd dreamt of. My mum had been a total star, and had gone to Neet's house, where her dad had let her in. When he'd left to go to the hospital, I'd been able to direct Mum all around the house to put up the banners Neet had made, blow up the balloons that she'd ordered, and best of all, bring the lemon cake round that she'd rustled up that afternoon after I'd tracked down the recipe. My mum was Phoebe-levels of badass. I seriously owed her one. Two. With women like her, Neet, Neet's mum and Olive around me, I was so cross that over these last few weeks I'd let myself think that I couldn't take matters into my own hands, and let situations own me rather than take control. This was my life and I needed to live it. As Mum said on the phone, it's not what happens to us, it's how we deal with it. And this was how I was dealing with my mistake from earlier – by owning it. I just had to hope that Neet put her trust in me and would go to the set. If she arrived, Holly (another total inspo) had agreed to do me a favour and take time out of her day to surprise Neet with the full glam works. Then Geli was going to drive her down to the beach, where Billy was setting up a projector and massive speakers, borrowed from his brother. All I then needed to do was get my mum to FaceTime someone this end, which we'd mirror on Billy's laptop, and then hopefully unleash the biggest Greek-English surprise welcome-home party for Neet's mum she could ever have imagined.

I just needed Neet to said yes.

To be there.

As quarter past six rolled round, I felt sick.

As twenty past six rolled round, I felt worse.

At half six, I realized how this was never going to happen.

Neet hated me.

And it made me so sad it hurt.

I got in bed, pulled the sheet over my head, and picked up my phone to message Mum to stand down. I'd cry if I tried to speak.

But then something came through: a picture from Holly of a shocked looking Neet.

SHE'D TURNED UP TO SET!

Without thinking, I leapt up and cheered like England had won the World Cup.

Holly had even made Neet's name for the back of the make-up chair out of white gaffer tape. What a legend!

I got two messages in quick succession.

BB: She turned up then!? 👍👍👍

He must have heard me. I replied with a massive smiley face. I was gutted things hadn't been able to work out with us, but right now it was hard to feel sad about anything, especially when the next message arrived.

NEETTOBEONTHATBEACH: I don't know what you're up to but . . . thank you.

She'd changed her name this morning before I accused her of being a terrible friend. I whipped up a picture from one of Jungkook's ab flashes with a speech bubble saying, "Meg told me to tell you there's no need to say thanks." And another saying, "And did I say how HOT you are?! Have the best night love me and all BTS."

Despite being stuck here, after I'd messaged Billy to say the plan was on, I threw myself back on my bed, and felt almost as happy as if I was out there with her.

Half an hour later Geli sent me another picture – I didn't even know his phone had a camera. It was a blurry photo of Neet, looking like an actual vision of everything that is good in the world, just with added kick-assness and the most amazing bright orange lipstick. She was grinning from ear to ear, a gazillion times more gorgeous than any pout. I swear I could spot the top of what looked like a sequin jumpsuit – Holly must have borrowed something from the film wardrobe. That woman was unstoppable. I loved her.

I messaged Holly to say all the thank yous, and sent Geli some serious love eyes.

I didn't even have FOMO, I was so happy that the plan was coming together. All they had to do now was get her to the beach spot I'd chosen, just down the road from here, next to the café with the big white wall. I'd suggested that Phoebe, Billy, Olive and even Alex and TJ gather for one last party, with Neet as the star attraction – and they were all up for it. I wasn't sure about inviting TJ, as I was still mad at him, but I did feel weirdly sorry for him being so alone out here, so Billy tried to get the message to him. Who knew if he'd turn up?

Knock knock.

I opened my door to find a serious-looking Dad. Was I in trouble for all the yelling?

"I need to have a word with you, young lady." Here we go. . .

"Come in." I held the door open. Resistance was futile.

"I don't need to come in. I'm only here to say one

thing." He cleared his throat. "I've spoken to your mother and . . . I know what you're up to." That wasn't a huge surprise – they told each other everything. "Now, don't go getting your hopes up, we still think you should be grounded." Mum *had* warned me, but my hopes hadn't got the memo and had been slowly drifting upwards anyway. Oh, well. That was that. Goodbye, rest of holiday. "But one person who doesn't agree is Olive."

I scratched at my sunburn, not sure where this was going. "She told me what really happened with TJ – and how you and Alex covered for him."

"Olive?!" That girl could not keep her mouth shut!

"Don't be cross with her." Easy for him to say! I'd just discovered my sister is a human sieve when it comes to secrets. "She very seriously made me promise, on the health of her latest slime unicorn creation, that I wouldn't say anything to anyone at work. And despite everything I think is ethically correct . . . I'm not going to." Well, that was a relief. So why was he here? "But . . . I *am* going to say sorry for overreacting. I was just so scared for what could happen to you. And, now that Olive has told me what you did, I still think you should be grounded for going in the sea that night without telling anyone first. But" – he put his hand on my shoulder – "I think maybe you should be ungrounded for how you and Alex tried to protect TJ behind the scenes. And for what you're doing for Neet tonight." He looked at his watch. "Now ... haven't you got a party to get to?"

I opened my mouth.

And shut it.

The shock was too real?! This was EPIC.

I was free! All because my sister had helped me out and made my dad change his mind? There must have been sunstroke all round!

I planted a massive kiss on Dad's face and gave him the biggest cuddle.

"Thank you!!!!!!!!!"

He smiled. "Eleven p.m. curfew, though ... and no swimming this time!"

CHAPTER
FORTY

Neet was due to arrive in three minutes and Mum had just messaged me saying she was all ready on her end.

I sprinted out the door in the full-on moping look I'd been rocking all afternoon: Dad's David Attenborough T-shirt, some bright blue baggy shorts, bare feet, my hair piled on head and puffy crying face. But then I sprinted straight back.

"Come on then, Dad!" He looked surprised to see me, but if I was going, so was he. As much as this was my last night with my friends, it was our last night together on holiday too. But I couldn't wait for him to do his slow parent things like lock up, so I had to leave him to catch up, as I sprinted along the beach, the sand hot under my feet. *Two minutes.* I video-called Mum as

I ran. "YOU . . . ALL . . . SET?" I yelled between puffs.

"Go go, Meg!" she shouted back, not even startled by what she was seeing. She'd put the banner up behind her, stringing it across Neet's hall. There were balloons everywhere. She'd done such an amazing job.

"MUM, YOU ARE . . ." Puff. ". . . A LEGEND!!!!"

She smiled. "Hurry!" She was looking out of the window. "The car's turning on to the street!"

I don't know where it came from, but I found another spurt of speed. I spotted a group of people outside the café. My friends had turned up! "Hold . . . fire . . . I'm . . . putting you . . . in . . . my . . . pocket!"

I ran as fast as I could. "Guyyyysssssss. . ." I hollered. They looked around to spot where the commotion was coming from, but when they realized the shouty, scruffy, possessed hairball was me, they started to cheer me on. Billy, Phoebe, Alex, TJ, Olive, all of them screaming wildly like I was finishing a marathon. These guys were the best. Alex gave me an extra wave and a smile, which I tried to return, although it was hard when I was gasping for air. Even though nothing was going to happen, it was still great to get to see him one more time, rather than leave it on the argument from earlier.

Olive skip-ran towards me, "You made it!"

I still had a little way to go and could hardly breathe.

"Thanks . . . to . . . you!" I spotted Billy. "Bill!" I grabbed my phone out of my pocket and threw it at him. "Meet Mum."

He knew exactly what to do – we'd planned it all out earlier – and just as Geli's car screeched round the corner, he got Mum to flip to the back camera and Neet's hallway popped up huge on the café wall. The projector had worked. The plan was coming together.

I ran to help him. "All OK?" I leant in so Mum could see me with him.

"This young man seems to have everything under control." Her voice boomed out as Billy grinned, chuffed. The speakers were working, then?!

"Shhhhhh." I held a finger up to my lips. "Neet's about to arrive and you're volume 100." Mum nodded, no real idea of the scale of what was happening this end, but it didn't matter – she always dealt with whatever life threw at her.

I checked Neet hadn't got out of the car yet and hugged Billy. "You" – I looked around at everything he'd set up – "are *next level*."

He grinned. "Can't have my favourite Dream Girl mutant going home with anything less than a Billy special."

"Seriously. You are the best. Your brother, too."

He laughed. "Oi. Let's keep this about me, please."

Olive squeaked. "Guys, she's coming. . ."

Neet still had no idea what we were up to, what all this was for. But as she walked out round the corner, and on to the beach, it wasn't just me who gasped – we all did. The sun was glinting off her sequins, and out of all the things I'd seen this holiday, this was the most film-star moment of them all.

Wow. Just wow.

Neet stopped as she realized there was a bunch of people waiting – and that at the front of them was me. I caught Geli's eye, and mouthed "*Efharisto*", which made him smile.

"Neet, step this way." I put my hand out. Everyone cheered as she walked towards me. I'd never seen her speechless – until now. I hugged her. "I am SO sorry."

She hugged me back, smelling of hairspray and expensive make-up and pure, wonderful Neet. It was so, so good to know we were friends again. "Forgotten already." Her heart was beating all quick-fire.

"I can't believe you did all this." We stepped back as she looked out at the beach, taking it all in – our friends, the party, everything. "All the best people are here."

But she hadn't seen the wall, and out of the corner of my eye, I could see a shadow behind the door. "Not ALL the best, Neet." I put my hands on her shoulders.

"Some of them are back home. Really home." And as she turned round, she saw the huge projection on the wall, just in time for the door handle to go down and slowly open. Everyone on the beach fell silent, but none of them could see what I could. Neet's eyes filling up. In fairness, I couldn't see that well either, because mine were too. "Is it?" Her voice was wobbling.

"Uh-huh."

I waved my hand discreetly at Billy, and he brought my phone over, as Neet's mum slowly hobbled through the door.

"WELCOME HOME, MUM!" Neet yelled at the phone. Neet's mum looked straight into the camera, put her hand over her mouth, and started to happy-cry.

Once the shock had settled a bit, her mum taking in the full scene at home and her daughter on the end of the phone, looking like a movie star on a beach packed with people there to celebrate this moment (my mum wobbling the phone as she cried behind the camera), we all started cheering, and hugging whoever was nearest. It was the best.

TJ even lifted Neet up on to his shoulders, bouncing her round, as she chatted to her family. Dad didn't even try and stop us; in fact, he was the one taking photos.

Once the call was over, and we all waved them off,

Neet requested we turn up the music, and together we danced and celebrated, everyone on a total life high. Geli's mates rocked up with some surprise chips and gyros – even Geli's friend whipping out his guitar and starting to wail didn't dampen our spirits. In fact, soon we all joined in – Alex's singing even worse than normal – as we tried to attempt a version of a local dance Geli was showing us.

I sent Mum videos from this end so she could see the amazing moment she'd helped create, and of course an extra one of a grinning Olive and TJ for her Facebook humblebrag. I'd managed to grab a quick word with him about Olive's tough time, and he told me he was going to post the picture on his stories. I was already gagging to see her face when it happened. Seeing as he seemed to be being a bit more human, and a bit less TJ, I'd even bitten the bullet and told him the truth about why I'd called off our date, and what I'd seen with Cara. He looked mortified, but I didn't need an apology; I just wanted him to know so he might not do it to someone else. Tonight wasn't about him; it was about Neet, and this amazing party for her mum. It was epic. I owed Mum big time. I owed Billy, too – so when he wasn't looking I put my entire collection of remaining spending money in a pocket in his rucksack. It wasn't much, but I left with it a scribbled note saying, "For vegan ice-cream only xx". I also sent a picture to Holly with the big news that the handiwork had led to the picture of Neet in the Troll light being shifted into second place for her favourite-ever profile photo. That had been in pole position for almost a year, so this was big news.

Telling the others I needed to wash off some sand, I walked down to the water's edge,

Truth was I just wanted a moment to take it all in.

I looked back at them all. At Neet, my dad, my sister, the friends I'd made. The people who didn't care if I wore my dad's T-shirt and had crisps in my hair. The strangers who had become friends and had come through when I needed them the most. The people who when I headbutted TJ didn't laugh about it on the internet – they cheered from the sidelines and told me it was going to be OK.

I turned my back to them and took a massive, grinning selfie, my sunburnt peeling head in full focus, all of them in the background, and I posted it. For the first time since the party I didn't care what anyone said or anyone thought, because I knew what I thought. That I was the luckiest person in the world.

And as the sun started to set, we began to make our way up to the spot Geli had shown me at that very first party for one final time. Phoebe came to say bye in case she missed us at the top. Their flight was only a few hours away and they had to head back within the hour. It was tough – I couldn't believe this could be the last time I saw her, although we both promised to stay in touch.

She headed off, leaving me alone with Neet.

"Thanks for all this." She was still in shock. "I can't believe you'd do all this for me!"

I snorted. "As if. It's like the tiniest drop in the ocean of what you do for me." I squeezed her hand. "I'm just so happy we could kind of be there when your mum came home."

She shook her head, a disbelieving smile on her face. "It was unreal."

"Talking of which." I stopped. "Geli. . ." I beckoned him over, stopping at the big rock that marked the start of the climb.

"Seriously, dude. I can't thank you enough for helping today. I can imagine this one wasn't the easiest to talk into coming. . ."

"I'm saying nothing." He smiled, knowing we all knew the answer was yes.

"There is one other thing. Alex. . ." I peered down the shore. He'd disappeared a while ago, but had just messaged to say things were good to go. Ah-ha – there he was, giving me a big thumbs up, a big grin on his face. "Yup, Alex has been working on something too. Come with me..." I jumped down off the rock and walked a few paces round the corner. Woah. He'd done good.

"What the..." Neet looked almost as taken aback as earlier.

A pathway of tea lights was flickering away, leading to a little patch of sand on the edge of some rock pools. "Apparently you can sometimes see the seals coming in to shore from here too..."

Geli nodded. Of course he'd know.

"But wasn't this..." Neet had figured it out. It was the date Alex and I had meant to have – when he'd told me earlier what he'd had planned, as amazing as it sounded, I knew that if he was up for it, it would be even more perfect for Neet and Geli. I'd been clear with him that tonight was about Neet – and even if I'd managed to wangle Dad into letting me go out, I wanted to spend it together with everyone. He'd not just understood; he'd worked non-stop to make it happen.

"Yup, but we thought you guys might want to..." Was I really going to say this? "Say goodbye or ... something." I knew they'd want to be with all of us, but also knew if they weren't given the chance for something to happen between them, neither of them would take that step.

"Just for a bit."

I couldn't tell who was more embarrassed – me, Neet or Geli. They agreed to go, and said they wouldn't be long. But as I watched them walk down the path, I noticed them reach for each other's hands.

"You pulled it out of the bag," I said after Alex made his way back to me. His white T-shirt was covered in sand, and sea, and bits of charcoal from where he'd been lighting a gazillion candles.

"Well..." He looked up at me, his gorgeous hazel eyes full of mischief. "Can we both remember all this effort was meant to be for you?"

"It still was, I promise." Making Neet happy, after all the stuff she'd been through, made me way more happy than if this had been just for me.

"Shall we?" He looked up at the path. "One last time?" I nodded. I'd loved our walks together, strolling and chatting about nothing. He looked at me and grinned. "By the way ... out of all the looks, this one is my fave."

I laughed. "With or without the face mask?"

He shrugged and laughed. "Either way works for me."

We walked up the path, both quiet and happy in each other's company, letting the mood slowly shift into something more sombre. The view was amazing, the sky the brightest pinky orange I'd ever seen. I'd miss this. I looked to my left – but I'd miss him more.

"Sorry for telling the others." Alex just came out with it. We'd only spoken about it over WhatsApp since this morning. "I promise you can trust me. I should have told you sooner." But he didn't need to explain. I'd spent the day thinking about it and I'd got it. We didn't know each other at the party, and back then I was happy to assume he was the serial snogger I thought he was. We'd all made mistakes. Plus, if he'd told me what he'd done, I would have freaked out, and never made friends with Billy, Geli or TJ. Or him. So in a weird way, he'd done me a favour.

"TBH, I'm kind of glad I didn't know." Truth was, I did worry he might think he was part of the whole stupid mission thing too, when actually how I felt about him was a million miles from trying to tick a box. "I still wish you'd never heard about that whole Megabite thing, though."

"And I wish you'd never stepped on that girl I was kissing, but, well..." He laughed. "What doesn't kill you makes a funny story, right?"

That was one way to look at it. We walked on a bit more, Phoebe and Billy's laughter getting louder. We both knew these were our last few moments alone together. Probably for ever.

Alex stopped. "There's something else I'm sorry about...
I'm sorry I didn't tell you how I felt sooner." He looked me
straight in the eyes. I swear I had to catch my breath as
he did. He had this way of looking at me like nothing else
mattered. "And I'm sorry we never got to have that date."

I was sorry too. The thought of what could have
been would be something I'd think about for ever. Alex
stepped nearer to me.

I became hyper-aware of how close we were.

How my face was so close to his.

How, if he looked down, and I looked up, we were
almost, almost touching.

My heart was thundering, but this time I wasn't scared.

I knew for certain that I wanted to kiss Alex.

And it would be OK.

Even if I unleashed a new level of accidental kissing
injury, I knew it would be all right. He'd make it all right.

"So..." His voice was soft, quiet. "I wondered if you
might like to finally finish that mission?"

The sea was smashing into the rocks below us; in
the distance was the sound of all my favourite people
having fun.

This moment was perfect.

He leant forward. I looked up.

My kissing curse was about to be broken...

Or not.

"Meg, do you know where the nearest loo is?!" Olive tripped down the path almost in to the middle of us. Alex and I leapt back. "Billy said it was here somewhere."

I blinked myself back into reality. The reality of me not currently kissing Alex. A reality that quite frankly sucked.

Instead Olive was here – happy, clueless Olive – and she was bobbing about. I could point her off in the right direction, down the dark path, and see what happened with Alex. Or. . .

"Sorry, Alex." I pointed into the dark. "Guess I'd better. . ." He knew what I meant. Head off with Olive. Finally give up on anything that could have happened.

Because if I left now, there would be no second try. He was going to have to get Phoebe and head back home. *Home* home.

He smiled. "See you around, Meg. And thanks."

"For what?"

He looked at me, but waited a few seconds before he answered, mulling the words in his head. "For making me change my mind."

"And thank you for – one sec, Olive." She was really fidgeting around. Not the romantic goodbye I'd dreamt of. "For being so dedicated to helping with the mission." I grinned and he did the same back, both of us understanding, feeling the same way. How good this almost was – us, this moment, everything that had happened so far, and what I wished more than anything was happening right now. "You went above and beyond."

And with a goodbye hug, my sister moaning about a wee, I said goodbye to Alex for the very last time.

THURSDAY

"Everyone got their seat belts on?" Dad turned round in the passenger's seat and looked back at us. When we realized we'd all got invites, we'd had to borrow the neighbour's people carrier.

Neet and I shouted "yaaasss" from the back row, where Olive was squidged in beside me. In the middle row were Neet's parents, and my mum was driving.

"Well, this is ridiculous." Neet flicked her hair with extra sass. Her mum had spent all afternoon helping us get ready. Everyone looked amazing, although Olive looked all kinds of extra with her blue clip-in mermaid hair. But what were you meant to do when your whole family got a handwritten invite from Trent Jameson to the premiere of *Emotional Baggage III: The Summer Holiday*?

"Say cheese, everyone." I swivelled round and tried to take a photo of us all. It was mainly my forehead, which had finally, after almost the whole summer holiday, recovered from my intense sunburn. Somehow I managed to get everyone's faces in the background. TJ said in his note that we had to keep our invitation secret, as there weren't enough for lots of crew and friends, so I saved it to post for later.

We set off to the motorway, Neet chatting to Oli as I scrolled through my photos. It had been quite a summer. After getting back from holiday, Neet and I had said yes to every single plan possible. Even the parties – *especially* the parties. And I'd loved them. What happened on Skotheos had made me realize something – it didn't matter what people who didn't matter thought. I couldn't control them; all I could control was me. Sure, I'd never got the second first kiss I thought would help change everything, but in trying to get it, I'd realized the only thing that really needed to change was how I felt about myself. I hadn't needed a kiss to prove anything. When I'd stopped stressing, and just been me, without even realizing, I'd made the best friends, organized the best plans and had the best time. It had been awesome.

Now I was back home, suddenly I wasn't Megabite any more: I was Meg who TJ tagged in his photos – and whose sister he tagged too. And all the people who'd been laughing at me now wanted to slide up in my DMs, including Sean.

Which is exactly what I thought I'd wanted – but now that it had happened, I didn't care. Because next week I'd be something else, someone else to them, and still the same old Meg to everyone I cared about – and most importantly, to myself.

I nudged Olive's leg. "I'm going to scream when I see you on screen."

She grinned. "Same . . . you looked terrifying."

Neet leant over. "Well, I'm going to scream, laugh, cry, stand up, EVERYTHING when I see you *both*, sooo . . . you have been warned."

We eventually got there three-and-a-half hours later, and pulled up in a multi-storey car park behind Leicester Square. We had to walk slowly as although Neet's mum's recovery was going really well, she still had to use a stick. She'd gone for a polka-dot one and had found the most awesome dress to match it – she was rocking the whole outfit so hard. I was so proud of everyone. My mum looked the coolest I'd ever seen her too – she'd gone for a fitted trouser suit, and Dad kept sneaking looks at her. I couldn't blame him.

Neet, Olive and I held hands as we pushed though

the crowds. I'd never been to London, and it was seriously busy. Where was everyone going on a Thursday afternoon?

But when we finally walked past all the bubble-tea shops, and bars, and souvenir shops, we turned into the big square – and came to a standstill. There was TJ's face, bigger than our house, plastered over the hugest cinema ever. Spotlights were swinging off the top of the building, cameras were everywhere, and hundreds of people were leaning over barriers screaming.

Woah.

We all took a moment.

"Well, this really is quite something." Neet's dad looked more than a little overwhelmed. Her mum straightened his bow tie.

"Just as well you look the part."

"Must have heard Dream Girl Four was coming," Neet said, prodding me.

Olive just squeaked. The TJ squeak had been retired since we'd come back to the UK, but was apparently making a guest appearance for the night. Together we walked across the square. Neet took a quick photo of the two of us to send to Geli. They'd been messaging all holiday. She wouldn't label it as boyfriend and girlfriend, because she was far too practical to think that it could work when one of you lived on a Greek island, but she did still grin in an unnerving way whenever I mentioned his name. I think she'd definitely done enough kissing on her final night of the holiday for both of us. The rash from his stubble didn't die down for two weeks. Not that she was embarrassed about it – she used to stroke it with a dreamy smile and say it was a reminder of him. Yup, my best friend was a weirdo. And I loved her.

The screaming crowd looked at our big family group suspiciously as we weaved our way through them and up to the barriers. Dad chatted to a security guard as Mum looked on impressed, and we got ushered through on to the actual red carpet. It really was a carpet that was red. What a weird thing?! Who invented that?

But as Olive and I said our names, the security guard put his hand out.

"Follow John, please." He called another guard over and said something discreetly into his ear. He nodded. I looked at Dad to check it was OK, but he was happy it was all above board. Trying not to be alarmed, Olive and I walked past the rows of photographers setting up, and were taken into a side room to wait. But what for?

We waited. And waited. Until it was almost time for the film to start.

"The plus one. Where is she?" A woman with a

clipboard ran in, shouting like she was directing traffic in rush-hour. "OLIVE JACKSON."

Olive stepped forward. "That's me?" The lady looked at her and ticked her list. "And Megan?" She checked again. "You're her chaperone?"

I nodded. I guess so? Without a moment to think, the woman opened the door.

OOMPH.

It was blinding. Camera flashes everywhere. The screams like one big wall of sound.

"Olive." TJ stepped forward, dressed in the coolest matt black suit, a white T-shirt underneath. I was relieved to see it was so tight I could make out chest hairs – reassuringly on brand. "I wondered if you..." He held up his arm. The crowd screamed even more. "Would you like to be my date for the evening?" Lights popped all over the place as the photographers and members of the public all tried to catch a glimpse of the girl he was talking to. My little sister. Luckily all the pandemonium meant TJ wouldn't be able to hear Olive squeak. I gave her a little push forward, until she took his arm. "And I must say, you look, what do you say here ... *quite brilliant.*"

I couldn't see her face. I hoped she was OK – that as confident as she was, this wasn't too much for her. But as

I watched, worried, she said something to TJ, and then, with both hands in the air, did a full Olive-spin, her blue hair and matching poofy blue skirt flying around her. TJ whooped, and as Olive started to pose for anyone who was watching, he stepped over to me.

He lowered his voice, trying to speak below all the noise. "Thanks for coming."

"Thanks for inviting us! All of us. This is. . ." I looked around at the scene – something I'd seen loads on TV and in celebrity interviews, and now I was actually in it. "It's just the best end to the summer."

"Didn't you bring a date?" TJ looked around. I shook my head at him. I knew he was winding me up. "I think we both know we didn't get plus ones."

He lowered his eyebrows, confused. "Hmmm, is that so?" He looked around. "I thought that was him."

I turned round to where there had been empty space. But where there had been empty space was something else.

Alex. A smiling Alex. All dressed up in a tuxedo. I'd never seen him in anything smarter than shorts, and oh my. In the words of Phoebe, I approved. So, so much.

He waved at me. It was all I could manage to stare back.

Wow. I didn't think I'd see him again. Let alone like this.

And, woah. Behind him was the coolest movie entourage I'd ever seen – Phoebe, Billy and Geli. If I smiled any harder, I'd strain a face muscle.

We'd all been messaging, but TJ had obviously told us to keep it a secret so it could be a surprise for us all. I bet he'd even helped with flying Geli over – the only other crew flown in were the most senior people.

I looked at TJ – the cheesy grin on his face told me I was right. "TJ! Why did you do all this?!"

He shrugged. "That's what friends are for, right?" The exact words I'd said to him that night we pulled him out of the water. And, not thinking about how many zillion photos would get taken, I gave him the biggest hug. Maybe Trent Jameson had been listening after all.

As soon as I let go, he got whisked away to walk the carpet and be interviewed, Olive trotting alongside him, like she was born for this.

When the coast was clear, and the photographers had lost interest in me, Alex walked over.

It felt so good to be with him in the flesh. "Megan Jackson. It is SO good to see you again." He put his hand out. "May I?"

I put my hand back in his. "You may." I hesitated. "Although I can't really walk in these shoes, so I apologize now for any disasters."

He smiled. "I've missed you." And I'd missed him too. After saying the happiest of hellos to the others, hand in hand, we walked the red carpet. Mitch, the assistant director, was in front of us. He had loo roll stuck to his shoe. We didn't tell him.

Neet's face when we got inside and headed to their row was priceless. She hadn't expected to see Geli ever again, let alone any of the others. This was the best day ever.

We all side-shuffled along the row to the empty seats that said 'Meg plus one'. Each chair had its own huge free popcorn, drink, and gift bag stuffed with summer inflatables. So VIP. Neet's parents and my mum were all so excited to meet Alex, Phoebe and Geli in real life, they wouldn't let them pass, chatting away until the lights went down. But our friends were just as excited to meet them too, and all wanted to chat to Neet's mum about how she was doing.

As they nattered, I spotted Holly looking incredible two rows in front. She climbed over the seats to come and hug us, and told Olive her hair looked even cooler than on the filming day. She was just as much of a star as I remembered.

When the film started to play, we finally sat down, but went on to break probably every rule of

A-list super-cool premieres, clapping and whooping throughout. But it was impossible not to. It was so weird seeing all the places I knew up there on screen in a huge Hollywood film. TJ's character was hilarious, but the best comedy moment was my mum full-on sobbing when she saw Olive. I would have found it more moving if Olive didn't keep yelling out, "It's me, it's me!" It was fair to say, as expected, I was truly grotesque in HD, and the director was right – my flying spit really was impressive. Alex still leant over and said, "Still would, though," which was both gross, and also weirdly hot.

I'd filled up way too much on the free drinks, so when the scene about TJ's mum chasing the wayward horse/chicken started, I popped out to the loo. But on my way back, as I tiptoed into the back of the screen, I bumped into Alex on his way out to find me.

And by the time the film ended, I couldn't stop smiling for three very different reasons.

I'd seen one of the worst best films of my life – I really would remember it for ever.

I'd laughed so hard, I'd cried at the credits. They were all photos from behind the scenes: Holly with her tongue sticking out, wearing the inflatable crown I'd left for her; Geli on his swing followed by another picture of Geli on the swing; Random Old Dude on his knee; Billy asleep, plate of melted ice cream in hand; and the last photo of them all, my dad after we'd left, on a banana boat, a hand in the air, having the time of his life.

But the third thing that happened was the most surprising thing of all.

Standing at the back of the cinema, away from everyone, I'd had my second first kiss.

And it was perfect.

Thanks to Alex I'd realized I'd been all wrong.

I'd never had a kissing curse.

I'd just never kissed someone as brilliant as him.

ACKNOWLEDGEMENTS

Ooh, what page is this? Awkward thank you page, that's what.

But ... books are a total team effort, and I couldn't not say a massive thank you to some particularly brilliant people who helped make this one happen. So, strap in and let's do this.

Gemma, you really are the best there is. Thanks for having me in your club, and for taking balloons on a train (metaphorically and literally).

And a huge thank you to the most amazing team at Scholastic, who always go above and beyond – most of all Lauren, editor extraordinaire, co-collaborator and all round lovely person. The biggest thanks for all your help and support.

Pete, I would happily read a book of just your mark-up comments. From the international ice-cream industry to car parks, your wisdom knows no bounds. Jamie, every cover you've done has been a total beauty and Meg and Bella would be nothing without you. Thank you. Emma, thanks for being a total star (and chicken joke saver). And the marketing and sales teams who make all this even more exciting, especially Emily, Ruth, Tanya and Harriet.

Holly and Lee – your beautiful wedding inspired the setting for this book, and gave me so many sunny memories to think about while staring out at the grey Hackney drizzle. Alexa, tell Jess and Ida they're the creative dream team – and thanks for the slime inspo. Pam, thanks for the cheerleading, and book-based medical advice. Superhuman indeed. Mollie – if you're reading this, a big hello! Jen, awkward hug for always nailing that BTS Army life. Dan – thanks for the baked-bean picture and pub chats. Let's never stop. And for all my friends who aren't here, but know who you are – you really are the greatest.

The bookish community is a lovely one, and I'm very lucky to have met such kind (and funny, always funny) people in Chelley, Jo, Jim, Beth, Simon, Perdita, Chloe, Ruth and so many more bloggers and authors too. Extra special shout-out to the Scholastic crew and Team Cooper. And an even special-er shout out to the amazing readers who have got in touch. If you're happy, I'm happy. Hope you liked this one.

Chris, thanks for always being my home (and rom-com guru). And my family, I love you to the moon and back. Always have, always will.

And the last word has to be to the coolest budding writer, treasure hunter and book spotter. You are ace and I hope this makes your name extra special to see. Thank you, ROSE!